Galhadria

Jan-Andrew Henderson

Black Hart Entertainment

Edinburgh. Scotland

Published by Black Hart 2022
Black Hart Entertainment.
6 Redgum Close, Bellbowrie QLD 4070. 5 Leven Terrace, Edinburgh

Cover by Panagiotis Lampridis (BookDesignStars)
Book Layout © 2017 BookDesignTemplates.com

Galhadria.
978-1-64826-920-2
978-0-6454957-0-6

Praise for Galhadria

A great read. I couldn't put it down - *Teen Titles*

Gripping from page one. Timeless - *Write Away!*

A cracking read - *The Sunday Post*

Fast, furious and gripping - *The School Librarian*

Skillful and well-paced - *Scottish Association of Teachers*

Enough plot to power half a library - *Scotsman Newspaper*

A winner. This book has it all - *Derby Telegraph*

Thrilling - *Newsround, BBC TV*

Appealing and authentic - *Sunday Herald*

A guaranteed bestseller - *The Afternoon Show*

Action-packed and highly imaginative - *Bookfest*

Fast-moving & inventive - *Scottish Book Collector*

Chapters

Part I

The Circus, The Sword and The Underground City

Faeries, elves, pixies, leprechauns. There are many names for that elusive race of humanoids; the Little People.

Kevin Farmer. *This Strange Planet*

Many of our ancestors lived in constant fear of offending the faeries... they were neither cute nor adorable, but dangerous, vindictive, cruel and not to be trusted for an instant.

Maurice Fleming. *Not Of This World*

The Grail

Warrior and child struggled over the brow of the hill, almost blinded by gusts of freezing rain tearing at their clothes. The warrior swayed and stumbled, trying not to lean on the small figure, for the child was already burdened by a clanking leather bag slung over one shoulder. The man's beard was matted with blood and his breastplate hung half off his chest, bent and ripped, as if it were tin foil.

They splashed, gasping, through a small stream. It was so dark they had not even seen it. The man sank to his knees, shaking fingers fumbling at the breastplate fastenings until the ruined armour dropped into the mud. Over the storm, and his own ragged breathing, he could still hear the roar of battle drifting up from the valley below.

The child looked back the way they had come and shuddered.

"I should be fighting alongside my clan," the warrior rasped. He tried to rise but his legs no longer supported him and he collapsed with a grunt of pain.

"No, Uallabh! We have to keep moving!" The child clasped the warrior's quilted tunic and tried vainly to pull the man to his feet. "We need to get the Grail to safety!"

The jerkin fell open, revealing a deep, jagged wound running from the man's shoulder to his waist. The child looked quickly away and saw a faint light was seeping into the sky above the eastern hills.

"It will be dawn soon." Tiny hands urgently clasped at the tunic again. "We only have to last a little longer."

An inhuman roar shattered the night and the child's head shot up, scanning the darkness, eyes wide with fear. Uallabh's hand went to the knife at his side and he pulled himself to his knees by sheer force of will. A riderless horse, lathered with sweat and blood, thundered out of the night. Eyes rolling in terror, it swept past them and vanished into the darkness again.

"The creatures must be following us," the man snarled. "You go. I will hold them off."

"They are still in the valley, fighting with your companions. Only one is on our trail." The child fished a silver cup from the leather bag and thrust it at the warrior. "But the one who chases us? A whole army will not stop her."

Uallabh looked down. Miraculously, liquid glittered inside the goblet, almost up to the rim.

"Drink from this," the child urged.

"Never!" The warrior pushed the cup violently away. "I will not be tainted by its dark magic."

"Listen to me," the child whispered urgently. "You are noble and pure of heart, or you would not be here.

You will stay that way if you do not attempt to use the powers the goblet gives you. I promise."

"What will it do to me?" the man asked.

"It will stop you ageing."

"I do not wish to be immortal."

"More importantly, it will cure your wounds. I need you!"

Uallabh looked intently at the child, his mouth set in a grim line. Finally, he reached out, took the cup and drank.

There was another horrific roar, much louder now. The child snatched the cup and thrust it back into the bag. Uallabh tried to get up again and this time, to his astonishment, rose easily to his feet.

"Go north. Hide the magic artefact," the child pleaded. "Then wait for me at the Glen of Roslyn, no matter *how* long it takes. I will come eventually."

The man picked up the bag and slung it over his shoulder. He stood fully upright and his eyes were clear and hard.

"And if this… thing kills you?"

"It will not dare risk the Dolorous Stroke. I promise that, too."

The Dolorous *what*, now?

"I have no time to explain!"

"Then I shall, reluctantly, do as you ask - though I curse the day we met."

The warrior took the bag and strode away without a backward glance.

The child crouched down in the wet heather and listened carefully. The sounds of battle were growing fainter but that was a good sign. It meant Uallabh's companions were pushing the monsters back. And the sky was definitely lighter. It would soon be dawn.

Perhaps everything would be all right.

A huge, yellow-eyed figure appeared over the crest of the hill.

The Drummer Boy

Charlie Wilson was a quiet boy. His parents moved around a lot and he didn't have many friends, so he kept himself to himself. He spent a lot of time sitting in his room playing the PlayStation or trying to beat his own high score on some computer game. When he grew up, he wanted to be either a computer programmer or an air traffic controller because, then, he'd get paid a lot to sit and press buttons all day.

"When I was young, I was out having real adventures instead of fooling around with some video game," Charlie's father said.

"When you were young, television hadn't been invented." Charlie snorted. "On the PlayStation, I can have totally amazing adventures. Be anyone I want."

And his father sighed and nodded because, secretly, he thought that didn't sound too bad.

He had no idea that Charlie Wilson was soon to have a totally amazing adventure. That, in the process, he would become an explorer, a magician, a detective and a grave robber.

Then, finally, he'd become a killer.

Just before term ended, Charlie came home to find his mother doing handstands in the hall - not that this was anything unusual - his parents were both professional acrobats. It was a career Charlie found highly embarrassing, so he pretended to everyone that they worked in a bank. He didn't much approve of his parents.

"Guess what?" his mother said, upside down. Her long dark hair brushed the hall floor.

"You found a new way to sweep?"

"Very funny." His mum gracefully flipped back onto her feet. "We've been asked to perform at the Edinburgh International Festival, up in Scotland. There's a whole show dedicated to physical performance."

"You mean it's a circus," Charlie sighed.

"Oh, it's much classier than that - not an elephant or clown in sight." Charlie's father stuck his head out of the living room and waggled his eyebrows. "This might be our chance to get famous."

Charlie had never heard of any famous acrobat and certainly didn't want his parents to be the first - they'd be absolutely insufferable. He was even more horrified to learn they were taking him to Edinburgh with them.

"We certainly can't leave you behind, tempting though it might be." His father patted the boy on the shoulder. "It'll do you good to go somewhere different. Bring you out of your shell."

"What do you think I am?" Charlie grumped. "A mollusc?"

"You'll love it." His mother did a somersault and knocked over the umbrella stand. "We'll only be there for three weeks, but it's the biggest arts festival in the world. There are street performers and jugglers and music and comedy and plays."

"And the bars stay open till three in the morning," his father added. "Not that it makes any difference to anything, mind you."

"We can do family things together for a change." His mother ruffled the boy's thick blonde hair before noticing that her nail varnish wasn't quite dry. "When we're not performing, of course. How would you like to learn to juggle?"

"I'd rather chew my own arms off." Charlie rubbed the pink sticky patch left on his head.

But it didn't matter how much he protested. His parents dragged him to Edinburgh anyway.

In Edinburgh, the City Council had shut down a narrow, neglected street in the old part of the city and erected a huge fibreglass tent in the middle - it stretched from a derelict concert hall on one side of the road to a set of abandoned tenements on the other. (Tenement was an old Scottish word for a tall building, his father explained). This was to be the special theatre where Charlie's parents and other acrobats would perform.

Two workmen stood watching the last of the scaffolding being removed. One was barely out of school, pale and scrawny, with so much acne he looked like he was permanently angry. The other was nearing retirement, skin brown and cracked as an oak door and thin white hair matted with plaster dust.

"Just like a circus big top, eh Jim?" the younger one said. "Only less impressive."

Jim nodded. He had long ago run out of things to say to his companion.

"Hey! You hear aboot Harry?" the teenager continued. He seemed to dislike silence. "Him and the lads were using a wee cellar at the bottom of those deserted flats fur their breaks - it's nice an cosy, know? And out of sight of the boss," he added with a wink.

Jim sighed and leant on his spade. The youngster took this as a sign of interest and kept going.

"He was foolin about wi one of the pneumatic drills an knocked a hole right through the cellar floor." The youngster sniggered. "An guess what? The lads said they found a tunnel under it."

"Aye." His companion didn't seem surprised. "I've heard stories aboot secret passages under these streets ever since I was wee."

"When wuz that? Nineteen oatcake?" the teenager's gurgling laugh turned into a fit of coughing. He pulled a cigarette from behind one greasy ear and lit it.

"There's a famous legend in Edinburgh." The elderly man continued without a change of expression.

"About a bunch of soldiers fixing up the dungeons in Edinburgh Castle, who found a hidden tunnel."

"I didnae hear about that."

"This was two hundred years ago."

"Oh." The youth thought for a moment. "I wasnae around."

"The army wanted to know where this passage went." Jim sighed and continued. "But it was awful small. So, they found a wee boy, gave him a drum to bang and chucked him in. The lad crawled through the darkness and the soldiers followed on top, right out of the castle and down the main street."

"Whit happened?"

"After about half a mile, the drumming stopped."

"Maybe he went on strike."

"More likely, he got stuck and died." The older man shrugged. "So, the army decided just to forget the whole thing. They hid the tunnel again and now everybody thinks it was just a daft story."

Jim held up a warning finger.

"But late at night, if there's no traffic about, you're supposed to hear phantom drumming coming from below these very streets."

"Load of nonsense." The teenager said cheerfully. "Let's go an get a mug of tea."

"All legends have a grain of truth in them, lad," Jim scolded.

"We'll find out soon enough," the boy grinned. "We told the council about the tunnel and it turns out there's nae official records of it. So, they offered us overtime, when this job's over, to have a wee dig under the rest of the cellars. See if we find anything interesting."

"That's a bit odd, eh?" Jim said thoughtfully. "These buildings are pretty old. They must have known about the tunnels back then but still built on top of them. And there's no records, you say?"

"Guy from the council told us they got destroyed about the same time the tenements were put up." The boy hefted an identical spade onto a skinny shoulder, impatient to get his tea.

"Nothing left but legends." The old man looked up at the deserted windows, dark and empty as soulless eyes. He scratched his stubbled chin and frowned.

"It's like somebody, long ago, wanted what's under this street forgotten."

The Tunnel

Once he got to Edinburgh, Charlie had to admit he liked it, especially the historic Old Town. It was built on a high basalt ridge leading up to Edinburgh Castle and its tenements and stone spires towered over the rest of the city. Charlie imagined the Old Town probably looked much the same now as it did centuries ago.

There were plenty of things to see and do in a city filled with flowering gardens, ancient courtyards, hidden alleys and vast museums. And Charlie's mother had been right about the festival as well. For three weeks, the city was packed with jugglers, magicians, unicyclists, human statues and hundreds of other performers, all dressed in weird and wonderful costumes to promote their shows. All the same, he wished he'd been allowed to bring his Nintendo.

There was one place he did find fascinating and that was the venue where his parents were performing. It was half theatre and half big top. Tent-shaped but made out of fibreglass, not fabric. Like a theatre, its walls were rigid and it had a door rather than an entrance flap. Yet it was as temporary as any circus, erected especially for the festival and destined to be taken down afterwards. Inside, there was no stage or curtains because, as his father explained, this place was specially built for *acrobatic* performances.

"None of your Shakespeare nonsense here, Charlie," his father chirped happily. "No men in tights running around shouting *thou hast killed me naughty knave* and waving plastic swords."

He pointed proudly to the girders, wires and poles that towered above them.

"When acrobats perform, it's a matter of life and death. There's real danger here."

"And that's a *good* thing?"

Charlie's father shrugged.

"Better than working in a bank."

In fact, there was more danger in this particular big top than he could have imagined.

"You can come and watch us practice if you like." Charlie's dad was still staring longingly upward. "Perhaps, one day, you can be part of the act."

"I've already seen you practise," Charlie muttered. He had lost count of the number of coffee tables his parents had broken leaping around their living room. "Anyway, it doesn't look all that dangerous to me. The high wire isn't all that high, is it?"

He jerked his thumb at the rope a few feet above their heads, a crisscrossing mesh dangling just below. "And there's a net."

Charlie's father glanced down at his son.

"That's not the high wire," he laughed. "Watch this."

He took a remote control from his pocket, pointed it at the roof and clicked a button. There was a loud hissing noise and a crack of white appeared, high above in the centre of the structure. The boy flinched.

With an electronic hum, the two halves of the big top roof slid slowly back from the middle, like a huge yawning mouth, until the building was completely open to the sky. There was another hiss and vertical poles, twenty feet apart and with a metal tightrope stretched between them, extended up and up through the gap that had been the roof and into the open air. Now, the tightrope looked thin as thread.

"*That's* the high wire," Charlie's father whispered.

"All right," the boy admitted, taking the remote control and inspecting it. "I'm impressed."

His stomach tightened at the thought of his parents balancing so high on the narrowest of supports - but he did like gadgets with buttons.

The theatre was erected across one of the many narrow little roads the inhabitants called 'wynds'. There were dozens of them sloping steeply down from the High Street into an area called the Cowgate – a run-down valley area festooned with pubs, much to the delight of Charlie's father. The boy goggled at the way that the big top was fastened to high buildings on either side of the wynd rather than being secured by guy ropes hammered into the ground.

"They look like an ordinary bunch of flats, don't they?" Charlie's father pointed to the abandoned and crumbling tenements on either side. "Only, they're not."

"I sense a boring story coming on."

"These tenements were built in front of a gigantic bridge," his dad continued. "They're so tall they made the structure behind almost invisible. This 'South Bridge' was constructed in the 18th century, so horses and carts could cross the Old Town without risking descending the steep slopes of the Cowgate valley. Under the massive arches, hundreds of stone chambers linked by passages were constructed – all easily accessible until the tenements hid them. They were supposed to be used as storage vaults, but people ended up living there.

"Why?"

"Overcrowding and poverty, mainly," his dad replied. "There's legends of people living in deeper tunnels that were dug into the Old Town ridge, even *under* the bridge."

"You swallow a guidebook?" Charlie frowned.

"They called it the Underground City," Charlie's father said solemnly. "Places where the very poorest people got stuck. It was a long time ago, mind you and it's all been built over, so even local people think it never really existed."

His father tapped the side of his nose.

"But I know it does."

"Oh yeah? How come?" The boy was suddenly interested. After all, he'd been playing Tomb Raider for most of the spring - and the idea of hidden passageways appealed to him.

Charlie's father looked surprised. It wasn't often he said something his son actually wanted to hear.

"Because the construction crew setting up the big top dug a bit of it up by mistake." He grabbed the boy by one arm. "Come and look at this."

He led his son over to a dark corner of the big top where another door lurked in the shadows. He opened it and they stepped into a short corridor. There was grubby plaster peeling from the walls and wooden slats and bare wires dangled from the roof.

"You can go from the big top right into the abandoned buildings and behind that are the bridge vaults themselves." His father opened a second door and ushered Charlie through. "It's like walking back in time."

They stood in a musty chamber with a low roof and uneven brickwork. It looked very, very old. The vault contained a pile of shovels and drills, a folding table covered in dirty cups and a large portable generator, which gave off an evil hum and smelled of burnt toast. The theatre construction crew had obviously used the little cellar to store their equipment and have tea breaks.

Charlie's father moved a mop, bucket and some plastic safety helmets stacked against the side of the generator. On impulse, he tried juggling three of the helmets but one bounced off the roof and hit his son on the head.

"Sorry, Chaz," he apologised. "Ceiling's a bit too low for that."

Charlie wasn't listening. Behind the mop and helmets was a ragged hole in the ancient brick wall. In the dim light of a makeshift bulb, swinging from the storeroom ceiling, he could see there was a tunnel below.

"Is that…"

"Part of the Underground City? I think it has to be." Charlie's father switched on a lamp attached to one of the safety helmets and shone it into the hole. A narrow, moss-lined passage stretched into the distance, as far as the beam could reach.

"I bet nobody's been in there for a hundred years or more." He knelt beside Charlie and looked into the passage. "It's way too small for any of the workers to fit inside. Have you seen how many sandwiches these guys eat?"

He stood up and began to practice juggling with the helmets again.

"I hear Edinburgh Council wants them to excavate the place properly but we'll be back home by then."

The boy stuck his head into the hole. There was a stale smell, similar to the one inside his parent's fridge. His mother and father weren't too big on cleaning.

"I bet I could fit in here." Charlie waved his hand about in the empty space.

"Don't even think about it." His father dropped the helmets with a crash. "I heard a story in the pub about a little boy who was forced into one of these abandoned passages and never came out again. They say you can hear his ghost drumming under the ground. I forget why he had a drum in the first place."

He scratched his head.

"To be honest, I don't remember much about that entire night."

He put the mop and helmets back to hide the hole once more.

"But there's no way you're going in there. God knows what trouble you'd get into."

Charlie's father was sure his son had no intention of venturing anywhere near the tunnel again. He'd rather sit in his room and play video games than have a proper adventure. He forgot that Charlie hadn't been able to bring his PlayStation with him.

The boy had already made a fateful decision. If he couldn't play *Tomb Raider* in the comfort of his own home, he would give the real thing a try. After all, it was better than wandering around Edinburgh on his own. He might even discover treasure in the tunnel or find a gold mine or something!

If Charlie had thought more carefully about his computer games, he would have realised there is a sort of rule regarding hidden treasure.

Wherever you find buried riches, you are also likely to come across something horrible guarding it.

The Juggler

Visiting a new place has an odd effect on people. Perhaps it's because nobody knows who they are, or their routine has changed, or maybe the air is just different. Whatever the reason, they sometimes find themselves acting quite out of the ordinary. That's exactly what was happening to Charlie Wilson.

The very next day, he got up, long before his mother and father, then went down to breakfast on his own. The family were staying at a local guesthouse and it was so early the boy was first into the little dining room. The walls were covered in tartan wallpaper and faded pictures of funny-shaped birds.

"Hello there, sonny! Would you like a wee spot of Scottish breakfast?" A plump waitress with a beaming smile appeared at his table.

"Scottish breakfast?"

"Aye. Bacon, sausage, fried egg, fried tomato, fried bread, mushrooms, potato scone, black pudding, fruit pudding, haggis, hash browns, beans, chips, tea, toast and jam."

"Do you have any Weetabix?" Charlie swallowed hard. "I was hoping to be able to move today."

"We've got porridge." The waitress didn't bat an eyelid. "It's grey and lumpy. Just like Weetabix."

"I'll have a glass of orange juice, thanks."

Charlie's parents thought of themselves as rather modern, as well as being very busy, so they allowed their son to pretty much come and go as he pleased. They had given him a mobile phone in case of emergencies but were sure he would never talk to strangers or go anywhere that looked even slightly dangerous.

"We should be thankful he's so ordinary, I suppose," Charlie's mother said to her husband. "When I was younger, I got into all sorts of scrapes, as you know."

"When you were younger?" Charlie's father sighed. "We got thrown out of the pub last night after you did the splits while hanging from a light bulb. But you're right. Our son's not like us. He's a sensible chap."

After breakfast, Charlie headed straight for the big top, intent on exploring the mysterious tunnel.

His father had given the boy a key for the theatre in case he wanted to come and watch the rehearsals. Acrobats couldn't exactly climb down from their trapeze to answer the door.

Charlie, however, had no desire to see his parents go through their act. He was convinced that, one day, they'd fall and break every bone in their bodies. But he knew the big top was deserted in the mornings. His parents hated to get up early and Charlie supposed that all performers were the same.

As soon as he was inside the big top, he made his way to the shadowy door at the back, crossed through the abandoned building and entered the bridge vault. He moved the mops and buckets away from the passage, took one of the construction helmets, switched on the light and fastened it on his head. It was far too big, but Charlie's thick hair acted like a cushion, which stopped the hard hat falling over his eyes.

He looked into the tunnel opening. The passage was damp and dark and he had no idea what was at the end of it. There might be a cliff or a bogeyman or, worse, the tunnel might get smaller and smaller until he found himself trapped forever. On the other hand, there might be some sort of forgotten fortune down there, like the stuff they found under the pyramids. What sort of super-computer could he buy then? It might be nice to own a yacht.

He put one arm tentatively into the dank opening and a cold draught raised goosebumps on his flesh. He shivered violently all over.

"Who do I think I am, Indiana bloody Jones?" Charlie withdrew his arm and backed away from the hole, shaking his head. "I wouldn't crawl down there if my life depended on it!"

He stood up and hurried back to the big top, still trembling from his sudden attack of the heebie-jeebies.

"I'll find a computer game store instead," he muttered. "See what the latest releases are."

He stopped in surprise halfway to the outside door. "Oh… eh. Hello."

In the middle of the theatre, shrouded in shadow, stood a girl in a short velvet dress. She was juggling. Not three balls or four, but six or even seven bright green orbs, glittering intermittently as they spun around her back and over her head.

"Hi there," the girl turned and spoke without missing a beat. "My name is Lilly."

She looked a little older than Charlie and her eyes and dress were as bright and emerald as the balls.

"I'm Charlie," the boy said awkwardly. "I didn't think anyone performed here in the morning,"

"I'm not a performer," the girl replied, her hands a blur of motion. "But my father's a magician. I'm practising to be as good as him."

"Really?" Charlie pointed to the spinning balls. "That's not magic, though, is it? It's just throwing things around."

Lilly arched an eyebrow and let her arms drop. The balls scattered across the theatre floor like startled frogs, vanishing under the audience chairs.

Charlie grimaced. Perhaps that hadn't been the right way to start a conversation.

"My parents are one of the acts here too," he said pleasantly, trying to begin again. "They're acrobats."

The girl nodded as if she already knew.

"Do you think you'll ever be as good as them?"

"Me?" Charlie laughed awkwardly. "I don't want to be an acrobat."

"I suppose." Lilly squinted at a trapeze hanging from the roof. "It must be frightening up there."

"It's not that I'm afraid," the boy retorted quickly, embarrassed by the misunderstanding. "I don't see the point in doing something dangerous just for the sake of it."

"Is that why you decided not to explore the tunnel?"

"What?"

"I've seen it too," the girl gave a sly smile Charlie didn't much like. "In the abandoned buildings at the back of the theatre. It's very dark."

The boy felt himself go red.

"What makes you think I'm interested in exploring some stupid tunnel?"

"You've got a hard hat with a light on your head."

"Yeah. Well, I *was* going to check it out," he blustered. "I... eh... just came back to make sure the theatre door was locked."

"It is." The girl walked over and straightened his helmet. "I'll keep an eye on the place, don't worry."

"Oh. OK then." At a loss for anything else to say, Charlie headed back to the storage vault.

He hunkered down beside the generator, staring into the tunnel once more. Surely he wasn't going to go in there just so he could prove to some weird stranger he wasn't scared?

The boy thought about his parents. He had genuinely never understood why they wanted to risk their lives swinging high above the ground. He asked his father once and the man had laughed gently.

"I don't want to grow dull and fat working as some salesman, Charlie," he explained. "You're only alive once, so you may as well really live."

The boy hadn't agreed. If life was so precious, what the hell was the point in jeopardising it? Besides, his father had been very clear that he wasn't to venture into the hole.

Only, he really wanted to know what was in there. Besides, the girl had practically dared him to go and she was undeniably pretty. His dad might secretly be proud that he was taking such a chance and, if he got into bother, he had his mobile phone.

The scales tipped. With a deep breath, Charlie knelt and slid headfirst into the tunnel.

The air was musty and the moss on the walls surprisingly dry and spongy, which made crawling easy. After a few dozen yards, he realised the little passage was beginning to widen. After thirty feet, the tunnel opened onto a chamber, this one large enough for Charlie to stand. A large archway cleaved the far wall with another passageway beyond.

"Woah! I really am in the Underground City."

He looked around in awe. The flashlight on his helmet lit up an ancient, curved roof dripping with thin fingers of hardened salt.

"This is well and truly the stupidest thing I've ever done."

He might be taking a chance, but Charlie Wilson wasn't stupid. He took a piece of chalk from his pocket (he had bought a packet especially the day before) and marked a crumbling but readable number 1 on the chamber wall. Then he set off down the new passage. He passed several openings into vaults of different sizes and the tunnel itself twisted left then right, other passages leading off like branches. Every time he took one, Charlie chalked another number so he'd be able to find his way back.

"Lara Croft was never smart enough to do this," he said proudly before tripping and falling flat on his face. The mobile phone flew out of his shirt pocket and bounced into the dark. As Charlie scrabbled after it, his helmet bumped against the stonework and one outstretched arm vanished into a cavity between wall and floor. He withdrew it with a shriek, just in case some big rat or land octopus was lurking inside.

"For God's sake!" he panted once he had calmed down a bit. "How many hidden holes are in this blasted place?"

He sat up and played the headlight over the little opening. It was no more than a few feet long, obscured by dirt and loose rubble.

"That's just great! I couldn't have aimed the phone down there if I was a champion darts player. How am I going to explain losing it to mum and dad?"

The answer, of course, was that he couldn't. He was going to have to try and rescue his mobile. The hole was half-hidden behind bricks and short straps of wood and Charlie began to move the debris to see if he could make a space big enough to reach into. Soon, he realised the gap was going to be large enough to fit his head and shoulders through and, though he really didn't like that idea, it meant he could see where the mobile had gone. After a few moments of cursing, he clenched his fists and stuck his head into the hole.

"Would you look at that?"

The light on his hard hat lit up a stairway leading down into the darkness. His mobile phone must have bounced all the way to the bottom. Charlie was aware that, bit by bit, he was going further than he had ever intended.

"I'm brave. I'm brave, I'm brave. My mother and father are brave and I can be brave too," the boy chanted, fastening the helmet strap tighter with trembling fingers. "Who am I kidding? I'm just a lot dumber than I thought."

He crawled through the widened hole, got unsteadily to his feet and made his way cautiously down the stairs.

At the bottom was another passage, with an uneven floor that sloped gently downwards. Charlie found his phone then, on impulse, carried on down the hill.

Despite himself, the boy was thrilled as well as frightened. He was finally beginning to understand how his parents must feel, swinging around on their trapeze. He was a bit disappointed, in fact, when the tunnel eventually opened out into a large vault, which seemed to signal the end of his journey. Charlie swung the light around but the doorway he stood in was both entrance and exit to the chamber.

The vault wasn't completely empty. A pyramid-shaped wooden frame and rusty iron hook leaned against one wall, there was a mound of rocks in the far corner and a waist-high circle of stone in the middle.

Charlie walked over to the brick circle and bent his head to shine the torch down. The beam lit up a thick layer of ash and lumpy grey remains of what must have once been coal.

"Looks like someone's been having a barbeque." Charlie raised an eyebrow. "Wouldn't be my choice of place for a picnic."

He turned and walked towards the smaller pile of stones. Though it was no more than a heap of rocks, it looked like it had been put there deliberately. He hesitated for a few seconds, then threw caution to the wind.

"The last time I came across a pile of stones, it was hiding something." The boy bent down and began to remove the rocks. "Doesn't seem right to come all this way and not see what's under this lot. Especially if it's a bag full of jewels."

The stones were piled on top of a rotting wooden board and once Charlie had uncovered most of the plank, he slid it aside. Underneath was a blackened hollow cylinder of metal the size of an oil drum. It looked like it had been rammed into a hole in the floor. Charlie peered inside and a grin spread across his dusty face. At the bottom of the cylinder was a square object wrapped in dark cloth. It looked like it might be some kind of box.

"Treasure!" he breathed. "About time."

Lying flat on the floor, he reached into the metal lined hole, grasped the coarse cloth and pulled it towards him. It was certainly a package of some kind, wrapped in the crumbling remains of what seemed like a huge leather glove. With shaking hands, the boy unpeeled the covering. Inside was a tatty book with a faded velum cover.

"Jeez. If I wanted to read something, I'd have gone to the library."

He gingerly opened the fragile cover and a slip of folded paper fell out. He couldn't tell from the light of the torch but he guessed it was yellow with age, for it crackled when he picked it up.

"A treasure map! Of course!" He unfolded the paper and bent his helmet closer to see what was written there. The words were hand-scripted but the letters were large and thick. It was easy to make out, even in the dim torchlight.

If you are reading this you are in mortal danger. Take the book, leev now and cover your tracks. I pray you are brave at hart and of good caracter and, if so, read on then do what you must. Hopefully, at the end, you will find a way to emerge victorious.

Charlie sat bolt upright.

"Mortal danger?" he gasped. "What does it mean, mortal danger?"

Then, the tapping began.

It was soft and faint, as if the sound came from a long way down, somewhere under the floor. Charlie's eyes widened and he sprang to his feet. The rapping was growing louder and it was getting faster. Though it still sounded far off, there was no doubt in the boy's mind.

The noise was heading this way.

Blood drained from Charlie's face and his bravado evaporated. He began to back out of the vault, stuffing the book into his shirt as he went. The rapping was more like drumming now, much louder and definitely heading in his direction. And it was approaching fast.

Charlie Wilson turned and ran.

His journey back to the surface was little more than a blur, for the terrified boy ran like he had never run before, breath hammering in his ears and the light on his head swirling sinister shadows across the passages. The chalk marks flew past. Five, then four, then three, then two, then one.

He sped through the corridors, bouncing off walls and stumbling over loose rocks. He plunged back into the little tunnel, ignoring scrapes on his hands and knees, as he frantically scrambled the last hundred yards. He didn't slow down until he had burst into the tool-filled vault and every mop, bucket and teacup had been piled back in front of the tunnel entrance.

Charlie took the helmet from his head and placed it on the vault floor with the others. His hands were shaking so badly he could hardly switch off the light. He sat on the floor, his chest heaving.

"Thank God I didn't have the full Scottish breakfast," he panted. "I'd still be down there."

He got unsteadily to his feet and opened the door leading back to the theatre.

"Nobody and I mean nobody, will ever make me go back into that tunnel," he promised, taking one last look at the covered up hole. "I'll never set foot in that place again as long as I live."

But, though he meant every word, Charlie Wilson couldn't have been more wrong.

The Book

Lilly was still juggling when Charlie staggered back into the theatre. He could have sworn for a second that she had at least a dozen balls in the air and what looked like a couple of mice as well. At the sound of the boy's wheezing, the whirling objects vanished into some hidden pocket performers always seem to have.

"Ah, you're back." Lilly smiled innocently. "Anything interesting down there?"

"Interesting?" Charlie slapped at his jeans and a cloud of white dust rose into the air. "I heard the ghost of that little drummer boy! The one that's supposed to haunt the place. My heart almost stopped."

He began to tell Lilly about the escapade but, to his annoyance, the girl started to laugh. She held up a hand to stop him.

"Charlie, Soon there's going to be a group of council workmen digging under the tenements from the opposite side of the bridge," she chuckled. "You probably heard them drilling an entrance."

"Sounded like drumbeats to me," the boy scowled. "I've never been so scared."

"A phantom drummer, eh? You should have stuck around. The rest of the band might have turned up."

Charlie ignored her sarcasm and pulled the book from under his shirt, releasing another cloud of dust.

"Anyway, I found this."

"Really? Let me see."

Charlie handed the book over and Lilly opened it.

"It's handwritten and the date inside the cover says 1824." She turned a page and read a little more. "It's the journal of somebody called William Makepeace."

"Like a diary?"

"Exactly."

"Is it a joke? Some kind of hoax?"

"There are parts of the Underground City that have been sealed for almost two centuries and this book's definitely old." Lilly shook her head. "See how dry the paper is."

She peered over the top of the pages.

"What are you looking so unhappy about?"

"I suppose this is real, too?" The boy unfolded the note and handed it to Lilly. "It was stuck inside the front page."

"It's the same type of paper." She read the message and looked up at him, eyes sparkling. "This is great!"

"Yeah. Fantastic. Especially the part about me being in mortal danger." Charlie pointed to the offending sentence. "What do you think it means?"

"Don't you see?" Lilly said excitedly. "The note's a warning to stop people going any further."

"It worked then," the boy snorted. "I came back soon as I read it."

"But think! Why would anybody leave a note like that?" Lilly waved the offending scrap of paper under Charlie's nose. "I bet it's cause there's something really important hidden down there. And only the stout of heart will be able to find it!"

She nodded as if this made perfect sense.

"That note's a warning but also a clue, see? There's something valuable right under our feet!"

A look of horror crossed her face.

"What if those council workers head towards it?"

"The speed most council workers work, they'll never get there."

"You said the note was inside this book." Lilly was obviously swept up in her grand idea. "Maybe the book says where the treasure is buried."

"You are getting totally carried away." Charlie held up his hands. "It's just some old diary, that's all. We should give it to a museum before it gets damaged."

"Well, we *could* do that." Lilly smiled a dazzling smile. "But it wouldn't do any harm to read it first. Eh? Where's your sense of adventure?"

"I left it in the tunnel."

"Look, it would only take a couple of days to finish. If there's nothing about treasure, you can hand it over to anyone you like."

"And if there is?"

Lilly shrugged. "Then… we can decide what to do next!"

"What the hell." The boy gave a sigh of exasperation. "Since you've got it all worked out, I may as well
give it a try."

"C'mon, Charlie." She gave him a nudge. "It *is*
quite exciting."

"Didn't they write really dull books in those days,
with big, long sentences?" Charlie took the diary back
from Lilly and opened it. "I'm not really into reading.
I like video games."

"What have you got to lose?"

"I suppose." He scanned the first page, scowling
with concentration. His frown deepened as he read out
loud.

*This iz the jurnal of myself, William Makepeace
aged about fourteen, (tho I am not sure which year I
was born, for I am an orphan) in which I am deter-
minned to tell of my life and adventurs, since it is my
grate desire to someday write a book of true im-
portanse.*

"I knew it!" Charlie groaned. "I've written school
essays that were shorter than his first sentence. And
who taught him to spell?"

"If he was an orphan in the Underground City, he
probably taught himself." Lilly arched a sarcastic eyebrow. "Think you could do that?"

The boy ignored her and began to read again.

I lived in the Canongate poorhouse until I found I was to be apprentised to MacPherson the Sweep - who wuz well known for ill treetment of boys in his employ. He would send them up the narrowest chimneys and, shood they become stuck, would lite fires under them to perswade them out.

"Ouch!" Charlie paused. "He's got to be making this up. Nobody's life is this bad."

"In those days, everybody's life was that bad. Unless they had money."

"I guess some things never change." The boy smiled thinly and began to read again.

One nite I escaped by leeping from the poorhouse roof into a drift of snow and remained buried until after dark. Finaly, half dead with cold, I made my way to the Underground City where all manner of criminals reside, and now make my living by means that I am ashamed to menshun...

"Wow." Charlie looked up from the book in astonishment. "This guy's had a hard time of it and I'm only on the first page. I wonder what he did that he's so ashamed of."

"Read the journal. You'll probably find out."

"It's too difficult." The boy protested. "I'll never get through it."

"Everyone has a story worth hearing," Lilly said. "You just need to be able to picture it."

She held out a fist.

"Maybe I can help."

She uncurled her fingers and blew across her palm. A cloud of glittering dust circled the boy's head.

"What are you doing!" Charlie waved his arms about, scattering the shining haze. "I got asthma, you know!"

"It's imagination. To help you read the book."

"It's glitter, Lilly." Charlie held up a sparkly hand in disgust. "Now I look like a girl."

"As you were so quick to point out, I'm only a juggler." Lilly shrugged. "What do you want me to do? Pull a rabbit out of my…"

"I'll read the book. All right?" The boy stuffed the journal back inside his shirt. "I'll let you know how far I've got by tomorrow. Where do you stay? What's your phone number?" He tapped his shirt pocket proudly. "I have a mobile. It's a Samsung."

The girl gestured around the tent.

"You can find me right here, every morning."

"Suit yourself." Charlie went to the door and unlocked it. He paused and turned back.

"See this mortal danger stuff? Just what kind of mortal danger do you think…?"

But Lilly was gone.

The Graveyard

After dinner at the guesthouse, Charlie's parents got ready to go to the big top and perform their act.

"Do you want to come and watch?" His father was pulling on a pair of yellow spangled tights.

"I think I'll stay in and read," Charlie shook his head. "Ehm. You're not going to walk through town dressed like that?"

"Don't worry, Charlie, everyone will be staring at your mother." Charlie's mum appeared to be wearing nothing more than three ostrich feathers. "And you don't need to wait up - we might go for a drink after the show. That's if we don't plunge to our deaths from the high wire. Hah. Only joking."

As soon as his parents were gone, Charlie pulled the diary from his bag, flopped onto his bed and began to read. William Makepeace had close, shaky handwriting and that made his long and badly spelt sentences even more difficult.

My best frend and constant companyun is a boy a little older than I, Duncan MacPhail, who it was my grate fortune to meet, for his strenth is admirable, his bravery beyond question and it was he who convinced me to give up my dishonorable profeshun.

Charlie felt his eyes drooping already. Hadn't this kid ever heard of full stops? He tried to remember what Lilly had said about using his imagination and concentrating on the story rather than the words. And Charlie had to admit, he wanted to know what this William Makepeace did that was so terrible, apart from not learning to punctuate sentences.

He looked at the book again.

I was sitting in Greyfriars Graveyard the first time I met Duncan, a fine spring day when the trees were heavie with white and pink blossums.

Charlie tried focussing on what the writer was actually saying. He pictured ornate gravestones and stately trees ruffled by a cool spring breeze.

Then the strangest thing happened. In his head, he could suddenly see a small boy sitting on a flat tombstone and writing in a book...

William Makepeace looked up as a scented blossom drifted past his head and landed on the velum-covered journal balanced between his scrawny knees. Two hundred yards away, through the scattered gravestones, he observed a group of mourners in black frock coats and tall stovepipe hats attending a funeral. The boy watched them from the corner of his eye, then quietly opened the book. He took a quill pen and inkpot from his pocket, dipped in the nib and carefully made some notes.

A shadow fell across the flat tombstone on which he sat and he looked up in surprise. Three angry-looking youths, one holding a stout club, stood over him - their burly forms blocking out the sun.

"We know what you're up to, urchin." One of the youths slammed his stick down on the flat stone an inch from the boy's knee. The mourners did not look round. "You're going to wish you'd never set foot in this graveyard."

"I'm already persuaded it was a bad idea," the boy said pleasantly, shutting the journal. "So I'll be on my way, gents, and we'll say no more about it."

"Think you're clever, don't you?" The largest of the three boys nodded to his ragged companions. "Grab his arms. I'm going tae teach this wee sod a lesson."

As the toughs moved forward to seize the boy, they heard a cough from behind a nearby tree. A tall youth stepped into the sunlight.

"I dinnae think that three big lads against one wee one is fair, nae matter what he's done," the stranger said calmly.

His hair was long and black and a thick tartan plaid was draped over his shoulder, then fastened round his waist with an ornate pin. His strange attire marked him out as a highlander - not a common sight in a city which still treated the fierce clans of northern Scotland with fear and mistrust. He kept himself between the sun and his assailants, making his features difficult to see.

"This is no your fight, friend." The largest youth stepped forward menacingly, shading his eyes with one hand. "Go about your business and leave us to ours."

"I don't mind if he joins in," William Makepeace said nervously. "In fact, I think it would even up the odds nicely. If he…"

One of the gang lashed out, the back of his calloused hand catching Makepeace a glancing blow on the temple and knocking him off the tombstone. Without a second's hesitation, the highlander launched himself forward, head down and arms spread wide. His shoulder crashed into the gang leader's chest and outstretched fists slammed into the stomachs of the henchmen on either side. Next moment, all three toughs were on the ground, gasping for air and the highlander was standing above them, brandishing the stick. In his other hand, a small but deadly-looking knife had appeared.

"Go on, get out of here afore I cut ye." He motioned towards the cemetery's iron gates, and the gang got unsteadily to their feet and ran. The knife vanished into the highlander's tunic as he helped the diminutive boy to his feet.

"Up ye get, wee man." He bent down and retrieved the fallen book. "Are ye all right?"

"I'm fine, thank you, and most indebted to your good self for saving me." The boy held out his hand. "My name's William Makepeace, but my friends call me Peazle. So do my enemies, for that matter. I obviously have quite a few."

The highlander shook the proffered hand.

"Duncan MacPhail from Aftonhouse. I dinnae have any enemies." He smiled. "At least, no alive."

"Then I'll count you a friend," Peazle said evenly. "May I have my journal back?"

"This is a funny kind of book now, isn't it?" Duncan opened the journal and looked at the first page. "I've been watching ye write in it. Yet there's nothing here."

He flicked through the remaining pages.

"Until you get tae the back, that is. Then there's a map of the kirkyard." He motioned to the crowd of mourners clustered around the open grave like unhappy shadows. "And you've made a wee tick, marking the spot where that funeral is taking place."

"It's my hobby," the boy said casually. "Funeral spotting."

The highlander's eyes narrowed.

"It's my guess you work for the Resurrection Men and that's why thon wee gang wished you harm." He looked at the stout stick, then back at Peazle. "I've heard stories of sic a thing - but never really believed they were true."

The Resurrection Men were the most despised of the city's many criminals, for they stole bodies from graveyards and sold them for unscrupulous anatomists at Edinburgh University to experiment on. To avoid suspicion, they often employed children as lookouts or had them mark out the sites of recently buried corpses. Then these body snatchers could return at night and find the grave, without falling over a dozen headstones in the dark.

Peazle was quick to defend himself.

"You think it's easy for an orphan living in this city? I have to eat, you know." He angrily snatched the book from the larger boy. "I pick pockets too, I might as well tell you. It's either that or get sent up some chimney for a living, or maybe suffocate down a Lothian mine, opening trapdoors for the coal carts."

"Calm down, my friend." The highlander placed a hand on the smaller boy's shoulder. "I know what it's like tae go hungry myself. I was forced to come down from the highlands because there's nae work to be had in the north."

He spat on the ground in anger.

"I've been here over a week and I must admit I'm faring little better."

"No luck?"

"Oh, I have a job in an iron foundry where I work fae six in the morning till eight at night for a few pennies. I sleep in a doorway because there are nae lodgings tae be had."

The pickpocket could see that Duncan's piercing blue eyes were ringed by dark circles and his fine cheekbones were made even sharper by exhaustion. It suddenly occurred to Peazle that his new friend wasn't nearly as old as he first appeared. He might only be a couple of years older than the pickpocket himself, perhaps fifteen or sixteen.

"I like it here because it's the only place in this overcrowded hellhole of a city where I can get a wee bit of peace." The highlander looked around at the laden boughs and lush green grass.

Peazle could see what he meant. Though dirty tenements surrounded the high walls of Greyfriars, the graveyard held only the funeral party, a courting couple and a few disrespectful urchins playing hide and seek. Tranquillity like that was rare in overcrowded Edinburgh, for famine and unsympathetic landowners had forced wave after wave of immigrants from the Scottish and Irish countryside to move to the cities. The population of the Old Town had doubled in the last thirty years.

"I spotted a hawk here yesterday," Duncan said. "A white one wi black tips on each wing. Ne'er seen anything like it before. Didnae look right in such a dirty sky."

The highlander grabbed a falling blossom and sniffed at it. But no fragrance could block out the smell of coal smoke and sewage that permeated the city.

"I come here a lot myself," the pickpocket replied. "Not just to spy on funerals," he added quickly. "I always sit here, on the grave of James Hogg."

He patted the stone on which he had been resting.

"He was a great poet, you know, and a man of learning. Yet he started as a humble shepherd, so I heard."

"Nothing wrong wi being a shepherd," Duncan scowled. "It was mah faither's profession."

"Listen, you helped me," the pickpocket said. "I'd like to return the favour. If you've nowhere to stay, you're welcome to lodge with me for a while."

Duncan thought for a second, then leaned behind a gravestone and picked up a small knapsack.

"Your hospitality is worthy of a highlander himself and I gladly accept. Where do you stay?"

"The Underground City."

"That sounds powerful grim."

"So does sleeping in a doorway. C'mon."

He led Duncan out of the graveyard, up the Old Town ridge and onto the High Street. For a few minutes, they pushed their way through crowds thronging between the bristling tenements, until Peazle turned down a narrow and steeply sloping alley.

"The South Bridge," said Peazle as they neared the bottom. "Home sweet home."

The boys stood in the shadow of the bridge's towering pillars, its grimy brick flanks studded with openings leading to internal vaults. Chambers which had been designed to hold goods and wares, but because of Edinburgh's horrific overcrowding, now held people.

The tenements that would eventually hide the vault entrances had not yet been built and Peazle and the highlander simply stepped from the street into the interior of the bridge. They made their way through a series of dark chambers and narrow passages lit by dirty spluttering candles. After a while, their eyes grew accustomed to the murky light and the boys could make out vagabonds and beggars huddled in the darkened corners.

"This is my present place of residence." Peazle stepped into a smoky chamber where three men were playing cards by candlelight. "It's smelly and dark and you might get murdered in your bed. But at least it's dry."

There was a squelch as he stepped through the doorway.

"Well, dry-ish."

"It smells tae high heaven." The highlander wrinkled his nose. "You actually pay for this?"

"I pay Merry Andrew." Peazle lowered his voice and indicated one of the card players, who slowly rose to his feet. Once he was standing, he had to stoop to avoid hitting his head on the roof.

"He's the biggest, so the vault belongs to him."

The pickpocket waved to the rough-looking man. His face was a rash of pock marks and grey stubble, except for where a large scar ran from ear to chin.

"Merry. This is Duncan MacPhail from the highlands. I want to share my space with him for a while."

Merry Andrew was far from merry. He looked like he could tear most men apart with his bare hands and was in the mood to do it.

"Oh, really?" he growled, his voice broken by a lifetime of loud cursing and cheap grog. "Suppose I don't want Duncan MacPhail in my hoose? You think this place isn't crowded enough?"

He towered over the two boys.

"I reckon I'll throw Duncan oot of my vault and charge you double for even suggesting it."

"Then Duncan might come back in the middle of the night and cut off your ears while you sleep." The highlander spoke softly but the small knife glinted in his hand once more. "If you're going tae make enemies sae easily, it's better tae keep them close so you can see what they're up tae."

There was a stunned silence. The other card players looked at each other and gave a low whistle. Merry Andrew glowered. Then he half-smiled. Finally, he laughed out loud.

"Well spoken, boy." He slapped Duncan on the back. "I like your spirit. Ha'penny a week and you can stay. I collect the money prompt each Friday."

Peazle finally let his breath out.

Later that night, Merry Andrew and his companions went to the local tavern to play dice. The highlander and the pickpocket sat talking in the candlelight.

"Where did you get such a fine book?" Duncan picked up Peazle's journal. "It looks expensive. I see you've a fine quill pen, also."

"Stole them from one of the bookstalls in Blair Street," the pickpocket admitted. "I always wanted to write something of value, like men of learning do. Taught myself to read in the poorhouse, I did.."

"I cannae read nor write myself," the highlander replied. "Where I come from, it was more important to learn how tae hunt and fight."

He lay down on the pile of rough sacks and straw that served as bedding in the Underground City.

"Still… it seems a shame to waste such a bonny volume."

"What do you mean?"

"Why don't you stop using it to dae the body snatchers dirty work? Keep a proper diary instead." The highlander blew out the candle, plunging the vault into darkness. "Someone might want tae read it years from now. Then you'll live forever."

"I doubt that," said the pickpocket. But he lay awake for a long time, smiling in the dark.

He had a proper friend at last and, to show his gratitude, he vowed to take Duncan's advice.

The Giant

Next morning, Charlie burst into the big top in a state of high excitement. Lilly was balancing three chairs, one on top of each other, at the end of her chin.

"I read the diary! Last night! Well, some of it. It was amazing... just like I was there. In fact, I don't even know if I dreamed it..."

He stopped in mid-tirade.

"Isn't that a bit heavy?"

"Itsh jusht an illushion," Lilly said without taking her eyes off the chairs. "You sheem very animated thish morning."

"It's this diary. It was written by a kid called Peazle, a real boy from two hundred years ago! He had a best friend, Duncan, who came down from the highlands to look for work in Edinburgh." Charlie spread his arms, trying to convey the enormity of what he was saying. "It was like I was *seeing* what went on."

"Musht be a quite a book."

"You don't understand. I can't explain it but some-how... I'm not just reading it. The book has only sketchy details and I only read a couple of pages but I still know what went on in their lives. Stuff that's not even written down."

Charlie pulled the diary from his rucksack.

"Listen. I have to go to Greyfriars Graveyard."

Lilly jerked her head back and the chairs collapsed in perfect formation, stacking neatly as they landed. Charlie blinked.

"Why Greyfriars Graveyard?" she said sharply.

"Eh? I want to see where Peazle liked to hang out. He used to write on the grave of some guy called James Hogg. Duncan liked it too because it had hawks, just like the highlands."

"Hawks?" Lilly scowled.

"Well, one hawk. White with black-tipped wings." Charlie held up the book. "You want to come?"

"No, I don't." The girl turned sharply away. "I have to practise."

"Are you OK?" Charlie asked.

Lilly ignored him and began to juggle again - seven balls, then eight, then ten, so fast they were merely a blur. When she did not turn around as he left, Charlie got the strangest feeling the girl was upset and trying to hide it.

Greyfriars was only a few hundred yards from the Old Town, but you could walk straight past without knowing it, for the cemetery was hidden by a high wall and ringed by old buildings. Charlie was lucky to spot the entrance, set back from the street between a pub and a row of small shops.

He let out a gasp as he walked through the wrought-iron gates. Dotted between the trees were carved grave-stones, now weathered with age. Behind that was a high backdrop of grey Victorian tenements, exactly as he had pictured them the night before. The boy strolled round the side of the squat, barn-like church that faced the gates. There was the flat tombstone that marked the final resting place of James Hogg, right where he knew it would be.

"This is more than a little weird," Charlie muttered, taking the journal from his bag.

The worn stone was warm from the summer sun and, on impulse, he lay down on it, looking around to see if anyone disapproved. But the graveyard, hidden behind its double barricade, seemed to be deserted - so Charlie opened the book and began to read.

Sunday is the only day when Duncan duz not wurk at the factory and so we arranged to mete on the High Street in the afternoon, for in the morning he was pay-ing his respects to a Gypsy girl who sings for mony in Blair Street and with whom he is much taken. I was in powerful good spirits for I had releeved more than one rich merchant of his gold snufbox that week...

Peazle walked slowly down the High Street, look-ing out for Duncan. Like all thoroughfares in the Old Town, the High Street was packed with people shop-ping and gossiping. It smelled strongly of sewage, for the ground was not paved and waste and rubbish were often thrown out of the windows at night. The air was filled with the shouts of fruit sellers and fishwives plying their wares from rickety wooden stalls planted in the stagnant mud. He finally found Duncan sitting on a stone stoop and looking glum.

"I presume things did not go entirely well with your girl this morning?" Peazle hunkered down beside his friend and tried to look sympathetic.

"She's no my girl, merely a pretty lassie whose company I like." Duncan poked dejectedly in the mud with his foot. "I'm fond of her and she can sing love ballads fit tae break a heart, but I'm a plain-spoken lad and no much for romantic talk."

"Well, don't ask me for advice. I'm too scrawny for courting. You fancy a bag of buckies?"

Peazle pointed to a stall selling little saucers of mussels covered in salt and pepper.

"I dinnae want to eat anything that looks like it came out of someone's nose," the highlander grunted.

Peazle bought a saucer anyway. He had taken to hanging around Edinburgh's bookstalls to hear what the learned gentlemen who browsed there were saying. Usually, he couldn't comprehend much of their sophisticated talk but would grab a silk handkerchief or gold coin from their back pockets as they strolled past. Last week, the pickpocket had overheard one gent say that eating fish made people smarter and decided seafood was his best bet for getting an education. Since mussels were the only kind of marine life he could actually afford, Peazle had taken to scoffing them whenever he got the chance.

The two boys sat on the cracked step while Peazle shovelled cold, slimy shellfish into his mouth and Duncan glowered at the thronging crowds. The highlander badly missed the solitude of his heather covered moors. Here, he could see only slivers of sky between the tenement blocks and even those thin patches were tainted by thick palls of chimney smoke.

Duncan would have liked to get out of the grimy, overcrowded city for the day but Peazle insisted he was scared of the countryside. The pickpocket had lived most of his life in slums and wasn't about to venture into a wilderness, where they might both get eaten by a wild animal. Especially a camel. Peazle was deathly afraid of camels after he had heard a learned gentleman state how bad-tempered they were.

"There's nae camels in the Scottish countryside," Duncan muttered. "I'm sure of it."

"Have you ever seen one?" Peazle asked.

"I dinnae even ken what a camel is."

"There you go, then," Peazle said triumphantly. "The countryside could be full of man-eating camels and you wouldn't know it."

Duncan wasn't giving up.

"We could go and climb up Arthur's Seat." The highlander pointed south to where a craggy hilltop could be glimpsed through the swirling smoke and chimney pots. "That's no exactly the countryside now, is it? You can see it from here."

Peazle looked at his friend in horror.

"You must be joking! When that thing blows up, I don't want to be standing on top of it."

Idling outside his favourite bookstall the week before, Peazle had been perturbed to hear two academics talking about Arthur's Seat being an extinct volcano with a vast network of tunnels underneath. Once he had asked around and found out what a volcano was, Peazle vowed never to set foot on the hill again. He was still trying to find out what extinct meant.

He half-heartedly offered the highlander a mussel but Duncan waved it away with a snort. Peazle could see his friend was in a foul mood but wasn't about to go climbing over a volcano just to cheer him up.

Duncan sighed loudly.

"Tell you what," the pickpocket said finally. "I'll buy us some decent food for tonight, eh? I've had a good week and it's time to sell what I've... eh... acquired."

He wiped greasy hands down his trousers and inspected his nimble fingers with pride.

"It means we'll have to go back to the Underground City for a bit, if you don't mind."

"If I'm getting something other than boiled turnip for supper, I'm willing tae trek through the very gates of hell."

"Funny you should say that," Peazle grinned uncomfortably as he stood. "C'mon, let's get this over with."

Duncan's mood was black as they marched back to the shadows of the South Bridge, stepped out of the sunlight and entered the familiar dark corridor that led to their vault. This time, however, the boys continued past the rude dwelling and carried on down the passageway. The highlander had never been in this direction before. He spent as much time as he could on the surface and was not inclined to delve deeper into the black, smelly corridors.

"Never thought we'd end up back in here on my day off," he muttered, tripping over a sleeping figure curled up on the tunnel floor. The passages, like every other part of Edinburgh, were festooned with down and outs who slept when they felt like it. And why not? In the permanent darkness of the Underground City, it was always night.

"Here we are," Peazle whispered finally, crouching beside a damp wall. "There's a set of stairs behind a little opening down here. Most people don't even know it exists."

His hunched form moved forward and, without warning, he was gone.

Puzzled, Duncan shuffled one near-invisible foot around in front of him where the wall met the floor and felt a small opening. He could have passed it a hundred times in the blackness without realising it was there. He sat down, wriggled his body through the gap and, leaning carefully on the slimy wall, inched slowly down a hidden stairway, feeling for each new step with his foot.

There was another tunnel at the bottom of the stairway and it seemed even darker than the one he had left, though Duncan didn't suppose this was actually possible. He heard a scratching noise to his right and Peazle's triumphant expression was lit by a crackling flame.

"Torches," the pickpocket said proudly, waving a stout stick that dripped flaming tar in alarming amounts. "Made em myself. You never know when the Old Town Guard will raid the place and I might have to make a quick getaway."

Duncan sighed. Edinburgh's Old Town Guard were mostly ex-soldiers well over retirement age. It was unlikely that they would bother raiding a den of vice-like the Underground City and weren't likely to catch more than a cold if they did.

In the light of the firebrand, the highlander could see this stonework was much older and cruder than the tunnels above and the walls shone with waterlogged moss. The smell was different, too. Not the stink of stale sweat and smoke that filled most of the chambers but a wet, earthy smell that reminded Duncan of the caves under highland waterfalls. Peazle moved away again and he followed, touching the walls and sniffing his fingers.

"This is no bad, actually!" he grinned. "Peaceful, ye ken? I cannae hear anyone. Why does nobody live down here?"

"It's too damp and cold, even for beggars and drunks," Peazle said. "As far as I know, there's only one person staying on this whole level and that's who we're going to see."

"Who might *he* be?"

"His name's Shadowjack Henry. A blacksmith by trade. He moved down here a couple of months ago. There's a well at the end of this level that's been blocked up for as long as anyone can remember, so Shadowjack set up a wee forge and opened the well to draw water. He makes metal trinkets and sells them to the market traders on the High Street. The forge makes the vault warm enough to live in and there's no one else down here to pay rent to. A nice wee set up, if you ask me."

"Sounds like it," Duncan agreed. "How is it I've never heard anyone mention him before?"

"You know how superstitious ignorant people are," Peazle said, as if he had the benefit of a fancy education. "There's some old legend about the well being haunted. Something about it leading straight down to hell."

Duncan stopped.

"Let's go back."

Peazle turned in astonishment. "Eh? What's the matter?"

"I'm not going intae any haunted place," Duncan said matter-of-factly.

"What?" Peazle spluttered, "I thought highlanders weren't scared of man nor beast! At least that's what you keep telling me about fifty times a day."

"Haunted stuff isnae man nor beast." Duncan shook his head. "Haunted stuff is witches and Kelpies and the Little People. In the highlands, you dinnae mess wi creatures like that, especially the Little People."

He folded his arms in determination.

"I cannae believe that you of all people would come down here, you that's scared of anything that moves."

"I'm scared of camels and volcanoes but that's scientific stuff," Peazle explained. "This is the 19th Century, Duncan. There's no such thing as Little People. Most of the trouble we get is from big people."

Duncan shook his head in exasperation but he was fiercely loyal to his friend and, after a stream of disapproving grunts, finally indicated to keep going.

For a while, the two boys walked without talking, the only sound being Peazle's tatty old boots crunching on loose stones and the rasp of his breathing. The pickpocket had to keep stopping to catch his breath. A lifetime of hardship, sleeping in the Underground City and a diet of turnip and salted beef hadn't done much for his health.

Duncan didn't try to hurry him, for the wiry high-lander was concerned about his frail friend and wasn't all that keen to get to where he was leading, anyway. Unlike Peazle, Duncan moved silently, as he had learned to do while stalking deer. Only now he walked without a sound in case something was creeping up on *him*.

Eventually, a flickering glow appeared at the far end of the tunnel and they could hear a muffled clanging, like a bell, growing louder. Peazle stopped and gave a long whistle.

The ringing stopped. After a few seconds, they heard a similar sound coming from the direction of the light, so Peazle signalled Duncan to carry on. At the end of the passageway, the boys turned a corner and a blast of hot, smoke-filled air seared their faces.

They stepped from the dark passageway into a bright chamber and came upon a sight that would have confirmed the worst fears of the other underground dwellers.

Shadowjack Henry stood in the middle of the red, shimmering vault, stripped to the waist and swinging an enormous hammer. He was so large he made Merry Andrew look like a midget and his massive torso, shining with exertion, bore the livid wealds of a hundred healed burns. He brought the hammer down on the glowing metal rod he was shaping and a shower of dazzling sparks flew into the air, vanishing into the fierce radiance that emanated from the blacksmith's forge.

Over the fire, a large metal smelting dish was suspended on a stout pole between two wooden tripods, powerful flames licking its sooty sides.

"My God," whispered Duncan. "We're in the doorway tae Hades itself."

Shadowjack looked round. Huge teeth split his bushy black beard as he grinned at the pickpocket.

"Peazle, my lad." He dropped the tool with a clang and raised a sweaty hand in greeting. The smile vanished as he caught sight of Duncan.

"Ah. I see you brought a visitor."

Shadowjack Henry flexed his considerable muscles and two bushy eyebrows closed ranks on his sweaty forehead.

"I don't get many visitors," he said coldly. "Being a private sort of person."

"This is Duncan MacPhail," the pickpocket gulped. "Don't worry, he's a good friend and one that I would trust with my life."

"That's the type of friend that you want, right enough." The giant smith looked the highlander up and down before turning back to Peazle.

"So, what have you brought for me, little man?"

The pickpocket pulled a canvas bag from under his shirt and emptied the contents onto the vault floor. Four snuffboxes glinted in the iridescent light. Shadowjack knelt and inspected them.

"Solid gold and good quality, as well. They'll make a pretty puddle once they're melted down. Well done, lad."

He went to a pile of bedding in the corner of the vault and rummaged inside.

"I'll give four shillings for the lot, as I'm in an uncommon generous mood."

The blacksmith smiled thinly and folded a few coins into Peazle's hand, his massive fingers enveloping the boys, like a shark swallowing a minnow. Shadowjack cast a sideways look at Duncan, to see if he had any opinion on the price, but the highlander was staring into the well. It looked harmless enough, just a round hole in the corner of the floor, with yet another wooden frame and pulley built over it. A rope and bucket sat nearby.

"Is this where you draw the water tae work your forge?"

"It is, boy." The blacksmith nodded. "And there are those who would like nothing better than for me to block that hole up again. Fortunately, I'm far too big to argue with."

He motioned with his hand.

"Don't fall in, though, for I won't venture down to rescue you."

"We're just going." Peazle wafted the air in vain, his face already running with perspiration. "Let's get out of here, Duncan, before I faint dead away with the heat."

The highlander was still trying to peer into the darkness of the well, so Peazle grasped his arm and ushered him quickly out of the vault. Shadowjack didn't bother to say goodbye.

"He doesn't much like others' company, especially strangers," the pickpocket explained as the scarlet glow faded behind them. "But I told you we'd eat well tonight."

He showed Duncan the pile of shillings.

"That well, back there?" his friend paused. "You can hear water running at the bottom."

"So what?"

"Water in a well doesnae run anywhere. What I heard was a stream."

"And that means?" Peazle looked none the wiser.

"I thought you were the scientific one," the highlander scoffed. "It means the water down there is coming from somewhere and going somewhere,"

He patted Peazle on the shoulder.

"It means there's another level underneath this one."

Charlie sat up with a start, not sure if he had been dreaming or simply lost in his own thoughts. The sun had gone behind a cloud and James Hogg's tombstone, wrapped in afternoon shadows, was cold against his skin. He sat up quickly and closed the journal.

Charlie knew exactly where Shadowjack Henry had once worked. He had been in that very chamber the day before and seen the remains of the blacksmith's forge. He recalled the discarded tripod and stone circle. The pile of rocks he had removed must have been covering up the well, sealed by some kind of iron plug. And just as well, for hadn't the terrifying drumming noise come from somewhere under it? Charlie shivered again and the sensation hadn't much to do with the temperature.

All the same, he looked up to see where the sun had gone and his shiver turned into a gasp.

Floating, far above his head, was a white hawk with black-tipped wings.

The Dungeons

Charlie returned to the guesthouse, his mind whirling. Like the last time he had opened Peazle's diary, the boy was not sure if he had imagined or actually witnessed the events in the past. But there was no doubt that he had actually seen a hawk, right here and now, identical to the one Duncan described two centuries ago. Perhaps the bird's descendants still nested in the area and, by some genetic fluke, bore the same markings. Then again, maybe all the hawks round here were white with black-tipped wings. Duncan didn't seem to know much about the lowland wildlife of Scotland and neither did Charlie.

Anyway, the boy had more pressing questions. How had Shadowjack Henry's well come to be blocked up - hidden under a pile of rocks along with Peazle's book? What was the mysterious rapping he had heard in the Underground City? And what exactly happened to the boys from the past?

By the time Charlie reached the guesthouse, his parents had left for their nightly performance at the big top. A little tray of biscuits and tea-bags were provided in each room, so the boy grabbed a handful of chocolate digestives, opened the journal, and lay down on the bed to read.

The next Sunday we arranged to mete in the after-noon once more, as Duncan had gone calling on his lady friend again and he seems to be creeture of habit. I was bored wating and knowing that the castle espla-nade was filed with gentlemen taking the air, I vowed to liten a few of their back pokets before returning to find my frend...

Edinburgh Castle was on the highest pinnacle of the Old Town ridge. The muddy road that led to it was steep and slippery and Peazle was wheezing like a don-key long before he reached the top. Eventually, the slope opened onto castle esplanade, an exposed area leading to the huge iron portcullis that fronted the mas-sive fortress walls. Since the other three sides of the castle overlooked sheer cliff faces, the esplanade was the only real way to reach the battlements - which left potential invaders horribly exposed. It was said that the approach was exactly the length an arrow could be ac-curately fired.

In peacetime, however, the esplanade's tremendous height made it the perfect spot for sightseeing. The area was filled with young men trying to impress lady friends by wearing their Sunday best and pretending to know the names of far off hills. Peazle strolled around like the city's scruffiest tourist, secretly eyeing them buying cups of flavoured ice for their paramours and watching where they kept their purses.

"A fool and his money are soon parted, and love makes a fool of the wisest man," the pickpocket said sagely. "Ooh. I must write that down."

While Peazle was spying on potential victims, Duncan sat at the bottom of Blair Street, listening to the Gypsy girl as she sang to the crowds. Like so many of the Old Town's narrow wynds, Blair Street sloped steeply down from the High Street until it vanished into the slums of the Cowgate. Each wynd had its own distinct character and this particular thoroughfare was lined with bookstalls and filled with what Peazle always referred to as 'learned gents', browsing idly among leather-bound volumes.

Near the bottom of the street, the stalls thinned out, and passers-by often paused to listen to the girl, for she had a voice that made words sweeter than any book. She and the highlander had struck up a friendship and he visited often.

This time, however, her tune was making Duncan melancholy. A lament about clans forced to leave their homeland after the doomed highland revolt of 1745. Even the girl's name reminded him of the highlands.

Heather.

Halfway through her refrain, Heather noticed Duncan's expression and broke off in mid-tune. She picked up a few grubby coins and, to the disappointment of the gathered crowd, came and sat beside him. Thick black hair swung across a radiant face as she lowered herself down.

"Is my singing making you sad?" She looked sideways at him.

"The song is," he replied. "All the more for being sung so beautifully."

"If you miss the highlands so much, why did you leave?" Heather asked. "If I might be so bold," she added quickly. She knew the highlander wasn't one to casually reveal his feelings.

But Duncan answered without any prompting, for the song had also reminded him of a great unfairness, and he felt injustices should always be brought into the open.

"The land my clan worked for generations was taken from them so the laird could use it for his sheep to graze," he said with undisguised disgust. "There was nae work anymore for the men who lived there."

"I'm sorry," Heather said. But Duncan hadn't finished.

"An outbreak of cholera five years ago killed many, my own faither included. The rest of my family booked passage for North Carolina tae start a new life in the Americas."

The highlander's face was expressionless.

"My mother wouldnae go."

"Why not?"

There was a long silence before the boy spoke again.

"I had a brother, little more than an infant. Ma used to leave him in the doorway of oor croft, wrapped in a wee tartan shawl, while she picked wild berries. I was supposed tae be watching him. I looked away for only a few seconds, I swear."

He kept his head bowed but the Gypsy could hear pain cracking his voice.

"When I turned back, he was gone."

Heather covered her mouth with a dainty hand.

"I thought it must be a wolf or a starving dog that took him and searched the moorland for days. It was nae use." Duncan's voice had suddenly grown hard and flat. "Ma would not accept that. She said my brother had been taken by the Little People."

"The faerie folk?" Lilly nodded, unsurprised. In those days, people still believed in such creatures.

"Aye. My mother died of the cholera some months after. Until that time, she stood in the doorway every day at dusk, calling my brother's name. Hoping the Little People might take pity and bring him back."

He looked up and smiled forlornly.

"They never did."

Pretending to stare at the view, Peazle stretched out his hand and slowly lifted the tailcoat of a young man who was chatting animatedly to his lady. A stiff breeze blew from the Pentland Hills across the esplanade and tore at the youth's clothes, making the pickpocket's practised manoeuvre impossible to detect. The wallet slid out of the back pocket and vanished into Peazle's vest. He gave a satisfied smile - the victim was so engrossed in his beau that the boy could have stolen his underwear.

As he turned to escape, the grin froze on his lips.

Two kilted soldiers stood behind him, pointing bayonets at his stomach.

Heather sat silently beside Duncan and, for a while, allowed the highlander his own thoughts. Eventually, she spoke again.

"Do *you* think the Little People took your brother?"

"I dinnae ken." The boy sighed. "At our clan gatherings, the old men used tae scare us with stories about them."

"It was the same with us Gypsies," Heather agreed. "According to our elders, the Little People have many names. Brownies, Elves, Faeries, Sprites, Imps and Pixies. Our legends say they used to live all over the world. But men began to spread across the globe and the Little People returned to their homeland of Galhadria."

The girl lowered her voice, as if some unseen being might be listening.

"They say that, in the quiet places of the earth, the Galhadrians sometimes return to dance or hunt - and it is a great misfortune for any man to come upon them."

Duncan was familiar with this part of the story. Children in the highlands had long been warned of 'Thin Places' - remote valleys and hilltops where the barrier between this world and the domain of the Little People were closest - though he had never heard the name Galhadria before. In these Thin Places, you might accidentally stumble on them dancing in the moonlight and, if you did, they would take you to their world. It wasn't that the Little People were evil, the old ones of the clan said. It was just that the wishes of men didn't mean much to them. Duncan supposed that was why they could steal a human baby without worrying what it might do to a mother or brother.

"We were told faeries sometimes take our children and leave one of their own in its place," he said. "And you cannae tell it's really one of the faerie folk until it grows up. Or sometimes they leave a horrible, deformed changeling. Or they dinnae leave anything at all. I wish I knew what was true."

He glanced round at Heather. The Gypsy girl was looking at the ground, her fists clenched.

"What's the matter, lass?"

"Nothing," she answered quietly. "I just think that legends can get mixed up over time. Even a small mix-up can change the meaning of everything, you know?"

Heather paused, as if she had more to say but, before Duncan could press her, she scrambled to her feet.

"I'd better give them another song. Something more cheerful."

She smiled and nodded towards another group of wealthy gents, milling beside the nearest bookstall. She began to sing again and the men gathered round and reached into their pockets.

Peazle had never been inside the castle before and, though he was truly impressed by the lofty battlements and smoke-blackened towers, he wished he could be anywhere else on the planet. The two soldiers marched him up the winding cobbled road into the very heart of the fortifications, past endless stone barracks, cannons and cooking fires. The castle hadn't seen conflict for half a century but was still a military garrison. Kilted recruits and officers in bright tartan trews and scarlet jackets stared as the pickpocket was escorted past. The air pulsed with the smell of roasting meat and the sound of shouted orders.

"What are you going to do with me?" he asked one of the soldiers timidly.

"If it were oop ter me, lad, oi'd probably joost shoot yer," the man replied in a thick Irish brogue. "Boot it's ter the doonguns oim taking yer."

"The dungeons!" Peazle squealed, then quickly regained his composure. Panicking wasn't going to help this situation. "I thought they were only for prisoners of war."

"Dat dey is," the soldier replied. "Boot we're not at war with anyone at present and, as it happens, there's a coople o men down dere from the town council. I reckon oil joost hand yis over to them."

He motioned with his bayonet towards an oak doorway set in a tower wall and the other soldier pushed Peazle through. Behind the door, a steep staircase wound into the bowels of the castle. The soldiers' tackety boots clattered on the stone as they followed Peazle round and round and down and down, past cold gaping chambers fortified with iron bars. In the darkness of some of the vaults, Peazle could hear murmuring in some language he didn't understand.

"Dootch smooglers," said the talkative Irishman. "Oi can't oondershtand a bloody werd they're saying."

The trio eventually arrived at a long corridor lit by thick, acrid candles. A group of men, two soldiers and two civilians, were clustered around a table cluttered with paper, trying to read in the flickering light.

"Sah! The tunnel don't show up on any of the charts we have!" a sergeant with a giant walrus moustache barked.

The civilians gave a little jump.

"There's no telling where it might lead. Might be a few feet or..."

"... Or it might lead right under our defences." His companion, an officer of some sort, folded hands behind his back. "We simply have to find out where it goes. Can't fit any of our men in there, you say?"

"No, Sah!" The civilians winced again. "Not even Private Hemmingway, an he lost his legs at Waterloo."

The sergeant thought for a second before adding, "And an arm."

The sergeant turned to Peazle and his guards.

"What might you be doing with that boy, private MacSorry?"

"Caught him stealing, sor. Wallets. Oop on the esplanade."

"That's not a military matter," the officer reprimanded.

"I know sor and I tot, since dere were two members of the town council here, oid bring him to dem."

The councillors, dressed in identical breeches and frock coats, looked up from their charts.

"It's not our concern either, soldier," one said. "Deliver him to the town guard. He'll most likely be tried by the magistrate on Monday."

The officer stroked his broad chin thoughtfully before speaking.

"What will happen to the boy?"

"It's a serious charge, pick-pocketing, if he was caught red-handed." The councillors went back to studying their charts. "He'll be deported to a penal colony in Australia, like as not."

"Actually, I was just testing these fine soldiers' powers of observation." Peazle raised his hand. "And very alert they were, too. I was going to put the money back…"

"Don't even bother, lad." The officer crouched beside Peazle and put a hand on his shoulder. "But there might be a way we could forget this whole ehm… incident."

"Oh, I don't think that's possible." One councillor glanced up again. "Boy broke the law."

"What I'm proposing." The officer ignored the interruption. "Is for you to redeem yourself by a bit of bravery. Like a little soldier, eh?"

Peazle nodded enthusiastically, not having a clue what the man was talking about. Encouraged, the officer continued.

"We've found a tunnel in the dungeons, lad, and we didn't even know it was there. We have to figure out where it goes - but it's too small for any of my men to fit in, see?"

Peazle nodded again, more slowly this time. He was beginning to understand what the man was getting at.

"So, if you was to have a little explore of this tunnel and tell us where it went, the army would consider this an act of patriotism. A great civic duty. Isn't that right, gentlemen?"

The councillors were nodding as well. Private MacSorry gave Peazle a thumbs up sign.

"True. A boy would be forgiven a bit of thievery if he was as patriotic as that," one councillor said slyly. "Wouldn't get sent to Australia, neither."

Peazle looked from one looming adult to another. They leaned towards him, moustaches bristling.

"All right," the pickpocket said wearily. "Show me the tunnel."

"Wait a moment. How will we know where he's gone?"

"Drum, Sah!" screamed the sergeant and the councillors jumped once more. "There's a tiny drum in the officers' mess. It was made for Colonel Grouper's little boy, before he blew his head off playing with a loaded musket!"

"Excellent, sergeant. Fetch the drum and a firebrand for the lad." The officer leaned further towards Peazle.

"We're going to make a hero of you son, rather than a villain," he whispered, not unkindly.

Charlie sat up in bed, covered in sweat. He was still fully dressed but his mother must have removed his shoes and put a cover over him when she came home. The curtains were open and he could see the moon shining behind the spires of Edinburgh.

"My God... the legend," he whispered to himself, remembering the rapping he had heard in the Underground City.

"*Peazle's* the little drummer boy."

The Descent

Charlie felt as if he had slept most of the day and night. Perhaps he had, for now he was wide awake, itching to get up and do something. He put on his shoes, stuffed the diary inside his shirt and went to the window. The Old Town was hunched in the middle of Edinburgh like a sleeping dragon, a heavy moon gilding its jagged outline.

Charlie looked at his watch. It was five-thirty in the morning. He unlatched the window and stuck his head out. There was a drainpipe a couple of feet to the left, but his room was on the second floor and it was too dark to tell whether the garden below was grass, soil or paving. Yet suddenly, he wanted to know. In fact, he wanted to know everything. And not just know everything but to feel everything too – that was the closest he could come to describing it. For the first time, Charlie Wilson really wanted to be part of the adventure rather than a spectator.

Almost without thinking, he pulled himself onto the broad window ledge and twisted round to grasp the drainpipe in both hands. He had never actually watched his parents perform the high wire act but had seen them practise many times. And he recalled his father's favourite phrase.

Hesitation is an acrobat's worst enemy.

With a deep breath, Charlie swung one foot over the pipe and planted it against the wall. He took his other foot off the sill and began to climb down, hand over hand. A minute later, he was standing on the dewy grass, not even out of breath.

"That was better than any video game," he said brightly, letting himself out of the garden gate and heading towards the Old Town. "What have I been missing?"

Edinburgh Festival's events went on until around one in the morning and the pubs closed even later. At this hour, however, even the most hardened partygoers had gone to bed. The streets were deserted.

Charlie made his way up the High Street and onto the castle esplanade. Far below, the lights of Edinburgh glittered like a swarm of fireflies, while the castle was a soaring block of darkness, casting a net of shadows over the esplanade and turning monuments and trees into sinister blobs. The boy felt like he was standing on another world.

Then, the first rays of dawn began to filter through the tall tenements of the Royal Mile, spotting the castle ramparts with light and laying golden strips along the concrete. They lit a low, bordering wall and Charlie went and sat on the ground with his back against it. As minutes ticked by, the castle slowly turned from black to charcoal to grey and the boy could make out the true outline of statues, railings and ticket booths. Eventually, it was light enough to read and he opened Peazle's diary.

He had to know what happened next.

The tunel was at the bak of the darkest deepest dungon and there was hardly room for even a boy of my small size to fit inside. I held the firebrand in front of me with one hand and dragged the drum behind me on a lether strap tied to my waste. The oficer had instructed me to stop every few minutes or so and bang the drum as loudly as I cood, so that he could hear where I was going. This prooved to be more difficult than he imagined...

The firebrand sputtered badly and the narrowness of the tunnel deflected the heat back into Peazle's face. He was forced to hold the torch as far in front of him as he could and crawl using his free arm. The leather strap attached to the drum kept getting tangled in his legs and the only way he could make a noise was to stop crawling and kick at the drum's taut skin with his feet.

The councilmen and soldiers at the entrance to the tunnel waited until the erratic banging was so faint they could hardly hear it.

"Sergeant," the officer said finally. "Take your men and scour the main courtyard. See if they can pick up the noise there. Put some out on the esplanade as well."

"Yes, Sah!" The sergeant stood to attention, then hesitated. "Beggin your pardon, Sah, but that drum the lad's dragging behind him fills the entire tunnel. If it comes to a dead-end, how's he going to get back?"

"This is a military garrison." The officer gave the sergeant a withering look. "We can't just have tunnels running who knows where. We need to know where it goes."

He turned and walked away.

Wriggling along the tiny passageway, Peazle was soon close to exhaustion. The firebrand in front of him was burning precious oxygen, what little air he could suck into his straining lungs was hot and thin, and his elbows and knees throbbed where rough stone had torn away the skin. Worst of all, he was gripped by a rising panic that was becoming harder and harder to quell. He wanted to scream in rage and fear and thrash at the walls - but knew this would use up even more air. Instead, he forced himself to lie still until he felt a semblance of calm return. Then he began to crawl forward once more.

When the pickpocket had almost given up hope, the little passage began to widen. Soon Peazle could crawl on his hands and knees, then manage a crouching shuffle. Finally, he was able to stand. He put the torch on

the ground, fastened the drum round his waist and untied the drumsticks strapped to his thigh.

On the esplanade, Private MacSorry sat on a low
wall, rolling a cigarette.

"MacSorry!" roared the sergeant. "I know the boy's
probably dead already, or his extremities are being
eaten by rats, but that doesn't mean you can give up
looking...." He stopped suddenly and held up a large,
scarred hand. "What's that?"

"What's what, Sir?"

"Silence, you horrible little man!" the sergeant
screamed. "How am I supposed to concentrate with
you wittering on!"

He dropped to his knees and pressed a hairy ear to
the ground.

"It's drumming, Private. That's what it is. Under the
ground." He looked up, moustache quivering and beckoned to the officer. "Sah! Over here!"

Peazle marched along the tunnel, firebrand raised
high. Occasionally he stopped and beat the drum for a
few seconds, but not very often, for the sound was
deafening in such an enclosed space. The boy was wary
of making a loud noise at the best of times. Pickpock-
ets, out of sheer habit, didn't like to attract unwanted
attention. And who knew what lurked in these passageways? Worse still, the tunnel had begun to slope

steeply down. Now, with every step, he was moving deeper into the bowels of the earth.

Then he came to a door.

It was ancient and thick, its misshapen oak timbers covered in dark mould. Peazle groaned in disbelief.

"What on God's green earth is this doing here? It must weigh a ton and I'll wager its hinges are rusted solid with age." He gave a half-hearted shove at the oak giant. "I bet Goliath himself couldn't shift it."

The door swung open without a sound and Peazle fell through into another passage. The barrier shut again and the pickpocket sprang to his feet, swiping wildly at the air with his drumsticks and screaming. But no hidden monster appeared and this tunnel looked the same as it did on the other side of the door. Regaining his composure, Peazle turned and inspected the barrier more closely. The torch lit up the hinges, ornate, finely crafted and looking like they had been made yesterday.

"No wonder they didn't rust." The pickpocket breathed. "If I'm not mistaken, they're solid silver and finer than any snuffbox I ever seen."

He ran his torch excitedly over the rest of the door – and found its surface was pitted with metal studs, glowing with a lambent beauty. They, too, were silver. Peazle grabbed a narrow rock and tried with all his strength to prise one off. The stud stayed put.

"Bother!" The pickpocket finally gave up. "Don't suppose there's much chance of stumbling on a crowbar." He stepped back and studied the door with growing suspicion. "Why would anyone go to the trouble of building such an ornate barricade way down here then make it so easy to get through?"

His eyes widened.

"Unless it only opens from one side!"

The pickpocket launched himself at the barrier and pushed with all his might. It didn't budge. He tried pulling on the silver studs but his hands just slipped off.

"Blast, blast, blast!!!" he sobbed. He attacked the door again, though he knew it was useless. He gave the unyielding wood one last kick, picked up the firebrand and continued, still cursing, down the tunnel. The unpleasant surprises weren't over for, before long, the tunnel forked. Peazle stared at identical passageways.

"Ach, both of these probably lead to certain death, so it doesn't matter which one I take."

He shrugged and went left. After a while, the tunnel split again and then again, so every few minutes he had to make a fresh choice. Peazle tried to pick the passages that didn't slope too much but each corridor twisted and turned and led inexorably downwards. Desperation eventually overcame fear and, as the boy marched, he began to beat the drum - berating himself with each stroke for agreeing to this insanity. He would probably keep descending until he died from thirst or reached Australia after all.

He turned a corner and stopped dead.

Once again, the passageway split in different directions but, this time, the left-hand passage opened into a large chamber. It seemed to have suffered a rock fall, for, on one side of the vault, boulders rose at a steep angle from floor to roof. The pickpocket's mouth fell open and the drumsticks dropped from his hands.

Scattered across the sloping hill of stones were a mass of breastplates and helmets - while swords, spears and arrows protruded between the larger rocks. They glowed coldly in the firebrand's light and Peazle could tell their worth at a glance. The weapons and armour, like the door studs, were made of solid silver.

The boy was looking at more wealth than he had ever imagined, and he could imagine a *lot* of wealth. He clambered onto the rockfall and ran trembling hands over the shining surfaces.

"This is the best thing that ever happened to me," he sighed, laying his cheek reverently on a gleaming breastplate. "Now I really do have to get out of here alive."

He cast an expert eye over the treasure until he spotted what he was sure was the finest piece. Near the ceiling, a beautifully engraved sword, complete with a jewel-encrusted handle, was wedged between boulders. The pickpocket scrambled to the top, grasped the handle and pulled with all his might. The sword gradually eased out of the narrow gap, remarkably light in his hand, smouldering with a steely blush that seemed to come from within.

"This will do nicely."

Peazle climbed back down the rock pile, the drum banging awkwardly against his knees. With a grunt, he unfastened a clasp on the leather strap and it crashed to the ground, then rolled off down the tunnel. Peazle fastened the sword in its place, picked up the firebrand and set off down the passage, whistling to himself. Now that he carried a weapon worth a fortune, the pickpocket was filled with a newfound enthusiasm.

Halfway down the Royal Mile, the sergeant took his ear from the ground and slowly stood up. On one side of his head, his hair, matted with mud, stuck out like a small explosion. The councillors and the officer looked at him expectantly.

"The drumming kept getting fainter, Sah, as if the boy was getting further and further underground." He took a deep breath. "Then it stopped."

There was silence for a few seconds before the officer turned to the councillors.

"It's not an escape tunnel - not if it goes down that far." He turned to the sergeant. "Order the men back to the dungeons and have them seal the passage up."

"Ehm. Begging pardon, Sah." The sergeant looked flustered, for he was not used to questioning his superiors. "Just because the drum stopped don't mean the boy is dead."

"No indeed, sergeant." The officer tapped an ivory-topped cane angrily against his leg. "But my priority is the defence of the castle, not the fate of some thief."

He turned his back, indicating their brief conversation was over.

"Yes, Sah." The sergeant motioned to MacSorry and his companions to follow and marched purposefully back up the High Street. He had seen children die before. The drummer boy of his own regiment had been swept away in a French cannon blast at the battle of Aurerstadt. He didn't approve, of course, but orders were orders.

Charlie opened his eyes. The whole of the esplanade was bathed in early morning sunlight and the brass statues lining the sides were shining like precious metal. He had long ago given up doubting what he was seeing was real. How that was possible was something he could ponder later.

"Breastplates and helmets and swords," the boy breathed softly. "All solid silver and encrusted with jewels."

He remembered Lilly's words when he had first shown her the note.

I bet it means there's treasure hidden down there…

"You said it, girl!" Charlie laughed, shutting the diary. Then the laugh died in his throat as he recalled what she had said next.

What if those council workers end up heading to-wards it?

Charlie sprang to his feet and raced down the High Street towards the big top.

The Forge

Charlie half expected to see Lilly juggling elephants or something equally bizarre when he burst into the theatre. Instead, she was sitting on the floor in her usual green dress, drinking a can of Coke.

The boy's face was red and sweating after running halfway down the Royal Mile, so Lilly held out the drink. He took a huge gulp and bubbles shot out of his nose.

"Charming."

"Listen!" The boy spluttered after three minutes of uncontrollable hiccupping. "There really is treasure in the Underground City. In a set of blocked up tunnels! It's in Peazle's journal. Ehm. Sorry."

He handed the can, overflowing with froth, back to Lilly. She looked at it in disgust.

"There's silver," Charlie continued. "Loads of it, according to this book."

"Told you." The girl allowed herself a triumphant smile.

"Yeah, but we're in trouble. Council workers will soon be excavating down there. You said so yourself." Charlie pointed to the back of the big top. "We need to get underground and find that treasure before they do."

"We? I thought I was just the lookout."

"I don't know about you," Charlie replied vehemently. "But that treasure would mean an awful lot to me. You've never seen where I live - it's small and cheap cause my parents hardly make any money. If you hadn't noticed, there isn't exactly a lot of work at the job centre for acrobats."

"Hey, hey." Lilly held up a hand. "Calm down and take a seat before you explode."

She pulled Charlie down beside her and he sat, chest heaving - trying to get his emotions, as well as his breathing, under control.

"For a start, you don't know if the council workers will end up anywhere near the treasure."

"They might," Charlie interrupted, running a hand through his hair. "All they have to do is break into the bottom tunnels."

"Calm down." Lilly took the boy's hand and stared earnestly into his face, her green eyes somehow soothing him. "Charlie, we don't even know if the treasure is still there."

The boy began to shake his head but she squeezed his hand tighter.

"The diary is almost two hundred years old, remember?"

He nodded sullenly.

"You need to read the rest of the book before you go rushing into the dark again." She gave one last squeeze before letting go. "Find out exactly what's down there."

"You're right." Charlie stood up and went to the ranks of chairs where the audience normally sat. He plonked himself down and pulled out the diary.

"What are you doing?"

"Taking your advice." He looked up. "I'm going to finish this. Go ahead and juggle if you want."

He bent over the book and began reading. Lilly pulled several multicoloured balls from her pockets and began to toss them in the air, her hands moving faster and faster, until the objects were no more than a whirling smear. After a while, the balls were joined by glittering stars, circling around each other like a tiny galaxy. One of the balls burst into flames without interrupting its mad spinning. Charlie didn't look up.

Lilly sighed. The balls began to vanish one by one. Their motions got slower and the stars glittered less brightly, then went out. Finally, only the flaming ball spun uncertainly on the end of the girl's finger. With a flick of her wrist, her hand enveloped the flame, snuffing it. The object dropped, smoking, to the floor.

Lilly walked over to Charlie.

"Budge up then," she said, sitting next to him. "Let's have a look."

The tunel seemed to be leveling out at last and I was no longer scared of meeting any monsters, or not very much. For I had my magnificent sword, which I intended to sell as soon as I cood find my way to the surface...

"Uh oh."

Peazle glanced up at his spluttering torch. The shadows in the tunnel were becoming thicker and darker, as the firebrand's flame grew lower. The pickpocket increased his pace but couldn't go much faster, for the extent of his ill health was making itself painfully obvious. The boy had a nagging stitch in his side, his breath was coming in broken gasps and the reduced light meant he stumbled on the uneven floor every few feet, sometimes sprawling headfirst across the pitted floor. On the fourth or fifth fall, he lay exhausted while the firebrand's flame faded to dirty red embers and the tunnel melted into terrifying blackness. Still lying on the floor, Peazle curled into a ball and began to cry.

Gradually, his sobbing turned to a shivering whimper, for the tunnel was cold and the heat Peazle had worked up during his earlier exertions was evaporating. He closed his eyes and pulled his elbows and knees in tighter, trying to shut out the cold, darkness and fear.

Lying perfectly still made him aware of something he hadn't noticed before. He could hear a faint, sinister hiss somewhere up ahead.

"Snake?"

Peazle's eyes shot open and one hand went instinctively to the hilt of his sword. He drew the weapon slowly from the leather belt and held it protectively in front of his face. To his astonishment, the sword glowed with a pale blue luminance, not as effective as the firebrand, but enough to let him see a few feet of the passage ahead. Peazle knew that lying doing nothing, no matter how scared he felt, wasn't going to solve his predicament - and *something* was making that hiss. It might be a giant underground snake but it might also be a wind blowing in from somewhere outside.

There was only one way to find out, so he struggled to his feet and started forwards, jabbing the weapon aggressively before him. Whenever the tunnel branched, Peazle listened carefully, then went in the direction of the noise. He knew he was choosing well for, at each fork, the sound got louder - though never as loud as the pounding of his heart.

The passage ended and Peazle found himself looking into a smooth volcanic chamber, triangular in shape and not much higher than his head. At the narrow end, a stream emerged from one rock fissure and rolled sluggishly through a gash in the floor, eroded by centuries of flowing water. At the wider end, it vanished into the darkness again. Peazle gripped his sword handle tighter, for the surface of the steam danced and sparkled with a strange red light that made the water look suspiciously like blood. The pickpocket had once overheard a conversation between two learned gents about Greek mythology, whatever that was. They recounted a story of how dead souls were ferried down an underground river and into Hades, which was guarded by a three-headed hound called Cerberus.

"Nice doggy," The pickpocket sank to his knees, clasping both hands in front of his face. "Oh, God. Please, please, get me out of this."

He closed his eyes, praying to whatever deity happened to be listening.

"I've always wanted to die rich, but not ten minutes after I *got* rich." He opened one eye and looked pleadingly upwards. "C'mon, I'll do anything. Just give me a sign."

An object came hurtling out of the blackness above and plunged into the stream, showering the pickpocket with icy needles of water. He scuttled back against the chamber wall, gasping with cold and thrusting his sword ineffectively in the general direction of the unknown attacker. The water broke again and a wooden bucket, tied to the end of a rope, emerged full and dripping from the watercourse. It rose jerkily back up and vanished into a glowing red hole in the chamber roof.

"Woah! Hey! Whoever's up there!" the pickpocket screamed at the top of his voice. "I'm down here! Here! Oh damn!"

He still held the silver sword.

He looked round in panic and, spotting a large boulder, ran over and pushed the sword into the shadows and covered it with stones. He whirled back, took a deep breath, jumped into the icy stream and waded to the centre of the chamber. Above him, he could now see a long, thin funnel rising twenty feet through the solid rock of the chamber roof, ending in a circle of red light.

Suddenly, he realised exactly where he was.

"Shadowjack! Shadowjack Henry! I'm down here!" the pickpocket yelled up the funnel. He waved his arms maniacally, though nobody above could possibly see him. "I'm at the bottom of your well!"

A bearded face appeared in the red circle far above.

"Peazle? Is that you I can hear, lad?" Shadowjack's voice echoed down the shaft. "How the hell did you get down there?"

The rope and bucket came hurtling down again. Shivering and crying, Peazle sat on the bucket, arms and legs wrapped around the sodden rope and Shadowjack Henry pulled him to safety.

A few minutes later, Peazle was sitting in the blacksmith's vault, wrapped in a woollen blanket and sipping a cup of hot ale. A pot of the sweet-smelling brew bubbled on the forge and the pickpocket's clothes hung, steaming, on the bar above. Shadowjack sat next to the boy, stripped to the waist, holding his own mug in a giant scarred hand. He listened intently, occasionally nodding, while Peazle told him about his underground journey. The pickpocket missed out the part about the treasure, however. He wasn't about to trust such a big man with so much wealth at stake.

"That's a fine adventure, without a doubt," Shadowjack said, when Peazle had finished. The two stared at each other for a long time until the blacksmith spoke again.

"If you go back to the surface, they'll probably just arrest you."

Peazle nodded bitterly.

"No. I don't think I'd be much of a friend if I let you go back up top." Shadowjack stroked his beard slowly, still looking keenly at the boy. The pickpocket couldn't see much friendliness in that stare.

They sat in silence for a while longer, Shadowjack watching him intently. Finally, Peazle couldn't stand it anymore.

"You know about the treasure, don't you?" he said bluntly.

"Aye, I do," Shadowjack admitted. "You think anything but treasure would keep me in this hellhole? I've not seen a bloody tree in months."

The giant stretched a burly arm over the forge and shifted Peazle's clothes so they wouldn't scorch. He took another gulp of his ale.

"I was a fine smithy, you know," he said. "Used to work out by Kelty, across the River Forth. I did all right when we was fighting Napoleon and the army needed cannon and cartwheels and the like. But, after the war, many that harvested the land left for the cities - for they have machines now that can do their work."

Shadowjack spat on the floor to show what he thought of mechanised farming.

"Me? I couldn't labour in some hot, cramped factory."

Peazle looked incredulously around the sweltering little vault.

"How on earth did you end up down here?"

"I went to Leith docks to enlist in the king's Navy. I'd got to like quite like cannon and thought I might make a good cabin boy."

Peazle frowned. He could never tell if Shadowjack was joking or just slightly insane. The big man carried on with his tale of woe.

"I was having a last whisky or three in one of the taverns there, when I overheard two Gypsy types talking in a corner. A mite the worse for the grog they were, and a bit louder than they intended to be. I only caught the end of what they were saying, but it sounded powerful interesting to me. Another ale?"

"No thanks."

Shadowjack poured more steaming liquid into the boy's cup anyway.

"One was telling the other some old Gypsy legend about how there was supposed to be untold riches hidden in a well under Edinburgh." Shadowjack took another large swig of his brew. The fact that it was still boiling didn't seem to bother him.

"Anyway, I'd heard from a beggar that there happened to be a blocked up well at the bottom of the Underground City."

"So you decided to abandon a life on the ocean wave and move here?" Peazle looked sceptical.

"To be honest, I can't swim." The big blacksmith grinned. "Besides, the only ship in port was a barge carrying treacle to Glasgow. So, I came down here, built a forge and opened up the well." He pointed to the forbidding hole in the corner of the vault. "Late at night, I'd climb down the shaft and search for the treasure. Took me a while to find it, though not as fast as you, eh?"

"Yes. I was born lucky." Peazle snorted. "So, how are you going to spirit all that silver away without anyone spotting it?"

"Simple. I'm melting it down in the forge."

"You're what!"

Instead of replying, Shadowjack padded over to the farthest corner of the vault and picked up a large knife. Peazle clutched his mug tighter. The blacksmith pulled a horseshoe from his pocket, scraped at it with his blade and held it out. Under the dirty iron surface, the metal gleamed brightly.

Peazle drew in breath sharply.

"Throw on a bit of dirt when it's hot and a silver horseshoe will look as drab and worthless as any iron one. When I've turned all the spoils into these horseshoes, I'll pile them on a cart and ride out of Edinburgh a rich man." He grinned slyly. "Your outfit's dry."

Warily, Peazle took the stiff, warm clothes and put them on while Shadowjack stood up and stretched. The movement put him between the pickpocket and the vault door. His shadow rose menacingly up the wall and flickered across the roof.

He was still holding the knife, its surface reflecting the blood-red glow of the fire.

"However, if anyone informed on me?" He looked darkly at the boy, and Peazle shrank back from the bushy gaze. "I'd find myself fighting off every thief and vagabond in the city."

"I wouldn't tell," Peazle said in a small voice. "Not ever."

"I want to believe that, lad." Shadowjack took a step forward. Peazle saw the giant was perspiring more than he ever had working on his forge. "I like you, boy, but that's an awful chance to take."

Peazle began to back away as Shadowjack advanced. His mind was working furiously.

"There is an *awful* lot of silver. Enough to make more than one person rich." He saw, to his horror, that the blacksmith was herding him towards the mouth of the well. "It can't be easy melting it down on your own."

"True." Shadowjack shifted the knife from one hand to the other, still moving towards the boy. "I have to fetch wood and coal for the fire but I don't like to leave the vault for more than a few minutes, in case someone stumbles on my little operation. That makes the job slow going."

"How many horseshoes have you made in the last month?"

"Six."

"I take your point." Peazle was at the edge of the well mouth now. He could hear the gurgle of the water below and feel cold air rising at his back.

"What if you had help?" he asked quickly. "You could be finished before you knew it."

"Help?" Shadowjack stopped and raised a thick black eyebrow.

"Suppose I was to go down the well and bring out the silver for you to smelt down. My friend Duncan could be a lookout. He's from the highlands. Nobody can sneak up on him unawares and he's handy with a blade if they did."

Peazle struggled to keep the fear out of his voice and sound as reasonable and business-like as possible.

"Shadowjack, there's enough silver down there to make all three of us wealthy a dozen times over."

The blacksmith tapped the blade against his cheek while Peazle teetered on the edge of the well.

"I agree, lad," he said. "You have a deal."

He shot out a meaty paw and grasped Peazle's hand. The force of his handshake lifted the boy away from the menacing hole and he bounced around on the end of the blacksmith's arm like a rag doll.

"Shadowjack," he said through rattling teeth. "Why didn't those Gypsies come looking for the treasure themselves?"

The shaking stopped.

"No idea, son," the giant blacksmith replied evenly. "Leith's a rough area. Maybe something… unfortunate happened to them."

He let go of the pickpocket's hand and gave a toothy smile.

"Off ye go. Find your pal and come right back. Don't ask any more daft questions."

And Peazle went, still shaking like a leaf.

The Gorrodin Rath

Charlie shut Peazle's diary with a snap.

"Well, that's that, isn't it?" he snorted. "They took the treasure and buggered off out of Edinburgh. I might have known we wouldn't be lucky enough to find it still down there."

"Don't be so sure." Lilly tapped the dirty old book. "If those guys rode into the sunset with the silver, then why was Peazle's diary in the Underground City?"

Charlie arched an eyebrow. "If I had that much money, a stupid diary would be the last thing on my mind."

"Even if it implicated you in stealing a fortune?"

"Ah. I never thought of that." Charlie pointed an appreciative finger at Lilly and opened Peazle's diary again. "There's still a bit more…"

Duncan, Shadowjack and myself began removing the silver. I wood take a piece of armour or a sword, carry it to the botom of the well and put it in the bucket. Shadowjack would haul it up, melt it down and beet it into a horseshoe shape. Duncan kept a lookout and fetched food and water and, by this method, working day and nite, we quickly transformed all the silver, until there were only a few pieces left...

Duncan sat on a pile of rags in the doorway of the vault where he and Peazle lived. The chamber was one of the last in this particular tunnel, an ideal place to keep watch, to see if anyone walked past, heading for the hidden staircase. The highlander didn't know why he was bothering. In the week they'd been working, not one person had shown the slightest interest in going anywhere near the blacksmith's vault. A combination of superstition and an understandable fear of an antisocial brute like Shadowjack effectively dampened the curiosity of any Underground City dwellers. Even the likes of Merry Andrew stayed away.

Today was the last day of their enterprise. The armour and weapons were almost gone and a huge pile of dirt-covered horseshoes were now piled in the corner of Shadowjack's chamber. The blacksmith had used all his savings to purchase a horse and cart, which was tethered in stables at the Pleasance Meadow, a few hundred yards away. At dusk, the trio would transport the booty to the surface, load it onto the cart and drive it through the city gates, claiming it was a delivery for the cavalry at Ruthven Barracks. Once they were out of Edinburgh, they would turn and head for Glasgow, where crooked merchants would pay a fortune for such an amount of pure silver. And it certainly was pure. In fact, it was the most beautiful material Duncan had ever seen.

Tomorrow, he would be a rich man. In a few days, he and Peazle would take their share and he would have the money to buy a plot of land in the highlands.

Yet, he wasn't happy. Everything had to be done in secret, for how could three peasants like himself, Peazle and Shadowjack claim to have honestly come by such a fortune? He would have to leave Edinburgh without telling anyone and adopt another identity, which meant he would never see Heather again. He could not bear to spend his life slaving in some Edinburgh factory, yet what was the use of having land when you could not use your own name? When you had no family or loved ones to share your riches with?

And why shouldn't he take someone? In fact, why couldn't he take Heather? He had always felt he had nothing to offer such a beautiful and talented girl. But soon, he would have enough money for both of them to live comfortably. Surely she must be tired of singing for a living in these cramped and filthy streets? She claimed to be a Gypsy, after all, so must share his love of open skies and uncluttered spaces. He could take her away and look after her properly.

His mind made up, he hurried out of the Underground City to find Heather, leaving Shadowjack and Peazle working, unawares, in the darkness below.

Shadowjack put on thick leather gloves and grasped the sides of the giant smelting dish, bubbling above the forge, hooked on a metal pole suspended between two wooden tripods. The blacksmith carefully tipped the container until a small amount of molten silver trickled into a curved iron mould on the vault floor. When it began to harden, he plucked the silver from the mould with iron tongs and hammered it into a proper horse-shoe. Sparks drifted through the air and singed the smith's beard, but he was used to this and paid no heed. Like Duncan, he was deep in thought.

It was a shame to have to split all these lovely spoils with the boys. Then again, he had to admit Peazle and Duncan worked hard. He certainly couldn't have pulled the job off without them. Besides, that Duncan was a tough character and Peazle wasn't stupid.

Ach, it was only money, after all. He just needed enough to get to America, find some unclaimed land and open his own smithy, for that was the work he loved. Shadowjack held up the finished horseshoe, swept it through a pile of soot and dirt and plunged it into the bucket of water, causing a mighty blast of steam to swirl around him.

Peazle sat at the bottom of the rock pile, trying to draw a proper lungful of air. In the last few days, his breathing had become more laboured and bouts of coughing racked his frail body. The boy's health was rapidly declining and he suspected he had tuberculosis.

Yet he had to keep going for, until he had a share of the treasure, he couldn't afford medical treatment. Thank goodness there were only a couple of pieces left.

He struggled to his feet but another fit of coughing forced the boy back to his knees. He wiped the back of one hand across his trembling mouth and it came away smeared red. The pickpocket clenched his fists, gritted his bloody teeth, and made himself stand. He picked up a helmet and, with a breathless sob, staggered back into the tunnel.

Heather was singing at the bottom of Blair Street, as she always seemed to be. It occurred to Duncan that, for a Gypsy, she seemed remarkably fond of staying in one spot. She saw him as he came down the hill, quickly finished her song and waved goodbye to the clapping gents. She gave Duncan a hug, standing on tiptoe to get her arms round his neck.

"Hey stranger," she said breathlessly. "I haven't seen you all week."

"Work, work, work, that's me." The highlander replied solemnly. He motioned for the girl to sit beside him. "Heather, I think we need tae talk."

"I thought you were ignoring me." She smiled and hunkered down. "Why so serious? Oh, I forgot. You're always serious."

The highlander smiled at the mild rebuke and took her hand.

"What would you dae if you had enough money to get out of Edinburgh?"

"I don't. Have enough money, that is."

"Suppose I got it."

"I've lived too long in this city to make wishes."

"I might... be on tae something." Duncan ran a hand through his long dark hair, unsure of how to finish. "Something that will make me... well... awfy rich."

"What are you talking about? Have you broken the law? Are you in trouble?"

"Oh, for goodness sakes!" The highlander thumped a hand on his knee. "I've aye been a plain speaker for I dinnae ken any other way."

He clasped her by the shoulders.

"Me and Peazle found treasure. At the bottom of the Underground City, under an auld well. We've almost finished taking it out and it's enough to make us all..."

His voice trailed away. Heather's face had gone white.

"What's wrong?"

"Treasure?" She put a trembling hand on the highlander's knee. "At the bottom of a well?"

"Incredible, isn't it?"

"Is it silver? Weapons and armour made of silver?"

"Aye, that's right." The highlander's delight turned to puzzlement. "Hold on a minute. How did you ken that?"

"Duncan. We *do* need to talk."

Shadowjack saw the rope suspended over the well jerk several times, a sign that Peazle was pulling at the other end. He put down his tongs and walked over to the hole.

"How many more, lad?" he shouted down.

"I've tied on a helmet. You can pull it up now." Peazle sounded exhausted. "There's only a shield left, but it's bigger than all the other pieces." There was a fit of coughing from the darkness. "I don't know that I can carry it, Shadowjack. It looks awful heavy."

"Go back to the rockfall and have a rest, wee man," Shadowjack shouted back. "I'll melt this piece, then climb down the rope and help you."

"Will do."

The helmet clanked back and forth against the sides of the shaft as the blacksmith pulled it up. When it reached the top, he leaned over the well mouth and untied it. As he finished unfastening the knot, a blast of frigid air hit him, rising from the black depths. Shadowjack shivered violently and dropped the helmet, then peered into the hole, bemused. He had been working in this vault, hauling water and bits of armour out of the shaft, for three long months and had never felt slightly cold before. Now, for some reason, the hairs were standing up on the back of his neck and his calloused skin was covered in goosebumps.

Peazle trudged back to the rockpile and lowered himself onto the floor. It seemed far chillier down here than it had ever been before. He set his aching back against a boulder, stretching and twisting to try and relieve the pain in his tired muscles. He picked up a little flask of whisky Shadowjack had given him and took a sip.

"Whooooeeeegh. Eugh! Eugh! Eeeeeeeeeugh!" He shuddered, putting it quickly down again. "I can't believe people drink this stuff for fun."

But he had to admit Shadowjack's 'medicine' had warmed him a little.

There was a sharp noise to his left and his head jerked up. A small stone tumbled down the rock pile and landed a few feet away. Peazle sighed in relief, unclenching his fists.

"I will be so happy when I get out of this place," he wheezed, sinking back. "My imagination is starting to get the better of me."

"We Gypsies know many stories, Duncan." Heather looked the highlander straight in the eye. "And, to be honest, most are just make-believe. Others we do not take lightly."

"It's the same in the highlands," Duncan agreed. "What of it?"

"There is a legend," she continued in whispered tones, "That I think you should hear about. According to the Gypsies, many centuries ago, one of the Little People was a great magician called Gorrodin.

"Little People again, is it?" Duncan frowned.

"Gorrodin was exiled from Galhadria for a reason I do not know. But his heart was filled with bitterness and he decided that, if he could not live in his own land, he would set up a kingdom on earth."

Lilly pointed to Arthur's Seat, always ominously present over Edinburgh's rooftops.

"In a great cavern under that hill, he created an army called the Gorrodin Rath and favoured them with a cup called the Grail, which bestowed eternal life on anyone who drank from it. But it also turned them into monsters. They terrorised the humans who lived in the area and, though the Little People disapproved of what Gorrodin was doing, they did nothing. Magical creatures do not fight each other, you see."

"Why not?" Duncan asked sourly. "We humans dinnae have a problem killing our own."

"I only know that this is a rule Galhadrians dare not break. They must not go to war with each other." She shrugged cynically. "Even if that rule did not exist, Little People love only music, dancing and merriment. They do not much care about men."

Duncan could see the reasoning behind that.

"Gorrodin had a daughter," Heather continued. "Who could not bear to see the evil done by one of her own kin. When a Scots army gathered to fight the Gorrodin Rath, she led them to a hidden cache of faerie silver, knowing full well that it was deadly to the dark creatures. The Scots forged it into weapons and armour, including a magnificent sword called Excalibur. This was given to the Scots leader Arturius."

"Excalibur? Arturius?" Duncan interrupted. "You mean King Arthur? I thought he was just a myth."

"It's myths we speak of," Heather said. "You must decide whether this one is true."

"Then carry on." Duncan nodded solemnly.

"Some of the Scots led a night raid on the Gorrodin Rath's stronghold and stole the magic cup. When the creatures - led by their mighty war chief, Mordred, gave chase - they were met by Arturius and the rest of his warriors. Mordred's army couldn't harm those Scots who wore silver armour and could themselves be killed by warriors wielding weapons made from faerie silver. Even so, the Scots were vastly outnumbered and the battle raged through the night until only a few fighters were alive on either side. The Gorrodin Rath were denizens of the dark so, when dawn broke, they fled through a tunnel into a cavern under Arthur's Seat."

She looked towards the top of the grassy peak.

"Arturius, though mortally wounded, led his few remaining men into the mountain after them. They sealed the entrance to the cavern with rocks and placed their silver weapons and armour in front, as a barrier to stop the Gorrodin Rath ever getting out. Even Excalibur was left there. It was a barrier the Gorrodin Rath could not cross, for they dare not touch it."

Duncan paled.

"The Scots searched and found another exit, so they melted down a few pieces of faerie silver and set them in a stout door to seal that as well. As a final precaution, they erected a fort at the entrance to always be ready, if the Gorrodin Rath got out. That fort eventually became Edinburgh Castle."

Lilly indicated the slope in the distance.

"Knowing he was defeated, Gorrodin vanished to the remote north and left his minions to their terrible fate."

"What happened to the Grail?" the highlander asked. "What became of the daughter?"

"Nobody remembers," Heather said simply. "Over hundreds of years, the treasure, the tunnel and Arthur drifted into legend - and the city of Edinburgh was built on top of them."

Heather bit her lip.

"If the tale is true, then it's not treasure that you're removing. It's the bars of an ancient prison."

She held out a hand.

"Duncan, I'm sorry…"

But the highlander was already on his feet and running towards the Underground City.

The Battle

Peazle stood up and stamped his feet. It was definitely much colder, too chilly to sit around any longer. At least, that's what he tried to tell himself. In fact, he felt incredibly vulnerable, sitting in a flickering pool of firebrand light. He hoped Shadowjack was almost finished melting the helmet. The pickpocket breathed in and, this time, he didn't cough. If he was careful and took things gently, he could probably get that last shield back to the bottom of the well on his own. A few steps then a rest, then a few steps. The hardest part would be getting it from the top of the rockpile. He'd just wait a couple more minutes to get his strength back, then he would give it a go…

Duncan raced through the Underground City, moving over the dark and uneven floor with the grace of a natural hunter. He powered into Shadowjack's vault and cleared the fiery forge with one leap, his foot catching the astonished blacksmith in the centre of his chest. The blow, with the force of a fifty-yard run behind it, caught the giant by surprise - and he toppled backwards with a grunt. As he crashed to the floor, Shadowjack lifted the heavy tongs to strike the boy, but Duncan's knife glinted in the firelight right below the smith's left eye.

"You make one move," the highlander spat, his face inches from the blacksmith's own. "And you'll never see the money you so badly wish tae spend."

"What is this treachery?" Shadowjack let go of the tongs and held up his empty hand. "Tell me quick. I've always played fair with you."

"You didnae warn us about the monsters!" Duncan wrapped his fingers in the blacksmith's bristling beard and pulled him even closer. "That's why the Gypsies you overheard never came looking for the treasure, isn't it? You told us about the silver, you treacherous dog, but you didnae tell us about the monsters!"

"Monsters!" the giant roared. "What are you babbling about, boy?"

"The silver guards a great evil! It cannae be taken oot!"

"Pah!" The blacksmith's eyes were almost bulging out of his head. "That stupid fairy tale? Only an ignorant peasant would believe something like that. I didn't even think it worth mentioning!"

"I believe in fairy stories," Duncan hissed. He lifted himself off Shadowjack's chest and stood up, still brandishing the knife. "I lost my brother tae the Little People. I'm not going tae lose my best friend too."

"You're brave to anger a man like me, highlander." Shadowjack sat up, his face red with rage. "Also very foolish."

He struggled to his feet and stepped forward, towering over Duncan.

"If I'm wrong, then I apologise to you, blacksmith, and my shame will be great." Duncan tucked his knife back into a leather sheath under his arm. "But I fear the worst."

"Nonsense!" Shadowjack fumed. "I'm on my way down to help Peazle take out the last piece of treasure right now. When we've brought it up, I want to hear no more of this ignorant tomfoolery."

"The last piece? Already?"

"Aye," Shadowjack scowled. "We're not all sitting around, thinking up daft children's tales, you know. That boy down there is working like a dog."

"Shadowjack, I beg you to trust me on this." Duncan moved to the well. "Stoke up the fire as high as it will go. Please."

He sat on the edge and grasped the rope.

"I'll explain when I return. If I'm being foolish, you can laugh at me while you count your money."

A self-mocking smile played on his lips, but his eyes burned into Shadowjack's with an intensity that made the blacksmith suddenly look down. Duncan slid over the well rim and into the darkness.

Shadowjack stood for a few minutes staring at the black hole and stroking his beard. Then he turned and began to quickly pile wood on the forge.

The shield made a grinding noise as Peazle slid it down the rock pile, but he knew the silver would be undamaged by the jagged stone. He had once overheard a learned gent claim that precious metals scratched and broke easily but this stuff seemed indestructible. Peazle was beginning to doubt these learned gents were ever right about anything. The shield slid off the last rock and hit the floor with a clang. The pickpocket began to drag it down the passage that led to the bottom of the well.

He had gone about fifty yards when it occurred to him that he had left Shadowjack's liquor flask back at the rockpile. Sighing, he trudged back to get it. He was stuffing the container inside his shirt when he heard footsteps pounding up the corridor in his direction.

"No need to hurry, Shadowjack. I'm managing just fine." He looked round as a running figure emerged from the darkness. "Duncan! What are you doing down here?"

The highlander slowed to a halt, his chest heaving.

"You all right?"

"Why wouldn't I be? Apart from coughing a bit, I'm fit as...."

Peazle's reply was drowned out by a deafening crack. A huge slab of stone shot out of the rock pile, like a cork from a champagne bottle, shattering into a thousand pieces on the cavern wall opposite. Duncan launched himself at Peazle, knocking the boy over and flattening him to the ground. The firebrand spun into the air and clattered across the floor as pieces of boulder rained down around them. A chunk the size of a brick hit Duncan between the shoulders and a thousand points of pain burst across the back of his head. He slumped forward on top of the pickpocket.

"Duncan! You're squashing me!" Peazle tried to roll the half-conscious highlander off, then froze as he peered from under his friend's motionless body.

An arm jutted out of a hole where the rock had been. It was long, powerful and twice the size of one of Shadowjack's powerful limbs. But this arm was so white it was almost translucent - hairless, with thick blue veins and spattered with patches of grey mould. And the hand on the end! It was more like a claw, curved, twitching and bristling with vicious yellow talons.

"Heaven save us!" Peazle whispered, thumping his groggy friend on the shoulder. "Duncan! Get up! Pleeeeeeeeeeeeeeeease!"

With a shudder, the rocks around the arm rose and parted and a head and shoulders burst out.

Peazle screamed.

The cranium was bald and misshapen, eyes sunk so far into the creature's doughy flesh, they were no more than malevolent little beads. The monster pulled its body slowly out of the gap, squat, wide and bent almost double - as if an eternity of squeezing through low passages had permanently curved the massive, knotted spine. It opened a cavernous mouth, revealing two rows of jagged teeth and stepped down from the rock pile, almost daintily. Its powerful sinewy legs ended in hooves, rather than feet.

Another head, equally ugly, burst from the rocks a few feet away.

"We have to get out of here!" Peazle hissed, twisting his friend's head in the direction of the aberrations and slapping his face. "Wake up!"

Duncan finally got his eyes to focus. With a grunt of agony, he pushed himself groggily to his feet, pulling Peazle with him. By now, a third, smaller creature had forced its way through the stones and the first two were clear of the rock pile, standing on the chamber floor itself.

"What in God's name are they?" Peazle whimpered.

"Gorrodin Rath." Imminent danger had sharpened Duncan's senses despite the pain. "We cannae let them get between us and the way back."

The monsters were crouching and stretching, sniffing the air and each other. Grabbing Peazle's hand, the highlander began to inch along the wall. "They dinnae seem to see very well, which is a wee blessing."

The two closest trolls glanced at the children and then over at the exit. With ugly leering grins, they moved to block off the boy's retreat.

"Nothing wrong with their hearing, pal." Peazle tried to shrink back further into the shadows, but it was too late. The third troll joined his companions and a fourth was beginning to emerge from the rocks.

"It's nae use. We're trapped." Duncan pulled out his knife and held it valiantly in front of them. "When I attack, you run to the right. Follow the wall. You'll only have a few seconds."

"When you attack!" Peazle grabbed his friend's arm. "Are you insane?"

"Nae point in both of us dying," Duncan said calmly, despite his racing heart. "Go tae the right, like I say."

The beasts looked at each other and one snorted loudly. The boys could smell a blast of foetid breath, for the nearest couldn't be more than twelve feet away.

"What if they understand Scots?" Peazle stammered. "You've just told them which way I'm going to go."

"Then choose your own path! Surprise me!"

"No, Duncan." The pickpocket picked up a chunk of broken stone. "You're my only friend and, by my soul, we'll live or die together."

The trolls edged towards the boys, hooves clicking on the stone floor and thin black lips curling back over drooling fangs. They hunched down and stretched their claws out - grunting, panting and waving their heads from side to side, in a sinister, snake-like motion. Duncan shifted the knife from hand to hand.

"Goodbye, Peazle," he said gently.

With a mighty roar, Shadowjack Henry barrelled into the cavern, swinging the silver shield around his head. The corner caught the troll nearest to him and half its malformed head vanished in a black oily cloud. The other creatures spun round, releasing a cacophony of ear-splitting screams, recoiling when they caught sight of the gleaming silver.

"To me, lads!" Shadowjack raced across the vault. The shield connected with the outstretched claw of one of the trolls and sliced it clean off - a white clutching hand flew through the air and landed at Peazle's feet. Galvanised, he and Duncan darted over to where Shadowjack was swinging the shield back and forth. At each thrust, the monsters shrank away, waving their arms ineffectually.

"Duncan, my boy," the blacksmith roared as the boys sheltered behind him. "I've decided there's no need for you to apologise, after all."

"Glad tae hear it," Duncan said as the trio began backing into the tunnel. "Now give me that shield."

"What?"

"Shadowjack, you said you'd trust me! Give it to me, then I need you to do exactly what I say."

Duncan grabbed the shield before the blacksmith could object.

"Run back to the well. Take Peazle, though you might have tae carry him."

Peazle was stumbling alongside them, coughing violently again.

"I've nae time to explain, but I have a plan. Climb back up to the vault and start melting the silver horseshoes in thon forge."

"Why? I mean… how many?"

"All of them, Shadowjack, or else we're dead. Go!"

The blacksmith looked like he was about to object, when another unearthly scream of rage rose from the chamber they had just left. Instead, he scooped Peazle under one meaty arm and set off. Duncan turned and faced the direction of the enemy, shield in hand, as the pursuing trolls clattered into the tunnel. Stopping when they saw his defence, they hissed, spat and screamed, yet dared not go any further. Duncan was facing his worst nightmare and felt like collapsing with pain and terror. But he was a boy with a long line of warriors' blood in his veins.

"Right, ye big Sassenach devils!" he yelled, for want of anything more appropriate to say. "Let's see you take on a highlander! Aye, you, wi your pasty faces and bad breath!"

The trolls retreated a few feet, snarling and gurgling amongst themselves. Bent and bloated bodies almost filled the corridor and Duncan and could see at least five of them crowding behind the leader. Two of the monsters turned and loped away, the tapping of their hooves fading into the distance. The highlander knew immediately what they were up to, for there were many branching corridors in this labyrinth. His adversaries were going to circle round and find another route to the well, catching Peazle and Shadowjack unawares and cutting off his own retreat.

There was nothing else for it. With a blood-curdling yell, Duncan charged at the enemy, catching the three remaining trolls off guard. Fleeing in panic, they tried to scramble over each other, spitting and clawing in an attempt to get away. Their bodies were too large to manoeuvre properly in such a confined space and Duncan swung the shield, catching the nearest creature square in the back. A huge gout of black liquid arched from between its shoulders as it fell, writhing and screaming. His second swing took the upraised arm from the second before the monsters thundered, squealing in terror, back the way they had come.

Duncan shouldered the shield, spun on his heel, and headed in the direction Shadowjack had gone.

Peazle was standing knee-deep in water at the bottom of the well when Duncan reached the chamber.

"Shadowjack's climbed the rope to the top and is melting the horseshoes back down again," he sputtered weakly. "Seems a shame, after all the effort we put into making them."

"Then get up there after him! These beasties will be here any second and I cannae hold them all off, no even with a silver shield."

The pickpocket shook his head.

"I haven't got the strength to climb, Duncan. Besides, I thought you might need this." He thrust his arm into the black water and pulled out a beautiful silver sword.

"Where in the name of all that's holy did you get that?" Duncan gasped.

"Hid it behind a rock a couple of weeks ago." Peazle tossed him the weapon. "Out of pure greed, y'know?"

Duncan looked at the sword reverently.

"My friend, ye never cease tae amaze me."

The bucket and rope came tumbling down the funnel and splashed into the water, narrowly missing the pickpocket.

"The horseshoes are melting away just fine," Shadowjack's voice echoed down. "Grab hold of the rope, lad."

"Take the shield with you." Duncan thrust it out. "Melt it down too. Melt everything that's silver. Then throw the rope back for me."

Too weak to protest, Peazle hoisted the shield on his back and sat on the bucket.

"Haul away, Shadowjack!"

Boy, bucket and shield rose, unhesitatingly, into the air - Duncan could hear Shadowjack grunting as he pulled. The highlander spun, sword in hand, in time to see the first beast slither into the chamber. Then another entered. And another. And another, until twelve of the monstrosities were bunched together in the vault. One gestured violently and the creatures began to fan out, gurgling and slobbering. They inched in both directions along the chamber wall until, eventually, they ringed the highlander. Duncan circled on the spot, holding out the sword, but knew he had lost. He could kill five or six, perhaps even more. In the end, however, they would overcome him by sheer weight of numbers.

The bucket landed in the water again and the trolls recoiled in surprise. That was the spilt second Duncan needed. He rammed his foot into it and grasped the rope with one hand.

"Pull, Shadowjack! Pull, or my life is over!"

Shadowjack gave a tremendous roar of exertion from above and Duncan shot into the air. Seeing their victim about to escape, the trolls rushed forwards en masse - the largest leaping into the air towards him, talons outstretched. Duncan swung the sword in a vicious arc and the creature's clawing fingers were sliced from its hand. The monster fell back into the water with a cry.

"You beasties are no gonnae hae any limbs left by the time I finish with you!" the boy shouted triumphantly, as he vanished up the funnel.

Peazle was waiting at the top to help Duncan clamber out of the well and into Shadowjack's vault. He gasped at the clouds of steam enveloping them - for the blacksmith had simply dumped the huge smelting dish onto the red-hot coals of his forge, then thrown in all the silver. The highlander could see the shield dissolving into a mass of bubbling molten metal that almost reached the top of the huge container. Shadowjack gave a whistle when he saw the sword.

"That's a piece and a half, no mistake. Can't believe we missed it the first time." He eyed the weapon hungrily. "You sure you want it melted down as well?"

"I dinnae think we'd better." Duncan held up the weapon in awe. "I'm wondering if this might be the legendary Excalibur itself."

"Aye. Right."

"I'll wager on it!"

"You have nothing left to wager with!"

"Could we get back to your plan, Duncan, whatever it is?" Peazle peered into the well. "These things are climbing."

"Tip out the molten silver." The highlander pointed to the dish. "Tip it doon the shaft."

"No!" Shadowjack held up his hands in horror. "That's our fortune!"

"And how will you spend it from your grave?"

Shadowjack groaned in disbelief, then grabbed a stout cudgel leaning against the wall. He rammed it into the glowing coals below the dish.

"Help me, then. Quick now, before this goes up in flames!" He leant his considerable weight on the staff and pushed. The boys ran to his side and hauled down on the cudgel as hard as they could. The container creaked slowly and lifted a few inches above the forge.

"Once more, boys. With all your might!"

Duncan and Peazle wrenched down on the staff again, with the desperation of people whose lives hung on a thread. The huge dish rose slowly out of the forge and toppled onto its side. Half a ton of molten silver surged out of the container and flowed into the well.

There was an unholy scream from inside the funnel as liquid metal engulfed the climbing trolls and swept them back into the depths. The creatures that filled the chamber below tried to escape when the molten mass hit the river at the bottom.

It was too late. A giant cloud of vapour, saturated with droplets of silver, filled the vault and shot along the tunnels at the bottom, enveloping the fleeing enemy.

In a matter of seconds, the rest of the Gorrodin Rath, who had survived for over a millennium, were blasted out of existence.

Shadowjack, Peazle and Duncan lay on their backs in the vault, gasping and laughing with joy.

"We did it!" Shadowjack thumped Duncan on the chest. "Poor as church mice again, aye, but alive all the same."

"No exactly." Duncan held Excalibur above his head. "This thing has a jewel set in it the size of a hen's egg."

"Poor or not poor, let's get out of here." Shadowjack sat up. "I, for one, don't intend to spend another day locked away from daylight. Not so long as I live."

He stretched out his arm, helped Peazle to his feet then reached back for Duncan. As he did so, a mournful howl rose from the depths of the well. It was a sound more powerful, nerve-jangling and, strangely enough, more human than any of the other creatures had made. Shadowjack froze in mid-pull.

"Oh my God." Peazle clutched the blacksmith's arm. "What was that?"

"Their war chief, Mordred, would be my guess," Duncan said flatly. "Clever beastie. He must have stayed well back while the rest attacked."

"How do you know all this stuff?"

"Never mind that. What will we do?"

"Whatever it is, we better make it quick!"

Shadowjack hauled Duncan to his feet with a mighty tug. The trio could hear hoofbeats growing louder, rattling down the tunnel towards the bottom of the well.

Mordred was coming.

"The dish!" The pickpocket indicated the container lying on its side. "It's still lined with silver. Looks like it might just fit in the well."

"Only one way to find out." Shadowjack flexed his mighty arms, picked up the container with a muscle-popping heave and slammed it into the hole in the vault floor. It slid down almost to its brim, where the lip prevented it sinking any further. Shadowjack stepped back, waving his hands in the air.

"Ooooh." He said through gritted teeth. "Still a bit hot, that."

"There's enough silver left crusted on the bottom of the dish to stop what's down there ever getting out."

Mordred knew it, too. There was another venomous roar from below, then the rat-tat-tat of Mordred's hooves thundering back down the passage as the monster searched in vain for another exit from the lower level. Duncan pushed at the smelting container with his foot but it didn't budge.

"You think there's any way that… thing can get out?"

"I doubt it." Peazle shuddered. "I imagine the soldiers intended to fill in the tunnel at the other end and, anyway, it's sealed halfway with a silver-studded door."

"What if someone removes the dish?"

"This vault already has a bad enough reputation. After all that unearthly screaming and drumming, I can't see anyone ever coming near it again."

"Just in case, we can block up the stairs that lead down here," Shadowjack said.

"Wait a minute." Peazle went to the back of the vault and fetched his journal. "Whatever that thing trapped down there might be, it's lived for a long, long time and isn't likely to die any day soon."

He opened the book and began to write.

"Gather as many loose rocks as you can to hide the well. I'm going to leave my diary here as a warning in case anyone ever finds this place again."

Shadowjack and Duncan silently scoured the vault and adjoining corridors for suitable debris while Peazle completed his journal. They wrapped the book in one of a Shadowjack's smelting gloves, left it in the dish, pulled a plank over the top and covered it with stones.

"I said you'd write something important one day." Duncan patted Peazle on the shoulder. The pickpocket didn't smile.

"I pity the poor soul who finds it," he said dolefully.

Then, with Excalibur wrapped in an old oilskin cloth, Peazle, Duncan and Shadowjack Henry walked out of the Underground City and into the sunlight.

The Bodysnatcher

Charlie turned the page but there was nothing else written in the book. He flicked through the rest of Peazle's diary but, from that point on, the pages were blank. He stood up, ignoring Lilly, and paced around the theatre floor. The girl sat and waited, running a small silver ball over her fingers from one hand to another. Finally, Charlie turned to her, tight-lipped.

"There's no way I'm believing that," he burst out. "There's no way I'm accepting there's some kind of monster still trapped at the bottom of the Underground City."

Lilly stayed quiet.

"I know what you're thinking," the boy continued. "That tapping I heard underground was the sound of Mordred's hooves. You think he heard me and came running up the passage below."

"You don't know what I think."

"Well, it's rubbish. That noise was council workers digging, just like you said."

"Could be." Lilly shrugged. "I wasn't down there."

"I don't believe in that kind of stuff! The journal must be a hoax."

"Sit down, Charlie," Lilly sighed. "Trying to make sense of this and walk at the same time is freaking you out."

The boy slouched back down and patted both knees, nervously blowing out his cheeks.

"Look," he said after a while. "Just suppose the diary is right. I'm just saying *suppose*. I'm not saying it is."

He began to get up again but Lilly pulled him back.

"Then let's suppose," she said. "What are you going to do?"

"Make sure nobody ever finds Shadowjack's vault again. Mordred's still trapped, isn't he? I'll go down and cover the smelting forge and… eh… I'll hide the stairway I found that leads to the vault. Put the stones back. Put everything back the way it was."

He smiled hopefully at the girl.

"If there is some sort of horrible creature down there, that'll keep him hidden for another two hundred years."

"I suppose it would," said Lilly. "If it wasn't for the fact that there are going to be council workers digging towards him. If they break through to the bottom level, Mordred will surely kill them."

"That guy stays angry a long time, eh?"

"Worse still. He'll be out."

"Couldn't we tell the police or the army or something?" the boy suggested.

"Tell them what? You discovered a thousand-year-old troll living under the streets of Edinburgh? They're not likely to believe that."

"I know the feeling."

"You have to do something."

"So what if he does get out?" Charlie was clutching at straws now. "How dangerous can he be? Magic or not, he's only one creature. This is the 21st century. The army has rockets and bombs and stuff."

"We're in the middle of a heavily populated city." The girl looked deep into his eyes. "What if he breaks out when your parents are performing in the big top?"

"What do you expect me to do?" Charlie leapt to his feet. "Take him on at hand-to-hand combat? I'm only a kid."

Lilly pointed to Peazle's diary.

"Two boys about your age once managed to beat a whole army of trolls."

"They had the help of a magic sword and a blacksmith the size of Mount Everest!"

With a flick of her wrist, Lilly sent the silver ball whizzing towards Charlie's head. He plucked the object out of the air, an inch from his nose, blinking in surprise.

"What the hell did you do that for?"

"Your parents are acrobats, you said? Look at how easily you caught the ball. You've inherited their speed and their eye."

"I'd rather my parents were big-game hunters and I'd inherited their guns. Am I supposed to fight this thing with my teeth?" He gave the girl a sarcastic sneer. "I've got silver fillings. Think that'll help?"

Lilly didn't get the joke.

"Only faerie silver will work against these kind of creatures, though you're on the right track. You have to think of what you have on your side, not what you don't."

"I've got you. Want to come into the Underground City with me?"

"Not a chance."

"Thought not," the boy said dryly, flicking the ball back. Thanks for your support."

"Charlie, I didn't mean it like that!"

"I got to think about this." The boy strode towards the theatre exit. "I have to go somewhere and work it out."

He opened the door, letting in a flood of sunlight.

"It's not that I'm stupid or a coward. It's just that I'm scared to death and I don't have a clue."

He stepped into the light without bothering to say goodbye. The door closed with a click, leaving Lilly sitting alone in the gloomy big top. She took out some more silver balls and began to juggle them - thirteen, then fifteen, then seventeen, spinning faster and faster, despite the half-light. One of the silver balls hit the edge of her finger and shot away at an awkward angle. She tried to recapture her momentum, clutching at empty air, but another ball deflected off her wrist and vanished under a chair. Next moment, the orbs were bouncing across the floor, away from the distraught girl.

Lilly looked at her hands sadly.

"I can't help him," she whispered to nobody in particular. "That's not fair at all."

Charlie was sitting in his room at the boarding house, staring at the wall and trying to formulate a plan, when his parents trooped in

"It's Wednesday tomorrow," his father announced. "Big top's shut, so we thought about taking you on a day trip. There's a pencil museum in Lerwick."

"I'd love to go," Charlie said.

"Really? You would?"

"Yes, but I can't." The boy thought fast. "I... eh... have to meet a girl."

"Young love, eh?" His father grinned. "You think a girl will be more fun than the pencil museum?"

"Don't tease him," Charlie's mum somersaulted onto the bed beside her son and they both bounced up and down for a few seconds. "What would you like to know about the facts of life?"

"Nothing, mother. We'll probably just go for a Coke."

"That's nice." His mother nudged him, wrinkling her nose. "Do you think about her a lot?"

"As a matter of fact, I've thought about nothing else for hours." Charlie looked up at the woman. "And I'm pretty sure she hasn't been very honest."

"Aw, baby." His mum suddenly looked serious, which didn't happen very often. "Are you going to be all right? You want to talk about it?"

For a second, Charlie considered telling his parents the whole story. He could give them Peazle's journal to read, then climb into bed and go to sleep. Let them work out what was real, what was not - and what he should do about it.

He looked at his father hopefully. His dad made a high whinnying noise, his cheeks vibrating violently.

"That's my impression of a horse," he said. "I can only do it from one side of my mouth."

Charlie groaned.

"It's fine," he said, patting his mother's hand. "Everything's OK."

"Have a talk with this young lady, son. Never let anyone walk all over you."

"I don't intend to."

"Good. Well, you have a fun time tomorrow. Dad and I can have a long lie and go shopping instead."

Charlie's dad sighed.

Finally, his parents went to bed and left Charlie to his thoughts. He desperately wanted to believe Peazle's diary was fake and that magic didn't exist. But he had seen these events, not just read them. What's more, he was convinced Lilly knew more than she was telling.

She should have been as surprised and horrified as he was. Instead, she calmly accepted it all.

Her reactions just didn't ring true.

He felt betrayed and even more lonely. He had come to think of Peazle and Duncan as friends. Now the diary was finished, he would never know what happened to them. Did they take Excalibur to Glasgow and sell it? Did they become rich liked they dreamed? Or had Peazle succumbed to the illness that was obviously killing him?

He took out the note and read it again.

If you are reading this you are in mortal danger. Take the book, leev now and cover your tracks. I pray you are brave at hart and of good character and, if so, read on then do what you must. Hopefully, at the end, you will find a way to emerge victorious.

"Not very helpful," Charlie scoffed. "I don't see a way to emerge victorious in the end. Couldn't you just have given me some bloody instructions?"

He frowned.

For Peazle hadn't written 'in the end'. The note said, 'at the end'. And though the pickpocket was a terrible speller, there was nothing wrong with his grammar.

Charlie's jaw dropped.

"It can't be that simple."

He opened the pickpocket's diary and flicked through it again. At the end was his hand-drawn map of Greyfriars Graveyard. There were little ticks scattered across the page, presumably marking the sites of recently buried corpses ripe for stealing. Looking closer, he saw that one plot was marked with a tiny cross rather than a tick.

He held the book closer and peered at the minuscule marking. Was it a cross?

Or was it a sword?

Charlie leapt to his feet, opened the boarding house window and climbed onto the sill. Without a second's pause, he swung out and clambered down the drainpipe. Soon, he was walking through the silent, deserted streets once more. He reached the big top, let himself in and felt his way to the little vault in the South Bridge where the workmen kept their tools. He took one of the construction helmets with a light on top, put it on his head and wrapped a short shovel in a splattered paint sheet. Then he let himself out of the theatre and strode through the Old Town until he stood at the gates of Greyfriars Graveyard.

The cemetery looked very different at night. The church seemed to be carved from squat, cold shadows and gravestones were scattered like blackened stumps of teeth. Charlie switched on the torch and made his way quietly round the church until he came to the grave of James Hogg, hidden in thick shadow at the bottom of the building. Hands shaking, he unwrapped the shovel, looking around to see if his actions might be detected. But the place was deserted and all lights were off in the surrounding tenements.

He opened Peazle's journal at the back and studied the exact position of the cross.

"Here we go," the boy muttered, "The last of the body snatchers."

He took a deep breath and plunged the shovel into the soil a few feet from the flat tombstone.

Nothing. The spade simply sank into the soft ground. Charlie withdrew the tool and pushed it in again a few inches to the left. Again nothing. He tried the right this time and, once more, the spade met no resistance. On the fourth try, the metal hit something solid.

Charlie began to dig around the spot and, a few moments later, could see an object glinting in his helmet beam. The sky was beginning to lighten, so he scraped hurriedly at the dirt and soon uncovered a beautiful, jewel-encrusted sword handle.

Hardly daring to breathe, he bent down, grasped the handle and pulled. Excalibur slid slowly and easily from the soil next to the grave of Peazle's hero and Charlie held the gleaming weapon in front of him.

"You knew!" he laughed, raising the weapon and saluting his companion from the past. "I don't know how you persuaded Shadowjack to part with this, but you knew. Someday, someone would find your diary. Then they'd need the sword."

He sat down on the flat gravestone, looking at the stunning object, and a great feeling of sadness welled up inside him. Partly, he was uncertain and scared. Partly, he couldn't understand how he had gotten into an incredible situation like this.

But mostly, he grieved for Peazle. If the boy had convinced Shadowjack and Duncan to bury the sword, then he didn't get rich after all. Without money, he wouldn't have been able to afford medicine. Charlie didn't think the pickpocket had lasted much longer after finishing his diary.

The boy felt a welcome warmth at his back as the sun began to rise over the eastern wall of the graveyard. He raised Excalibur above his head and let the rays of a new day dance along its blade.

"Thank you, my friend," he whispered.

He stood up and made a few practice cuts in the air with the weapon. He had no idea how to wield a sword but Excalibur was light and, somehow, felt right in his hand. He edged his way around Hogg's grave, slashing at imaginary foes, imagining he was Arturius, surrounded by the army of Gorrodin Rath. He clutched his heart.

"You got me, pesky varmints!" he croaked, staggering back and forward. "But, before I die, I'll chase you down these tunnels to the very gates of hell and seal you in."

Charlie stopped, Excalibur quivering in the air.

"Just a second. Why would the Gorrodin Rath retreat into a tunnel, where they knew they could be trapped?" He lowered the sword. "If they were losing, why didn't they just run away?"

He thought back to Peazle's diary.

As dawn broke, the Gorrodin Rath finally fled and took shelter in the caverns under Arthur's Seat.

Charlie looked up at the golden orb getting higher over the graveyard wall.

As dawn broke.

A grin of comprehension spread slowly across his face. There was something the Gorrodin Rath feared as much as faerie silver.

They were afraid of daylight.

The Monster

Charlie stepped into the theatre, construction helmet in one hand and paint cloth in the other. Lilly was sitting in the empty front row of chairs, exactly where the boy had left her the evening before. Her face was pale and drawn and she looked like she had been there all night.

"Where's your father, Lilly?" Charlie asked.

"Eh?" The girl was taken aback by this unexpected question. "I don't know."

"I mean, where's your father on that?" The boy pointed to a huge poster adorning the theatre wall. It advertised acts performing at the big top during the festival and was printed in fancy, circus-style lettering.

BLACK HART ENTERTAINMENT PRESENTS:
THE EDINBURGH FESTIVAL ACROBATIC CIRCUS!

The Flying Pollock Brothers
Bert the Human Bullet
The Bouncing Brucies
Skulina: Mistress of the Wire
The Wonderful Wilsons

Dazzling Derek and Deekie Bob the Wonder Dog

"I remember my dad telling me this attraction is just for acrobats, apart from Deekie Bob the Wonder Dog, of course." He walked over and studied the poster more closely. "I thought your father was supposed to be a magician performing in this big top, but I don't see him advertised."

"It must be a typo," Lilly shrugged.

"How did you know ordinary silver wouldn't work against Mordred?" Charlie kept going.

"What are you talking about?"

"Yesterday, you said only faerie silver could beat Mordred. But you hadn't read that part of the book, so how did you know?" Charlie strode towards her. "How come I never see you anywhere except inside this theatre?"

"Why are you hounding me like this?" Lilly backed away.

"You said your father is a great magician. Where is he?"

"Stop!" The girl held up her hands but the boy kept advancing.

"You're Gorrodin's daughter, aren't you? The girl who led the Scots to the faerie silver." He pointed an accusing finger. "I imagine you're also Heather, the singer Duncan liked so much."

Lilly went white.

"You're one of the Little People." Charlie shook his head and laughed mirthlessly. "Now, *there's* a phrase I never thought I'd hear myself say."

"You seem to have it all worked out." Lilly managed to sound impressed and resentful at the same time.

"Actually, it was a guess." The boy looked sheepish.

"It was a good guess."

"Why didn't you tell me right away?"

"Oh, I don't know." Lilly pulled a face. "Probably cause you'd think I was nuts. You had to read Peazle's book before you'd believe."

"You put a spell on me. That's why I was able to witness what happened in the past whenever I opened the diary."

"You said you didn't like reading."

"Fair enough." To the girl's surprise, Charlie chuckled. It seemed like nothing was impossible anymore. He would just have to get used to it.

"The diary said Heather had dark hair but yours is red. I suppose that's magic too?"

"No, it was dirt. You think 19th century Gypsies could afford shampoo?"

This time, Charlie laughed, then reached out and took her arm. She flinched as if she wasn't used to being accepted.

"It's fine. Sit beside me." Despite her deceit, the boy found it impossible to stay angry with Lilly. Besides, he needed answers fast. Any information he could get from the girl might now save his life. He flopped down on a chair and she sat next to him, looking at the floor.

"Why have you stayed here so long?" Charlie asked. "Why don't you live in Galhadria with the rest of the Little People?"

"I can't go back. Not after what my father did."

"Where exactly is he?"

"I really don't know." The girl wouldn't look up. "He deserted me long ago and hasn't been seen since."

"I'm sorry about that." Charlie took her hand.

"I loved him, you know. But I had to try and make right the great wrong he did."

"Are you telling me you've hung around the entrance to the Underground City for millennia?" The boy squinted at her. "Just to stop Mordred and his gang getting out?"

"Partly because of that." The girl put a trembling hand to her mouth. "I also thought, someday, my father might come back."

"I got to admire your patience." Charlie gave her hand a squeeze.

"I like living in Edinburgh," She waved her hand dismissively. "And I want revenge, no matter how long it takes."

"Lilly," the boy said evenly as he could. "If you're a magician's daughter and one of the Little People, why didn't you use your powers to fight Mordred? Why are you trying to make me do it instead?"

Lilly finally looked up, her eyes wide and green.

"Magical creatures must not fight other magical creatures. It's called the Dolorous Stroke - a law so old, we no longer even think about it." She leaned forward earnestly. "But I know if I break it, something terrible will happen."

She shook her head miserably.

"I can't help you."

"I know, I know." The boy couldn't hide his irritation. "And Little People don't care much for humans either. You like to dance and sing."

He curled his lip.

"For a magical race, you Galhadrians don't actually *do* an awful lot."

"You're not even supposed to know we exist." Lilly gripped her mortal companion's hand so tightly the boy winced. "Charlie, I'm doing my best! I've kept people out of Mordred's way for centuries. Now I'm trying to save the lives of these workmen."

"Yeah. By sending some kid to take on Toothy Mctoothface."

"No. There's something different about you. I don't know what it is - but it's sort of… magical as well."

"Aw, you're giving me a big head." Charlie grinned again. "Look, he's just one creature. We call in a bomb threat and the army will be here in no time. They're bound to make short work of him."

"Not unless they have bullets made of faerie silver," Lilly sighed deeply. "And you're missing the point.

Mordred is proof that magic exists. If he gets out, your whole race will believe, once again. And men are far more advanced than they used to be. Your scientists might even find a way to make our magic work for *them*."

"Would that be so bad? Could solve a lot of the world's problems."

"You've developed weapons that could destroy your own planet, Charlie. That's *without* spells." Lilly arched an eyebrow. "What do you think?"

She jabbed a thumb at her chest.

"How long would it be before they discovered a way to reach Galhadria and come hunting my people again?"

"I take your point." Charlie picked up the paint cloth and unwrapped Excalibur, its blade glowing a ghostly blue in the dim light of the big top. Lilly gasped when she saw it.

"No point hanging around here then, is there?" He lifted the sword above his head and plunged it back down. The blade sank into the stone floor as if it were made of butter. Charlie let go and Excalibur quivered and sang, vibrating like a huge bee sting.

"I've got a monster to fight."

"Do you have a plan?"

"Sure." Charlie stood up and placed the helmet with the flashlight on his head. "I'm counting on Mordred laughing himself to death when he sees me."

"Let me fix this." Lilly rose and fastened the strap of the hard hat under the boy's chin. She had to stand on her toes to reach and the top half of her body pressed against his chest. She felt cold.

"So, what do I call you?" Charlie said. "A Little Person?"

"You call me a friend," She slid her arms around his waist and gave him a tentative hug, her head resting lightly on his shoulder.

"You have your parent's courage," she whispered in his ear. "Remember, you also have their skill. Use it."

She leaned back and kissed him quickly on the lips, then held him by the shoulders, at arm's length, like a general inspecting one of her troops. Charlie was surprised to see the girl's eyes glistening.

"If I don't manage this…" he began.

Lilly put a finger to his lips.

"These are the first tears I have shed since my father vanished," she said softly. "Please don't die."

Suddenly the boy felt more confident, more powerful and more loved than he ever had in his life. He lifted his hand to touch the girl's cheek, just once, then walked towards the door at the back of the theatre.

"Your sword!" Lilly motioned towards Excalibur, still upright and vibrating.

"I don't need it. Not yet."

Charlie smiled and stepped through the door.

Lilly came back to the weapon and crouched beside it, admiring the intricate carvings on the flawless blade. She clenched her fists in a little gesture of triumph.

"He does have a plan," she said to Excalibur. "I knew he would."

Charlie searched around the little vault where the council workers kept their supplies until he found a small pulley he had noticed on his first visit. He put it in his pocket, took a length of nylon rope from a shelf and wound it around his waist. Then he moved the debris covering the tunnel entrance, slid inside and began crawling back towards the lower levels of the Underground City. He knew he could easily find Shadowjack Henry's vault again. All he had to do was follow the chalk marks he had made on the wall less than a week ago.

He could hardly believe it. Seven days ago, he was an ordinary boy living a normal life. Now he was marching down a hidden tunnel to do battle with an ancient monster. He wasn't the same person anymore, for the old Charlie wouldn't even have stood up to a school bully. But this was not some petty classroom squabble. It was a noble and valiant quest. The kind of thing he had always imagined doing.

He still wasn't sure it was worth fighting a monster for.

When he reached Shadowjack's vault, the boy stood outside the doorway for several minutes until his breathing was under control and his heart had stopped pounding. Once inside the chamber, he would have to work quickly and calmly, if he were to have any chance of succeeding. Or staying alive, for that matter.

"Hesitation is an acrobat's worst enemy," he said to himself and stepped into the chamber.

The hard hat's beam lit up the wooden triangle and iron hook - the old apparatus Shadowjack Henry once used to draw water for his forge. Charlie dragged it to within a few feet of the well, positioning the set up between the blocked hole and vault doorway. He unwound the rope around his waist, threaded it through the detachable metal pulley he had brought and fastened the pulley to the wooden triangle. He took the end of the rope and tied it to the ancient hook. The metal was rusty but still solid enough for his purpose.

The rope and pulley system now formed the basis for a crude winch and he slid the hook under the rim of the metal cylinder that blocked the well. He stepped back, wound the rest of the rope back around his waist, and began walking towards the exit.

The rope tightened.

Charlie gritted his teeth and kept going. The pulley jiggled and there was a grinding sound from the metal dish. The boy pulled harder, though each tug tightened the rope around his waist and forced air from his lungs. The metal dish groaned again and the rim slid up a few inches. Charlie grunted, trying to find a proper foothold, throwing himself against the rope, fighting for air, sweat prickling his body. His feet slipped with each step, so he seemed to be walking on the spot. He bent his head and strained even more.

The dish rose a foot out of the well.

"Aaaaaaaaaaaaaaaaaaaaargh!" Charlie roared, staggering forwards, fists clenched and veins standing out on his forehead. "Come on! You rotten, stupid... COME ON!"

With a horrendous screech, the container lurched out of the hole in the ground and landed with a crash, demolishing the wooden frame. Charlie collapsed face down, his outstretched hands scraping along the floor, lacerating the skin on his palms. In an instant, he was back on his feet and unwinding the rope. He glanced over his shoulder. The metal dish lay on its side and, right behind it, the boy could see a gaping black hole in the floor.

The well was open.

Charlie listened. At first, the only thing he could hear was his own ragged breathing. Then he caught a noise, faint and far away. It sounded like drumming, but he knew now it was hoofbeats.

Mordred was coming.

The boy darted out of the vault and sped back through the tunnels. His arms and legs were pumping with all their might, but he concentrated on keeping his neck rigid, the beam of light steady and pointed down. If he stumbled and fell on the uneven floor, he would lose precious seconds, which might make the difference between life and death.

A blood-curdling roar echoed through the corridors behind him. With a cry of fear, Charlie sprinted faster. Reaching the bottom of the steps, he scrabbled up, slipping on the wet stone, using his hands to propel himself forwards. But he was going too fast to judge distance properly. As he launched himself through the little hole at the top, his helmet cracked on the jagged brickwork and the light smashed, plunging him into utter blackness.

Charlie's bout of terrified swearing was drowned out by another monstrous bellow, much closer than the last. The boy scrambled to his feet and began stumbling along the corridor, one arm scraping along the wall, the other waving blindly in front. The best he could now manage was a hesitant shuffle. Mordred would catch him long before he reached the big top. He didn't even know how to get back now, for he couldn't see where the tunnels forked, never mind the chalked numbers telling him which passage to take.

He stopped, taking deep breaths, trying desperately to calm down. Wiping tears from his eyes, he peered into the blackness in a vain attempt to see something, anything, that might give him a clue where the next turnoff lay.

And there it was. A glowing pinpoint of light punching a tiny hole in the darkness! Letting go of the wall, the boy staggered towards the glow, arms flailing in front of him, his stumbling run gathering momentum until it ended in a headlong dive. His lungs emptied with a painful whoosh as he landed heavily on the floor, outstretched fingers closing around a little sparkling object.

It was a juggling ball. Next to it was a handheld flashlight.

"Thank you, Lilly!" The boy switched on the torch. The beam lit up a numbered fork to his left. It was only two feet away.

There was another howl from Mordred, right behind Charlie. Then the boy was off again, racing up the passages, hurling himself around dark corners and crawling along the last narrow tunnel like a jet-propelled mole. He burst into the maintenance vault, tearing the construction helmet from his head and flinging it across the room.

He could hear a horrific rending of stone as something much larger and a thousand times stronger than he was forced itself into the other end of the tunnel. Then Charlie was in the big top and racing for the exit, grasping Excalibur as he went past. The sword slid from the stone as easily as it had gone in and, seconds later, the boy was standing with his back to the theatre entrance, weapon held in front of his face.

The door that led to the workman's vault flew off its hinges with an explosion of shattered wood and Mordred stepped into the big top.

"Oh. My. God."

Charlie's face turned chalk white as he saw his opponent for the first time. Mordred was the height of a reasonably tall man, and there, any resemblance with humanity stopped. He had heavily muscled arms reaching almost to his knees and spade-like hands ended in a rash of vicious yellow talons. The creature's legs were short and thick and there were hooves where his feet should be. His body was maggot white, hairless and laced with thick blue veins.

But it was his face that shocked Charlie most. Mordred's angular head was bald and his jaw jutted forward like a mechanical scoop, lined with dozens of piranha-shaped teeth. His ears were disproportionately large, set flat against a smooth scalp, while the rest of his features were almost non-existent. The creature's nose was no more than a hole in the front of the face and his eyes had retreated far into his skull, two glowing points of hatred burning deep within waxy flesh.

Mordred took a few lurching steps towards the boy, raising his talons as he approached. Charlie lifted the sword over his head and pointed it towards the beast, like he had seen ninjas do in Kung-Fu movies. He hoped it looked impressive.

"You're not getting past me. I don't care how big you are." He tried to sound bold and manly but the words came out as a series of trembling squeaks. "You never heard of David and Goliath?"

The monster halted. A strange gurgling sound rose from somewhere inside its chest and the jutting mouth split into a hideous upturned slash. Charlie realised, with growing horror, that the creature was laughing.

Then things got worse.

"Brave boy," the troll gurgled. "Even if you do hold the Great Sword."

Mordred's speech was thick and vibrant, buzzing like a swarm of feasting flies. Despite his terror, Charlie was surprised to notice the creature had a distinct Scottish accent.

He gripped the sword handle tighter and cleared his throat. It occurred to him that Mordred hadn't spoken to a human in two centuries and might be inclined to chat before tearing him limb from limb. Mordred looked around the big top with what Charlie presumed was a satisfied grin.

"You better go back where you came from before I chop you into bits," the boy croaked.

"Mordred cannot pass while you have the weapon, as you surely know," the creature hissed back. "But he does not need a door to escape. The poor walls of this dwelling are not like the thick stone of the prison where he suffered so long."

Mordred headed for the side of the big top, ignoring Charlie.

"He shall tear his way out with bare hands."

The boy kept quiet, Excalibur tight in his trembling fist. Mordred raised a taloned claw. Charlie held his breath.

The creature stopped, sniffing suspiciously at the air around the wall. He turned his white, mottled head and stared malevolently at his adversary. Hairs rose on the back of Charlie's neck.

"Clever. Soooo clever," the troll growled. "It is daylight outside, is it not? You have tried to fool Mordred, daring little fellow."

He cantered back over to the centre of the theatre, clicking sharp talons together, considering his situation.

"Smart little boy," he muttered. "But Mordred can wait for night to fall. After all, he has waited for fourteen centuries to be free. Can you imagine that?"

"Not really." Charlie shook his head.

"No. Mordred can hardly imagine it himself, nor does he want to." He hunkered down in the middle of the big top. "After such a time, he can pass a few more hours, heh?"

He laughed a bitter, gurgling laugh again.

"I'll fight you," Charlie said in a tiny voice. His legs were trembling so badly that he could hardly stand, and he felt sick and dizzy with fear. "As you said, I have the sword."

"A Galhadrian is behind this," the creature whispered, tapping its head with a claw. "You would not dare do it on your own."

It clicked talons together again.

"Stalemate," it murmured. "Mordred fears Excalibur, that is true. Yet, you cannot catch him, for he is fast. He will wait."

"Hopefully, that will give you time to stop speaking about yourself in the third person." Charlie put on a false show of bravado. "It's really irritating."

The creature grinned, revealing three rows of teeth.

"At nightfall, Mordred shall simply slice his way through these puny walls to freedom." He began to plod towards the back of the theatre. "You cannot guard every inch."

"I don't intend to." Charlie looked up to make sure he was in the right position. Six feet above his head, the safety net for high wire acts stretched from one side of the big top to the other. He bent trembling knees, tensing the muscles in his body, then leapt into the air, slashing as high as the sword could reach.

Excalibur's blade swept through the steel ropes fastening the net to the wall as if they were thread. With a loud twang, one side of the mesh swept down, draping itself over Mordred.

Charlie charged forward with a yell, as the creature spun, snarling in anger. Though the safety net was made of wire and coated with toughened rubber, the creature's talons sliced through the mesh as easily as Excalibur had. Mordred's arm shot out and grasped one of the metal posts that roped off the performance area. He plucked it from the theatre floor as if it were a weed, the securing bolts popping out of the concrete like bullets.

He flung the spike at the boy.

Charlie dived as the post rocketed towards him, hunching his shoulders and tucking in his head, the way he had seen his parents do a hundred times. The metal bar whizzed past, inches over his hunched form and Charlie straightened out of the dive in time to see Mordred reaching for another post. With a grunt, he threw Excalibur straight at the creature.

Mordred roared in defiance and launched himself sideways, rolling as effectively as Charlie had done, though the movement tangled him even more in the safety net. Excalibur sliced harmlessly past and clattered to the back of the theatre.

Now the beast was between Charlie and his only weapon.

"The child has lost the Great Sword!" he cackled, slicing at the net again. "The child is lost too."

But, instead of turning back, Charlie headed straight for Mordred. The creature slashed wildly at the net, trying to free its arms properly and the jagged rows of teeth slavered as they bit down on the wire strands.

With every atom of his strength, Charlie leapt again, arms outstretched like a soaring bird, up over Mordred's head. The monster thrust one tangled arm skyward, claws glinting, but the boy tucked his head down again and flicked his legs up. With a grace and skill that would have delighted his parents, he twisted in the air. The boy arched over Mordred's outstretched arm, somersaulting perfectly and landing on his feet on the other side of the monster.

Momentum kept him going and he staggered to the back of the theatre, grabbed Excalibur from the floor, jumped and slashed again. The other side of the safety net pinged away from the wall and enveloped the creature once more. With a ferocious howl, Mordred tore into the new mesh folds with teeth and claws. They fell away like torn spider webs.

"Mordred will be free before you can reach him!" he crowed.

"I'm not coming near you." Charlie reached down to a prop table, half-hidden in the shadows, and picked up a small black box. He pointed it at the big top roof.

"Welcome to the 21st century," he said, the tremble gone from his voice.

He pressed a green button.

With an electronic whirr, the two halves of the theatre roof began to separate. Mordred's head shot up and he gave a wail as a line of sunlight appeared on the theatre floor. He struggled out of the net and lumbered towards the back of the theatre, but now Charlie and Excalibur stood between him and the only way back to the tunnels. Behind the creature, a widening band of light danced and sparkled on the chrome and plastic of the theatre fittings.

The monster looked at Charlie, clasping its clawed hands together as if in prayer. Tiny eyes, filled now with sadness and fear, burned into the boy. Charlie felt a sharp pain in his chest.

For a fleeting second, he had seen something terribly human in that stare.

"Clever little fellow," Mordred whispered softly, as the sunlight reached him. "He is victorious."

Charlie's eyes widened. Watching the light hit Mordred was like witnessing some deformed snowman caught in an inferno. The troll dissolved in front of his eyes, gobbets of flesh sliding from its body, hissing and bubbling, the way fat melts in a pan. Turning his head upwards and stretching out his mighty arms, Mordred let out one last agonised roar.

"MORGANAAAAAAAAAAAAAAAAAAAAAA!"

The sound echoed round and round the big top, until the monster was gone, leaving nothing but a pool of rancid flesh on the floor.

Charlie dropped Excalibur, his chest heaving.

"Dad was right," he said morosely. "This trip has certainly brought me out of my shell."

Sinking to his knees, he began to cry.

The Thin Place

Charlie's palms hurt, though they had finally stopped bleeding. His tears had dried up too - and he sat quietly in the middle of the big top floor, looking like an exhausted clown. His face and hair were white from dust in the Underground City and the knees and elbows of his clothes were worn away by crawling through the tunnel. His dishevelled appearance fitted the surroundings perfectly. The door to the workmen's vault lay scattered in pieces across the floor, and so did bits of Mordred. There was a metal pole sticking out of one of the big top wall supports and the roof was gaping open to the sun.

The roof! Charlie leapt to his feet, pointed the remote control and clicked. With a grinding sound, the metal flanges, high above, closed again. Anyone outside would simply presume the mechanism was being tested. The boy looked at his watch and was surprised to see it was still only 6.30am. Good. Not many people would be about, especially in this quiet little street. Hopefully, Mordred's dying yell would be mistaken for the Geronimo-style roar of a practising acrobat.

The boy was so exhausted he could hardly think straight, but getting the hell out of this wrecked tent, undetected, certainly seemed a priority. He wondered where Lilly was.

He gave the control box for the big top roof a wipe with his T-shirt, in case the police were inclined to fingerprint it, prised Excalibur into the gap between the doorframe and the theatre door and sliced through the hasp of the lock. Now investigators might think the big top had been broken into and vandalised. Charlie wrapped the sword in the paint cloth and stuck his head nervously out of the door. Nobody was about. He hurried up the sunlit wynd and turned the corner onto the High Street without seeing another soul.

At this time in the morning, even the High Street was quiet and the few passers-by didn't pay much attention to Charlie's tousled hair and torn clothes. After all, the festival was filled with performers dressed in weird and wonderful costumes to promote their shows. Right now there was a lone figure dressed as a penguin plodding down the other side of the road.

He had to figure out what to do with Excalibur. The sword was worth a fortune, he had no doubt, but what use was that to him? If he tried to sell it, there would be all sorts of very awkward questions, like what was a young boy doing with a two-thousand-year-old sword made of a metal science couldn't explain? If Lilly was right, a magic blade wasn't meant for human eyes any more than Mordred had been.

The fairest thing the boy could think of was to put Excalibur back where he found it. The graveyard was bound to be empty at this time of day. He could go straight there, replace the sword and be back in bed before his parents woke up. Tucking Excalibur under his arm, he headed for Greyfriars.

When he arrived, there was a small figure standing outside the wrought-iron gates, pressed against the wall as if trying to stay hidden from anyone in the cemetery.

"Lilly?"

"Get over here." Lilly motioned nervously to him. When he got close enough, she reached out and pulled him away from the gates. "Are you OK?"

"Mordred's dead." Charlie tapped his hand on the paint cloth, sharing credit with the hidden weapon.

"I guessed that, otherwise you wouldn't be standing here." She clasped the boy's arm and hugged him triumphantly. "You are something else, know that?"

"Thank you," Charlie blushed. There was so much white dust caked on his face that Lilly didn't notice.

"Where are you going now?" she whispered. "Are you going to put Excalibur back?"

"I am," the boy said miserably. "There goes my yacht."

"Not so loud!" Lilly hissed. "Listen. It's all very noble, what you're doing, but it's not a great idea for you to go in there."

"Why not? I've been before."

"Exactly!" Lilly glanced around nervously. "You saw a white hawk with black-tipped wings and there's no doubt it saw you."

"So?" Charlie screwed up his face. "I'm not a dormouse."

"The hawk is a lookout." Lilly scanned the clear blue sky. "For us. For the Little People! Greyfriars is a Thin Place, Charlie. You know what that is?"

"I remember from Peazle's diary." The boy thought for a second. "It's a place where the line between this world and Galhadria is almost non-existent."

"I presume my people let the sword lie hidden in Greyfriars in the hope someone would, someday, use it to defeat Mordred. Yet they are determined to remain a secret to humans."

Lilly tugged at the paint cloth.

"What do you think will happen if you go waltzing back in there now? They'll know you've killed him."

"So soon?"

"You're still alive, aren't you? Plus, you've got bits of troll stuck to your boots."

"Oh, yeah." Charlie looked down. "Think that'll come off?"

"Even worse, you worked out who I am." The girl looked at him imploringly. "You go in there and you'll never come out."

Charlie scowled.

"You Galhadrians aren't exactly big on gratitude, are you?"

"No, we're not." It was Lilly's turn to go red. "As you so perceptively put it, we aren't big on anything except dancing, singing and enjoying ourselves. Helping others isn't high on our agenda."

"Why don't you take the sword in for me, then?" The boy held out the weapon.

"I can't!" Lilly stepped back. "My people don't approve of me hanging around on earth. If I set foot in a Thin Place, they might force me back to Galhadria with them."

"What's wrong with that?" The boy pushed the sword towards her again. "You've put right what your father did wrong. Well, you used me to put it right."

"I had to Charlie!"

"I understand." He patted her arm. "But while I'm being blunt..." He looked apologetic. "I don't think your father is ever coming back."

"Neither do I," Lilly replied sadly. "I hoped someday he might return to rescue his followers." A sudden cold wind rustled through the gate. "But I've gotten to quite like it here and, as you reminded me, we Galhadrians aren't big on gratitude."

"Well, I am." Charlie tucked the weapon back under his arm. "And I'm putting Excalibur back where it belongs."

He pushed at the gate and the iron lattice swung open with a creak.

Lilly hesitated, then stepped away from the wall. She fished in her pocket, brought out a small silver whistle and handed it to him.

"If you're ever in trouble. I mean real trouble, just blow. I'll be there for you, I promise."

"What about your no interfering with people rule?"

"I'd say it was a bit late for that. Besides, I owe you."

"I think I know why you want to stay on earth." The boy grinned and gave her a knowing wink. "After all this time, you're more human than Galhadrian."

"And you're more magical than any person I ever met. In all sorts of ways."

She threw her arms around the boy. He held her awkwardly with one arm, the other still clutching the paint cloth.

"Goodbye Charlie." She kissed his cheek. "I hope we'll meet again."

Lilly turned and ran. Halfway down the street, she gave a small skip.

Charlie watched her, heading further and further into the distance, until she looked just like any other girl in the world.

The shovel was where Charlie had left it, lying next to James Hogg's grave. The boy unwrapped Excalibur and stood over the denuded area where, the day before, he had scraped away the soil. There was a large flat rock, half-hidden under dirt, probably a remnant of some headstone that had fallen over and been covered. But the boy knew Excalibur's power and plunged the sword down anyway. It sank easily into the stone and the packed earth below, up to its hilt. Charlie hoped it hadn't gone through the remains of poor old James Hogg as well. He bent over to pick up the shovel. Once he had covered the handle, Excalibur would remain hidden for many years. Perhaps centuries.

"My goodness, there's an old friend," a voice said at his ear.

Charlie almost fell over. Two boys were standing behind him. One was short and thin, the other tall and muscular with long black hair. But it was their clothes that gave Charlie the biggest start. The short boy was wearing a bright yellow waistcoat, plus fours and a bowler hat and the taller one was resplendent in full highland regalia.

"We wanted to give you a proper welcome," said the bowler hat. "So we dressed up in our finest togs."

"Aye, we didnae want tae scare you," added the one in the kilt.

Having just won hand-to-hand combat with a vicious monster, Charlie was more astonished than alarmed. He simply stared, his mouth hanging open.

The shorter boy stepped forward.

"The name's Peazle," he said, "And this is my friend Duncan." He shook Charlie's unresisting hand. "Pleased to make your acquaintance."

"I know who you are." Charlie's face twisted into an incredulous smile. "I recognise you."

He let go of Peazle's hand.

"I can't believe this. Are you ghosts? You feel solid enough."

"Oh, we're real," Duncan laughed and Peazle giggled as well.

"How can that be?" The boy was as delighted as he was mystified.

"It's quite a… eh… strange explanation," Peazle said. "I take it you read the diary?"

Charlie nodded.

"What did you think of the writing style? You can be honest."

"Peazle!" The highlander glowered at his friend. "Just tell the story."

"Yes. Sorry. Well, when we beat the Gorrodin Rath…" Peazle hooked both thumbs into the waistcoat in preparation for his tale.

"Most of the Gorrodin Rath," Duncan broke in, nodding graciously at Charlie. The boy beamed with pride.

"Most of the Gorrodin Rath," Peazle continued. "Anyway, we came here afterwards to bury the sword."

"Even Shadowjack?"

"Aye, he tagged along too." The boys from the past looked at each other knowingly.

"Peazle was dying of the ague," Duncan said solemnly. "And the wound I received from the falling rock was more serious than it first appeared. I think Shadowjack intended to wait until we were not fit tae resist, then dig the sword up again. I admit I was for selling it myself and buying my friend here some precious time. Yet Peazle wouldnae hear of it."

"What happened?" Charlie sat down on a headstone, enthralled. He was going to hear the end of Peazle's and Duncan's story at last.

"We buried the sword and were about tae go," Duncan began. "When we were surrounded by a group of Little People."

"And they're not so little," Peazle broke in. "Let me tell you that, for nothing."

"With Excalibur under the earth, we had no way tae defend ourselves," Duncan continued. "They took us back to Galhadria, Shadowjack as well - though he wasnae best pleased about it. We've been there ever since."

"But you're still young."

"That's the great thing about living in an enchanted realm," Peazle smiled. "Long life and good health. I've had two hundred years to study, more than anyone on earth. I always wanted to be a man of learning."

The pickpocket sat on the tomb next to Charlie and put his arm around the boy's shoulder.

"There's so much I want to discuss with you. I'm particularly interested in mapping genomes and DNA splicing." Peazle's eyes were bright with excitement. "How broad is your knowledge of genetic engineering?

You must have seen programmes about it on your marvellous invention, the television?"

"Not unless they made it into a cartoon."

Peazle grunted. Charlie turned to Duncan.

"What have *you* been up to for two hundred years?"

"Looking for my brother."

There was a long, uncomfortable silence.

"The Galhadrians claim to have nae knowledge of him." The highlander said coldly. "I search their land anyway."

Charlie removed Peazle's arm from his shoulder and stood up.

"What are you both doing here?" he asked warily.

"Like us, you know too much about the existence of the Little People for them to allow you to roam free on earth." Duncan's expression was impossible to read. "We've been sent to bring you back with us to Galhadria."

"I'd rather not, actually." The boy backed away.

"They thought we would be the best ones to fetch you," Peazle said sheepishly. "It's not so bad there, really. Galhadria is beautiful and I owe the Little People my life. They're courteous enough to us and don't interfere in our lives."

The boy was talking rapidly, trying to convince himself as much as Charlie.

"There are rivers and mountains for Duncan and books for me to read, and we can look after you."

"Not a chance." The boy shook his head vehemently. "I don't want to sound mean, but you were both orphans living in poverty. I actually have a life."

"Charlie, if you don't come with us, they'll take you themselves."

"Then they'll have a fight on their hands." Charlie spat. "I'm out of here."

"ENOUGH!"

The voice was low and clear and seemed to come from thin air. There was a bright shimmer around Hogg's grave, like a heat haze. Then the area behind the tomb seemed to rupture. A narrow shaft of blue light split the fabric of the air and a stranger stepped through it and into the graveyard.

He was tall and slender, with red hair cascading around an angular face. Piercing green eyes matched his emerald tunic and he wore a green kilt with a short sword fastened to his thick leather belt.

"That's Jack Thane," Peazle whispered. "One of Galhadria's greatest sorcerers."

"The hour grows late," Thane said, bowing politely to Charlie. "Soon, humans will begin to enter this place."

His hand whipped out at lightning speed and grabbed the boy's arm. The fingers gripped like iron and a bone-deep numbness spread from Charlie's elbow to wrist.

"You have done us a great service and will be treated well, yet your fate cannot be altered. You must come with me."

Duncan and Peazle looked at each other and hung their heads.

"Take the sword back to Galhadria, highlander," the stranger instructed Duncan. "That is where we all belong now."

With a glowering look at the Galhadrian, Duncan bent over, grabbed Excalibur's hilt and pulled. The sword didn't budge. The highlander planted his feet firmly on the ground, put both hands around the handle and pulled until he was red in the face. He gave up and stepped back, dumbfounded.

"It winnae move," he said.

"What?" The Galhadrian let go of Charlie. "Stay there."

He walked around the flat tombstone to where the sword handle protruded from the soil. Charlie looked at the graveyard gate. It was a hundred yards away, half-hidden by the church and he had no doubt Thane could catch him long before he got there.

The wizard stood over Hogg's grave, clutching the sword. Charlie shuffled a few steps towards the flat tombstone and, as he did so, caught Peazle's eye. The pickpocket shook his head slowly, warning the boy not to try anything. Charlie held his gaze. Peazle shook his head again. Charlie shaped his mouth into one unspoken word.

Please.

Peazle bit his lip, then nodded. Duncan caught the silent exchange and, without a change of expression, edged closer to his friend.

The Galhadrian was pulling with all his might on the handle of Excalibur, but the sword had not moved an inch. He stood up, the exertion on his face changing to incredulity.

"How did you achieve this?" He stepped onto the flat tomb and towered over the boy. "What have you done?"

"Now!" Peazle shouted - and he and Duncan leapt. The boys hit Thane with a flying tackle and all three tumbled off the tombstone in a tangle of arms and legs. Charlie launched himself forward, cartwheeling over the gravestone, landing in a crouch on the other side. He grabbed the sword handle and pulled Excalibur out of the ground with one fluid motion. The Galhadrian swept Duncan and Peazle away as if they were toys. He was on his feet in an instant, face contorted with rage.

Charlie pointed the sword at his chest.

"I've already killed one magical creature today," he snarled. "Do you want to be the second?"

Thane was barely listening. He stood transfixed, staring at the sword in the boy's hand. Duncan and Peazle struggled to their feet, equally astounded. They had expected Charlie to run for the exit.

"You took the sword from the stone," the Galhadrian said, awe in his voice. "When I could not."

"So what?" Excalibur did not waver in the boy's hand. "Is this a trick?"

"Excalibur has a power of its own," Thane said. "It will not let me wield it… and yet you can. I do not understand."

He held up his hand in a gesture of truce.

"Perhaps some of the Gorrodin Rath still live. Or you have formed a bond with the weapon for reasons I do not yet comprehend. Whatever the cause, Excalibur's work is not done here and, therefore, neither is yours."

"Really?" Charlie snorted. "I think I've done all the work I'm going to do for you."

"That is your choice." The wizard bowed low. "But the sword will remain here, in case you need it someday. You may bury it and return to your world. I will not interfere."

Charlie looked at Peazle and Duncan.

"His word is good," said Duncan. "I'll vouch for that, at least."

"I trust you will not speak of this," Thane glowered at the boy. "Or I shall return and your punishment will be great."

"My lips are sealed." The boy lowered Excalibur. The air around the grave had begun to shimmer again.

"Then, farewell, Master Wilson." The wizard motioned curtly to Peazle and Duncan.

"Come," he said brusquely, stepping into the light without a backwards glance.

Duncan smiled at the boy.

"Good luck, Charlie." He hesitated, then followed the wizard through the gateway to Galhadria. Peazle stopped at the entrance to the light.

"Until we meet again, my friend." He doffed his hat and vanished into Galhadria.

Charlie saluted him with his sword until the shimmer in the air faded away.

Charlie's mother and father were sitting on a couch eating breakfast, when their son walked into the guestroom. The boy's hair was matted with dust and grime, his mud-spattered clothes were ripped and dirty and there was a large bloodstain down one side of his shirt.

"What on earth happened to you?" his mother said, dropping her spoon. "Are you all right?"

"I've been practising." The boy plonked himself on a chair between his parents and put an arm around each of them. "I want you to teach me to be an acrobat."

His parents stared at him, then at each other.

"Well, that's great, Charlie," his father said, unable to keep the pride out of his voice. He patted his son tentatively on the back. "In fact, it's fantastic!"

"We'd be delighted, Charlie." His mother smiled at him warmly. "There's plenty of stuff to learn, but we'll start whenever you like."

"I've had a hard day." The boy let go of his parents, sank back wearily and closed his eyes. A slow smile spread across his face.

"But tomorrow? I think I'll start with a bit of juggling."

* * * *

Deep in a cavern, far to the north, a creature stirred, misshapen ears pricking up on its hairless head. From far away, the cry of her dying kin, born on wind and wave, wafted down to wreck her centuries-long slumber.

One tiny eye opened in a mass of white flesh.

Morgana was awake.

Part II

The Clan

In Scotland, the Templars, specifically the St Clairs, were the guardians of holy relics... one suggestion is that the Grail Cup is hidden in the St Clairs' Rosslyn Chapel, near Edinburgh.

Cassandra Eason. *The Encyclopaedia of Magic & Ancient Wisdom.*

Some folklorists believe that King Arthur once lived and fought in Scotland... Possibly he was a Celtic Cavalry leader with a swift-moving force.

Raymond Lamont-Brown. *Scottish Folklore.*

Gary MacMillan

Something was hunting Charlie Wilson.

It was lunch hour and he was sitting alone in the shadow of the science building, a secluded port-a-cabin near the edge of the school grounds. The structure was perched on the brink of a steep, scrub-covered hill and was Charlie's favourite spot. Just below the crest of the slope, he could look right across the town of Fenton to the patchwork of farmlands beyond. And nobody could see him.

Or so he thought.

At the foot of the hill, under a tangled thicket, hate-filled eyes glared up at the boy. Drooling black lips stretched back over needle-sharp teeth and the creature stalking Charlie began to inch uphill, gently worming through the stalks of bushes so the green tops wouldn't move and alert its prey.

Charlie reached into his schoolbag and pulled out a red notebook with his name and address written on the front. His English teacher had given the class a writing assignment - *What I Did on My Holiday* - and he was having real problems with it. Not because he thought it was a boring topic.

Quite the opposite, in fact.

He opened the notebook and looked at what he'd written so far.

MY HOLIDAY
by Charlie Wilson

I spent last summer at the Edinburgh Festival in Scotland. My parents were performing in a show. Edinburgh had lots of old buildings and a big castle in the middle of the town. I met a girl called Lilly who was one of the Little People or Galhadrians, as they call themselves. She turned out to be hundreds of years old.

I discovered some hidden tunnels under the city and found an old diary there. It belonged to a pickpocket called Peazle, who lived in the 19th century. Long ago, he and his friends, Duncan and Shadowjack Henry, found monsters called the Gorrodin Rath trapped in the tunnels. They managed to destroy them, but they missed the leader, Mordred. Lilly was staying around to make sure Mordred never got out. I quite liked Lilly.

Anyway, I found King Arthur's sword, Excalibur, and killed Mordred with it.

That was my summer holiday.

"Can't see that I'll get A+ for this," he muttered to himself, tearing out the page and crumpling it into a ball. Nobody would believe the story was true. Besides, he had promised Lilly he would keep the existence of Galhadrians a secret.

"I'll just have to make something boring up instead," he sighed.

The creature was now halfway up the slope, belly low to the ground and claws digging into the dirt, as it pulled its body through the foliage. It uttered an impatient gargling growl and saliva spilled over its glistening jaws onto the torn earth.

Charlie was about to start writing again when he heard a rasping voice floating over the crest of the hill.

"What you looking at, eh? You looking at me?"

The boy recognised it immediately and groaned to himself. The voice belonged to Gary Macmillan.

Gary Macmillan was the school bully, a pasty-faced youth with bad teeth and oily hair. He was also broader and stronger than most boys his age and stood at least a head taller than the others in his class. Charlie scrambled up the incline and peered over the top. Macmillan had a smaller boy pinned against the wall of the building. Behind him stood the bully's two sidekicks - Watson and Brogan - sniggering behind their leader like hyenas waiting for scraps.

"I seen the way you were looking at me," Macmillan sneered. "Now I'm going to have you."

Gary Macmillan's victim kept his eyes down, afraid to anger his attacker further. His lip was trembling as he tried his best not to cry.

The old Charlie Wilson would have ducked quietly down again rather than interfere. After all, Macmillan was twenty pounds heavier than he was and had two thugs helping him. But the summer adventure had changed him. He was no longer the kind of boy to walk away from something so wrong.

The creature was hauling itself through the last few yards of thinning undergrowth when Charlie put his notebook back into his schoolbag and stood up. It flattened itself to the ground with an enraged hiss, as the boy turned and walked away.

The bullies had their back to Charlie and didn't notice he was there until, heart pounding, he stepped between Brogan and Watson and tapped Gary Macmillan on the shoulder. As the youth looked round in surprise, Charlie hit him as hard as he could, right between the eyes. The bully staggered backwards several feet before landing flat on his back. Seeing his chance, Macmillan's victim turned and fled.

Brogan and Watson stared at the newcomer in astonishment. Nobody had ever dared pick a fight with Gary Macmillan. Charlie turned on them.

"What you looking at, eh?" he leered.

Macmillan staggered to his feet, his expression of pain turning instantly to one of rage. Before he could advance, there came a roar from behind the group.

"Wilson! What do you think you're doing?" A large, hairy hand landed on Charlie's shoulder, spinning him around. He found himself looking at the bearded face of Mr Swift, the school's Physical Education teacher.

"I came round the corner just in time to see you hit that lad," Mr Swift fumed. "I trust you have a good explanation for your conduct?"

Charlie shrugged.

"Ehm… I didn't know you were about to come round the corner?"

Mr Swift turned bright red.

The boy looked over his shoulder as the PE teacher hauled him off to the headmaster's office. Gary Macmillan was glaring after them, face still contorted in anger.

I'll get you for this, the bully mouthed.

Hidden by bushes, the creature bit into Charlie's forgotten schoolbag with a fury Macmillan could never match and silently tore it apart.

The Silver Bear

That night, Charlie's father came to his room. He sat on the bed and looked awkwardly around, picking up half-finished plastic models his son had been working on and putting them down again. Finally, he exhaled loudly as if he had been holding his breath.

"I got a phone call from the principal at your school today. He said you hit a boy."

Having run out of models to study, Charlie's father began to scan the posters of pop stars on the wall. He wondered how some of them got their hair to stick up like that.

"Did you punch someone called Gary Macmillan?" he asked at last.

"Yes, I did."

"Care to tell me why?"

"Because he's a bully," Charlie said defiantly. "He picks on smaller kids and they're too scared to tell anyone about it." Despite his bravado, the boy's voice began to quiver.

"Now he and his friends are going to be after me, because I tried to help. I'm scared, dad."

"Why on earth did you get involved?"

Charlie had been thinking about this all day and could only come up with one answer. After all, he had fought another monster for the very same reason.

"It was the right thing to do," he said simply.

Charlie's father looked taken aback. He glanced up at the ceiling, which he always did when he was lost for something to say. Then he reached out and gently touched the boy's face.

"For what it's worth, son, you've made me very proud."

He stood up and put his hands in his pockets. Charlie remained sitting on the bed and both looked at each other. Charlie's father walked to the bedroom door and opened it, then paused, rubbing his chin thoughtfully.

"You know, Charlie. There are two great virtues a man can have. One is knowing what is right. The other is doing what is right. Today, you showed you have both."

"Yeah," the boy scowled. "I'm going to get a total pasting for it, too."

"Unfortunately, virtue often has to be its own reward," his father admitted before he left.

"Is that supposed to cheer me up?" Charlie muttered to the closing door.

An hour later, there was a gentle tap and his mum slipped quietly into the room. The boy looked up from his book and raised an eyebrow. His mother and father were good to their son but seemed to prefer each other's company. For both to visit in one night was an unusual occurrence. Charlie's mother plonked herself onto the bed in the same place where her husband had sat not long before.

"Your dad and I have had a talk," she said. "He thinks we've been very selfish, dragging you from place to place, just so we can do the things we want. You never get a chance to settle down."

Charlie couldn't argue with that. His parents often moved around the country, chasing the small number of jobs open to their rather unusual profession. The boy had changed schools several times in his few short years and it had been hard for him to make any real friends.

"That's going to change," his mother continued decisively. "You don't like Fenton much, anyway, do you?"

"Not really."

"Then we'll move one last time." Charlie's mother caught the look of resignation on her son's face and raised her hand. "But this *is* the last time, I promise. We've decided to go to Birmingham and we're staying put when we get there."

"Really?" Charlie couldn't keep a note of suspicion out of his voice.

"Really. Your father has decided to get a steady job." She smiled at her son's astonishment and ruffled his hair. "To be honest, he never liked wearing those spangled acrobat's tights much. He just did it to please me."

She lowered her voice to a whisper.

"He'd probably rather work in a bank."

"Are we going to go soon?" Charlie asked, thinking of Gary Macmillan.

"Why wait? Your father is going to look for work tomorrow and I'll sort out somewhere for us to live. We can stay with my friend Shirley in Birmingham for the next few days while we get things finalised." His mother gave a knowing wink. "So you don't have to worry about this bully anymore."

Charlie blinked rapidly. His parents weren't big on planning ahead but this was a snap decision, even by their standards.

"It's all a bit sudden,"

"Remember what your dad is always telling you?" his mother said. "That hesitation is an acrobat's worst enemy? There's no point in saying something unless you're willing to act on it."

"What will *you* do in the city?" the boy asked tentatively.

"I was thinking of becoming a nightclub singer." Charlie's mum pushed her hair over her face and struck a provocative pose. "I look too good in spangles to give it up."

The boy grinned despite himself. He knew his mother could never do anything normal. She let her hair drop back down and looked solemnly at him.

"Joking aside, your father is making a great sacrifice for you," she said quietly. "You know why?"

Charlie shook his head.

"Because he's not afraid to do the right thing either. And because you're worth it."

As she spoke, she reached around the back of her neck and unfastened the silver chain she always wore. On the end dangled a small, exquisitely carved metallic bear.

"I notice you've taken to wearing a little whistle around your neck," she said. "I don't even know who you got it from."

Charlie stayed silent. The whistle had been a parting gift from Lilly. But he couldn't exactly tell his mother that.

She gently reached out and fastened the chain around the boy's neck. The bear clinked against the whistle with a musical ring.

"I got this from *my* mother." She tapped the glittering amulet. "It's the most precious thing I own in the whole world."

"I can't take this." Charlie tried to unfasten the clasp. "Not if it means so much to you."

"No, it's yours now. To show how much I love you."

Charlie's eyes filled with tears. His parents had never acted like this before. He gave the bear a grateful squeeze and tucked it into his pyjama top.

"I'll never take it off," he said.

"You'd better not. It's very lucky and the most precious thing I own, so you must take care of it."

Charlie's mum cleared her throat loudly and gave his hand a brief pat, as if she had used up all her emotions for one night. Then she kissed him quickly on the cheek and left.

"If this keeps up, I'll be wearing more jewellery than a New York gangsta," the boy mumbled. But he was secretly happy, for each token was proof someone cared for him.

He lay awake for a long time, staring at the ceiling and smiling to himself, all thoughts of Gary Macmillan banished from his mind. He was too excited to sleep so, eventually, he got out of bed and went to the window. Charlie's parents didn't have a lot of money and the street where they lived was rather run down, dimly lit and lined with small uniform gardens. Their own small plot was overrun with weeds, ringed by untidy bushes. Charlie's parents weren't big on gardening. The boy stretched, yawned, and looked down into the undergrowth.

A pair of yellow eyes stared up at him from a tangle of shrubs.

The boy's heart leapt and he felt the hairs rise on his neck. He let out a shuddering breath and instinctively grasped the chains around his neck.

"It's a cat," he whispered to himself. "Of course. Just a cat."

But he knew it was far too big to be a cat. And as his eyes adjusted to the dusky light, he could now make out a large, thick body. The creature slid sideways and vanished into the darkness below the garden wall. Seconds later, the front gate swung violently open and slammed shut. He had a brief glimpse of something bobbing through the shadows and down the street.

Charlie scanned the rest of the road but dirty orbs of streetlights revealed nothing out of the ordinary. Finally, he went back to bed.

"It must have been a dog, then," he frowned. "A big dog. Or maybe a badger."

Clutching the bear and whistle, he closed his eyes tightly. He still couldn't sleep - but now he had a different reason.

The Wilsons' front gate had a strong spring and a child-proof latch that clicked shut automatically.

Whatever let itself out of the garden had to have hands.

In the Whale Room

The man in the green tunic sat on a polished stairway in a great silver chamber, his head resting wearily in his hands. He was tall and thin with long dark hair. Goose feathers threaded through the turned down tops of his leather boots marked him out as a great wizard.

There was a hesitant tap on the massive oak door at the other end of the chamber and the sorcerer quickly straightened his back. He nodded towards the door, which swung silently open. A small boy stood in the brightly lit entrance, like Jonah, peering into the glistering jaws of a mighty whale.

The high vaulted chamber was as lofty and ornate as any Cathedral and the giant silver arches that soared to the roof resembled the ribs of some massive leviathan, so the chamber was known as the Whale Room.

The boy squared his shoulders and marched over to the wizard on the staircase. The newcomer was small and wiry, wearing a brightly patterned waistcoat and bowler hat. In his hand, he carried a large metal briefcase that looked strangely at odds with his eccentric clothes.

"I ought to have picked up a pair of sunglasses on my trip," he said, squinting around the dazzling interior.

The sorcerer stood up and descended the stairs to meet him.

"Welcome back to Galhadria, Master Peazle." He lifted his hand in greeting.

"Thank you, Jack Thane."

The wizard indicated for Peazle to sit. There was no furniture in the Whale Room, so the boy perched on the bottom step with the briefcase on his knee, like some miniature insurance salesman in fancy dress. Though they shone like polished glass, the steps were not slippery and the chamber, despite its vast size, wasn't cold.

"Well then, Peazle." Jack Thane tilted his head inquisitively to one side. "What have you brought from the world of men this time?"

The boy set the case on the mirrored floor and popped the latches. He opened the lid and stood up again. In each hand, he held a gun with a short, thick barrel.

"These are called BK-8000 semi-automatic pistols," he replied, awe and fear equally evident in his voice. "Human weapons. Absolutely no recoil. Each can fire a single shot or a three-bullets-per-second burst with ten settings in between and they have a range of almost quarter of a mile. This is the weapon of choice if you want to absolutely, positively kill every single.... eh... person in the room."

"Your skills as a thief have not diminished, I'm glad to say," the wizard nodded. "Did you spirit these away from the tent of some great warrior?"

"Actually, I ordered it on the internet." Peazle scowled, unsure whether the wizard was joking or not. "I'm not a pickpocket anymore, Master Thane. I'm more of a... scholar."

Jack Thane grunted.

"Show me," he said. "Show me this semi-atomic plimsol."

"Show you?" The boy looked around the spotless hall. "In here? You sure?"

The wizard nodded.

"All right." Taking a deep breath, the boy tightened his finger on the trigger and swept one of the guns in an arc above his head. The weapon made a rapid put-putting rasp, no louder than air being let out of a balloon. Forty feet up, gouts of silver erupted from the walls of the Whale Room and danced and spun in the air. The gun was suddenly silent again, and Jack Thane and Peazle watched as metal shards dropped to the floor with a musical clatter. The boy looked embarrassed, as if he'd broken some elderly aunt's favourite vase. He blew a pale wisp of smoke from the pistol's barrel.

"It's almost like magic," he said by way of an excuse.

"Almost." Thane agreed, waving his arm in a casual way. The boy jumped as if he had received an electric shock and looked down at his hands. He gave a short gasp. The gun, like the rest of the room, was now solid silver. The case, ammunition and spent cartridges around his feet were also silver. A deadly fortune scattered across the floor.

"Now, *that's* magic," The Galhadrian sniffed.

"If you don't mind, I'd like to go to the great library and return to my studies." Peazle put the gun back in its case and snapped the lid shut. He looked as if he was about to say something else, then thought better of it. But nothing escaped the attention of Jack Thane.

"Speak your mind, friend," he snapped brusquely. "This place has too many secrets already."

Peazle stood up, clutching the case to his chest like a shield.

"Science is mankind's magic," he said defiantly. "You must realise that, someday, men will also be able to turn lead into silver. And more than that, I fear."

The wizard suddenly looked tired. He sat slowly down on the step again, a movement that put his eyes level with those of the standing boy. So he closed them.

"Peazle... I need you to go back to the world of mankind right away," he said gravely. "There has been a rather unfortunate... development there."

Jack Thane opened pale green eyes again and fixed them on his little companion.

"You mean something terrible has happened." The pickpocket scowled.

"You could put it like that." The wizard considered the best way to elaborate and finally decided just to start at the beginning. He took a deep breath and began.

"Long ago, a creature of great evil walked the land of men. Her name was Morgana. Like her son Mordred, she was leader of the monsters known as the Gorrodin Rath."

He saw fear ignite in the pickpocket's eyes. Peazle had fought the Gorrodin Rath when he lived on earth. He still had nightmares about it.

"She vanished during a great battle with a knight called Arthur and I thought her dead. I believe now I was wrong."

Thane's lips twitched. He didn't like being wrong.

"I think she has returned."

"What? Where?" Peazle looked around to make sure that Morgana wasn't lurking in a corner.

"I don't know that either," Jack Thane admitted bitterly. "My fellow wizards still doubt she is alive but I am sure. And dark creatures have been seen on earth...."

"What has all this got to do with me?"

"I believe Morgana has sent her foul minions after a certain human child. I want you to rescue him."

"In that case, you should send someone bigger. Like yourself, for instance."

Jack Thane shook his head in irritation.

"Magical creatures do not fight each other, Peazle, you know that."

"I know, I know," the boy sighed. "And you Galhadrians don't interfere in the lives of men." He stole a sideways glance at the figure in green. "So, you want to send a lowly human."

The wizard waved his hand again and the silver wall behind Peazle began to glow softly. The pickpocket turned in time to see a faint picture forming. It seemed to be a boy lying on a bed. Peazle couldn't be sure, for the details were unclear, as if he were looking through a frosted window.

"When you first came to my land," Thane said. "How long ago was it?"

"You took me to Galhadria nearly 200 years ago." Peazle sounded annoyed the sorcerer didn't remember. "And, yes, in doing so, saved my life."

"Now it is your turn to save the life of this child."

"Do I *want* to save him? Is it dangerous?"

"Morgana is an enemy of both Galhadria and mankind. Let me impress something upon you. Fail and we all may be doomed."

Jack Thane pointed to the wall behind and Peazle turned again. The frosting effect had gone and Peazle found himself looking into a bedroom decorated with posters of pop stars and model spaceships hanging on wires. The boy was sitting on his bed, head bowed, idly playing with two little chains around his neck. At the end of one chain dangled a little silver whistle. The other held a silver bear.

"Odd bits of jewellery," said Peazle. "Nice quality too," he added, betraying his expertise as a former crook.

"The boy does not realise it, but he holds the key to Morgana increasing her powers a hundredfold. Don't let that happen, Peazle."

The child on the wall raised his head and the pickpocket's eyes widened in recognition.

"Yes. I believe you met him once." The wizard smiled thinly.

"His name is Charlie Wilson."

The Wasteland

Charlie woke in an excellent mood, though it was muted by exhaustion, for it had taken him a long time to drift into sleep. He was delighted by his parent's unexpected attention and the possibility of leaving Fenton. What's more, it was Saturday and he wouldn't have to go to school and face Gary Macmillan. The day after, he would be in Birmingham with mum's friend Shirley. To settle down at last!

The boy was still uneasy about what he had seen in the garden. He might have dismissed it as a trick of the light, if he hadn't witnessed so many strange and frightening things last summer. Dragging himself wearily into the shower, he wondered if his life was ever going to be the same again.

He had no way of guessing things were about to get a hundred times worse.

The shower woke him properly and he got dressed and ran down the stairs to have breakfast. There was a note in the middle of the kitchen table, weighed down by a half-eaten sausage.

Off to the job centre. Don't go anywhere.
Love, Mum and Dad X.

"Rub it in, why don't you?" Charlie poured himself a bowl of cornflakes. He was by no means sure his father really wanted to work in a bank and didn't want to be eternally reminded of the sacrifice his parents were making to ensure he had a more stable life. Anyway, his mother and father would have discovered by now that the job centre was shut on a Saturday. Most likely, they'd have gone to the movies instead.

Before his summer escapade, Charlie would happily have obeyed his parents and spent a whole day on his PlayStation. Now he didn't feel like sitting at home in front of the TV when he could be out doing something. Trouble was, he lived in Fenton and there really wasn't anything to do. Charlie could either hang out in the little town square, where everyone would see he didn't have any friends - or go and explore the surrounding countryside. It was an easy choice to make. He put on his hiking boots, got a rucksack out of the cupboard and filled it with the meagre contents of the fridge. Charlie's parents weren't very big on food shopping.

On impulse, he turned his parent's note over and wrote on the back.

Sorry. Gone to do something VERY important —
Charlie xxxx

He hadn't a clue what that important thing might be, but it sounded good. Then he shouldered the rucksack and let himself out the front door.

A few hundred yards up the street, a narrow alley between houses led onto a patch of wasteland, followed by a stretch of allotments. On the other side of the cultivation was a railway line and, beyond that, nothing but farmland and rolling hills.

He started walking in that direction, unaware he was heading into a trap.

Halfway down the street, he heard a rustling noise from behind the hedge he was passing. The gardens in his road were bordered by waist-high walls but this particular house had been empty for some time. The garden was choked with long weeds and fronds of unruly foliage tumbled over the crumbling brickwork. The bush nearest him rustled again. Charlie put his hands on the wall and peered over, trying to see what kind of animal was making the undergrowth tremble. Maybe there was something trapped. He leaned over further, trying to get a proper look.

"Get away from there!"

Startled, Charlie leapt back from the wall, whirling around to see who had shouted.

A boy stood at the end of the street, right in front of his house. Charlie had gone too far down the road to see him properly, but he could have sworn the stranger was wearing a bowler hat. He took a few hesitant steps towards the figure, which was now waving its arms wildly.

There was a roar from the other end of the street and Charlie spun again. Gary Macmillan and his two companions were racing towards him. They had been lying in wait behind a set of garages at the end of the road! The boy looked back towards his house, but the figure in the bowler hat was gone and the gap was closing rapidly between himself and the bullies, tearing up the deserted street.

The sensible thing would be to run back to his house, but what if he couldn't get the key in the lock before Macmillan reached him? What if the boy in the strange hat was part of the bully's gang and hiding in his garden? Making an instant decision, Charlie sprinted across the road and bolted down the narrow alley that led to the allotments. The alley twisted twice, and Charlie bounced off wooden fences in his haste to take each corner as fast as possible.

He shot out of the other end and onto the patch of wasteland. In front of him, ringed by a tall wall, strips of carefully tended land sloped steeply down to the rail line, each belt planted with rows of cabbages, strawberries and potatoes and dotted with garden sheds. A narrow path wound around the side of the allotment beside a thick strip of high briar bushes, giving the plots some protection from the wind.

Charlie was about to take that route when he remembered that it ended in a high wire fence separating the lower reaches of the allotments from the railway at the bottom of the hill. The boy's parents had warned him never to climb the fence or cross the tracks, where express trains thundered past at deadly speed.

But staying on the path was just as dangerous, for it doubled back up the hill and came out at the far end of the waste ground, close to where it went down. If Macmillan followed him, while his sidekicks made for the other end, they would have him trapped.

What was the last thing Gary Macmillan would expect him to do? Apart from stand and fight, of course. He scanned the communal gardens quickly, looking for an alternative route - but the strips of carefully cultivated land offered no hiding place.

Unless!

In the closest allotment was a large, green compost bin. He remembered his parents' words. *Hesitation is an acrobat's worst enemy.* Without another thought, Charlie pulled open the lid. Inside were grass cuttings and torn up weeds, but they only came halfway to the top. He hauled himself inside and shut the top just as Gary Macmillan and his gang burst out of the alley. Wrapped in sudden darkness, the boy curled himself into a ball and tried not to breathe too heavily - no mean feat, with rotting cabbage leaves tickling his nostrils.

Macmillan took in the allotments and the path with one glance. He motioned Watson and Brogan to circle the wasteland and ran off down the path in the direction he was sure his quarry had gone.

Charlie stayed put, still trying to get his ragged breathing under control, listening to the fading footsteps of his pursuers. He guessed Macmillan would take a couple of minutes to reach the bottom of the hill. By that time, Brogan and Watson would be far away as well. Then he could leap out of the bin and make a dash for his house. Wrapped in oppressive darkness, he counted silently, trying to judge the best moment to break for freedom.

Gary Macmillan was halfway down the incline, panting with exertion, when he came upon a boy sitting among the brambles. The stranger was small and wiry and wore a brightly coloured waistcoat and bowler hat.

"What you looking at?" Gary Macmillan snarled, his standard opening line for any new person he met. The boy didn't reply.

"Has anybody come past in the last few minutes?" The bully advanced threateningly on the stranger, to emphasise the fact he wasn't going to stand for silence, evasion or lies. The boy didn't seem too concerned.

"Not a soul," he replied calmly, hands in pockets. "Though I did see a child climbing into that green compost bin, way up there. Which, I must say, was a tad unusual."

He nodded to his right and Macmillan followed the gesture with his eyes. There was a clear view of Charlie's hiding place further up the hill.

Gary Macmillan wasn't the type to trust anybody, especially someone wearing a flowery waistcoat. His hand shot out and grabbed the smaller boy's arm.

"You come with me and we'll check," he said. "If you're lying…"

He left the sentence unfinished, but there wasn't much doubt about what he would do if the bin turned out to be empty. The boy shrugged and calmly let the bully escort him up the path. Macmillan let out three piercing whistles as he walked. Watson and Brogan heard the call and hurried back. Both accomplices had armed themselves with sturdy fence posts.

"You sure you three are going to manage against one wee lad?" the stranger remarked casually, eyeing the vicious-looking weapons. Gary Macmillan shot the boy a warning look.

"Keep hold of him," he motioned to Brogan, while he picked up a rock. "We'll shut his smart mouth in a minute."

The boy with the bowler hat and colourful waistcoat shrugged again.

The Cat Palug

Charlie was finding it harder and harder to breathe inside the compost bin. The lid of the container was almost airtight, the smell of rotting vegetation overpowering, and he could feel tiny bugs beginning to crawl over his face and into his sleeves. He was certain his asthma was about to play up. Surely the bully was far enough away for him to leap out and make his escape? He tensed his muscles and got ready to heave the lid open and dash for freedom.

Something crashed against the side of the container and it tilted precariously to one side before settling back with a thump. Charlie gasped in terror and inhaled a mouthful of grass. As he tried to dislodge the lid, spluttering and coughing in panic, the side of the container buckled. This time, the bin toppled over with a crash, the lid flew open and Charlie was catapulted out, along with an avalanche of half-rotted vegetation. The boy's fingers scrabbled frantically in freshly tilled soil and he scrambled to his feet, eyes wide with terror.

He saw Gary Macmillan and his henchmen, but they were almost twenty feet away. And, between him and the bullies, was a sight that defied reason.

It looked like a cat, but larger than any feline the boy had ever seen. Its ears were set back flat on a spade-shaped head, and its eyes were not almond-shaped but rounded, like those of a human. It was sitting up on powerful back legs that ended in viciously clawed feet. It was obvious that the creature, not the bullies, had tipped over the compost bin. Gary Macmillan and his sidekicks, coming through the allotment gate, stopped in their tracks, their faces mirroring Charlie's fear.

Instead of front legs, the cat had arms. Arms that ended in wide, hairless hands.

"Oh my God," breathed Watson. It was the first time Charlie had ever heard him speak.

The cat creature whirled around in surprise, ears angling forward. It gave an evil hiss, like a sputtering fuse. The bully's henchmen took several steps back, their faces even paler than normal.

Gary Macmillan didn't have many virtues but he certainly wasn't short of courage.

"What are you looking at?" he snarled at the creature, though his voice was a lot higher than normal. Then he launched his rock at it. The cat gave a high-pitched wail and sprang towards them, spitting and snarling. Out of habit, more than any sense of bravado, Brogan and Watson leapt forward to defend their leader, swinging the jagged fence posts at the creature. It flailed its powerful arms, knocking the weapons aside. Macmillan bent quickly and picked up another rock. From behind the bullies a small figure, one Charlie hadn't noticed in the confusion, darted around the battle and sprinted over. As he approached, Charlie got a proper look at his face.

"Peazle?" he gasped.

"Glad to make your acquaintance once more." The boy doffed his bowler politely. "Now run."

He grabbed Charlie by the arm and pulled away. The bullies, swiping wildly at the hissing cat, didn't notice their prey was escaping.

Charlie and Peazle sprinted, stumbling and gasping, onto the wooded path and headed towards the railway track. Halfway down the slope, Charlie looked back in time to see Gary Macmillan and his sidekicks fleeing into the alley. Brogan's torn shirt was flapping wildly and Macmillan's arm hung limply by his side. There was no sign of the monster.

"Faster!" Peazle hissed. "That thing doesn't want them, or they'd be dead. It wants you."

He reached the bottom of the hill and launched himself at the high wire fence that cordoned off the railway track, climbing swiftly to the top and reaching down for his companion.

"I can't cross the railway line," Charlie shouted. "I'm not allowed. It's dangerous!"

"You think *that* creature isn't dangerous?" Peazle yelled back, hauling at the boy. "What do you suppose it's after you for? A kiss?"

He toppled over the top of the mesh fence, grabbing Charlie's collar and pulling him along. Charlie lost his grip, almost plummeting down the other side and onto the track. Peazle caught the boy and pressed him against the wire until he could get a proper handhold. The pickpocket was a lot stronger than he looked.

They leapt down onto the railway embankment as the creature exploded out of the undergrowth. It hit the fence with such ferocity Charlie thought it would scythe right through. The chain link rattled violently but didn't give. The cat creature glared maniacally at Charlie, only inches away, lips curled back into its stubby face and spittle drooling from snarling fangs.

Then it began to climb.

"Come on!" Peazle pulled Charlie away from the fence, where he had been transfixed by the creature's stare. "Up the other side, for God's sake. Or it will be upon us!"

He ran across the tracks and leapt onto an identical wire fence on the other side. Charlie went after him. His legs felt as if they were jelly and his arms seemed to have lost the power to pull him up. The creature was almost at the top of the first fence, which it had scaled in a fraction of the time the boys had taken. It let out a howl of triumph. Except...

It wasn't a howl. It was the wail of a train.

Seconds later, the Birmingham Express rounded the corner. The creature somersaulted over the top of the fence in a perfect arc, using powerful arms the way a gymnast would. As it landed on the other side, the train swept past, obscuring the cat from the boys' view. The chain of the fence rattled and swung, and Charlie had to use all his remaining strength to stop himself being plucked off his perch and sucked under the thundering wheels.

"Will you get up here!" Peazle reached down and grabbed his companion by the hair. "A train isn't going to stop it!"

He yanked violently and Charlie scrambled after him, wincing in pain. In a few seconds, they were over the top and plummeting down the other side. The boys hit the ground as the last carriage of the express whizzed past. Suddenly visible again, the cat creature bounded across the tracks and began to rapidly scale the second fence.

"We can't outrun it!" Charlie sobbed.

"We don't have to." Next to the fence was a narrow road lined with more bushes. Peazle dived into the nearest thicket and hauled out a mass of shiny chrome. "I always plan ahead."

"Bikes?" Charlie gasped.

"What were you expecting? A helicopter?" Peazle vaulted onto one bike and held out the other. The creature was already on the top of the second fence, so the boy jumped onto the proffered cycle and began to pump the pedals, gathering speed. The cat hit the ground and lurched towards them. It moved with awkward but speedy lunges, using massive forearms to pull itself along, knuckles folded, swinging its short legs under the furry torso the way an ape would. Now, it was Peazle who was in trouble, his bike wobbling as he tried desperately to keep it under control.

"What's the matter?" Charlie yelled over his shoulder.

"I grew up in the 19th century! I'm not exactly used to bicycles!"

The pickpocket was veering from one side of the road to the other, the creature only yards behind.

"That's what you call planning ahead?" Charlie groaned.

Peazle ignored him, putting his head down and pedalling furiously, grim determination etched on his face. The creature leapt, arms outstretched, but the bike straightened and shot forward. The cat missed him by inches, landing heavily and rolling across the tarmac. The pickpocket steadied his handlebars at last and the two boys gathered speed, leaving the creature, gasping and spitting, rolling on the tarmac behind.

"Nothing to it," Peazle cried gleefully. "All I had to do was find the scientific principle behind these velocipedes. Pedal like hell."

He grinned as the bikes crested a rise. The boys soared down the hill and away from danger.

"Course, it helps to have a Cat Palug chasing you."

"A what?" Charlie panted breathlessly, the wind whistling through his thick hair.

"A Cat Palug." Peazle waved behind him, though the creature was now too far away to see. The bike wobbled dangerously again and the pickpocket quickly returned both hands to the handlebars.

"I suppose I have some explaining to do."

"You think?" Charlie changed gears. "I'd certainly say so."

Waiting for the Train

After a couple of miles hard pedalling, they came upon a bus stop and Peazle slammed on the brakes. The bike went into a violent skid and vanished into a ditch. The pickpocket emerged a few moments later, pulling twigs from his hair. He fished a large fob watch from his pocket and glanced at it.

"You should dump your bicycle, too," he said, as if his loss of control had been meticulously thought out. "The autobus will be here any minute."

Right on cue, the blue and white bulk of a Birmingham corporation bus appeared in the distance.

"We're getting a bus?"

"Faster than a bicycle. That creature behind does not tire, like you and me. Do not think, for a moment, it has given up the chase."

Peazle held out his hand and waved down the approaching vehicle. The bus ground to a halt and its double doors slid open.

"I hope you have some money."

"Where are we going?" Charlie dropped a handful of coins into the driver's palm as the pickpocket ushered him inside. The other passengers stared at their dishevelled appearance or, perhaps, Peazle's outlandish bowler hat and waistcoat.

"My parents will be back soon." Charlie protested. "They'll wonder where I am."

"Right now, the Cat Palug is wondering where you are as well. That's what is praying on *my* mind."

Peazle and Charlie sat down and the pickpocket looked nervously at the open bus door. Finally, it hissed shut and the vehicle pulled away.

"What was that thing?" Charlie whispered.

"A Cat Palug? One of the dark creatures of old. I doubt anyone has seen one for hundreds of years." Peazle shook his head in disbelief. "Yet it came right into a town to get you."

"I should go back. Tell my mum and dad."

"Tell them what?" Peazle laid a hand on his friend's shoulder. "That you were attacked by a moggie with hands?"

He looked out of the window nervously.

"Even if they believed you, nobody else would. Then you'd all be in mortal danger."

"How do you know Gary Macmillan and his gang didn't scare it off? They scare most things off."

"Those boys we left behind?" Peazle dismissed the idea with a wave of his hand. "They're only alive because three youths mauled to death in a little place like this would draw too much attention to the thing that killed them."

"But they saw it. They'll tell."

"Would you believe if you hadn't witnessed it?" The pickpocket tried to wipe away the grime that covered the window but only succeeded in smearing it around. "Besides, I get the feeling those young gentlemen are not known for telling the truth."

Charlie could see the logic in that.

"I'm sorry, my friend." Peazle dejectedly scrubbed at the large stripe of dirt that now adorned his sleeve. "The only way to keep you and your parents safe is to get as far away as possible."

"Got anywhere in mind, or are we just fleeing in general?"

"I thought I'd explain once we were on the train." The pickpocket pushed his face against the pane and tried to see past the muck.

"The train?" Charlie grabbed his companion and pulled him around. "What are you talking about? I'm not taking any train."

Peazle stared at him with eyes that seemed sad, tired and very old. But then, he was old, Charlie remembered. Though he still looked like a boy, the pickpocket had been alive for almost two centuries.

"There are dark creatures hunting you, Charlie. They have been sent by Morgana, last of the Gorrodin Rath. We must flee."

"Hold on!" Charlie shook his head vehemently. "*Mordred* was the last of the Gorrodin Rath." He gave a shiver. "I killed him,"

"Morgana is Mordred's mother," Peazle said flatly. "And far more deadly."

Charlie went white.

"That's why she's after me? Because I killed her son?"

"You're not exactly her favourite person," Peazle agreed. "Yet, that is not the reason she is hunting you."

He leaned close and whispered in the boy's ear.

"She is looking for the cup."

"The only cup I've got has a picture of the X-Men on the side. I bought it in Woolworths."

"The Grail cup. The source of her power."

"*I* don't have it. I don't even know what it is."

"I believe you," the pickpocket said. "Yet you are the only lead Morgana has, for the cup was stolen from her by a certain young girl."

He shrugged.

"And you were the last person to see her."

"Her?"

"Yes," Peazle replied evenly. "Morgana is searching for your friend Lilly."

Charlie sat in miserable silence, glaring past Peazle at the gritty window. Ploughed fields and hedgerows, flickering past gaps in the dirt, were gradually being replaced by the red bricks and trimmed gardens of Birmingham's suburbs. He had the horrible feeling that his old life was passing away like the greenery. He pulled his mobile phone from his jacket pocket and began to dial.

"At least I can call my parents," he said brightly. "Let them know what's going on."

He stopped dialling and smiled sarcastically at Peazle.

"Once I work out exactly what *is* going on."

"Ah! A mobile telephone. Don't get it near my head." The boy gingerly took the phone from Charlie and studied it. "Amazing! Though I must admit, I am puzzled by this modern desire to send text messages. I thought the telephone was invented so people could talk to each other."

He reached up and pushed the mobile through the open ventilation window.

"What are you doing?" Charlie jumped to his feet, but the phone had already shattered into a hundred pieces on the road behind.

Peazle seized Charlie's arm and gripped hard. Grimacing in pain, the boy was forced down into his seat.

"Listen to me, Charlie!" Peazle hissed. "Listen well! Morgana will think nothing of using your parents as bait to get to you. Do you understand?"

He squeezed tighter and the boy winced again.

"She hopes to use Lilly to find the cup. She hopes to use you to find Lilly. And she will use your parents to get to you. Morgana is following a trail. A cold one, certainly, but these are the clues she has. Your mother and father are only safe as long as you don't communicate with them!"

"I've no idea where Lilly is." Charlie blinked back tears. "This isn't fair."

"I know that only too well." The pickpocket let go of Charlie's arm and stared angrily out of the window once more. "That's life, though."

The low, spacious houses had now gone and highrise flats and factory chimneys signalled they were entering the heart of the city.

"You've risked your life twice to save me," Charlie said. "Once last summer and once today." The corrugated roof of Birmingham train station slid into view, visible through the narrow gap between the grime and the top of the window. "But, come on, Peazle! I can't just leave my parents not knowing where I am."

"Their anguish will surely be great," the pickpocket agreed. "Morgana will sense this, know they are not in touch with you and leave them be."

The bus shuddered to a stop.

"You and I have both seen Mordred." The pickpocket whispered, narrowing his eyes. "Do you really want your mother and father to come face to face with his kin?"

Charlie stood, breathing heavily.

"Let's go," he said shakily. "We've got a train to catch."

The Policemen

Charlie's mother and father had only been home for minutes when the doorbell rang. To their surprise, two policemen stood on the front steps.

"Mr Wilson.?" The lead policeman was short and portly, with a small black moustache. He looked a bit like a traffic warden who had put on the wrong uniform.

"Yes?"

"I'm Sergeant Plune and this is Constable Valentine. Sorry to disturb you, but we're investigating a rather strange report." The policemen looked uneasily at each other. "See, eh… we picked up a trio of young boys a short while ago. They were covered in bruises and lacerations. Some of them rather serious."

The policeman rubbed his forehead, unsure of how to proceed.

"The kids seemed rather… eh… hysterical. They… um… claimed they'd been attacked by a large cat."

"A cat?"

"A cat, yes." The policemen looked at each other again. "According to the boys, a cat with hands."

"A cat with hands." Now it was Mr and Mrs Wilson's turn to look at each other.

"Excuse me, officer," Charlie's dad looked puzzled. "Cats don't have hands."

"Yes, I know that." The policeman was growing visibly more uncomfortable. "Thing is, they say your son was a witness."

"Was he hurt?" Charlie's mother pushed past her husband.

"No, madam. Apparently, he got away. Now, normally, we wouldn't pay any attention to such a wild tale - but the boys' injuries are quite serious. Is there any way we could talk to your son? Get his side of the story."

The policemen looked as if they were ready to continue the conversation inside the house, but Charlie's mother didn't move from the doorway.

"He isn't here right now," Charlie's father said. "Of course, we'll call you as soon as he comes home."

"Any idea where he might be?"

"Out playing, I suppose." Charlie's father shook his head. "He's a very sensible boy, though. I'm positive he wouldn't be involved in anything... naughty."

"I'm sure he wasn't. But we *would* like to talk to him." Plume removed his hat and polished the brim. "One boy's arm was broken in four places. Never seen injuries quite like it." He replaced the hat and shadows hid his eyes again. "We'd just like to get to the bottom of this."

"Of course, officer." Charlie's mum gave an innocent smile. "Like my husband said, we'll give the local station a ring as soon as he appears."

"No need, madam." The taller officer at the back spoke for the first time. "This house is on our beat. We'll be back in a couple of hours. Sort it out then."

"Of course." Charlie's father seemed dazed. "But a cat with hands? How ridiculous."

"Ridiculous. Yes. Of course. I'm sure your son can clear it all up." The officers nodded gravely and walked back down the garden path.

Charlie's father closed the door behind them. Charlie's mother was already running for the kitchen, her face white. She snatched a note from the table and held it up.

Gone to do something VERY important – Charlie
xxxx

Charlie's father was heading up the stairs, three at a time.

"Where are you going?" she called.

"To get coats," he said. "We're going to look for our boy."

Charlie sat in a dark corridor at the back of the railway station, sandwiched between a broken photo booth and a pile of empty boxes. He had cleaned up as best he could in the station washroom and was now eating the Cornish pasty he'd packed in his rucksack - though his mouth was too dry to enjoy the taste. A few feet away, crowds jostled in and out of fast-food bars, streaming towards and away from their trains. The air was filled with chattering and shouting and charged with all the emotions of a mass of humanity saying hello and goodbye. The boy looked down. His hands were shaking so badly that bits of pastry were strewn in a circle around him.

Peazle emerged from a crowd of suited commuters. He crouched next to Charlie and flourished two tickets in his face.

"The train for Edinburgh leaves in ten minutes. I got us first class."

"Best to go on the run in comfort, eh?" Charlie whistled sarcastically. "Where did you get the money for that?"

"I am a master pickpocket, you know." Peazle cocked his head and listened to the distorted mumbling coming from the loudspeaker overhead. "Two centuries of technological advancements, and you still haven't figured out a way to make station announcements intelligible."

"If you don't tell me why we're going to Edinburgh, you won't be intelligible either." Charlie grabbed his companion by the waistcoat. "Cause you'll have my fist in your mouth."

"I have arranged to meet my master there."

"Your master?"

"As you know, I live in the land of Galhadria now," Peazle sighed. "Galhadria is ruled by a circle of great sorcerers. The Lords of the Western Wilderness they call themselves."

"That's pompous."

"They're mighty wizards, not some Rotary club." Peazle tucked one of the train tickets into Charlie's pocket. "I work for Jack Thane, the most powerful of the Lords. You met him briefly."

"And he sent you?"

"Jack Thane has no desire to see a monster like Morgana gain more power." The boy gave a half-hearted smile. "So, he told me to rescue you."

"You're not exactly the seventh cavalry." Charlie looked through his fingers at the small figure seated opposite him. "Unless you have a cunning plan."

The pickpocket shrugged modestly. "You know what a Thin Place is?"

"It's a gateway to Galhadria."

"Yes. There are only a few open Thin Places left in this country, and most are in desolate parts of the north. But there is one in Edinburgh."

"In Greyfriars Graveyard? Yeah. I saw it once."

"We will go there and you will retreat to the safety of Galhadria."

"What!"

"It's only for a little while."

"And what are *you* going to do?"

"Find Lilly. She's the next link in the chain. Then, hopefully, the cup itself. Once it is safe in Thane's deepest stronghold, Morgana will have more to worry about than chasing after some small human."

The pickpocket gave a wide smile.

"You'll be able to return to your parents." He prised Charlie's hands loose and helped the boy to his feet. "But we're not safe yet. We have to leave straight away."

"Are you sure Lilly has this stupid cup?" Charlie brushed the last crumbs from his jeans and slung the rucksack over his shoulder. "Or even knows where it is?"

Across the platform, a grimy locomotive gave a dragon-like hiss and backed out of the station, its clacking staccato growing more confident as it gathered speed.

"The cup belonged to Lilly's father but had fallen into the hands of the Gorrodin Rath." Peazle was looking awkwardly at him. "Few people could have stolen it from them. Lilly did."

The pickpocket leant in close to Charlie's ear, as if he were ashamed to say it.

"After all, she's Morgana's child too."

The Potion

Being on the train was a lot better than travelling by bus. The first class compartment was almost empty and the seats were huge and smelled faintly of aftershave. Best of all, the windows were clean and the boys had a clear view of fields, rivers and towns clattering past.

Peazle would have been content to stare out of the window all day. He had never been on a train. The Galhadrians had no railways, happy to walk or ride steeds wherever they needed to go. They were immortal, after all, and felt they had all the time in the world.

Charlie allowed his companion to gaze across the landscape while he ordered coffee and Kit-Kats from a passing trolley. The boys silently sipped their steaming drinks and Charlie nibbled on a chocolate bar.

"Yes?" Peazle turned away from the view.

"I'd like to know how my friend's mother turned out to be a monster that's looking for me." He wiped his mouth with a napkin. "Lilly neglected to mention it."

"It's hard to know where to begin." The pickpocket took another sip of his drink. "I never actually tasted this coffee stuff before. It's making my hair stand on end."

"Start at the beginning."

"All right," Peazle nodded. "What do you know of the Gorrodin Rath?"

"Nothing I like."

"Bear with me." The boy formed a triangle with his fingers and tried to look learned. "What do you know of their history?"

"Only what Lilly told me. Do you remember her at all? She was alive when you lived in Edinburgh, too, but you knew her as Heather."

"Yes." Peazle thought back to the 19th century when he and his friend Duncan stayed in Edinburgh's Underground City. "She was Duncan's friend more than mine, though he did not know she was an immortal."

"She didn't tell me much." Charlie, too, was recalling when he had first met Lilly. "Said her father was a great magician called Gorrodin, who lived in Galhadria hundreds of years ago. He... went bad, I suppose you'd say. Abandoned Lilly, left Galhadria and created an evil race on earth called the Gorrodin Rath."

"Go on."

"They were trapped in underground caverns by a knight called Arturius. Gorrodin fled and hasn't been seen since. You killed most of the surviving Gorrodin Rath and I got the last one eight months ago."

He drained his coffee and crumpled the cup with a flourish.

"End of story. Or so I thought."

"It's not the end of the story." Peazle sighed. "It isn't even the right story."

"Lilly wouldn't make up something horrible like that." Charlie felt an unexpected lurch in his stomach. "Not about her own dad."

He hesitated.

"Would she?"

"Lilly doesn't *know* the truth." Peazle scratched his chin uncomfortably. "But you need to, if you're going to help her."

"So, what *is* the truth?"

"Jack Thane gave me this." He reached into his pocket and pulled out a small phial of thick green glass with a wax stopper. "Drink it. It will allow you to see into the past and know what really happened all those centuries ago. It's not as nice as coffee, though."

Charlie nodded, not particularly surprised.

"Lilly pulled a similar trick on me when I first met her. That's how I knew so much about your adventures back then."

"My escapades pale beside what you're about to witness." Peazle snapped his fingers at a passing conductor. "Another of those truly excellent beverages, my good man."

He turned back to Charlie and reached for his Kit-Kat.

"Drink some potion. I already know the story, so I'll stick to coffee."

Charlie uncorked the phial and took a swig.

"Aaaaaaaaaargh! It tastes like medicine." He grabbed Peazle's cup, took a gulp and recoiled. "*How* many sugars are in this?"

"Lilly was right about one thing," the pickpocket continued. "Gorrodin was indeed her father - and one of the greatest wizards in Galhadria. At one time, he was also a Lord of the Western Wilderness." He took a sip, shrugged, and added another sachet of sugar.

"He was alive in the days when Galhadrians walked on earth and long before that. When the Little People finally withdrew to their own world, he was one of the few still free to visit mankind."

"What's Galhadria like?" Charlie interrupted.

"Eh?"

"You've been living there ever since you were taken. What's it like?"

"It's an awful lot better than the place I came from." Peazle shrugged. "Rolling hills, snowy peaks, vast forests - that kind of thing."

He gestured out of the window, where a wooded incline swept majestically down to a stream below. Half a pram and two litter bins protruded from the water.

"Looks a bit like Earth without the pollution and overcrowding."

Charlie looked out. The gorge had been replaced by row after row of identical houses, grey pebble-dash below each window stained with dark patches as if they spent most of their time crying.

The boy turned quickly away from the sight.

"Go on," he said.

"Gorrodin had a fondness for mankind, though they were little more than savages at that time. I mean, we're talking hundreds of years ago. One day, it occurred to him that he might help humans be better than they were. In the area now known as southern Scotland, he gathered together the bravest and noblest of the race and forged them into a tribe."

"Hold on!" Charlie tapped on the table. "I thought Galhadrians didn't interfere in the lives of humans?"

"Absolutely," Peazle nodded enthusiastically. "The other Lords were furious. But Gorrodin was a powerful sorcerer and the best they could do was banish him."

"To the place where he wanted to be, anyway?" Charlie said mockingly. Both boys giggled.

"Yes, he wasn't too concerned," Peazle said. "But things got out of hand."

He stopped laughing and carried on.

"Gorrodin's tribe flourished. Everyone was equal there, a beacon of light in what came to be known as the Dark Ages." The pickpocket was obviously warming to his story - but Charlie noticed the boy's voice was starting to sound a little thin - and he looked slightly blurred. Charlie wondered if that was the potion or the effect of drinking Peazle's coffee.

"The magician appointed a human leader, Arturius, to rule his tribe, warriors dedicated to bringing peace to the land. Their home was called Taneborc, roughly where Edinburgh is now. Arturius is now better known as King Arthur and Taneborc drifted into legend as Camelot."

Charlie shook his head, trying to clear it, but the scenery outside the window seemed to be melting and reforming. He knew it was Thane's magic at work, so he surrendered to its spell.

Dirty factories faded away and he could suddenly see a large, thatched village, surrounded by a barrier of raised logs. Smoke rose from a communal fire in a central clearing, a series of long wooden outhouses held pigs and cattle and, on a distant hill, there stood a stone fort.

Out of the corner of his eye, he could see a cloud of dust rising behind a glittering column of riders, cantering out of the distance towards the village. There was a flurry of shouted activity and the gates of the stockade swung open for the approaching horsemen.

"All legends have a grain of truth at their centre, and the legend of King Arthur is no different." Peazle's voice came far away now. "You ought to know that more than anyone."

Charlie was no longer listening. His body was still on the train but his mind was swooping over the emerald fields towards Camelot. He noticed a white hawk with black-tipped wings sailing alongside him and knew, from past experience, birds like these were the eyes of the Galhadrians, keeping watch.

The conductor arrived with more drinks and stared questioningly at the motionless boy.

"He always sleeps with his eyes open. Weird, isn't it?"

Peazle smiled at the astonished official and emptied four sachets of sugar into his new cup.

Mordred

Charlie found himself floating into a wooden chamber at the centre of the stockade. Smoke wafted up from a cooking fire through a hole in the thatched roof. At one end was an enormous round table circled by seated warriors.

A man strode into the building, smiling broadly, and raised a gloved hand in greeting. He was tall and broad, not long into his twenties, yet he bore himself with confidence and dignity. Around his muscular shoulders hung a bearskin, held at the throat by a silver Roman clasp and a short sword hung on his waist. Behind him stood two warriors. One was even taller, with a ring of fiery red hair and moustache to match. The other was older, grey streaking the thin hair that bordered his sallow face. The young man bent his knee briefly to the packed earthen floor, then stood. A woman with short black hair and pretty features emerged from the shadows. She grinned and gave the newcomers a little wave.

At the opposite end of the room a short, stocky knight rose at the table, a plain circlet of gold resting on his forehead. He, too, was young, but his bright blue eyes were edged with dark creases, the mark of a man who carried more responsibility than his years warranted.

"Welcome home, Mordred, my friend," he said warmly. "News of your victory has preceded you."

Charlie drew a sharp breath at the mention of the newcomer's name.

"My Lord Arturius." Mordred acknowledged the compliment with a brief nod. "We met the Pictish army at Longmuir and crushed them. Our northern borders are safe."

He unfastened the bearskin and swept it over his shoulder.

"Uallabh. Pelinore. Take your places with our comrades."

The two companions sought out empty spaces at the table. Those on each side slapped their backs and pushed food and drink into eager hands. Arturius raised his goblet and winked at Mordred.

"Peace in our times," he said. The other knights held up their goblets in agreement and swallowed heartily. Mordred raised his cup but merely sipped. The action did not escape the man sitting to the right of Arturius. He was older than most of his companions, though his actual age was impossible to determine. Like the king, his eyes were disturbingly bright - green rather than blue - matching the cloak that covered his torso.

"You are troubled after such a victory, Mordred?" he said softly.

"In truth, Gorrodin, I am," Mordred replied. "The Picts are a warlike race and I feel that this defeat will merely fuel their hatred."

He swallowed his drink half-heartedly.

"I worry that, years from now, my sons will still be fighting our battles. All in the name of peace."

Gorrodin nodded and stroked his long chin. He was one of the few clean-shaven men at the table.

"You think I should use my magic to destroy the Picts forever, young friend? Aye, and subdue the Angles and Britons in the south. In fact, anyone else who threatens us?"

Mordred nodded enthusiastically and several others at the table banged the wood in agreement. Gorrodin glanced around and held up a hand.

"You will always have enemies as long as violence, selfishness and greed fester in the hearts of men. Would you have me banish all those too? Would you want me reaching inside everyone, without permission, and making whatever changes I please?"

A portly knight named Bahlain let out a belch of protest and several of his companions began to laugh.

"Say, for instance, I didn't like people being rude while I was trying to make a point."

Gorrodin swept a hand through the air and the laughter stopped instantly. Battle-hardened warriors looked at each other in astonishment and growing fear. Their mouths were open and full bellies shuddering, but no sound came from their lips.

The room was deathly silent.

The wizard clicked his fingers and gasps of shock and amazement shuddered through the hall, as the men found they could speak again.

"If I alter your world too much, it becomes *my* world," he said to the hushed men. "You must change it yourselves, I'm afraid. And you can - for your own Lord Arturius, who I call Arthur, has more greatness in his heart than my magic can ever match."

He suddenly looked humble.

"You all do."

The Knights of the Round Table were neither philosophers nor politicians, yet this was a sentiment they understood. As one man, they rose and toasted Arthur, then Mordred and each other. Arthur walked around the table, nodding to each man, finally sitting beside Mordred.

"Party seems to be going well," he said.

Mordred grunted, then brightened as the woman who had waved earlier approached.

"A clever trick by Gorrodin, I thought," she said, brandishing a half-eaten chicken leg and wiping her lips daintily. "I always wanted to see the Round Table quiet for once."

"I am glad you are amused, mother. However, I fear it was an empty speech by your wizard, for all its cleverness." Mordred took the chicken leg and bit into it. "If you two weren't romancing, I'd have argued him into the ground."

The woman snorted.

"Not so empty, I fear." Arthur was suddenly solemn.

"My Lord?" Mordred asked quizzically.

"Gorrodin is right," Arthur said. "We must prove we can create a better world without the waving of a magic wand."

He hesitated, then straightened his back.

"That is why Gorrodin is leaving us."

"I am going too." The woman looked at the ground. "For you know that I love him."

"And I, her." Gorrodin appeared from nowhere and laid a hand on Mordred's shoulder. The young warrior jumped, hand reaching instinctively for his weapon.

"I wish you wouldn't do that."

"Despite my youthful appearance, I am old beyond your understanding," the wizard said softly. "Yet I have never loved the way I love your mother, Morgana. As you pointed out, I could wave a hand and make you accept this. Instead, I ask for your blessing."

For the second time, Charlie drew a sharp breath. This woman was Morgana? He didn't understand, for he could see no threat from the charming figure standing in front of him.

Mordred stood slowly until he was level with the wizard. The two held each other's stare.

"You and I do not agree on many things, sorcerer," he replied. "But we concur that my mother is an exceptional woman - and I fully trust her judgement in everything."

Morgana flushed bright red. Mordred reached out and clasped Gorrodin's hand.

"You have my blessing."

"You will not be forgotten, my friend." Arthur looked around at the revellers, each one loyal, brave and true, if slightly drunk. Uallabh was standing on the table, plaid round his waist, proudly showing his neighbours a battle scar on his bottom.

"I have talked to my men and we are agreed that, in honour of your memory, we will take your name."

Arthur bowed.

"From this day, we shall be known as the Gorrodin Rath."

The Picts

Charlie felt himself plucked from Taneborc and spirited across time and space, quickly and smoothly as a bird gliding through air. Again, there was the hawk with the black-tipped wings, hovering beside him.

They flew north for miles, heading years into the future, until they landed beside the window of a small but elegant stone dwelling. Behind the boy, a low and level moor rose gently to nudge a line of cliffs and a tall waterfall plumed from the rock like a gigantic horse's tail.

He heard giggling coming from the other side of the house and stuck his head around the corner to see who it was.

There was Lilly, a couple of years younger than he remembered, playing with a small dog. Charlie quickly ducked his head back, though it was obvious by now he was merely a spectator and couldn't be seen.

He peered through the windowpane into the glowing interior. He was fairly sure that 7th-century houses didn't have glass - or metal window catches, for that matter. This must be the home of the wizard, Gorrodin. Sure enough, the sorcerer was sitting at a table with

Morgana, her dark hair shimmering in the firelight's glow.

Gorrodin held a small wooden cup between his hands.

"Magic is a powerful force and it can warp and change those who try to master it," the man was saying. "For that reason, even great wizards keep their powers, not within themselves, but in a special talisman. This one belongs to me."

He tapped the side of the cup and silver liquid bubbled up inside, filling the vessel almost to the rim.

"I call it my Grail," he continued. He pushed the cup towards his wife, but his face was troubled. "Morgana... Our daughter Lilly has my blood in her veins, so she is magical, too. We will outlive you by thousands of years and I cannot bear that thought. If you drink from this, you will be like us."

"I don't know if I want to live forever." Morgana stared at the innocent-looking beaker.

"Nobody lives forever." the wizard smiled softly. "But immortals do live a long, long time."

"Then I will drink, for one lifetime with you and our daughter is too short."

Morgana reached for the cup but Gorrodin laid his hand gently upon hers.

"After this, however, you must never touch the Grail again." He pulled nervously at his chin. "It is not yours to use."

"Of course." Morgana bowed her head but not before Charlie spotted the sad look in her eyes. Gorrodin noticed it as well.

"That was not an insult," he continued. "Humans and magic must not mix. It is too strong and corrupts them in a most terrible way."

He lifted his wife's head and smiled at her.

"But I have no fear." He spread his hand in front of his wife's face, drawing it into a smile. "Look. I wave my hand and the power of the Grail is yours to command. Because I trust you never to use it."

Morgana lifted the cup and drank.

Charlie found the scene swinging away like a revolving mirror, only to be replaced by an almost identical one. Lilly was further off, taller now, and her dog was no longer a puppy. He glanced in the window. Morgana was sitting writing at the table. There was no sign of Gorrodin.

He heard a rumble in the distance that transformed quickly into the thunder of horses' hooves. Morgana's head lifted, a look of consternation on her face. She rose to her feet and headed for the door.

Charlie skirted the house and arrived at the front at the same time as Morgana emerged into the sunlight. Her hands shot to her mouth as she spotted whooping horsemen galloping across the moor towards her daughter. Their faces were daubed with blue and each was heavily armed.

"Picts!" Morgana breathed. "A war party!"

Lilly had spotted the horsemen and was sprinting back towards the safety of the house - but it was obvious the raiding party would catch her before she reached shelter. Morgana was about to head for her daughter then, realising the same thing, turned and darted back into the house. Charlie ran towards the girl before remembering he could do nothing to help.

"Fetch Gorrodin!" he shouted at the empty doorway. But, if the wizard were around, he would have already been defending his family. Lilly was still racing for the house. Her dog turned and bounded towards the attackers in a desperate attempt to save his mistress.

The hound didn't stand a chance. After a few desperate lunges, it vanished under the oncoming hooves.

Lilly skidded to a halt, rage written across her childish face. She stretched out her hands and the leading Pict was catapulted backwards off his steed. She thrust her arms forward again and another rider went down. The remaining Picts yelled louder and spurred their horses on - there were far too many in the raiding party for the girl's fledgling magical powers to stop.

Lilly turned to run again, but a wooden axe came hurtling through the air and embedded itself in her back. She fell forward onto the heather, a gout of blood erupting in the air.

Charlie sank to his knees, his face ghostly white.

With a triumphant whoop, the leading Pict dismounted his horse and advanced toward the dying girl.

He never reached her.

Charlie could not feel the force that rushed past him, nor did he understand what it was. All he saw was a rippling in the air and ferns and heather curling in on themselves, as if subjected to immense heat. The shimmering path reached the Picts, turning them instantly to black outlines that broke and drifted into the moorland.

Charlie whirled. Morgana stood in the doorway, holding Gorrodin's Grail. She ran to her daughter, still clutching the cup, and knelt beside her. With a shudder, Morgana pulled the axe from Lilly's back and placed her hand over the spurting wound. She drank from the cup again, whispering hysterically to herself. The blood pouring between her fingers instantly stopped and, when she removed her hand, her daughter's wound was gone. Lilly's shallow, laboured breathing evened out until it became deep and regular.

"Sleep, my child," Morgana whispered. "When you awake, you will forget this dreadful thing." She hesitated. "Nor will you remember I broke my sacred promise to your father and used his Grail once more."

She clasped, then unclasped, her fingers and a small, glinting object appeared in her hand. She fastened it around her sleeping daughter's neck.

It was a tiny silver whistle on a chain.

"If you are ever in trouble again, my daughter, blow the whistle and I will come."

She stroked Lilly's cheek, rose and walked back to the house. Charlie paused to make sure the girl was all right, then trotted into the interior after her mother.

Morgana was replacing Gorrodin's Grail on a shelf. As she let it go, her hand trembled. Then she reached out and stroked the wooden surface as gently as she had touched her child moments before.

She turned and Charlie took an involuntary step back. For a brief second, he had seen something flicker in her eyes - a glint that had not been there before. A more experienced observer might describe it as the first kindling of lust, or desire without bounds. Charlie only had one word for it.

Evil.

The Break-In

Sergeant Plune and Constable Valentine returned to Charlie's house at the end of their beat, as promised. Fenton was a small rural town and didn't have a lot of crime, so the 'handy cat' - as they jokingly called it - had been the highlight of their day. The two men had spent most of their shift trying to figure out what had happened.

"I still say those kids were hallucinating. Experimenting with drugs," Constable Valentine opened the Wilsons' garden gate and the two policemen strolled up the path. "The Macmillan boy is never out of trouble."

"I've never seen a hallucination break anyone's arm." Sergeant Plune knocked briskly on the front door. "Could be they came across some weird animal that escaped from a zoo. I saw a red panda once on TV and it had little fingers and thumbs for climbing trees. Mind you, that was in China."

He knocked again and the front door swung gently open.

"Mr and Mrs Wilson?" The policemen peered into the dark hall. "Are you here?"

There was no reply. As their eyes adapted to the gloom, they noticed that the occupants' telephone table was lying on its side.

Motioning for his companion to follow, Sergeant Plune moved cautiously into the house, crossed the hall and opened the living room door. Constable Valentine heard the sergeant gasp and looked over his shoulder.

The room looked as if a tornado had cut through it. Bookcases and chests of drawers lay on their sides, contents spilling out over the floor. A storm of paper, ornaments and knick-knacks were strewn across the room. The policemen quickly unfastened their batons and Constable Valentine hurried up the stairs while Plune inspected the ruined living room. He noticed several items of jewellery lying on the floor next to the contents of an upturned box. This house hadn't been burgled. It had been torn apart during the process of a frantic search. Sergeant Plune picked a spangly pair of tights from the floor and gaped at them.

Valentine's head appeared over the bannisters above. His raised eyebrows told Plune the bedrooms were in the same state.

"Nobody up here. No sign of the kid or the mother and father."

"What the hell is going on?" Sergeant Plune turned to see Charlie's parents standing in the doorway, look-ing, open-mouthed, at the wreckage of their house. He quickly dropped the tights.

"Mrs and Mrs Wilson," he said. "Eh… any news from your son?"

Charlie's parents shook their heads.

"Then I think we'd better call Birmingham main branch." Plune pulled out his police radio. "Don't touch anything up there," he shouted to Constable Valentine, then tapped the antennae thoughtfully against his teeth.

"This is a lot more serious than some damned cat."

Events were flowing past Charlie as if history were a river. He saw Morgana practising sorcery with the Grail whenever Gorrodin and her daughter were absent. To the boy, it was obvious that everything good about the woman was being consumed by the magic inside her. Gorrodin obviously could not, or would not, see it.

The scene melted and changed. Now Gorrodin and Morgana were having a furious argument. The wizard stormed out of the house, anguish screwing up his face, heading towards a cave near the waterfall. His wife strode after him, tears streaking her cheeks.

"You have deceived me, my love," he shouted. "You promised not to use the Grail!"

From a leather bag at his side, he withdrew the wooden cup.

"It pains me, but I must keep the talisman where you cannot touch it. I shall seal it in this cave."

He tossed the Grail into the darkness and chanted a few words. With a crumbling shudder, the sides of the crevasse began to grind shut. Morgana stood behind her husband, fists clenching and unclenching in desperation.

As the cave entrance grew narrower, she stretched out her arms, fingers wide. The Grail shot out of the tiny gap in the quickly closing walls and into her hands. Gorrodin turned, eyes wide, as Morgana thrust out her arms again. The wizard flew backwards like a rag caught in some violent gale, vanishing into the cave. His cry of anguished betrayal was cut off, as the rocky sides slapped shut.

Morgana sank to her knees, clutching the Grail as if it were a lost child. Without a backwards glance at the place where her husband was now entombed, she rose to her feet and strode away across the valley.

Charlie heard a small sob and looked around.

Lilly had been watching the whole scene, hiding in the heather.

Charlie flew through time and space again, south to where Edinburgh would, one day, stand. They saw Morgana arrive at Camelot with the Grail and how her return threw Arthur's tribe into disarray. Many knights welcomed Morgana warmly, for Northumbrian tribes from the south and Picts from the north were continually attacking. The Gorrodin Rath sorely needed help.

Arthur, however, wished to have nothing to do with the Grail. What's more, he did not believe Morgana's explanation that Gorrodin had returned to Galhadria and entrusted her with its powers to use in the Rath's defence.

Mordred, on the other hand, was tired of fighting endless battles. He accepted his mother's ruse without question and was happy to use Morgana's magic to right the wrongs of the world. Reluctantly, Arthur took his most loyal followers and left.

And so, as Charlie looked miserably on, the Round Table was destroyed. Mordred, Morgana and their supporters drank from the Grail and tried to use its magic. Like Morgana, they became obsessed with their new powers.

Months ticked by in seconds and the boy watched, with mounting horror, as the Gorrodin Rath began to change. The more they practised forbidden magic, the more it altered them. They slowly transformed into dark creatures, troll-like in appearance, who could not bear the light of day. They no longer farmed the land but retreated into underground caverns, emerging at night to seek the easiest food they could find. Their former race.

The Gorrodin Rath had become cannibals.

Arthur slumped on a rough wooden throne, his face creased with lines of anguish. Charlie stood beside him, unable to do anything but watch. The flap of the tent opened and a warrior stepped inside and knelt.

"There is a young girl here to see you, my Lord."

"I have no time for an audience with children."

"She claims to be Gorrodin and Morgana's daughter."

In an instant, Arthur was on his feet and hurrying outside, Charlie right behind. There, in the bustle and sun-dappled smoke of the knight's camp, stood Lilly. The girl was grimy and bedraggled but standing tall and proud, as the daughter of a wizard should, in the presence of her king.

"Are you really who you say?" Arthur began. Then his voice trailed off. One look at the girl's emerald eyes told him all he needed to know.

"What has happened to Gorrodin, child?" he said gently

"My father is trapped in a cave to the far north, my Lord, and I do not know how to free him. So, I have sought you out. I am half Galhadrian and know the ways of the Little People, but my powers are still weak and the journey south was dangerous. I am truly sorry, but it has taken me many months to reach here."

Arthur crouched beside the girl and took her hand. Passing warriors stopped and looked in amazement at the sight.

"You must rest," he said. "We will talk once you have recovered."

Lilly shook her head.

"My anger burns too bright," she replied. "And it may be that I can aid you." She reached inside her tunic and brought out a lump of shining metal. "My father's race loved jewellery and finery, you see."

Arthur looked puzzled.

"When they abandoned earth, they left much behind, for Galhadria has no shortage of such treasures." The girl gave a small smile. "Not far from here, according to my father, was a hidden cache of fairy silver. I have found it for you."

"And?" Arthur looked none the wiser

"Fairy silver is deadly to dark creatures, the very things my mother and her followers have become. You have forges here, do you not?"

Comprehension began to dawn on Arthur's face and he nodded.

"Make weapons and armour from the silver," the girl continued. "If you strike without warning, you can enter the caves where the creatures live and rescue my father's Grail before they realise what is happening. It is the source of their power and they will be much weakened without it."

Arthur motioned to the gathering warriors.

"Assemble the men and have our blacksmiths stoke the campfires!" he shouted, flinging a cloak around his shoulders. "I want my warriors to form a war party. We will strike swiftly and take the cup."

He smiled warmly at the girl.

"Hope has come amongst us, at last."

The train whistle blew loudly and Charlie was back in the compartment again. He stared at Peazle, wide-eyed. The pickpocket blew on his coffee and tendrils of smoke ducked and curved around his lips.

"This wasn't the story Lilly told me!" Charlie stammered. "She claimed her father deserted her in Galhadria, went to earth and created a private army of monsters called the Gorrodin Rath. She said her dad was the bad guy."

Peazle sipped his drink, staring awkwardly at his companion over the rim of the cup.

"There is an explanation." The pickpocket looked grim. "But I fear you will not like it."

"No surprises there, then,"

The pickpocket drained the last of his coffee and looked solemnly out of the window again.

"We must be in Scotland," he said. "It's raining."

Charlie stared down at the stained Formica table. He felt sad and betrayed.

"Why did Lilly tell me some totally made-up crap about Gorrodin leaving her?" he said finally. "Why did she never mention Morgana being her mother? Why didn't she go back and try to rescue her father?"

Peazle sighed heavily. He raised his hands ineffectually and put them back on the table again.

"Drink, my friend. You may as well know everything."

So, Charlie did.

The Last Stand of Arthur

Charlie found himself in the distant past, once more, standing on a dark, heather covered escarpment, battered by rain. A line of mounted men looked warily up at the craggy hill in front of them. Cold rain was falling, plastering long hair to scalps and running down nervous faces. For a few moments, the rays of the setting sun burst through the clouds and danced across a bristling row of silver swords and spears.

The warriors struggled to control the horses, for the animals were rolling their eyes in fear, frantic hooves churning purple thistle heads into the mud. One horseman tugged powerfully at his reins, forcing his struggling mount closer to Arthur, marked out as their leader by the silver ringlet on his head.

"It is only moments till the sun sets, my Lord," he cautioned. His long red hair was braided and his face daubed with a war mask of deep blue spirals. Charlie recognised him as the knight called Uallabh, made up for battle.

"Forgive me, sire, but I do not understand," he continued. "We have stolen back the cup. Are we to throw that advantage away by fighting in the dark and at the bottom of a hill? We could not be in a worse defensive position."

Arthur did not look around.

"The Gorrodin Rath have become thieves, murderers and nightcrawlers," he said sorrowfully. "Only if they are sure of victory, will they commit their whole force to battle."

"And if they win?"

"By that time, the Grail will be gone. After all, I am entrusting one of my finest men to guard it."

The painted warrior was taken aback.

"My job is to fight with you, sire."

"The Grail must be kept from Morgana, old friend." Arthur looked unwaveringly into Uallabh's eyes. "I trust none but the greatest knight I have ever known."

Uallabh blinked rapidly, his jaw tight. He seemed about to speak again, but Arthur shook his head to cut him off. With a grunt, the warrior wheeled his horse around and stared angrily at Lilly.

The girl stood in the fading light, clutching her father's wooden cup. Arthur raised a gloved hand and pointed to his silent friend.

"Uallabh will get the Grail to safety," he smiled. "Even if he is none too pleased about it."

The sun slid behind the western hills. A long black shadow crept slowly over the small army and up the side of the hill, enveloping them in darkness.

"Listen."

At first, the men could hear nothing but the hiss of the rain and the whinnying of terrified horses. Then a sound like wind howling through a mountain pass drifted out of the darkness, growing louder and louder, until it was a nerve-shredding roar.

Shapes began to appear on the crest of the hill, black and monstrous. They almost blended into the darkness were it not for the red glow of their eyes and the gleam of vicious fangs and teeth. Eventually, a solid mass of deformed bodies filled the horizon.

Arthur seemed calm and only those closest to him saw the knotted muscles of his jaw and the movement of his lips, as he uttered a silent oath.

Then he straightened, raised his spear and spurred his reluctant steed towards the enemy. Giving an inhuman scream, they rushed down the slope.

With a spirited war cry, Arthur's doomed army lifted their weapons and charged after him.

Charlie was whisked into the air and away from the carnage erupting below, where monsters and men rushed together with a fury that made him screw shut his eyes. The moon raced across the sky, accompanied by the clash of steel and the screams of dying men and horses.

The boy floated down to the top of a nearby hill. Lilly and Uallabh were struggling towards him, almost blinded by the gusts of freezing rain soaking their clothes. The warrior swayed and stumbled, trying not to lean on the small figure, for the girl was already burdened by a leather bag slung over her shoulder. Uallabh's beard was matted with blood and a bronze breastplate hung half off his chest, bent and ripped as if it were tin foil.

They splashed, gasping, through a small stream – it was so dark they had not even seen it. The warrior sank to his knees and his shaking fingers fumbled at the breastplate fastenings until the ruined armour fell from his chest. Over the storm, the hiss of the stream, and his own ragged breathing, he could still hear the roar of battle drifting up from the valley below. Lilly looked back the way they had come and shuddered.

"I should still be down there, fighting alongside my comrades," the warrior rasped. He tried to rise, but his legs no longer supported him and he collapsed with a grunt of pain.

"No, Uallabh! We have to get away!" The girl clasped the warrior's quilted tunic and tried vainly to pull the man to his feet. "We have to get the Grail to safety!"

The jerkin fell open, revealing a deep, jagged wound running from the warrior's shoulder to his waist. Lilly looked up and saw a faint light seeping into the sky from the east.

"It will be dawn soon." Tiny hands urgently clasped at the tunic again. "We only have to last a little longer."

A merciless roar shattered the night and Lilly's head shot up, eyes wide with fear, scanning the darkness. Uallabh's hand went to the knife at his side and he pulled himself to his knees by sheer force of will. A riderless horse, lathered with sweat and blood, thundered out of the night. Eyes rolling in terror, it swept past them and vanished into the darkness again.

"The creatures must be almost upon us," the warrior snarled. "You go. I will hold them off."

"The Gorrodin Rath are still in the valley, fighting with your companions. Only Morgana is following." The girl fished Gorrodin's wooden Grail from the leather bag, waved her hand over the top, and then thrust it at the warrior. "But my mother... a whole army will not stop her."

Uallabh looked down. Miraculously, liquid glittered inside the goblet, almost up to the rim.

"Drink from this," Lilly urged.

The warrior pushed the cup violently away.

"Never!" The warrior pushed the cup violently away. "I will not be tainted by its dark magic."

"Listen to me," the child whispered urgently. "You are noble and pure of heart, or you would not be here. You will stay that way if you do not attempt to use the powers the goblet gives you. I promise."

"What will it do to me?" the man asked.

"It will stop you ageing."

"I do not wish to be immortal."

"More importantly, it will cure your wounds. I need you!"

Uallabh looked intently at the child, his mouth set in a grim line. Finally, he reached out, took the cup and drank.

There was another horrendous roar, much louder now. The child took the goblet and stuffed it back into her bag. Uallabh tried to get up again and this time, to his astonishment, rose easily to his feet.

"Go north. Hide the Grail," Lilly said. "Then wait for me at the Glen of Rosslyn. No matter how long it takes."

The warrior took the bag and threw it over his own broad shoulder. He stood fully erect and his eyes were clear and hard.

"And if this... thing kills you?"

"It will not dare risk the Dolorous Stroke."

"The *what*, now?"

"I have no time to explain!"

"Then I will do as you ask." The man nodded once and strode away without a backward glance.

Lilly crouched down in the heather. The sky was definitely lighter now and it would soon be dawn.

A huge figure appeared out of the blackness.

The girl allowed a horrified groan to escape her lips. In the months she had been travelling, magic had corrupted Morgana until she was unrecognisable. She was almost twice the height of a man, with a torso so large and muscular, it was more beast-like than human. Malevolent eyes, deep in a knobbly skull, bobbed above a snarling mouth bristling with fangs. Blood dripped from a gaping wound in her abdomen.

Lilly raised her hands and a bolt of light shot from her fingers. It struck Morgana in the chest and threw her backwards into the heather. Seconds later, the creature was on its feet, unscathed by the blow. The thick white lips pulled back in a scornful sneer.

"You're too late," the girl said. "The Grail is gone and I do not know where."

"So, you too, hate me," Morgana snarled. "Would stop me from possessing what is rightfully mine."

A heavily taloned hand shot out, pointing at the little girl.

"Then let the man who caused this grief take the blame." The claws twitched and Lilly went rigid, as if some invisible hand had her by the throat.

"You will believe your father, the mighty Gorrodin, deserted you and caused all this misery." Her voice dripped with contempt at the mention of her husband's name. "You will forget me, for you are not worthy to be my daughter."

She opened her hand and the girl sank to the ground, unconscious.

"Sleep, Lilly," she whispered.

She looked around, sniffing the air. But Uallabh and the Grail were gone and dawn was breaking. With a roar of fury, she stretched her hands to the sky where the hawk still floated. With a screech, it plummeted from the sky in a ball of flame.

"And I do not like being spied on," she hissed.

Then she headed across the heather to find a place to hide and heal, leaving her minions to their fate.

Charlie sat up bolt upright, giving a small squeak.

"*That's* the thing chasing me?"

Peazle nodded.

"Her own mother?" he breathed. "Lilly's mother did that to her?"

"Lilly truly believes the story she told you," the pickpocket said. "She thinks her father caused the death of Arthur and the curse of hatred is heavy upon her."

The pickpocket looked solemnly out the window. A ruined castle slumped on a nearby hilltop, beaten into a shapeless pile of stones by the passage of time.

"Why didn't the Lords of the Western Wilderness come through a Thin Place," Charlie snapped. "To tell her the truth?"

Peazle's look of consternation changed to something that resembled anger.

"The Lords of the Western Wilderness always disapproved of Gorrodin meddling in human affairs. They were happy to see both him and the Gorrodin Rath out of the way."

"I'm not going to like this." A horrible feeling grew in the pit of Charlie's stomach. "Am I?"

"Having Lilly stay under Morgana's enchantment suited the Lords well." The pickpocket swallowed hard, as if he had eaten something distasteful. "They let her keep watch over the remaining Gorrodin Rath, waiting for her father to return to free them - so she could have her revenge." He sighed. "Though the Lords knew very well he was trapped for eternity."

"How could they do something so rotten?"

The conductor, passing by, gave them a dirty look, then hurried off before Peazle could ask him for more coffee.

"Lilly is only half Galhadrian. She's also half-human." The pickpocket looked ashamed. "The Little People do not care much for humans. They care even less for half breeds."

"And these are the guys you work for, eh?" Charlie shot back. "Well, I tell you what. I don't care much for Galhadrians.

"To be honest with you, Charlie," Peazle grunted. "I don't either."

Inspector Archer

Their train was travelling along the coastline when Peazle spotted a distant grey mass that was Edinburgh, twenty miles away, on the other side of a curving bay. Charlie had been silent for a long time, taking in all that Peazle had told him. The pickpocket stared glumly at the sparkling water. He knew his companion must be in turmoil and had no idea how to ease his anguish.

"What I don't understand," Charlie said, as if on cue. "Is why Morgana has waited all this time to go after the Grail again."

"I've got no idea, though I know she was severely wounded." the pickpocket said. "She killed the hawk who was keeping an eye on her, so the Lords of the Western Wilderness lost track of her movements. They assumed she died when the sun came up, but she may have been strong enough to survive in daylight. Or found some kind of shelter."

He crumpled the empty coffee cup.

"Something obviously woke her. Jack Thane is certain she is alive and searching for the Grail. It was the source of her power and she will always desire it."

"And I'm her only link?"

"I fear so. You were in the wrong place at the wrong time." Peazle scratched his cheek awkwardly. Charlie remembered that the boy had also seen the horror of the Gorrodin Rath first-hand.

"What am I going to do?"

He leant forward on the table, head in his hands. The train was now threading its way through the out-skirts of Edinburgh. The centre of the town might be filled with stately Georgian homes, lush parks and magnificent churches, but the suburbs were as bleak and industrial as any other city.

"Morgana is controlling the last dark creatures left on earth," Peazle continued after a while. "She will keep sending them after you so long as you remain in this world. Your only option is to hide."

They were plunged into darkness as the train roared into the long tunnel that ran under the centre of the city. Charlie and Peazle held their breath and gripped the hand rests of their seats until the leather squeaked. They had no great love of tunnels. When they emerged into daylight, sheer rock rose steeply from the tracks to Edinburgh's magnificent castle, hundreds of feet above. Peazle shivered, remembering he had once been a prisoner there.

"In the meantime, I shall attempt to find Lilly."

Charlie fingered the silver whistle on the chain around his neck.

If you ever really need me, blow this, the girl had told him, last time he saw her.

"I know how to do that," he muttered to himself.

A few minutes later, the train pulled slowly into the city's Waverly Station.

Sergeant Plune sat at the dining table in the Wilson's kitchen. A tall, bald man with a pockmarked face took off his brown raincoat, entered and introduced himself as Inspector Archer of Birmingham CID.

"I've talked to the parents and no valuables have been taken, not that these people had much to steal. All the rooms were torn apart. Whoever went through them seemed pretty angry and the boy's bedroom was the worst. There's still no sign of him."

"Do the parents have any idea why their house was ransacked?" Plune asked, secretly thrilled to be part of such a big operation.

"They say they haven't a clue," the Inspector replied. "To be honest, they're more worried about where their son might have gone. According to the mum and dad, he's a very sensible lad."

The Inspector looked longingly at the electric kettle, undamaged, on the breakfast bar. Plune took the hint and got up to make a cup of tea.

"This one's got me baffled," Inspector Archer admitted. "It's just plain weird. Especially when you take into account that crazy story about some wild cat."

He took Charlie's note, sealed in a plastic bag, from his pocket.

"Then there's this. It seems to indicate the boy left of his own accord." He looked down at his notepad. "For now, we'll have to treat him as a runaway and start checking local bus and train stations."

He heard a cough from the doorway and turned. Charlie's father was standing there, his expression taught.

"I'm going to look, too," he said. "I've been calling his mobile every ten minutes, but there's no answer and the tracker app doesn't seem to work."

"All the more reason to stay put." Inspector Archer put down his mug of tea. "You have to be here in case your son tries to contact you or comes back."

He indicated to a policeman standing in the hall. The uniformed man moved to escort Charlie's dad away.

"Crime scene, you know?" the Inspector said apologetically. Charlie's dad glared at the steaming mug, snorted, and strode off.

"You find any fingerprints?" Sergeant Plume said quietly, and the Inspector nodded.

"All over the place. Mr and Mrs Wilson aren't big on dusting." The Inspector dismissed these potential clues with a shake of his head. "They belong to the occupants. Strange thing is, there are animal hairs all over the house, but the Wilsons say they don't own a pet."

He caught Sergeant Plume's alarmed expression and looked around again. This time, Charlie's mother was standing in the doorway. She fixed the Inspector with a steady gaze. Archer was about to rise and usher her out, but the intensity of her stare pinned him to the seat. Mrs Wilson was very beautiful, he thought, and he noticed her eyes were the deepest, brightest green he had ever seen.

"Find my son, Inspector," she said, her look never wavering.

"I will, ma'am," he said.

"No. Promise me. Promise you'll find him."

Inspector Archer was an experienced investigator and had seen too many missing person cases end in tragedy. He knew no such oath could be kept, so he never made one. He opened his mouth to say something neutral, but the woman's gaze was making the hairs on his neck stand on end. There was more than anguish in that look. There was an intensity that was almost hypnotic.

Even so, Inspector Archer would never understand why he said what he did.

"I promise."

The boys alighted and hurried out of Edinburgh's Waverly Station. The sky was beginning to darken and a cold wind whipped at their clothes. Charlie immediately looked to where the Old Town sloped up from the rest of the city, the site of his incredible adventure the previous year. Peazle looked as well, taking in the castle, the Gothic steeples and ancient tenements that lined the Old Town ridge, casting serrated shadows over the city. They brought back no fond memories.

"Looks much the same as it did when I saw it last," he grunted. "Two centuries ago."

The streetlights suddenly came on, bathing them in a yellow glow. The pickpocket pulled Charlie back into the shadows, glancing nervously up and down the busy street.

"We have to draw as little attention to ourselves as possible," he hissed in a stage whisper. "Morgana could have eyes anywhere."

"If she does, they'll be blinded by your waistcoat."

"I love this attire," Peazle replied defensively. "But I probably should steal a proper vestment, eh? It's getting a bit chilly."

"Nick a proper hat while you're at it." Charlie fished an apple from his pocket and bit down. He hadn't had a real meal all day and realised he was starving. Being back in Edinburgh, the place where he had already defeated one monster, seemed to have rekindled his spirit of adventure.

"What now?" he said through a mouthful of fruit.

"We need somewhere quiet to lie low till nightfall," he said.

"How about the Underground City?"

"How about I punch you in the snoot?"

"I was joking."

"The Great Sword Excalibur should still be in Greyfriars Graveyard, where you hid it last summer,"

Peazle said. "We're going to wait until it gets dark properly and dig it up."

"What do we need Excalibur for?"

"It had the power to slay Mordred. I'd like to have it to hand, wouldn't you?"

"Oh yeah. It'll increase your chance of survival from none to just-about-none." Charlie gave a wink. "But I have a little surprise that's going to make our job a lot easier."

Before the pickpocket could stop him, he pulled the silver whistle Lilly had given him from around his neck and blew into it.

There was silence.

"Oh. Maybe it's blocked." The boy held the whistle up to the streetlight and tried to see inside. He put it in his mouth again.

"What are you doing?" Peazle jumped forward and knocked the whistle away. "You want every bobby in the city turning up to see what the commotion is? They won't be able to help us!"

Charlie tried to point out that police didn't use whistles anymore, and he was summoning another type of help entirely, but Peazle grabbed his protesting companion and dragged him away from the station entrance and up the steep hill that led into the Old Town.

Charlie was disappointed. He wanted to see the look of amazement on the pickpocket's face when Lilly suddenly appeared. Had she lied about helping him?

Peazle was so intent on hurrying them into the anonymity of the Old Town's bustling back streets that neither boy noticed a white hawk with black-tipped wings hovering in the dark sky above. Nor did they see a crouching shape in the deepest shadows of a nearby alley.

If they had, they would have realised that no amount of darkness could disguise the size of its outline.

The figure seemed almost too big to be human.

Greyfriars

There was no point in going into Greyfriars before dark in case they bumped into sightseers. No one had been buried in the graveyard for over a century, but it was picturesque and historic, so people often visited during the day. The boys went instead to the City Restaurant, an upmarket fish and chip shop with chrome fittings and red leather seats. Charlie ordered dinner and Peazle took off his coat - a fur-lined parka that he had 'borrowed' from a washing line behind one of the Old Town tenements. The waitress politely ignored his multicoloured waistcoat. Halfway through the meal, the pickpocket sat back and folded his hands contentedly over his stomach.

"If I'd lived and died in the 19th century, like all the other people I knew, I'd never have tasted fish in batter or Cokey Cola. Life just isn't fair, sometimes."

"Tell me about it," said Charlie sourly.

"Ach, you're lucky in many ways. You live in a world of scientific advancements the people in my time couldn't have dreamt of." The pickpocket was unable to contain his passion. "Have you ever used an electric toothbrush?"

"How do you know about stuff in my world if you live in Galhadria?"

"Jack Thane sends me here, now and then - though not nearly often enough. I always have to come straight back or face his wrath." Peazle got a second wind and shovelled another huge forkful of mushy peas into his mouth. "Pass me some more of that... tomato sauce, is it called? Wondrous stuff."

"How do you get back and forward?"

"Thin Places, of course. They're few and far between, but I have a map."

"Why exactly does Jack Thane send you on trips to Earth?"

"You think I'm a spy, Charlie?"

"Just curious." The boy nibbled at a chip. "Listen, Peazle, I appreciate this Thane guy has a lot of confidence in you - sending a fourteen-year-old boy to save me from a rampaging monster.

"I've lived two centuries, by the way, but your sarcasm is noted."

"But why aren't the Lords of the Western Wilderness helping you?"

"Magical creatures do not...."

"Magical creatures do not fight magical creatures, I know!" Charlie waved a handful of chips at the pickpocket, who tried to ward off flying ketchup. "But WHY?"

"The Little People don't talk about it," Peazle said, leaning forward. "But I'm small and folk tend not to notice me. I hear things I'm not supposed to. Plus I love to study. The Lords have a great library and I find things there."

"Like what?"

"Long ago in Galhadria," Peazle leaned even closer. "There was a terrible civil war. When it was finally over, the greatest sorcerers of the land plotted to make sure it would never happen again."

"The Lords of the Western Wilderness?"

"The very same," the pickpocket replied. "Gorrodin was one at that time. Together, they wove a great enchantment. I'm not sure of the exact details, but it worked something like this... Should two magical forces ever take sides against each other again, whichever side struck the first deadly blow would ultimately lose."

Peazle laughed cynically.

"It was called the Dolorous Stroke and the Lords thought the threat of it enough to guarantee peace forever."

"Magical creature must not fight magical creature - the rule no Galhadrian can break." Charlie nodded. "That's where it comes from."

"It does. It is ingrained in their culture."

"All right, I can see that." Charlie conceded. "But it doesn't explain why the Galhadrians are determined to stay hidden from us humans. We're not magical."

"The Lords have powers you couldn't imagine," Peazle pointed to a small TV, high on a bracket behind the café counter. The sound was off, but Charlie could see armed soldiers in Khaki surveying the aftermath of a bomb blast in some Middle Eastern country. A bleeding child was being pulled, crying, from the wreckage of a burning car.

"Men have immense power, too, Charlie. It's called science. And that power is growing faster than you can control." Peazle looked sadly at his dinner companion.

"They're afraid of us."

The pickpocket pulled a fob watch from inside his waistcoat and looked at it.

"The graveyard should be deserted by now." He stood and put on his coat. "Let's get the sword."

It was Saturday night, and the streets of the Old Town were filled with revellers out enjoying themselves. Nobody paid much attention to the two boys, especially since Peazle's new parka covered his outlandish waistcoat and the hood partly obscured his bowler hat. The pair finally reached the gates of the walled graveyard, set back from the houses, lit dimly by one distant streetlight.

They were closed.

"That's just great," moaned Charlie. "Somebody must have started locking it at night."

"All the better." Peazle stepped up to the gate, pulled a small cloth bundle from his pocket and removed a sliver of metal.

"Sometimes, I think I chose the right profession after all." He bent over and, a few seconds later, there was a click and the gate slowly swung open.

"Two hundred years may have passed, but basic lock design is still the same." He ushered Charlie into the graveyard and secured the gates again.

The boys moved cautiously between the gravestones, hands stretched in front of them, trying to get accustomed to the dark. They skirted the black mass of Greyfriars church and crept through the inky shadows until they reached the area where the poet, James Hogg, was buried. Eight months ago, Charlie had concealed Excalibur at that very spot.

"How are we going to dig the sword out?" hissed Charlie. "I can't see a bloody thing."

"You think I wouldn't come prepared?" Peazle trotted over to one of the nearby mausoleums, a solid block of darkness resting against the graveyard wall. There were several clinking sounds and the iron door of the upright tomb swung open as easily as the cemetery gate had. Moments later, a torch beam cut across the distance between them.

"Greyfriars is a Thin Place, remember?" the pickpocket's voice floated gleefully from behind the beam. Seconds later, he was back, carrying two torches and a shovel. "I planted these in that mausoleum a couple of days ago. I would have dug up Excalibur myself, only you seem to be the only person who can pull it from the ground. It seems to have bonded with you."

He shone the torch beam into his own face and Charlie saw his curious expression.

"Why do you suppose that is?"

"I haven't got a clue." Charlie took the spade and plunged it into the earth behind James Hogg's headstone. Peazle lit up the spot so the boy could see where he was digging.

"Me neither. And if the Lords of the Western Wilderness know, they haven't told me." The pickpocket sounded faintly annoyed.

Metal clinked against something solid and Peazle bent closer, directing the flashlight beam into the hole. The hilt of a sword protruded from the soil. Charlie grabbed it, pulled, and Excalibur slid easily out of the ground.

"This might be a bad time to bring it up." The boy held the gleaming sword in the air. "But I'm not going to Galhadria. I'm coming with you to find Lilly."

Instead of objecting, Peazle motioned for silence, listening carefully.

"Shhhhhhh. Do you hear something?"

"Don't be freaking me out, bro."

"I heard the gate rattling."

"Then let's get out of here. Could we use the Thin Place, after all, but come out somewhere else?"

"I'm not opening a Thin Place if a bunch of drunken teenagers are about to come staggering around the corner."

"What if it's Morgana that comes round the corner?" Charlie hissed. But Peazle had snapped off the flashlight and was already moving away, crouching low to the ground. Charlie sighed and followed him, scurrying after the dark, bobbing shape.

They rounded the corner of the church. A full moon floated just above the sharp points of the closed cemetery gates, its pale light bleeding down onto the empty path. There was no sign of any intruders. Peazle stopped and straightened up.

"Perhaps I am being a little over-cautious," he began. "What's the matter?"

Charlie was staring in horror at the pickpocket. Or rather, what was behind him. A huge shape was rising above the nearest gravestone, moonlight silhouetting its hulking form. Two massive arms arched over the top of the tomb, reaching out for the boy.

"Peazle! Get down!" Charlie shouted, leaping forward. The pickpocket's childhood instinct for survival kicked in and he threw himself to the ground. Charlie leapt onto his friend's back and used the leverage to propel himself high into the air, swinging his sword as he went.

Inches from the creature's massive head, Excalibur's silver blade clashed against another sword, as a second figure shot up behind the gravestone. Sparks flew from the clashing weapons, the monster fell backwards with a yelp and Charlie went somersaulting over it, landing awkwardly on his side. In a second, he was on his feet again, weapon held in front of him.

"My compliments!" The swordsman facing him was a tall youth with long dark hair. "You handle that weapon as if ye were born wi one in your hand."

The boy spoke in a thick northern accent, one that Charlie remembered from their brief meeting eight months ago. Peazle rose to his feet, grinning.

"Duncan?" He shouted gleefully. "Is that you?"

"It is indeed." Duncan sheathed his sword and shook the pickpocket's hand. "Your wee pal almost took the head off Shadowjack here."

The enormous figure sat up, shaking its head. A toothy smile split the darkness.

"Is this all the thanks I get for keeping an eye on you two all night?" Shadowjack Henry laughed.

The Worms

The introductions were brief. Charlie sheepishly shook hands with Duncan and stared at Shadowjack. He had never seen a man as large as the blacksmith.

"What are you two doing here?" the pickpocket beamed.

"Jack Thane came calling," Duncan said. "He asked if we'd help you escort this boy tae safety." The highlander indicated Charlie. "And perhaps fight a monster or two. Sounded simple enough."

"After all that time in Galhadria, I was dying for a change," Shadowjack added.

"We've been following since you arrived in Edinburgh, tae make sure none of Morgana's agents were right behind. Nae sign of any trouble, though." The highlander sounded a little disappointed. "So, what now? Back through the Thin Place and nae real adventure?"

"I, for one, am keen to get out of Greyfriars." Shadowjack Henry looked longingly towards the cemetery entrance. "Something bad always seems to happen here."

"Shadowjack?" Charlie looked up at the ugly iron tips of the barrier. "How did you get in?"

"Young Peazle here must have picked the lock," replied Shadowjack, patting the boy on the shoulder so hard the pickpocket's knees buckled.

"That I did," Peazle said warily. "I also secured it behind me."

Duncan looked sharply round.

"It was open a minute ago," Shadowjack looked bewildered. "I strolled right in."

The highlander's sword slid from its scabbard and glistened in the moonlight. The cemetery was ringed by a fifteen-foot stone wall - even a giant like Shadowjack couldn't scale it – and the gates were the only way in or out. The highlander cursed himself silently for not spotting the obvious.

Greyfriars Graveyard was the perfect place for an ambush.

"Damn!" Duncan hissed. "This is a trap!"

And he turned and sprinted towards the Thin Place.

"Go!" shouted Shadowjack, pushing Peazle in front of him. "Little man. That torch, throw it here! You and the highlander, on our flanks!"

Charlie tossed his flashlight to the blacksmith. Duncan was on the right of the group, sword in hand, so Charlie moved to the left, brandishing Excalibur as he ran. The group dashed across the graveyard in silence, leaping over tombstones, the torch beam bobbing in the darkness. Peazle pulled a notebook from his parka pocket as he fled and vainly tried to shine his wavering light on it.

"I've got the incantation for opening the gateway to Galhadria written down," he panted.

"You didn't memorise it!?"

"It's about nine yards long!"

"The Thin Place is straight ahead," Duncan said, clearing a high gravestone with an effortless hop. "Better get incanting."

"Wait!" He skidded to a halt, holding his sword to the side to stop his comrades' advance.

"Make up your mind!"

"Shine your lights on the ground."

Shadowjack and Peazle did so.

"What foul magic is this?" Shadowjack breathed.

The earth in front of Hogg's grave seemed to be coming alive, seething and writhing, as if the bodies buried underneath were trying to break free. The party watched in horror as twigs, bones and rocks breached the churning, broken soil.

Worms began to boil to the surface. Thousands upon thousands of them.

"Back! We have to go back!" Peazle whirled and shone the light the way they had come. But the soil behind them was erupting, too.

"We'll be swallowed by the earth!" he wailed.

Duncan scanned the graveyard, refusing to panic.

"Into that tree," he pointed. A thick oak twisted out of the ground next to the graveyard wall, less than twenty yards away, the branches curving over the top of the barrier and into the darkness. Without looking backwards, the highlander slammed his sword into the scabbard on his back and darted to the tree. He climbed swiftly, uttering only a few quiet grunts and was soon scrambling through the middle branches. Seconds later, Shadowjack, Peazle and Charlie were clawing their way up the trunk behind him, ignoring the rough bark that tore their elbows and knees.

"Watch what you're doing with Excalibur," Peazle squealed. "You almost had my eye out."

"I'm trying to hurry you up."

"Tell the big lump in front of me!"

"Another few feet and these branches won't hold my weight," Shadowjack shouted, accompanied by cracking and breaking sounds, as he tried to force his way through the intertwining limbs. His foot hit Peazle in the head and the pickpocket dropped the flashlight. Charlie glanced down as it hit the ground.

The base of the oak looked to be anchored in a stormy brown sea and a gap was appearing at its base, as the earth sucked into itself, like sand in an hourglass. The torch sank into the widening hole and vanished.

"Climb higher!" Charlie screamed. "They're trying to bring the tree down!"

Shadowjack and Peazle were fighting their way through the middle of the foliage, Peazle wriggling through the branches like an eel while Shadowjack simply hauled the limbs out of their supporting wood and tossed them away. Duncan had reached a stout overhanging branch and was edging his way along it.

A few more feet and he would be able to touch the top of the graveyard wall.

"We're almost there!" the highlander yelled encouragingly.

The oak gave a tortured groan and lurched back a few feet. Duncan yelped and slipped from his perch. He grabbed a branch as he fell and managed to hang on, swinging by one arm, his face a tight mask of pain. Below him, a great gap opened in the earth, a monstrous black mouth.

Then the tree was falling and Charlie realised the trunk he was clinging to would crush him when it hit the ground. A tall, angel-topped monument rose up on one side and he vaulted sideways towards it, thrusting Excalibur in front of him. The sword slid into the stone and Charlie's breath was slammed out of his body as he hit the monument. But he kept hold of Excalibur, feet scrambling for footholds on the smooth marble. There were none and, suddenly, he was hanging just above the boiling earth, both hands clutching the hilt of the sword. He silently thanked his parents for teaching him their acrobatic skills.

The oak hit the earth with a mighty crash. From the centre of the branches, Shadowjack's torch beam still wobbled and spun as he, Duncan and Peazle clawed their way through the broken foliage and back onto the trunk. All around the toppled tree, the earth frothed and jumped, as millions of worms seethed and chewed at the bark, trying to reach the stranded humans. To

Charlie's dismay, he realised both his gravestone and the fallen tree were beginning to sink into the churning mud. The monument gave a sudden drop and he almost lost his handhold. Burning bile rose in his throat.

"Please God, I don't want to die like this," he cried softly to himself.

As he prayed, a shaft of light cut across the graveyard. Not the weak beam of a torch - but a shimmering beacon. Charlie twisted his head to see where it was coming from.

A tiny figure stood, far away, at the gates of the cemetery - bathed in brilliant luminescence. It raised one hand, made a fist, and brought it down forcefully. Every tombstone in the graveyard, between the stranded party and the gates, fell flat with a dull thump and a blast of cold air swept through Charlie's hair.

There was a shout of triumph to his right as Duncan leapt off the sinking trunk. He landed on a flat gravestone, shaking an army of worms from his boots in disgust.

"This is our way oot!" he shouted. "But they'll no stay above ground for long."

Then he was off, leaping from flattened tombstone to flattened tombstone. The others did not need any prompting. Charlie hauled Excalibur free and launched himself into space. He landed on his back and saw stars. Within seconds, worms were swarming over his arms and legs, pawing at him like a million squirming fingers. With a moan of revulsion, he tried to roll towards the closest toppled gravestone. He put one arm out and it sank into the earth, up to his shoulder. Slimy, wriggling bodies surged over his face and he pulled back his arm, hidden by a mass of quivering worms. He thrust Excalibur in front of him and the earth itself seemed to recoil from the Great Sword. Scything the weapon back and forth, he groped the last few feet and flopped onto the cold stone. Turning his head sideways, he caught a glimpse of his companions fighting for their lives.

Peazle had jumped off the tree, only to sink up to his waist in churning grubs and worms. He was screaming in terror, arms raised above his head. As he slid into the earth, Shadowjack came thundering past. Reaching out one mighty arm, he grabbed the shrieking pickpocket by the hair and pulled with all his might. With a wail that put his earlier efforts to shame, Peazle shot out of the ground. Shadowjack stuck him under a beefy arm and began hopping from one tombstone to another, zigzagging towards the gate.

Charlie's tombstone was now being lapped by an ocean of squirming pink flesh. It dropped a few inches, then the boy was leaping from gravestone to gravestone, trying not to slip on squashed, oily bodies, heading towards the exit. He reached the safety of the concrete driveway, right behind the others and collapsed in a heap. Beside him lay Peazle, Duncan and Shadowjack, all pulling worms from their clothing and hair and gasping with relief.

The bright light had gone and only the faint yellow illumination of the streetlight allowed them to see when the last of the twisting pink bodies had gone.

A small figure stepped from the shadows.

"Did someone whistle?" The voice was weak with exhaustion but Charlie recognised it immediately. He rolled onto his stomach and looked up.

"Nice timing, Lilly."

"Fashionably late." The girl gave a small smile and nodded politely. She turned to the highlander.

"Hi there, Duncan."

"Hello again, Heather. I mean, eh… Lilly."

"Whatever you're called, I thank you from the bottom of my heart, lass." Shadowjack got up and bowed, pulling a last fat worm from his beard. "Before we make more formal introductions, is there anywhere I could have a bath?"

"We tried tae lodge at an inn earlier," Duncan said sheepishly. "But Shadowjack got stuck in something called a revolving door."

"I'd never been in a fancy hotel before," Shadowjack said proudly.

"I can take us to lodgings." Lilly stepped out into the street, looked around and beckoned for the others to follow.

"Stay in the shadows, though. You look as if you've crawled out of your own graves."

An hour later, Jack Thane stood among the ruins of Greyfriars Graveyard. Lord Math was beside him - a black velvet cloak protecting her from the cold. Beyond them, a third shadowy figure crouched behind a gravestone, sniffing the ground. All three were bathed in the pale blue glow of the Thin Place, shining in the air like an upright pool. It also lit up the flattened headstones and fallen trees.

"They did not make it to Galhadria, Thane," Math said smugly.

"Charlie Wilson's whistle summoned Lilly, as he hoped," Thane replied. "Regretfully, it also alerted Morgana as to their exact whereabouts."

Thane knelt and studied the ground. "It's possible they will try to get through the Thin Place tomorrow."

"Would you?" Math grunted sceptically, looking at the broken headstones surrounded by a sea of dead worms - the earth, an expanse of flayed brown skin, turned inside out. "The worms will still be here and the area crawling with humans, too, I'll wager."

"Perhaps that is for the best." The wizard gave a sly smile. "Peazle is no fool and that is why I sent him. He has persuaded the Wilson boy to come north and now he has found Lilly. I imagine they will search for the cup itself rather than immediately retreating to Galhadria."

Math sniffed.

"Does the awakening of one long vanished creature really warrant all this... excitement?"

"Have you no eyes?" Jack Thane snapped, sweeping his arm across the devastation. "Look at this."

He dipped his fingers into the ruined earth and lifted a dirty clod thick with dead worms.

"Morgana should not have this kind of power."

"True." His companion frowned. "But she does. In which case, do you really think the boy and his companions can stay alive long enough to make it back?"

"As you can see, they are not food for the worms yet." Thane shrugged. "But you are right. I do not see how they could ever succeed."

Jack Thane stood, releasing the handful of soil as he rose.

"No matter. If Lilly knows where the Grail is, she would not reveal it to us, for we have treated her badly. But she may show its whereabouts to the Wilson child and I will be watching."

"If their quest is so important, perhaps we *should* act to help."

"The rest of the Lords will not agree to our interfering on earth, as you know. By the time we convince them Morgana is as great a threat to us as she is to mankind, it will be too late."

He snapped his fingers at the creature behind the tombstone. The Cat Palug stepped into the light, glaring at him with baleful yellow eyes.

"I have started the Wilson boy running." The Lord gave a rueful smile. "He has led Peazle to Lilly, as I hoped. Let us also hope they retrieve the Grail and reach another Thin Place before Morgana's forces catch up with them."

"Are you so sure the girl knows where it is?"

"I am not." Jack Thane attached a leather leash around the creature's neck and straightened up. "But she is our best bet and, as I say, I shall be watching."

With a gentlemanly bow, he took Math's arm. As if they were going for a moonlight stroll, the Galhadrians stepped through the Thin Place and vanished.

Hotel Huntingdon

The night brought a strange mixture of joy and sorrow. At first, the very fact they were alive had been cause for celebration. Lilly took the others to a nearby hotel - the Huntingdon - tall, modern and expensive. The bedraggled party tripped pensively into a huge black and white tiled lobby and tried to look inconspicuous behind a group of spiky potted plants, though Shadowjack would have had as much success if he had been hiding behind a twig. Lilly walked briskly over to the reception desk, where the counter staff were whispering suspiciously to each other. She waved her hands a few times and the blazer-clad receptionists suddenly looked blank, as if they weren't quite sure who they were. A few minutes later, Lilly, Peazle, Duncan, Shadowjack and Charlie found themselves on the top floor, being escorted to the Penthouse Suite by an equally bemused porter.

"I must learn how to do this magic stuff," Charlie said, racing around the huge rooms, opening and closing every door he could find. "This cupboard is bigger than my whole house."

While the rest explored their plush surroundings, Lilly announced she was going to find fresh clothes and food. While she was gone, the others took turns to clean up in the huge white bathroom. Shadowjack was unimpressed by the invention of the shower.

"It's just a wee hose sticking out of the wall," he shouted. "What happens if I turn this red lever here? Yeeeeeaaaaaaaaaaaah!"

Lilly staggered back in, laden with plastic bags advertising the hotel shop.

"How did you persuade reception to open the store at one in the morning?"

"I made them think it was one in the afternoon." She upended the bulging bags and provisions and clothes tumbled out onto the floor. Charlie noticed that the girl had dark circles under her eyes. True, it was late, but it occurred to the boy that he had never really seen Lilly perform this much magic before. It seemed to require immense effort on her part.

Soon, they were all lounging on the thick white carpet, drinking Coke and eating crisps. Each of the boys now wore jeans and woolly jumpers, though Peazle still had on his bowler hat and Duncan had wrapped the tartan plaid around his waist.

"I don't suppose you could swap this for one in plum?" Shadowjack inquired, tugging his sweater.

"Think yourself lucky," Lilly sniffed. "When I told the staff your chest size, they thought it was a joke."

Now that they were all comfortable, Peazle introduced Shadowjack and Duncan formally to Charlie and everyone thanked Lilly again for saving their lives.

"I came when I heard Charlie's whistle, just as I promised," said the girl matter-of-factly. "I didn't expect to be called so soon, or to find all of you with him." She looked around the assembled group with a raised eyebrow. "Just what is going on?"

"A simple errand, lass," Shadowjack emptied an entire packet of prawn cocktail crisps into his mouth. "We've got to find some goblet and bring it back to Galhadria."

The girl frowned, as if something were scratching at the edges of her memory. Charlie nudged Peazle.

"You've still got some of that potion you gave me, don't you?" he whispered.

The pickpocket nodded.

"What would happen if you gave it to Lilly?"

Peazle's eyes widened and he got quickly to his feet.

"Would you accompany me to the balcony, Lilly?" he said, holding out his hand. His voice sounded casual, but the tips of his fingers trembled. "There are a few things I... eh... need to show you, and you might appreciate some privacy."

Before the girl could protest, he took her gently by the arm and led her away.

Duncan and Shadowjack looked at Charlie, puzzled.

"What was all that about?" said the giant, opening another packet of crisps.

"Lilly's about to find out some rather horrible things," Charlie said flatly.

"Like what?"

"It's hard to know where to start." He held up one hand and ticked off facts. "One. For fifteen hundred years, she thought her father was a traitor. Turns out he was actually a hero. Two. The Lords of the Western Wilderness could have set her straight and didn't. Three. Her mother is the monster who's chasing me and almost killed us tonight."

There was silence for a long time. Duncan's face darkened and he bowed his head. Shadowjack stared into his empty crisp packet, his bushy brows knitted together.

"Poor wee lassie," he said eventually.

Peazle came back in, shutting the balcony door behind him.

"That was quick." Charlie looked up, surprised.

The pickpocket bowed his head.

"She remembers everything," he said quietly.

Charlie and Duncan began to rise, but Peazle stopped them.

"She wants to be left alone," he said, shaking his head. "Said she'll see you in the morning."

"And what then?"

"I don't know." The pickpocket flopped down on one of the beds. "She may know where the Grail is. It didn't seem the right time to ask."

For a while, the four talked softly to each other, though, every now and then, one or the other cast a glance at the patio door leading to the balcony. But the door was smoked glass and it was dark outside. They could not see Lilly.

Peazle, Shadowjack and Duncan caught up with the last hundred years. Though they had been friends on earth, they had gone their separate ways in Galhadria. In a land without telephones or emails, the three companions soon lost touch completely.

Shadowjack had set up his forge on a rolling green meadow and become an expert at working faerie metals into jewellery. His work was much prized by the Galhadrians. Peazle had spent his time studying art and science. The Lords of the Western Wilderness kept an extensive library in their great stronghold of Castle Alclud on the edge of Galhadria. In return for access to their books, the pickpocket was sent on 'errands' such as the one he was engaged in now.

"That's a lot of work just to get a library card," Charlie said sarcastically.

Duncan told how he had travelled the length and breadth of Galhadria, looking for his missing brother, taken as a baby two hundred years ago. Highland lore was full of tales about how the Little People used to steal human children. Though the Galhadrians swore these were nonsense, the highlander still searched. He had never found him.

Charlie related his adventures and explained why he had to leave his parents. The others instinctively looked towards the balcony again.

Eventually, the conversation drifted to more mundane matters. Duncan couldn't believe that a kilt now cost £400 and looked like a skirt and Shadowjack wanted to know what a prawn was. They lay on the soft, deep carpet, talking and slowly getting to know each other again until, one by one, they drifted off to sleep.

All but one.

The Balcony

A bank of heavy purple cloud crawled sluggishly across the night sky, bruised by the spires and tenements of Edinburgh. The smoked glass door slid quietly open and Duncan stepped out onto the hotel balcony. A gust of wind arched around the side of the building and tugged at his unruly locks. Lilly was perched like a small green bird. on the stone parapet that bordered the balcony, staring sightlessly into the night. Duncan walked softly over and peered into the street. A car horn honked intrusively in the darkness.

"Sixteen hundred years," Lilly said. "All that time, I believed my father had deserted me."

"Aye. And now you know he didnae." Duncan spread his hands. "Better you were wrong for a thousand years than right about your paw being a traitor."

"He's been trapped all this time and I never tried to rescue him." Tears glittered in the girl's eyes. "I deserted him!"

"A spell was cast upon you, Lilly." Duncan put out his arm and touched her shoulder. It was cold as the night wind. "You must find your father and explain that. You say he is a great wizard. He, of all people, should understand."

"He'll understand the Lords of the Western Wilderness left both of us to rot. His anger will be great."

Lilly shivered. The highlander climbed onto the parapet and crouched beside her small figure. Together, they watched the red taillights of cars gliding past a hundred feet below. On top of the ledge the wind was stronger, and the tartan plaid snapped and fluttered in the breeze. Lilly saw that the boy's sword was still fastened to his back. Duncan noticed her glance.

"It doesnae feel right unless I'm wearing it," he said simply.

"That's a shame."

The highlander nodded and draped the plaid back over his weapon.

"I have spent two hundred years looking for my missing brother without success," he said, finally. He looked up at the few stars visible through angry clouds and ran a hand wearily through his hair. "That's no nearly as long as you've been apart from your kin."

Lilly looked sideways at the highlander, his hair blowing in the wind, dark as a raven's wing.

"To the Devil with Jack Thane and his orders," he said. "I will go with you if you wish to free your father. You have my word."

With a grunt, he hopped down from the ledge and held out his hand. The girl hesitated, then smiled and allowed him to escort her from the perch. She stood behind the highlander, using him as shelter from the biting wind. Duncan had forgotten how small she was.

"You look younger than I remember," the high-lander said. "But I know that's because I am older."

He smiled at her briefly, though smiling no longer seemed natural to his face.

"I remember you as Heather, the Gypsy who captured my heart and saved my life." He unwrapped the plaid from around his waist and draped it over her shoulders. "But she is gone. Now you are Lilly - a lassie who needs her father."

He bowed stiffly.

"Half Galhadrian you may be, and God knows I have nae great love for your race - but I am at your service."

Lilly darted forward and kissed him on the cheek while his head was at her level. Duncan stood up, surprised and pleased. Lilly bowed in turn.

"I gratefully accept your help, highlander."

The balcony door slid open and Duncan's hand automatically went to his sword. Peazle stood in the entrance, bowler hat in his hand, fingers drumming nervously on the brim.

"May I intrude?" he asked.

"You were listening behind the door?" Duncan's eyes narrowed in irritation.

"Old habits die hard." The pickpocket turned and faced Lilly. "I understand that you want to rescue your father, but we have to get you to safety. You have shown yourself and now Morgana will be after you."

"Yes. And you led her straight to me." Lilly looked the pickpocket in the eye.

"I'm sorry for that." Peazle straightened his shoulders and stared back defiantly. "But it's all the more reason why you should seek refuge in Galhadria. I, however, have been tasked with finding the Grail Cup. If you know where it is, tell me and I will endeavour to retrieve it before Morgana."

"I have a better suggestion." The voice came from behind them. They turned to see Charlie standing a few feet away, just inside the sliding door.

"Why don't we find the Grail ourselves, then take it to its rightful owner?" He stepped forward. "We can free Lilly's father and give him back his talisman."

"The Lords of the Western Wilderness have their flaws, granted." Peazle slapped his hat in exasperation. "But they are powerful sorcerers and can protect us from Morgana."

"So could my father if he had his cup back," Lilly protested.

"Are you sure?" Peazle asked. "He once loved your mother, remember?"

"So did I." Lilly's voice was cold.

"The more I hear about these Lords of the Western Wilderness, the less I trust them." Charlie broke in. "I say we find the Grail, take it to Gorrodin, and ask for his help instead."

A shadow fell across Charlie as Shadowjack Henry moved into the doorway behind him. He gave Lilly a bristling smile.

"What is this?" Peazle sighed in exasperation. "A party?"

"You have saved my life twice now, wee lass, once from Mordred and once from Morgana." The black-smith stepped onto the balcony, moved Peazle and Charlie gently aside, then bent on one knee before the girl. "I, too, will help you find the Grail and return it to your father."

"Listen, old friend." Duncan placed his hand on the pickpocket's shoulder. "Jack Thane has sent you on a bad errand. Away back and tell him that his underlings have mutinied. He'll not blame you."

Peazle shook his head and a slow, unexpected smile split the boy's face.

"Why tip him off at all?" he said mischievously. "As long as I stay with you, Jack Thane will assume we're still trying to get back to Galhadria through an-other Thin Place. After all, Greyfriars is hardly safe."

He stuck the bowler back on his head and set it at a jaunty angle.

"I can't let you go on an adventure like this without me. You'd never make it."

Duncan smiled a genuine smile for the first time since returning to his old home.

"Then we are a clan," he announced proudly. "Our loyalty is to each other."

"If that's settled, can we please get some sleep?" Shadowjack Henry yawned. "Tomorrow, we have to search for this blessed Grail with God knows what chasing us." He turned hopefully back to Lilly.

"Unless you know where your father's cup is."

"I have absolutely no idea," she said. Then she gave a dainty smile.

"But I know someone who does."

Hunting Charlie Wilson

Charlie and his companions woke early with a new sense of purpose. They would find the Grail and free Lilly's father. With his help, they would defeat Morgana and be at liberty to do what they wished afterwards. Of course, Morgana looked to be a formidable enemy, and each secretly worried what the Lords would do about this deception - but they were comforted by the fact that they were together. It seemed right somehow.

"As you say, highlander, we are our own wee clan." Shadowjack Henry stretched and rubbed his bushy black beard. "We stick together, no matter what may befall us."

Duncan smiled to himself as he pulled the new jumper over his head. Even Lilly seemed cheerful - relieved to know the truth, more than angry at what had happened to her. Charlie supposed her Galhadrian half allowed the girl to shrug off such shattering misfortune. And she was obviously delighted at the idea of being reunited with her father.

"So, where do we start?" Duncan asked as they packed their belongings. Lilly had made a morning trip to the shops and brought back sleeping bags, tents and rucksacks. The highlander was eager to be off and looking. He considered himself rather an expert at searching.

"I gave my father's talisman to one of Arthur's men - a warrior named Uallabh. He promised to meet me at the Glen of Rosslyn." Lilly picked up Excalibur and slid it into a long plastic tube used to hold fishing rods. Duncan did the same with his own sword, smiling with approval at how well this disguised the weapons.

"When was this?" Shadowjack asked, fastening his rucksack.

"I'm not sure. Sometime in the early 7th century?"

The rest stopped packing and stared at her.

"He won't be dead," she protested. "He drank from the cup. He's immortal now." She paused and gave a worried shrug. "If he didn't try to use the powers the Grail gave him… he's eh…. probably still human."

Shadowjack snorted and gave the strap of his rucksack a mighty tug. It snapped off in his hand.

"Shoddy workmanship they have these days," he grumbled, reading the label on the pack. "Where is Taiwan anyway?"

"Lilly," Charlie said tentatively. "What makes you think he'll still be waiting after thirteen centuries? I'd have got a bit fed up by now. You know. Maybe figured that you weren't actually coming."

"He was one of Arthur's greatest warriors." Lilly gave him a disapproving look. "He gave his word."

Charlie, wisely, kept quiet. Peazle looked up from a map he had been studying.

"There's a village called Rosslyn about twenty miles from here. It has an ancient chapel overlooking a glen. That the place?"

"Sounds like it." Duncan shouldered his rucksack and picked up his fishing tube. "Can you magic us there?"

"Not a chance." Lilly gave a sigh. "I may be the daughter of a great sorcerer but I have no talisman of my own and I'm only half Galhadrian. That little trick in the graveyard last night took all my strength – and it was just tipping over a few headstones."

Duncan accepted this stoically.

"How long will it take to walk?"

"No need," Peazle grinned, folding the map and tucking it inside his shirt. "There's a wonderful new invention called the autobus. You'll love it."

Charlie's party trooped out of the elevator and through the hotel foyer. Lilly blew the morning staff a kiss as she waltzed out of the door and into the sunshine. Puzzled by the appearance of such an odd-looking party, the staff looked up the hotel register. There was no record of anyone booking in the night before.

Inspector Archer sat alone at his desk. His tiny office was painted a dull olive and filled with cheap metal furniture. In the corner were overflowing boxes of files, along with a kettle, a bag of sugar and some dirty cups. A small television hooked to an ancient video machine crackled in one corner of the room, playing footage taken by a CCTV camera mounted at Birmingham's central train station. In his hand, the policeman held the statement made by Gary Macmillan. It was short and to the point. Macmillan wasn't keen on talking to the police at the best of times, especially when it involved describing an attack by a cat with hands. Already, he was a laughing stock at school, a situation he found necessary to rectify by using his fists.

The Inspector wasn't interested in some cock-and-bull story about a mutant cat. But he was very interested in the bully's insistence that Charlie Wilson had run off with a boy wearing a bowler hat and bright yellow waistcoat.

Archer yawned, stretched, and then glanced at the TV once more. The yawn froze on his face. The footage was jumpy and grainy but there was no mistaking what he was watching.

Two young boys, one wearing a bowler hat, were crossing the screen, heading for the train due to leave for Edinburgh. The Inspector looked down at the photograph Mrs Wilson had given him of their son. It was hard to see the other boy's face but the Inspector was in no doubt who his companion was.

Charlie Wilson.

The clan piled onto a bus for Rosslyn and Shadow-jack and Duncan made straight for the back seat. Both sat with their noses pressed against the grimy brown windows, watching the wonders of the world roll past.

"Hey Charlie." The highlander pointed into the air. "Why is that wee bird flying so slowly?"

"It's a plane." Charlie glanced up. "It's far away. People fly inside them all over the world."

"Aye, right. And my Uncle Fraser became the Queen of Sheba."

Shadowjack's seat squeaked and strained as he squirmed around, trying to see out of all four windows at once.

"What an amazing place the planet is now!" he mar-velled, a grin splitting his bristling beard. "What great happiness such marvels must bring. I'll wager there's no more famine or disease or war."

Charlie and Lilly glanced at each other.

"There are no more blacksmiths, that's for sure." Peazle looked up from the *Guide to Scotland* he had stolen in the bus station. Shadowjack gave a dismissive snort.

"I don't care. After this is over, I'm learning to be a bus driver."

"What have you found?" Charlie looked at the book over Peazle's shoulder.

"There's a castle and a chapel at Rosslyn Glen." He read. "They were built in the 15th century. The castle's just a ruin now but the chapel is still intact. Famous for the ornate carvings inside… eh… what else?"

Peazle tried to hold the book steady, as the bus rattled out of Edinburgh and into the countryside.

"The chapel was the headquarters of the Knights Templar… I read about them in the library at Galhadria… they were an order of ancient knights dedicated to doing good." He looked around to make sure everybody appreciated his breadth of knowledge, but Shadowjack and Duncan were waving to cars through the back window and Lilly had fallen asleep.

"I'm listening," Charlie said apologetically.

"Hmmm. According to legend, the Knights Templar were alleged to have used the chapel as a hiding place for…" The pickpocket looked up at Charlie, tapping the book nervously.

"A hiding place for what?"

"The Holy Grail."

Charlie sat back, blinking rapidly.

"Holy smoke."

"You don't think?"

Charlie smiled thoughtfully.

"Lilly once told me that all legends get twisted over the course of time." He spoke quietly so as not to wake the sleeping girl. "But they always have a grain of truth at the core."

"I can see where this legend might come from." The pickpocket held up the open guidebook. "Lilly gives her father's magical cup, called the Grail, to one of

Arthur's warriors and arranges to meet him at a valley called Rosslyn." He winked. "Now there's a chapel in the same place that's supposed to be the hiding place for surprise, surprise… a magical cup called the Grail. Our mysterious warrior will surely be long gone, but he was certainly around at one time."

Peazle shut the book with a snap, and Lilly opened her eyes.

"Are we there yet?" she yawned.

"No," Charlie smiled, patting her arm. "But we're an awful lot closer than we were."

Rosslyn

Rosslyn Chapel was half a mile from the village of the same name - a small building with graceful stone buttresses and arches that seemed ornate as lace. It sat on the edge of Rosslyn Glen - a precipitous and heavily wooded gorge - with an expanse of level farmland behind it. Swathes of bulging greenery locked together to hide the valley floor, but the clan could hear the hiss of a river churning far below the thick canopy.

Duncan immediately placed himself outside the chapel door, the best place to keep watch for anyone following them. Shadowjack had bought a disposable camera in the gift shop and wanted to try taking pictures of the view. Peazle sat in the church garden under a weeping willow, reading his guidebook about the area, while Charlie and Lilly ventured inside.

The church was almost empty - the only other occupants were a couple of Japanese tourists with camcorders and a few parishioners sitting silently in pews near the front. Charlie and Lilly strolled around the interior in respectful silence. Daylight shone through the stained glass, patterning the pillars with spatters of coloured light and illuminating multiple carvings of saints and devils threatening each other across the aisles. Charlie stood on tiptoe and peered at one of the angels. Its face was rendered almost expressionless by the erosion of time, but he thought it looked a bit like Lilly.

"Wow. Everything here is so old," the boy said, gently touching the angel's smooth stone cheek.

"Not as old as me," Lilly answered quietly. Catching Charlie's worried look, she wrinkled her nose and gave him a devilish wink. "But I don't look it."

They wandered in and out of sweeping arches, gazing up through motes of sun-speckled dust to the majestic beamed roof high above. Lilly let her eyes drift and gave a sudden gasp. Charlie looked around. The girl was squinting through the sunlight at a small stone gargoyle leering out of the wall. Peazle wandered in the front door.

"It's called a Green Man." The pickpocket studied the carving with scholarly interest. "They're carvings of ancient pagan deities - you find them in very old churches - left over from the times when Christianity hadn't quite stamped out ancient superstitions and beliefs. Pictures of primitive gods and goddesses mainly."

"You really have studied a lot in the last couple of centuries, haven't you?" Charlie looked impressed.

"Actually, I read it in the guidebook."

"This isn't a carving of a man, green or otherwise." Lilly reached out and tapped the grimacing stone face, withdrawing her hand quickly as if she expected it to bite. "It's Morgana."

There was a creak of old oak as one of the worshippers at the front of the church slowly stood.

"Fashionably late, Lilly?" he drawled.

At the sound of his voice, the girl stiffened.

He was a big man, almost as tall as Shadowjack Henry and just as impressive. He wore a long black coat, expensively cut, over a black leather waistcoat with gold buttons. His thick red hair was pulled into a severe ponytail and he sported a waxed handlebar moustache the same bright colour.

"Nice threads," Peazle remarked.

"He looks like a ginger Zorro," Charlie whispered.

"Who's Zorro?"

"Hold on a minute." The boy frowned. "I recognise this guy!"

Lilly did as well.

"Uallabh?" She took a faltering step back, hand rising to her mouth.

"In the flesh." The tall man stepped up onto the back of his seat and strode gracefully towards them over the tops of the pews. His boots were as black and shiny as the rest of his outfit and silver tips on the heels gouged little chips from the wood as he walked. The other parishioners looked up in horror and tutted loudly but Uallabh did not even spare them a glance.

"Pay no attention," he said, hopping off the last bench and giving a small salute to Lilly. "After all, I helped build the place."

"You look good for a thousand years old."

"I've lost weight."

Uallabh's voice was slow and languid, as if the centuries had rounded his accent the way it had the stone around him. He looked and sounded more like a Wild West gunfighter than a Celtic warrior of old. He nodded his fiery head in the gargoyle's direction.

"Had that put there to let you know I'd been around. If you ever came back, that was."

He smiled, but his lips were thin and bloodless and the warmth didn't reach his eyes. It looked uncannily like the sneer on Morgana's rocky face.

"You must hae a great deal of patience."

Uallabh turned sharply. Duncan stood in the doorway, sword in hand. Shadowjack Henry lurked behind him, his huge figure blacking out the sun.

"You can't pull out a weapon in a church!" Charlie gasped, horrified.

"Patience? Oh, I do indeed," the tall warrior replied calmly, paying no attention to the boy. He held up his hands to show he was unarmed. "But, to be honest, I haven't been around lately. Over the centuries, I've travelled to quite a few lands. Yes. Done quite a few things."

He lowered his hands and turned back to Lilly.

"But I come back every few decades… to check on the place."

"It's quite a coincidence that you turned up at the same time as us," Peazle said.

"Oh no. I guessed you were coming."

"How?"

"You'll see." The tall man smiled his narrow smile again and glanced around. The Japanese tourists were pointing camcorders in his direction. He glared at them until they turned away.

"Too many prying eyes here, Lilly." Uallabh hooked his arm through the girl's and led her towards the chapel doorway. "I've rented a cottage nearby."

He cast an unhurried eye over the rest of the party.

"Do you trust your entourage?"

"They're not my entourage. They're my friends."

"Ah," Uallabh said casually. "I have no friends myself."

Politely, he stepped back to allow Peazle and Charlie out of the chapel before following them into the sun. He pointed in the direction of a smallholding, just visible through the trees, on the other side of the valley.

"They may come if you wish," he said to Lilly. "You go first."

"He's a bit tetchy, isn't he?" Charlie hissed as the party set off.

"Maybe he doesn't like women to be late," Peazle whispered back.

"Maybe he's oot of his wits." Duncan led the way, hand on his sword.

The forest grew thicker, the hiss of the river louder and fat flies buzzed around their heads, as the sunlight struggled to penetrate the canopy of leaves. The highlander glanced back. Uallabh was at the rear, walking side by side with Lilly. She was trying to ask him questions, but he didn't seem to pay her much attention. Instead, his eyes darted from side to side, checking each tree and bush.

It occurred to the highlander that the tall warrior had never once turned his back towards any of their party. Duncan was wary by nature but Uallabh's caution seemed excessive.

The boy nodded to himself and tightened the grip on his sword hilt.

Uallabh was expecting trouble.

Inspector Archer rang the Wilson's doorbell and was answered by the sound of running feet. The front door jerked open and Charlie's father stood there, blinking. He looked as if he hadn't slept all night.

"Is my boy all right?" he said, naked fear in his eyes. "Have you heard anything?"

"I have tentative good news, Mr Wilson." Inspector Archer removed his hat and peered into the hall. "Is your wife around?"

"No. She's out searching the town for any sign of Charlie."

"Mr Wilson. Your son was captured on CCTV getting on a train for Edinburgh yesterday - apparently boarding of his own accord." The policeman hesitated. "He was accompanied by a boy wearing a bowler hat. You know any kids who wear something like that?"

"I don't keep up with children's fashion trends," Charlie's father replied witheringly. "And my son isn't the type to just take off."

"Do you know any reason why he would want to go to Edinburgh?"

Charlie's father shook his head.

"We took him there last year but he didn't seem to enjoy it much." He looked doubtful. "I... eh..."

"Anything at all would be helpful."

"He met a girl there that he seemed to like, except we don't know who she is. And he's seemed... I don't know... different since. More serious." Charlie's father smiled wanly. "I didn't think he *could* get more serious."

"So he might have secretly gone north to see this girl?"

"Not without telling me. It's not like I'd object if he wanted a girlfriend."

Inspector Archer shut his notebook without writing anything in it. He hadn't expected to learn anything new.

"Your son's details have been circulated to the Edinburgh police," he said gently. "All we can do now is wait."

Charlie's father put a hand on his arm.

"I don't know the Edinburgh police." His grip was tight, betraying the hidden strength all acrobats have. "But I think I know you. I've looked into your eyes and I've seen a good man. A man who cares. I want you to lead the investigation."

"I'm with Birmingham CID, sir. The police up north know the terrain."

"Fine." Charlie's dad let his hand drop. "In that case, I'll go myself."

"I'd strongly advise against that." Inspector Archer began. But Charlie's father cut him off.

"I understand," he said. "And you understand that I can't take that advice."

It struck Archer that, behind the dishevelled appearance and meek manner, Charlie's father was as handsome as his wife was beautiful. And he was dealing with his grief and worry with a calm dignity that the Inspector rarely saw. He wondered what the boy was like. For the second time, he felt compelled to do something against his nature.

"Give me three days," he said suddenly. "It's the best I can do." He put the notebook in his pocket and shuffled awkwardly on the doorstep. "Mr Wilson. What do you make of this cat with hands business?"

Charlie's dad looked out across the suburban landscape.

"Him thought there was come into this land griffins and serpents," he quoted. "And him thought they burnt and slew all the people in the land."

"Pardon?"

"It's from *Le Morte d'Arthur* by Mallory. The point is, Inspector, it doesn't matter what kind of monsters are out there. All that matters is that we fight them."

The Inspector looked impressed.

"You're certainly a well-educated acrobat, Mr Wilson."

"Like you, I prefer action to words." Charlie's dad gave a grim smile. "That's why sitting doing nothing hurts so much."

Uallabh's Escape

Uallabh's cottage was clean and simple, with old-fashioned whitewashed walls and sturdy oak furniture. Curious about his new ally, Charlie glanced around, looking for the warrior's personal things - but there were no pictures on the walls and no mementoes on the dresser, window sill or table.

"I have enough memories," said the Uallabh, following the boy's gaze. "I don't need reminding of the things I've seen."

"Are you expecting trouble?" Duncan pointed to a profusion of bolts on the inside of the door. The highlander ran his hand over one, sniffed his fingers and wrinkled his nose. The locks were either new or had been oiled recently.

"I'm always expecting trouble," Uallabh muttered, sitting down on the only chair in the room - carefully positioned, Duncan noticed, so it wasn't in a direct line of any windows. The rest of the clan unfastened their rucksacks and flopped down on the polished wooden floor. They were getting used to rooms that didn't have enough seating for all of them.

"So, Lilly. I take it you have come for your father's cup?" From the casual way Uallabh asked, it was obvious he already knew the answer.

"Yes," Lilly nodded. "I got a little delayed."

She looked around. The rest of the clan were watching them both intently.

"Eh… what exactly did happen all those years ago?" Peazle piped up. "If you don't mind us asking?"

"Aye," Shadowjack joined in. "Lilly told us how you ran from the Gorrodin Rath…"

"I did not run," Uallabh interrupted. "I was ordered by Arthur to take the Grail to a place of safety."

He turned to Lilly.

"I wanted to return and help." The warrior lowered his head in shame. "But I swore an oath…"

"I understand," Lilly said, her eyes fixed on the ground. "Morgana put a curse on me. Took away my memory and made me blame my father for everything that had happened."

Uallabh raised an eyebrow. "But you remember now?"

"I knew nothing until yesterday." Lilly smiled gratefully at Peazle, who shrugged and went a little red. "In some ways, I wish I was still in the dark."

"And what happened to the monster?" Uallabh said brusquely. He had the same forthright manner as Duncan, or perhaps he did not want Lilly to dwell on her pain.

"A picture paints a thousand words." Lilly flexed her fingers and took a deep breath. "I'm not much of a sorcerer but I can do a few basic tricks." She held her tiny hands out and slowly opened her palms. A shimmering picture began to spread across the far wall, congealing into a sharp image like ripples settling on a pond. The others looked at it in amazement – all except Peazle, who had seen Jack Thane work the same spell.

The clan found themselves looking at a battlefield. The constant hiss of the rain was mingled with the cries of the dying and the ring of metal upon metal. Strewn across the sodden moor were the bodies of perhaps fifty Gorrodin Rath, the downpour washing blood from their misshapen white corpses. Round each monstrous carcass lay a dozen or more of Arthur's warriors, weapons still clenched in their lifeless fists. For the first time, Charlie understood just what a sacrifice these men had made in taking on Morgana's army. Yet, despite horrific casualties, they drove the Gorrodin Rath towards the caves of what would eventually be named Arthur's Seat.

A hulking figure came tearing across the heather behind the unsuspecting men. The clan flinched. As Lilly had stated, its face was a replica of the carving on Rosslyn Chapel wall.

"My mother," said the girl sadly.

Morgana ran with long jerking strides, straight for a group of warriors clustered around a fluttering pennant. It wasn't hard to guess who she was trying to reach.

Arthur and his men turned as Morgana approached them and the warriors clustered around their leader in a vain attempt to protect him. Morgana's windmilling claws ripped the defenders apart and she lunged at Arthur just as the knight swung Excalibur at her. Morgana gave a shriek and staggered back, scrabbling at her side, inky gore spurting through her fingers. Arthur stepped away, one hand clutching at his chest, blood seeping from a great gash just above the breastplate. With a look of surprise, he sank slowly to his knees and toppled over.

There was a sharp exhalation of breath from Uallabh's chair.

"My Lord," he said, his voice trembling. It was the first time the clan had heard him show any real emotion.

Morgana retreated from the carnage, still trying to stifle the flow of blood. She turned and loped away, roaring to her own army as she retreated. But the Gorrodin Rath had seen their leader attack the enemy rear and they rushed at Arthur's warriors with renewed fury. Charlie shuddered involuntarily. He spotted Mordred swinging a huge bloody club, leading the charge against his assailants. Surprised by the sudden advance, the humans fell back - though they recovered quickly and launched themselves forward again with a determination that easily matched their foes.

"The sun is coming up!" Charlie pointed to the wall. The mountain tops behind the battlefield were beginning to glow with soft golden light.

The Gorrodin Rath had spotted the sunrise, too. With a furious roar, most turned and fled for the safety of the caves, while a few of the most loyal grouped around Morgana, begging her to save them.

The monster closed her eyes and spread both claws, muttering an incantation. A shimmering blue light appeared beside her and several creatures stumbled through. But the effort took all Morgana's power and the luminescence quickly faded again.

Abandoning the rest, Morgana turned and vanished over a hilltop, seeking Lilly and the cup.

"Where did Morgana go after she had dealt with you?" Charlie asked Lilly. "How did she remain hidden for hundreds of years?"

"I presume she had enough strength to open a Thin Place one more time," Lilly replied. "Go through it herself before she succumbed to her wounds."

"Jack Thane thinks she ended up in the land of Toth," Peazle said.

"Toth?"

"There are lands tae the west and north of Galhadria." Duncan counted off exotic names on his fingers. "Alabarra and The Wooded Kingdom in the north and west. Monshorn to the south and Toth in the east. I have never been there."

"There are impassable mountains separating Toth from Galhadria," Peazle confirmed. "A huge wall guards the only pass, but I was not allowed to see it."

"I wonder what brought Morgana back after all this time?" Uallabh's direct question showed his warrior instinct was keen as ever. None of them had an answer but Charlie noticed that Lilly gave a little glance in his direction. Everyone but Uallabh was aware he had killed the creature's son. It suddenly occurred to him how similar the two had looked and a horrible thought sprang into his mind.

"It's hard to tell the females of the Gorrodin Rath from the males," he said.

"So?"

"What if some of those creatures escaping through the Thin Place were female?"

Peazle suddenly realised what the boy was getting at.

"If they were, the Gorrodin Rath may have been breeding for over a thousand years, hidden in some far off land." His face paled. "If that were so, how many of them might there be now?"

Duncan pulled his sword closer to him.

"Enough for a great army," he said slowly.

The Cup

Shadowjack Henry went to the window and looked out. Rosslyn Glen was lit by a late afternoon sun, filtering through the trees and setting the tops aflame with golden light. For a second, he remembered his old life on earth, working a forge in a valley not unlike this one. He stroked his beard, then turned to Uallabh, sitting in his chair, fingers laced casually over his chest.

"What's your story, warrior?" he asked.

Uallabh drew a deep breath through his nose and let it out again. When he spoke, his voice was neutral.

"I was entrusted with guarding the wizard's cup after we took it from the Gorrodin Rath," he said. "I drank from it, as you know."

The others nodded.

"I can still die in battle but I'm no longer affected by the passage of time." The warrior gave a wry smile. "As much a curse as a blessing, let me tell you. But it was the first and last time I used the Grail - I had no desire to end up like the Gorrodin Rath."

The others were in full agreement with that sentiment.

"I guessed Lilly would not make it to Rosslyn Glen, not after what I had seen."

345

Uallabh sat straight in the chair and tilted his head back, staring at the ceiling. The room was growing darker as the sun sank and he slowly blended into the shadows.

"I had nowhere to go. My Lord and my clan were destroyed and all that was left was my solemn oath to them. I took a ship to France and travelled without purpose. But word had spread of the treasure I carried. No matter where I went, I was followed by those who sought that power. I killed many times and nearly died just as often. After a few hundred years, that can get a little tiring, even for a fighter."

For the first time, Duncan looked at Uallabh with sympathy. He, too, knew what it was like to travel strange lands and hold little hope in his heart.

"I tried to carry on the work my Lord Arthur had started," the warrior continued. "I founded an order of knights - the Templars - recruiting only those famed for their virtue, piety and chivalry."

Peazle nudged Charlie and pointed at the *Guide to Scotland*. He gave the boy a quick told-you-so look. Uallabh uttered a snarl of derision.

"I was not Arthur," he said, finally. "My knights became corrupted by lust for the very thing they were supposed to guard."

"What happened?" Charlie said with a sinking feeling.

"They turned against me," the warrior replied calmly, as if he were discussing the weather. "So, I destroyed them."

The party sat in silence, heads bowed.

"I did not mean to cause you such pain, Uallabh," Lilly said softly.

"In the 15th century, I returned to Rosslyn and established this chapel," the man continued as if he had not heard. "I was going to hide the Grail here in case Lilly ever came back."

He gave the girl a wink that seemed ghoulishly at odds with his expressionless voice. "However, legends about me had spread and, of course, men came looking. Lawless knights. Bounty hunters. Desperate men. All seeking the power of the cup."

He uncrossed his legs and slowly stood.

"I travelled the world again, taking the Grail with me wherever I went. To this day, there are secret societies on earth who know my identity and what I have. They still send men to search for me."

He stood beside Shadowjack Henry and looked with him out of the window.

"I kill them too."

Shadowjack put a hand on Uallabh's shoulder. The warrior did not seem to notice.

"But you knew to come back here, now? After all this time." Duncan could not keep the suspicion from his voice. "Just before we arrived?"

"A few months ago, I was living in Prague," Uallabh said. "I like it there. Lots of old buildings. But I can't stay too long in one place, for people grow suspicious when I don't age. That's why I can't have friends or a family."

Charlie saw Lilly's shoulders tighten. Talking about families was definitely a sore point with most of the clan.

Uallabh walked across the room and opened an oak door. Beyond was a bedroom. The clan could see a long black shape taking up half the floor. With a start, Charlie realised it was a coffin, its lid fastened with an enormous lock. Uallabh smiled grimly.

"I hide the cup in this when I travel. Customs officials are very keen to look in a trunk. Coffin's a different matter."

He fished about inside his waistcoat and pulled out a key on a leather thong around his neck. Watching the tall figure immaculately dressed in black, standing nonchalantly next to his coffin, reminded Charlie of a picture he had once seen in a book.

A picture of Count Dracula.

He wondered how many other legends Uallabh had managed to start in his time on earth.

The warrior was now bending over the coffin and unlocking it.

"About six months ago, the Grail changed."

"Changed?"

"I didn't know what it meant," the warrior said. "But guessed it prudent to come back here... just in case,"

He lifted the creaking lid with no small effort.

The rest of the clan trooped through to the bedroom and peered excitedly into the chest. Lilly was almost holding her breath.

The coffin was lined with white velvet. At the bottom was Gorrodin's wooden cup.

"It's been like that ever since," the warrior said.

Lilly stepped back, her mouth open.

The Grail was softly glowing - gilded with beautiful, lambent flame.

The Eastern Wall

Jack Thane stood on top of the Eastern wall, staring into the pale grey morning. A brisk breeze ruffled his long dark hair and the goose feathers topping his boots. He put his hand on a shining silver rail and leaned out. The wall was so high that it was almost impossible to see its lower reaches, even if they had not been shrouded in morning mist. But he glimpsed the flash of a white hawk with black-tipped wings darting and swooping far below him.

No matter how many magical feats he might see, the wall never failed to impress him. It was as high as the sheer snow-topped peaks on either side - though the Lords' magic kept the curving structure free of ice. On either side, the craggy tops of the Fanfall Mountains stretched into the distance - an impassable natural barrier that separated the western edge of Galhadria from the desolate and forbidding land of Toth.

The wall stretched across what had once been a great pass - the only way through this impenetrable mountain range. At the base was an enormous, barred gate that had once allowed travel between the two countries. It had rarely been opened in the last centuries

- for a long time dark creatures had prowled Toth and it was no longer safe for Galhadrians to enter.

Turning, Jack Thane stared back into his own land. Far below, he could see Castle Alclud – home to the Lords of the Western Wilderness - looking no bigger than a child's toy. Its myriad spires and minarets were slatted with shadows. It sat at the base of the Fanfalls and the morning sun had not risen high enough for its beams to dance across the walls and bring them to life. He let his eyes follow the path from the castle to the base of the wall, where a precarious staircase, cut from sheer stone, zigzagged up the surface.

He saw two small figures, fellow Lords, moving slowly up the steps hundreds of feet below. Though they were too far away for him to make out their faces, he recognised both from their ways of walking. One was their leader, Tom Lincoln. The other Jenny Haa.

They could have flown up in an instant, but Jack Thane had recently insisted the Lords of the Western Wilderness not use magic unless they had to. Their powers were immense but their magic was not infinite. And Thane knew they would soon need all the sorcery they possessed to keep the enemy at bay.

Lords of the Western Wilderness. Jack Thane sorely disliked that title. As a young man, he had roamed the green hills of his world, coming and going as he pleased. He had been a master of the lyre and was often asked at villages he travelled through to host dances. He would strum into the night while maidens danced and men brought him cups of wine made from the finest fruit in their vineyards.

That was an age ago. Now, he was stuck here, at the farthest corner of his domain, with only other sorcerers for company - protectors of their world. The Lords neither sang nor danced and they talked of nothing but pills and potions.

Tom Lincoln and Jenny Haa suddenly appeared at the top of the wall. They had tired of walking and had spirited themselves up the last half mile. Jack Thane frowned. If they knew how much magic they were going to need in the coming months, they would not use any on such trivialities. He bowed in reluctant greeting.

"You are early, Master Lincoln."

"I am," Tom Lincoln replied brusquely. "And I would like to know what is so urgent that you have called me to the top of this wretched place." He waved a dismissive hand in the direction of the mountains. "There is nothing to see here."

"If only that were true." Thane sighed theatrically, raising his eyes to where the sun was beginning to disperse the grey haze in the sky. "In truth, I'm afraid to even look down."

"I did not know you were fearful of heights," Tom Lincoln replied sarcastically. He was impatient to be back in Castle Alclud, where he had more important tasks to perform.

"If that were all I was scared of, I would still be asleep." Thane pointed over the edge of the wall.

"Look down into Toth again, Master Lincoln, for the morning mists are clearing."

Grunting sourly, the sorcerer bent his short, thin body and peered over the side of the wall. At first, he saw nothing. Then, gradually, the haar dispersed and patches of the dull olive landscape of Toth started to show. He gave a gasp.

"There is movement!"

Jack Thane nodded. Jenny Haa pushed back her green hood and she also squinted over the parapet.

"It was the same yesterday," Thane said.

The last traces of mist had dissipated and Tom Lincoln's eyes widened as he took in the magnitude of what he saw. At the end of the pass was a mass of slowly moving white and grey, as if Toth were covered in a carpet of maggots. Though the distance made the creatures below smaller than insects, their numbers were vast. The sorcerer was looking at an army. Not simply hundreds, but thousands of monsters, milling around.

"The Gorrodin Rath." He whispered in horror.

"I had hoped this time would never come," Thane sighed. "Despite all my plans and preparations, I never really believed it would happen."

"But it is day!" Lincoln's face betrayed his puzzlement and anger. "They cannot come out in the day!" He struck the wall a furious blow with his fist and Jenny Haa flinched, stepping quickly back from the edge.

"You have eyes." Jack Thane was unmoved by this display of temper. "They have the power."

"They cannot!"

"Will you still not believe?" Thane cried angrily. "For months, I have been trying to convince the other Lords. I tell you, the Dolorous Stroke has been struck!"

Jenny Haa put a hand to her mouth.

"I do not know when or how," the sorcerer continued. "But it must have been done by one of our people - and against the Gorrodin Rath. That is why their leader, Morgana, has awakened and her wounds have healed. That is why the Rath have grown so strong."

Tom Lincoln stood back from the wall. The evidence was right below him and he could not ignore it. Jack Thane was right and no amount of protesting would change that.

It was time to act.

"Have the Gorrodin Rath tried to escape Toth by using Thin Places?"

"They have searched. But I sealed all those in Toth centuries ago."

"And the wall?"

"To reach us, they must overcome it. But it will take all our powers to keep it standing and the enemy will grow ever stronger. Eventually, we will not have the strength to keep them at bay."

"I trust you have a plan, Master Thane? You have never been the patient sort."

"Of course." Jack Thane bowed meekly. "But it depends on a human pickpocket and his ragtag friends."

Jenny Haa looked fearfully over the wall again.

"I do not understand," she said. "The Gorrodin Rath are trapped in Toth. How could one of us strike a blow against them? Why *would* we?"

Jack Thane shot out a hand and grasped her arm. His face was set in a determined grimace.

"That is no longer important," he said with quiet menace. "But we will *not* use any more magic until the Gorrodin Rath attack. Understood?"

He turned and stormed off down the staircase without looking back.

The Getaway

"Uallabh, I wish to free my father and return the Grail to him."

Duncan moved a little closer to Lilly as she made her announcement. Uallabh had killed everyone else who came looking for the cup and the highlander didn't want his friends to be next. Uallabh opened a cupboard door and removed a long black cloak from a plastic hanger.

"If I knew where your father was trapped, I'd have handed back his accursed cup centuries ago." He fastened the cloak around his neck and slipped his arms through short, wide sleeves. Now, he looked even more like a vampire.

"There is one small problem," Lilly said. "Morgana is back and seeking the Grail to increase her power."

"As I said. Many have sought to take the cup from me. They have all failed."

"Nobody like Morgana."

"The only time I saw nobility in my fellow men was when Lord Arthur and his sorcerer Gorrodin were around to guide them." Uallabh pulled on a pair of black leather gloves. He drew himself erect and smoothed down his cloak. "You want to return the

Grail to your father? Tell me where he is and I'll be happy to take you."

"Take us?"

"Yeah. I've got a van outside." Uallabh pulled a set of keys from inside his cloak and jingled them. "How do you think I lug that coffin around? On a mule?"

"I'm not sure of the exact location where my father is trapped," Lilly sighed. "So much has changed over the centuries."

"How about a hint?"

"It was the northwest."

"That'll do me." Uallabh headed for the door. "We can work it out later when we're far from this place."

Night was falling when the clan left the cottage. The woods were tall stripes of darkness and a thick cloud of floating insects attacked a bare electric light suspended above the back door. They had drawn lots and Charlie got the short straw. His rucksack now contained the Grail, carefully rolled inside a sleeping bag.

"That makes you prime target numero uno," Peazle smirked.

"I've got the power of immortality in this bag," Charlie said, awestruck. "I wonder what it would be like to live forever?"

Peazle looked at him with something akin to pity.

"Charlie. At the moment, you're the only one here who won't."

The boy stopped in his tracks. He hadn't thought of that.

"Immortality's not what it's cracked up to be," Uallabh led them down the crunching gravel path where a white transit slumbered at the end of the wooded drive. "Should I bring my coffin? You can sit on it in the back of the van."

"Thanks… but I'm used to the floor."

"It's bound to come in handy for something."

"No doubt," Shadowjack snorted. "We can use it if one of us dies."

There was an awkward silence. The big blacksmith grimaced at his own stupidity.

"I think we'll leave the coffin behind." Uallabh took out a flashlight as he reached the van, shone it carefully around the surrounding forest, then over the vehicle. Along the side in black lettering, the clan could make out the words.

U. St Clair. Antiques.

"Everything looks safe."

"Nice touch," said Shadowjack, slapping the logo on the side. "Though I just made a wee bet with Peazle that it would say Exterminator."

He gave Uallabh a friendly smile. Uallabh sniffed and tried a half-hearted grin back, but only one side of his mouth curled up and it looked more like a sneer. He was evidently out of practice at being sociable.

"Sit with me, highlander," he said, handing Duncan the keys to the vehicle. "You look like a natural fighter and you never know what we might encounter. There's enough room for the rest of you in the back. I have one last errand to do in the house."

He trotted towards the cottage. Duncan looked at the keys and then at the passenger door. There was a little silver circle below the handle - that must be a lock. He tried two or three different keys until one fitted. He turned it and the door clicked open.

"Who says I cannae handle modern technology?" The highlander gave a thumbs up.

"Duncan?" Lilly interrupted the highlander's smug observations. "Turn and look at the woods. Do it slowly."

The highlander cautiously twisted his head.

A dozen pairs of glowing eyes stared at them from the blackness between the trees. Whatever was watching couldn't be more than fifteen yards away. Duncan inched around until he could see in the other direction. Shadowjack was standing near the back of the van, rucksacks scattered around his feet. Charlie and Peazle were hiding behind him, staring fearfully into the forest. Uallabh came out of the cottage, closed the back door and came striding towards them. His step faltered as he realised something was badly wrong. A glance at the forest stopped him dead.

One set of eyes blinked and moved forward, the creature behind it taking shape, as it emerged from the trees. It was a large dog, fur matted and dirty and cracked flesh showed through bare patches of mange. The hound's slavering mouth was drawn up over yellow fangs and white spittle dripped from its foaming muzzle. It emitted a low, trembling growl that made the hair stand up on Charlie's neck.

"Does it have a name tag?" Peazle said timidly.

"No unless it reads Hound of Hell." Duncan looked longingly at his sword, still inside the fishing rod holder next to the pile of rucksacks. Shadowjack took a tentative step towards the nearest canvas sheath - the one that held Excalibur. The dog growled again and tensed its hind legs. Other glittering eyes began to move closer and the clan could make out the outline of several more large canines hidden among the trees.

"Don't move, Shadowjack," hissed Duncan urgently.

"I'm a statue."

"This is Morgana's doing," Lilly breathed.

"We're only going to get one chance," Uallabh's voice remained calm despite the predicament. The dog swung its head towards him and gave a low snarl but didn't move any closer.

"Charlie, can you drive?"

"I'm fourteen."

"In that case, wait until I give the word," the warrior continued. "I want you, Peazle, Lilly and Shadowjack to pull open the back doors of the van, jump inside, and close them as quick as you can." He turned his head in the highlander's direction, careful to keep the rest of his body motionless. "Duncan. You get in the front and unlock the driver's door for me."

"How do I do that?"

"What?"

"The only motor vehicle I've ever been in is an autobus. And that was four hours ago."

Uallabh let out a groan. The dog took another step forward and shook its head menacingly, white flecks curling around its neck like a shimmering collar. Duncan could see it was working itself up for an attack - and that might come at any second. He had no doubt the other canines, still lurking in the trees, would be quick to join in.

"Look in the passenger window," Uallabh said softly. "Do you see a square, grey catch on the driver's side?"

"I see it."

"You pull that.

"Got it."

"Now everybody, when I shout *go,* get yourselves into that van as if your life depended on it. Which it probably does."

Uallabh seemed to have a knack for finding humour in grisly situations.

Duncan was still peering in the passenger window, trying to adjust his eyes to the darkness inside. He tried to see into the back of the van but it was separated from the front by a curtained partition. He noticed the driver's window was rolled down a few inches and his eyes darted down to the driver's seat. It seemed to have some kind of dark covering. So did the passenger seat. And the dashboard.

They were covered in feathers.

The highlander pushed himself away from the car with a cry.

"Go!" roared Uallabh, startled by Duncan's sudden movement.

"Uallabh! Wait!"

The highlander was too late. Uallabh was already racing for the driver's side of the van. As he shot past, Shadowjack reached round, hauled open the van's back doors. Lilly sprang onto the runner board, ready to dive inside.

She got no further. A great inky mass surged from the interior of the van, enveloping her completely. With a strangled cry, the girl was catapulted backwards through the air, her head and torso completely hidden by a rustling, quivering black cloud. Peazle and Charlie threw themselves at the ground, but Shadowjack was caught in the surging wave, his top half obliterated by blackness.

"Crows!" he bellowed, swiping at the air, his voice muffled by hundreds of flapping wings. "They're attacking me!"

Lilly dropped out of the blackness like a stone and crashed to the ground as the flock of black crows swooped upward in a perfect arc. Shadowjack sank to his knees beside her, his beard bristling with feathers and his face covered in tiny lacerations. Uallabh skidded to a halt, looking confused.

The dog seized its chance and lurched forward, bounding towards Lilly's unconscious body. Duncan ran for his sword. Peazle and Charlie pulled themselves to their feet and got between the girl and the slavering animal as the rest of the hounds burst from the woods. Each was wild and scabrous and every bit as big as their leader. Duncan appeared at Peazle's side, his own sword in one hand and Excalibur in the other.

There were four sharp cracks behind them and the lead dog and three others jerked sideways and crumpled into the ground. The others stopped in confusion, ears flat against their snarling skulls, stomachs pressed against the earth. Duncan whirled around.

Uallabh was clutching a smoking pistol in each hand.

"Swords were all very well in your day, highlander," he chuckled as the dogs reversed, snarling, back to the trees. "This is the 21st century."

The crows attacked again.

They came down at rocket speed, with a sudden rush of air and the deafening beating of wings. Seconds later, the clan were enveloped in a whirling black mass. They tore frantically at the feathered air as claws and razored beaks raked their faces and hands, each jab drawing fresh blood. The dogs stopped retreating, turned, and crawled towards them again.

"The van!" Uallabh shouted. He fired several times up into the swirling cloud, then threw himself to the ground. "Crawl under the van!"

Charlie and Peazle dropped to their stomachs and wormed their way backwards, wriggling under the vehicle, dragging Lilly with them. The gravel ripped at their hands and knees, but the damage was nowhere as severe as the birds were causing, slicing at the back of their heads and battering them with their wings.

"I knew I shouldn't have packed my bowler hat away," Peazle cursed. "I need a helmet."

"I don't fit!" Shadowjack had tried to squeeze his massive body under the vehicle but he was too large to get more than the bottom half into the protected space. His arms were slapping at his exposed head, trying to stop the crows from reaching his eyes.

But the birds were now ignoring them and concentrating on the pile of rucksacks instead. They pecked and clawed at the fabric and several crows grasped the straps of Charlie's bag, flapping furiously as they tried to lift it off the ground.

"They're after the Grail!" Charlie shouted.

It was more than the boy could bear. He had abandoned his old life and his parents to get his hands on Gorrodin's cup. Lilly lay unconscious and bleeding beside him and he and his friends were trapped under a van by a bunch of birds, watching feral dogs closing in on them like sharks circling a sinking ship.

"Sod this."

Charlie hauled himself out from under the van, put his head down and ran straight into the throng of frenzied birds. He grabbed the rucksack and hauled as hard as he could, popping the straps from the beaks of the screeching crows. The boy kept going, carried through the flock by sheer momentum. The birds rose behind him, a tattered black cloak lined with beak and claw, ready to swoop back down and smother him.

There was only one place to head.

"No! Not the house!" he heard Uallabh shout. But it was too late. He hit the back door of the cottage and burst inside.

The birds turned and streamed after him, pouring through the open door right behind the terrified boy. Shadowjack, Peazle and Duncan rolled out from the van, ready to go after their friend.

"Look at the woods!" Uallabh cried from under the van. A black-gloved hand stretched out from behind the back wheel, waving a gun in the direction of the forest.

Now there were over twenty pairs of eyes staring malevolently from the trees. The gloved hands pulled the trigger of one gun, then the other. The weapons clicked uselessly.

"I've run out of ammunition."

"Bet you wish you had a sword now," Duncan remarked scathingly.

The dogs attacked again.

The Coffin

Charlie tore through the living room, a split second ahead of the screeching black torrent and shot into the bedroom, slamming the door behind him. The wood shook and buckled as the combined weight of hundreds of crows slammed into it. The boy desperately looked around for something to wedge under the handle but the room was empty, except for a bed and the coffin.

"What kind of person only has one chair in his whole sodding house?" he wailed, as the door splintered and burst. With an acrobatic leap, the boy flung himself headlong into the coffin, reaching up and hauling the heavy lid down behind him - severing the wings and beaks of the leading birds, who were trying to struggle through the closing gap. Only one made it inside before the top slammed shut. In the pitch darkness, Charlie felt the furious creature worming its way up his body, trying to reach his face.

"One against one this time," he said with a grimace, grabbing the crow and wrenching at its neck until it snapped.

A noise like thunder reverberated through the claustrophobic blackness and the satin around him began to vibrate. Charlie covered his head with his hands.

The birds were attacking the coffin.

The pack of snarling dogs burst out of the woods and pelted towards Shadowjack, Duncan and Peazle. Peazle tossed one sword to the blacksmith and Excalibur to Duncan, who caught it gingerly and gave an experimental swing.

"Just like old times, eh?" Peazle had hauled a rucksack onto his back and was fastening another to his front.

"Padding," he explained.

Then the dogs were on them. Duncan and Shadowjack stood back-to-back, feet planted wide apart, while Peazle danced between them, trying to stay out of the way of their swinging swords. The dogs raced around the party, leaping forwards, then jerking back, snapping at the air with slavering jaws, trying to get hold of the easiest target. Duncan was a fine swordsman and Shadowjack made up for his lack of expertise by sheer bulk - but Peazle had only the rucksacks for protection. The pickpocket desperately twisted and turned, trying to kick at snarling muzzles that drew closer with each rabid lunge.

"Uallabh!" Duncan took a swipe at one bounding dog and it skidded sideways with an agonised yelp. "What are you doing? We can't hold them off forever."

There was silence from under the van. Uallabh was nowhere to be seen.

"That sneaky bissom! He's abandoned us!" Duncan thrust angrily to the left and speared a slavering hound. As he twisted the blade to free it, another dog leapt onto his exposed back, fangs inches away from his face. Shadowjack elbowed it into the air and the hound snapped at Peazle as it landed, almost taking off his hand.

The pickpocket was near to crying. A large greyhound leapt past him, fastened itself to Shadowjack's side and bit deep into his flesh. With a roar, the blacksmith brought a meaty fist crashing down on its head. The dog went rigid and dropped away.

There was a rapid succession of shots from somewhere behind. Three of the hounds spun away from the attack and collapsed, writhing on the ground. Duncan risked a glance in the direction of the shooting. Uallabh was standing by the cottage, fumbling in his pocket.

The dogs peeled away and headed for him before he could find more bullets and reload. Instead of ammunition, however, the warrior pulled a small square object from his pocket. It was a sturdy Zippo lighter and Uallabh flicked it to life with a practised roll of his thumb. A jerk of his gloved hand broke a pane of the window and he tossed the lighter through.

The dogs were now only feet away, their legs a blur of motion. As the leading hound leapt for his throat, Uallabh threw himself to the side, rolling twice and scrabbling behind a stack of logs.

The house exploded.

Huge yellow fireballs billowed out of every window. The dogs were engulfed in mid-stride - half the pack wiped out instantly in the flaming inferno. Even Shadowjack was knocked flat by the force of the blast, bowling over Duncan and Peazle as he fell. Ash and burning feathers floated all around them, coating the white van and settling on the blackened corpses of the charred hounds. The few survivors broke off their attack and slunk back into the woods, howling mournfully as they went.

Ears ringing, Peazle lifted his head from the gravel and stared in disbelief at the cottage - or what was left of it. The explosion had blown out the windows and destroyed the masonry surrounding them. The front door was a warped, smoking lump lying yards away from its blackened frame. The strength of the blast had been so great it had extinguished the flames instantly, but the entire building was reduced to a charred hollow. Nothing inside could have survived.

"Aw, Charlie," Peazle moaned, burying his face in his hands. The pickpocket had dragged the unwilling boy on this adventure and had got his friend killed. A clogging wad of regret rose in Peazle's chest and he burst into tears.

Uallabh, face blackened by ash and dirt, pulled himself up from behind the log pile.

"What have you done?" Duncan rose unsteadily, swaying from side to side, sword clutched menacingly in his hand.

"I turned on a gas canister when I left the house. First rule of staying hidden is leaving no evidence."

The warrior stumbled over the smoking ground to the broken remains of the bedroom wall and peered into the murky gloom.

"I left a candle burning. By the time the gas reached the flame, we should have been well on our way." He wiped his forehead with the back of his hand, leaving a sooty stripe. "The birds must have blown it out with their wings. Had to finish things off myself."

"You killed Charlie!" Shadowjack and Peazle were on their feet and Duncan looked ready to turn his sword on the warrior. Uallabh squinted through the smoke into the ruined bedroom. He seemed gruesomely calm.

"You know, they don't make coffins now like they used to," he said conversationally. "Had mine for 200 years - specially manufactured by the finest craftsmen. Lead lined, it is."

He pointed nonchalantly into the shattered room.

"Could even withstand an explosion."

The rest looked into the smouldering bedroom. In the centre of the charred floor lay the coffin, still intact. As they watched, the lid slowly creaked open and Charlie sat up, holding his rucksack. He looked around at the devastation, blinking.

"I like what you've done with the place," he said. "Not a bird in sight."

Uallabh's van hurtled through the night, keeping to the smallest, most secluded roads, always heading north. Peazle sat in the front seat beside the warrior, a map of Scotland on his knees.

The rest of the clan were in the back. Lilly was finally awake, lying with a wet towel pressed to her head. Apart from that, she was virtually unscathed, having spent the entire battle out cold under the van. The rest looked like death warmed up, their clothes covered in grime, faces and hands lacerated by beaks and teeth. Uallabh had tied a bandage around Shadowjack's bloody midriff - a task that had emptied the van's medical kit of gauze. Fortunately, the wound was not deep enough to be serious.

"We'll stop and rest somewhere when we get further away," the warrior shouted back. "We can't be too careful - as you now probably agree."

"Can we clean the van out when we do?" Charlie poked around the floor with his foot. "All these feathers are bothering my asthma."

"I can't believe you booby-trapped your own house," Peazle said to Uallabh, not without admiration.

"Standard practice."

"I can't believe I couldn't fit under the van," Shadowjack growled. "I'm definitely going on a diet."

The rest roared with laughter. Even Uallabh beeped his horn in appreciation. Only Duncan seemed solemn. He crouched beside Lilly and helped press the towel against her broken skin.

"We barely survived that," he whispered. "And why were we attacked by animals?"

"Morgana must have been directing them from Toth. Some animals are easy to control - especially lower creatures like worms or starving, confused ones like stray dogs." Lilly felt the lump on her head and winced. "Carrion birds have always done the bidding of the darker forces - but usually as spies and thieves, not fighters."

"Either way, it means Morgana knows where we are."

"She'll always have some idea as long as there are crows in the sky," Lilly conceded. "Every time we do something predictable, or stay in one place too long, she'll scrape together whatever she can control and assault us with them."

"At least she's not close enough tae fight us herself," Duncan said, always thinking of tactics.

"Thank goodness for that." The girl winced at the thought of battling her mother again. Then she frowned.

"Do you know how much power it must take to mount attacks like these from the other side of a Thin Place?"

Duncan didn't.

"The Lords of the Western Wilderness themselves couldn't do it." Lilly took the cloth from her head and dabbed at some of the blood on Duncan's face. She leaned close so the others wouldn't hear.

"My mother never had power like that before, Duncan. Not even with the Grail."

"So, what has happened?"

"I don't know." Her voice dropped even lower. "But if she gets her hands on the cup now, her abilities will be Godlike."

Duncan smiled grimly. "Then we'll have tae make sure she doesnae."

There was more laughter from the other occupants. Charlie had found some crisps and was refusing to give Shadowjack any, despite his pleas. Lilly pressed her knuckles against the side of her head and closed her eyes. Duncan wasn't sure if she was concentrating or just in pain. He sat back and rested his head against the metal skin of the van. The vehicle's movement made his teeth chatter and he gritted them together until his jaws ached.

He was deeply troubled. For a start, he did not trust Uallabh. During the fight at the cottage, the warrior had glanced in the bedroom window before he blew the house up - but how could he have been sure Charlie was safe in the coffin? Duncan had the horrible suspicion Uallabh was merely trying to save his own skin.

And he was beginning to realise how formidable an adversary Morgana was. She was obviously clever and there was every chance she would guess where they were heading.

If she did, Duncan had no doubt there would be another ambush waiting for them when they got there.

Archer's Holiday Plan

Superintendent Lipton's office was painted battleship grey and smelled of cigarette smoke. It was like sitting in a giant ashtray, Inspector Archer thought. Across the dingy walls were splattered photocopies of wanted men and missing children, an arcade of black and white faces who had gotten lost one way or another. A large water cooler burped rudely in the corner.

"You've put in for a week's holiday, eh?" The superintendent scratched his yellow-tinged moustache and glowered at the Inspector's timesheet.

"I'm owed three."

"Where were you thinking of going? Venice? The pyramids? Butlins?" The superintendent tried to sound jovial, but Inspector Archer could sense a policeman's mind at work behind the seemingly innocent question. He decided to tell his boss the truth.

"I thought about going to Edinburgh. Heard it's pretty up there."

"Going on your own?"

"Who would I take?"

The superintendent picked up a small folder and flicked through it.

"This case you were working on. Charlie Wilson. Missing, eh?" He read quickly. "The boy was spotted taking a train to Edinburgh, along with another kid wearing...." he frowned over the top of the file. "A bowler hat. It's all very Oliver Twist."

Inspector Archer didn't reply.

"It's been reported to the authorities up north, Archer," the superintendent carried on. "Well out of your jurisdiction, I'd say."

Inspector Archer held his superior's stare.

"I'm going on holiday. That's all."

"Still... I'm sure you intend to say hi to the local police in Edinburgh. Just to keep your hand in." The superintendent's moustache bristled. It could have been a small smile or a disapproving tightening of his lips.

"I might. Professional courtesy, after all."

"You've handled plenty of missing person cases. What's so different about this one?"

"I don't know." Archer let his eyes drop. "Just a hunch, sir, that's all."

The Inspector dropped the file back onto his desk.

"It's your holiday. You earned it. Do what you like."

"Thank you." Inspector Archer stood and made for the door.

"Inspector."

"Yes, sir?"

"Policing is about facts and hard evidence. Hunches don't work in the real world."

"I know, sir."

"Enjoy your vacation."

"I'll try."

Archer went out and closed the door. Superintendent Lipton sighed and shook his head, put away the file and lit a cigarette.

Charlie woke with a strangled gasp. His arms were pinned to his sides, and the air around him was bright and red. For a second, he thought he was back in Uallabh's coffin, surrounded by the flaming fireball that had destroyed the warrior's house.

He realised he was wrapped in a sleeping bag and daylight was glowing through the canvas sides of his tent. He struggled free of the bag and stuck his head through the flap. The morning sun was moving through the trees, cutting bright swathes across a misty clearing. The rest of the clan sat around a small fire, sipping coffee from tin mugs. Uallabh's van was parked at the edge of a rutted track that petered out where the clearing began.

"What time do you call this to be waking?" Peazle shouted cheerfully.

"The later I get up, the less of the day there is to get chased around by God knows what," Charlie replied sourly, climbing out of the tent and accepting a steaming mug.

"What's for breakfast?" he grunted, rubbing his eyes. "Berries and grubs?"

"There's still some prawn cocktail crisps." Shadowjack held out a crumpled packet. "I brought about twenty bags at a service station. I've become quite partial to them."

"We're trying to work out exactly where we're going." Duncan looked up. He, Uallabh and Lilly were bent over a map of Scotland, laid flat on the dewy grass and held down by rocks.

He turned to Lilly.

"Describe where you lived with your father."

Lilly was staring intently at the map as if it were a jigsaw puzzle she didn't know how to complete.

"In the northwest highlands somewhere, beside a huge waterfall. He's in a cave nearby." She scanned the chart from coast to coast. "But there were no maps in those days - and the names of places have changed over the centuries. There are dozens of waterfalls marked here. I can't tell which one it is."

"Was there anything unusual about it?"

"Yes. My father picked it because there was a Thin Place nearby."

Charlie glanced at the chart. "I don't think *The Collins Touring Map of Scotland* lists those as a method of getting around."

"Not really a morning person, are you Charlie?" Peazle rummaged in a bright blue rucksack. With a happy sigh, he pulled out his prized bowler hat and doffed it at them.

"I thought you threw that blasted thing away."

"Good job I didn't." Reaching inside the brim, the pickpocket pulled out a crinkled piece of parchment and tossed it to Uallabh. The warrior unfolded it and laid it on the grass. It was another map of Scotland, but this one had no roads or towns or any names at all. Instead, dotted over the surface were strange blue or gold spirals.

"A faerie map," Uallabh said with a tinge of awe in his voice. "I've heard of them. Never actually thought I'd see one."

"I got it from Jack Thane," said the pickpocket proudly. "See those little swirls? Those are Thin Places - the blue spirals are the ones that can still be used. There are very few left and they're almost all in the far north. Probably because there are fewer people there."

The clan gathered excitedly around the maps and compared them.

"Only one big waterfall has a Thin Place anywhere near it - and it's an open one! Here, near the northwest coast. On the modern map, it's called Eas a Chual Aluinn Falls. - the highest waterfall in Britain."

"It's pretty remote."

"It's pretty hard to pronounce," Charlie scowled. "The nearest waterfall to my house is called Tumbley Dell."

Peazle circled the point on the map with a black pen. "Whatever it's called, that's where we're heading."

"Perhaps not." It was Uallabh who spoke and the rest of them looked at him in surprise. The warrior was studying the modern map carefully.

"Morgana can't know for certain where we're going," he said. "But she's bound to guess that Gorrodin's prison might be on the list."

Duncan nodded. He had already come to that conclusion himself.

"She knows what our van looks like and the northwest of Scotland is pretty desolate country. Great for a trap, if we're caught on some isolated country road."

"Then what do you suggest?"

"I suggest we fool her."

The War Council

Uallabh leaned forward and tapped the faerie map.

"As Peazle said, there are very few Thin Places left open - but there is a cluster of them here in the far northeast. Up near this little town of Wick." He shifted his attention to the modern map. "And lo and behold, there's a rail line not far from here that runs north and ends at Wick."

"But the rail line runs up the *east* coast," Lilly protested. "We want to be heading for the west."

"I know. So, what would Morgana think if we took that train? What would the Galhadrians think, for that matter? Don't forget, they must be wondering how we're getting on."

"They'd think we still intended to take the Grail to Galhadria - through one of the Thin Places!"

"Exactly. So, let's board that train. Suppose Morgana has an ambush waiting at Eas a Chual Aluinn Falls. If her spies report we're heading northeast instead, she'll likely change plans - move her forces to stop us reaching the Thin Places there. That should even the odds a little."

"I can see where you're going with this," Duncan said approvingly.

"I can't," Shadowjack mumbled through a mouth-ful of crisps

"The rail line hugs the east coast for most of the journey but, right here, it veers inland to avoid crossing the Dornoch Firth." The warrior traced the route with a calloused finger around a wide estuary jutting into the Scottish mainland. "The farthest point it moves inland is this wee station here, Lairg. No more than a village."

Peazle tapped the rim of the bowler hat thoughtfully against his lips.

"Lairg is about the same latitude as Eas a Chual Aluinn Falls."

"Exactly. What if one of us sneaked off the train there carrying the Grail? Headed west on foot? It can't be more than 40 miles to the Falls, as the crow flies."

"Try not to use that expression."

"Sorry."

"I know that area," Duncan broke in. "It's not too far from the lands of my childhood."

In his head he was picturing precipices and glens more accurately than any map could portray them. He closed his eyes and made some mental calculations. "I could make it in a day and night's hard march."

"Meanwhile, the rest of us leave the train at Wick and try to keep out of Morgana's way. By the time her spies notice that Duncan is missing, he may well have reached Gorrodin and freed him. Then Gorrodin uses the Grail to rescue us."

Uallabh sat back and sipped his coffee.

"It's risky, I admit."

"Risky isn't the word for this plan." Shadowjack scratched his beard. "It's more…."

"Suicidal?"

"Insane?"

"Doomed?"

Everybody looked at the maps, willing them to somehow produce an alternative.

"I havnae got a better plan," Duncan sighed. "Does anyone else?"

Nobody did.

"Then let's break camp and get moving." Uallabh was already on his feet and dousing the fire. "You never know who might be watching."

Charlie and Duncan took down the tents. Lilly folded up the faerie map and Peazle tore off the section of the touring book that contained Eas a Chual Aluinn Falls and stuck it in the inside rim of his hat. Shadowjack began cleaning out the mugs with ash from the dead fire.

"A day and night staying ahead of Morgana," he said to Charlie with a note of concern. "When we get to Wick, we better stock up on crisps. What flavour is your fav…." His voice suddenly trailed off.

A large crow was watching him from the long grass a few feet away.

"Charlie," he whispered. "That black beastie's been listening."

He lunged forward with surprising swiftness for a man so large. But the crow was already airborne, wings fluttering like black cloth. It deftly avoided Shadowjack's outstretched arms and rose steeply into the sky with a victorious caw, growing smaller with each beat of its wings.

A blur swept up over the top of the nearest tree and collided with the vanishing black shape. As the astonished clan looked on, the crow spun sideways, trailing an arc of blood, then dropped like a stone. It landed with a thud on top of Uallabh's van.

A white hawk with black-tipped wings floating serenely in the air where the crow had been. It banked in a long, leisurely turn and then hovered again, watching the clan. Charlie looked vainly around for a rock to throw - he was sick and tired of being spied on by stupid birds - no matter who they reported to.

He heard a sharp crack to his right. The hawk remained motionless in the air for a second, then its wings folded and it fell from the sky, crashing to the ground a few feet from the campfire.

Uallabh lowered his pistol and tucked it back inside his coat.

"Like I say. You never know who might be watching."

He picked up his pack and lugged it to the back of the vehicle.

"I washed this van yesterday," he grumped, sweeping the crow off the hood with a contemptuous swipe.

The rest silently finished stowing the tents and picked up their remaining possessions. Uallabh beckoned to Duncan and the highlander climbed into the passenger seat beside the warrior. Peazle walked over and looked down at the dead hawk. The once-proud bird lay in the wet grass, a lump of bloody feathers.

"I told you, Jack Thane," he muttered to himself. "We have a different kind of magic here."

He stuck his bowler hat on his head and climbed into the back of the van.

The Lords of the Western Wilderness sat at a round table in the Whale Room. Jack Thane, Tom Lincoln and Jenny Haa were there. So were the other Lords - Prestor John, Gideon, Will Thorn, Mabon, Math and Baubi Ross. All waited in nervous silence until Lincoln raised a hand to formally begin their meeting.

"We are in grave danger, my friends." The old man's voice was quiet and strain had deepened the wrinkles on his face. "The unthinkable seems to have happened. The Dolorous Stroke has been struck - against the Gorrodin Rath."

There was a muted gasp from the other wizards. Will Thorn rose, face red with anger. He was the youngest of the Lords and his dark, darting eyes were as quick as his temper.

"Who could have struck such a blow but one of us?" There was a murmur of agreement from some while others shouted their own questions.

"When was this deed done?"

"How do we know for sure?"

"ENOUGH!" Tom Lincoln bellowed and the outcry died down. "There will be time enough for recriminations if we survive. In the meantime, we must use every scrap of our powers to keep the Western Wall strong and the Rath contained."

He looked across at Jack Thane.

"One of us has already taken it upon himself to put an…operation into effect," he said bitterly. "It may afford us some small reprieve. You have the floor, Master Thane."

Jack Thane stood and gave a business-like bow.

"The Dolorous Stroke was designed to destroy the side that struck it." Despite this gloomy prognosis, the sorcerer seemed remarkably confident. "I, for one, am not going down without a fight."

Will Thorn and Prestor John nodded and the others muttered in agreement.

"The Stroke has awakened Morgana, leader of the Rath, and bestowed on her immense authority," Thane continued. "She hopes to increase that advantage even more by regaining Gorrodin's Grail."

There was an icy silence from the rest of the table. Gorrodin's name was never mentioned among them. Jack Thane paid no attention to their discomfort.

"Even without the Grail, she will triumph over us. But if she regains the cup, source of her original power, her victory will be swift and complete. Therefore, I have sent a party of humans to keep it from her."

The rest of the sorcerers were leaning forwards, eyes narrowed, listening intently.

"They have already located Gorrodin's daughter - the only link to the cup - and are trying to bring her back to safety. I am not sure of their present location, but I presume they are heading for a cluster of Thin Places in the north of Scotland."

"You presume?"

"The hawk following them has not reported back," Thane said. "A victim of Morgana's forces, I imagine."

"What do you actually *know*?" Lincoln snapped.

"They have been joined by Uallabh, one of Arthur's original knights." The wizard hesitated, then plunged on. "It is possible they may even have the Grail itself."

"I cannot believe you would entrust the fate of Galhadria to a bunch of humans!" Gideon stood, hands wide, entreating his companions. "We should send one of our own to find and escort them back to Galhadria."

"None of us can leave anymore." Baubi Ross spoke quietly. "From now on, it will take the power of our combined talismans to keep the Rath at bay. We can no longer interfere, even if we want to."

Jack Thane permitted himself a superior smile.

"We must trust that the humans will thwart Morgana while I try to find a way to snatch victory from our sure defeat. As a young friend of mine once said, they have a different kind of magic."

Nobody at the table smiled.

"It does not matter." Mabon scolded. "If the Dolorous Stroke was used by a Galhadrian against the Gorrodin Rath, they are destined to win. It's as simple as that."

"Grail or no Grail, I have a plan," Thane insisted. "I cannot divulge the details right now…."

"Why not?" Will Thorn objected. "Is this a play for power? How do we know it was not *you* who instigated the Stroke?"

"Or you!" Thane was quick to turn the accusation to his advantage. "It could have been any of us. In which case, I prefer to play my cards close to my chest."

"None of *us* are traitors." Thorn stammered.

"What of the Wilson child?" Math broke in. "He used Excalibur to kill Mordred. Could that not be the Dolorous Stoke?"

"Excalibur may be magical, yet it is simply a tool." Gideon shook his head. "The boy is a mere human. It was not him."

"If any of you have another strategy, I'd be happy to hear it," Thane snapped. "If not, let me try and save us in my own way."

The rest lapsed into sullen silence.

"Enough squabbling." Tom Lincoln brought proceedings to a close. "I agree the humans most likely move is to head northeast, to reach the Thin Places there. We will send what meagre forces we can muster to guard those and assist in their safe passage to Galhadria. This meeting is adjourned."

He banged a gavel sharply on the table and the sound rang ominously through the Whale Room.

"In the meantime, let us prepare for war."

Part III

The Dolorous Stroke

*And so there grew great tracts of wilderness,
Wherein the beast was ever more and more. But
man was less and less, till Arthur came.*

Alfred, Lord Tennyson. *Idylls of the King*

*To him the long years and ages have been but as
days. He lies in magic sleep. But the day will
come when the strong enchantment that bound
him will be broken, and he will come forth to behold the changes that have been wrought by
more potent arts than his, and all the wonders of
this later time.*

Charles Henry Hanson. *Stories of the Days of
King Arthur*

The Clan

Inspector Archer stood at the entrance to Waverly Station, staring up at the famous towering silhouette that was Edinburgh's Old Town. Crowds of shoppers surged in and out of the stores lining Princes Street, fat plastic bags of shopping clunking against each other. They hardly glanced at the tall, bald man in a suit and tie, raincoat draped over one arm, gawping like a tourist. The castle rose above the bustling thoroughfare, as it had done for a thousand years, ancient and serene.

Archer turned to a uniformed policeman strolling past.

"Could you tell me the way to the nearest station officer?"

"It's about ten feet behind you, sir. You just came out of it."

"Not the train station." Inspector Archer pulled out a worn brown wallet with a gold badge inside. "The nearest police station."

The locomotive to Wick was an asthmatic old diesel, chugging sluggishly through the mountain passes of the Scottish highlands, pulling three dingy carriages. Even in the 21st century, there were few people living in the far north, so transport to and from remote areas was infrequent and poorly maintained. Since it was a weekday, the only other occupants of the carriage, apart from the clan, were an old man in a flat cap and a stout woman wearing a large tweed coat, accompanied by a young boy and girl. The mother was absorbed in some glossy magazine and occasionally passed a soggy, homemade sandwich to her offspring. Both children sat with their foreheads flat against the greasy carriage window, chewing placidly and watching grazing cattle glide past.

"How much farther now?" Shadowjack yawned loudly, stretching huge muscular arms, which almost spanned the breadth of the carriage.

"Where are ye headed, son?" The old man doffed his cap. He wore an olive Barbour jacket and green Wellingtons - a postcard-perfect picture of an elderly countryman.

"Someplace called Lairg," Shadowjack replied.

"It's the next stop, but we're still twenty-odd miles away." The old man jerked his thumb towards the window. "This is the Pass of Shin."

The giant leaned across him and looked out, then withdrew his head sharply. The train was winding its way along a narrow ledge not much wider than the locomotive itself. A few feet beyond, the ground sheared away, dropping through a chaotic mass of trees to a dark, frothing river.

"Name's Paul Jessop, by the way," the old man said amiably.

"Shadowjack Henry."

"Sounds foreign."

"I was born just outside Glasgow."

"Aye. Foreign." Paul Jessop said with a knowing smirk. "Born and bred in the north, myself. Never got off in Lairg, though. Bit too cosmopolitan for my liking." He gave the blacksmith a jokey wink. "It's got a visitor centre *and* a caravan site."

Shadowjack nodded politely, then pretended to go to sleep.

Charlie Wilson had a seat to himself. Uallabh and Peazle were sitting together on the other side of the aisle, both engrossed in their own thoughts. Duncan and Lilly were in front of him, talking to each other in low tones, while Shadowjack was beyond them - he was so big, he needed two seats for himself.

It was the first time since this insane adventure had begun that Charlie had time to think properly about his situation - and wasn't sure he wanted to.

He was worried about his mum and dad. They must be frantic by now, wondering where he was. And he was terrified of what might happen next. He had almost died twice already, and who knew what dangers were still waiting for him?

And, looking at Lilly and Duncan together, he realised he was jealous. Lilly was laughing at something Duncan had just said, and Charlie could smell the faint freshness of her red curls bobbing above the seat back. The highlander might seem gruff and serious, but he was also smart and brave - as well as being two hundred years closer to Lilly's age than Charlie. The boy had to keep reminding himself that Lilly was as ancient as the hills they were passing - and only half-human. She looked so young and so... pretty.

There was no point in fooling himself. He was no more than a child to her. Twice now, Lilly had manipulated him into some suicidal scheme to further her aims. As he well knew, Galhadrians weren't big on gratitude. Yet he would continue to help the girl, if only because he felt it was the right thing to do.

He looked around at his companions - marvelling at what a mixed bunch they were. Why were they all participating in this crazy adventure? Lilly had an obvious reason - she wanted to free her father. But the rest had little to gain. Duncan had been forced to abandon his all-consuming search for his brother. Peazle was betraying his own master, Jack Thane and would, doubtless, be punished for his treachery - if Thane were as callous as he seemed. Shadowjack had given up the peaceful life on his forge to lend assistance - though he had never met Lilly before. And Uallabh seemed to hold no love for humans or Galhadrians, yet had come along too.

There seemed to be only one plausible reason for everyone's folly.

They were lonely. He, Lilly, Peazle, Duncan, Uallabh and even Shadowjack Henry.

Now they had each other. Each time they risked their lives for their companions, the bonds between them grew stronger. Charlie glanced over at Uallabh, sitting tense as a statue on the other side of the aisle. An overhanging branch slapped the side of the train, and the warrior jumped, hand moving instinctively to the pistol inside his leather coat. As he slowly relaxed, he noticed Charlie watching him. His steely gaze fastened on the boy - a chilling, ice-blue stare that was the last thing many men had seen. Then he suddenly crossed his eyes. Charlie gave a muffled snort of laughter.

No. They were not lonely when they were together. They were the clan.

Jack Thane entered his chambers and drew back the veils surrounding the main room. Golden light was wafting through an open window, and a soft breeze carried the smell of ripe apples across his living space. Thane frowned.

On a chair in the centre of the chamber sat Math, sheathed in black velvet, hands clasped demurely on her lap.

"I don't remember inviting you to my rooms, Mistress Math," the wizard said curtly.

Math walked to the window, where dying sunlight framed her white hair and turned it rich copper.

"Being one of the Lords bores you, Jack Thane," she said. "Does it not?"

The sorcerer was taken aback at first, then gave the question proper consideration.

"I could think of more enjoyable ways to pass the centuries," he admitted.

"I agree." Math absently batted an insect that dared venture too near her face. "But we cannot be out there dancing and singing with the rest of the Galhadrians and ruling them too."

"I would say they require very little ruling," Thane said blackly, sinking onto the eiderdown bed. "They don't exactly do a lot."

"Yes. I preferred Galhadria before the civil war, myself. Back then, our people were more adventurous. More… passionate."

"And the most adventurous and passionate were the ones who rebelled and were destroyed. What you say is close to treason."

Math laughed dismissively.

"You were very quick to spot that the Dolorous Stroke had occurred," she continued, deftly changing the subject.

The Dolorous Stroke. Thane frowned again at the mention of this ancient spell - designed to prevent another uprising. It stated that, should two magical forces go to war, the first side to kill one of the enemy would be destined to lose. And it had been struck against *their* enemy, the Gorrodin Rath. Which meant they were doomed.

"If you have a point, get to it," Thane said.

"You were also quick to act on that discovery. You make a good leader in time of crisis, as the other Lords are now aware."

Jack Thane narrowed his eyes.

"What are you insinuating?"

"I notice you are fond of vanishing from time to time, Jack." The use of a sorcerer's first name alone was a breach of etiquette, but Thane was too intrigued to care.

"I revisit my former haunts occasionally, for old time's sake. What of it?"

"Is the land of Toth one of your old haunts? The place where Morgana has gathered the Gorrodin Rath to march on us."

"I have been there." Jack Thane was more guarded now. "I felt someone should keep watch on them, as I always considered the Rath a serious threat. Now I am proved right."

"Indeed you are." Math continued staring out of the window. "You didn't happen to… eh… cross the path of some of their warriors on your trips? Perhaps… kill one."

Jack Thane rose from the bed and drew himself to his full height. His hate-filled look would have turned a lesser adversary into a trembling wreck.

"You accuse me of the Dolorous Stroke!"

"I am only saying out loud what some of my companions are muttering to themselves." Math was undaunted by the wizard's piercing stare.

"Do you think I am some novice to be goaded by a scattering of troll-men? That I would sacrifice my own people to a war we cannot win?"

"Of course not," Math replied soothingly. She turned from the window, cloak billowing around her. "But if you were responsible for the Dolorous Stroke, Jack Thane, I'm certain you had a good reason. Perhaps to put in motion your *secret* strategy, one you claim will allow us to cheat certain defeat."

Jack Thane regarded her warily.

"I have an idea I am sure will work," he said slowly. "The fact that I keep it to myself does not mean I caused the conflict which must surely come."

"The Dolorous Stroke cannot be overturned by any magic, no matter how strong," Math reminded him. "Possessing the Grail will not change that, for it can't be used against Morgana. Gorrodin shared its power with her when they were man and wife, remember?"

She narrowed her eyes.

"There is no way for us to win that I can see."

"It is not merely Gorrodin's cup I seek." The wizard tapped his nose. "The boy Peazle has a secret mission only I know. And it will save Galhadria, I promise."

"You are positive?"

"I am."

"You were always too much like Gorrodin, Jack." Math reached out and touched Thane's cheek. "Brilliant and decisive, yet impetuous and arrogant. The mark of a leader, I suppose."

"What are you saying?"

"That I will back you, if this plan is successful. Support you, should you wish to rule."

Her voice suddenly hardened.

"If you fail, however?" She withdrew her hand and slipped it into the folds of her cloak.

"You will die on the Great Wall, defending Galhadria with the rest of us."

The Journey North

Lilly and Duncan kept their voices low.

"I'm not sure about Uallabh's plan," the girl said quietly. She looked out the window at the formidable rocky screes that made up so much of highland scenery. "As soon as Morgana realises we've left the rest of the clan and headed for my father's prison at the Falls of Eas a Chual Aluinn, she'll send her forces straight back there. They may well beat us to our destination."

"I'm nae scholar, but I see you're referring tae me in the plural."

Lilly took his hand and smiled.

"I thank you for the noble gesture, highlander," she whispered. "There is a password to open Gorrodin's prison, but it only works when used with the Grail. You are human and the cup can change you if you try to weld its power." She tapped her chest proudly. "I intend to go with you and open the cave. I will be there to see my father's suffering ended."

She waved her fingers in front of the highlander's face. Glittering sparks drifted between the tips.

"I may not have much magic but certainly enough to keep up with you, no matter how fast you think you can travel."

Duncan stared out the window while he considered the girl's words.

"I dinnae like it," he said finally. "But I can see that you coming along makes sense." He grinned broadly. "Besides, I cannae protect you if you're stuck up in Wick."

"I need no protection," the girl bristled. "Rather, I thought I might look after *you*."

The trees had thinned out as the train topped the Pass of Shin and the purple peaks of a distant mountain range rose slowly over the horizon. Mossy boulders soaked up the light, and sparkling streams crisscrossed the wrinkled olive landscape.

"You are a brave and noble man, Duncan Mac-Phail." Lilly looked at him with admiration. "People like you and Charlie make me proud to have human blood in my veins."

"Let us hope it stays in oor veins and doesnae end up staining the ground."

They noticed the locomotive was gradually slowing down. Finally, the train shuddered to a halt with a tired hiss.

"Is this Lairg? I don't see any station." Shadowjack pressed his face against the glass, trying to look a little further ahead. The pass was behind them now, and the train was sitting motionless in an unbroken sea of heather.

"There's probably another locomotive up ahead, or the points need changed or something." Peazle tried to demonstrate his knowledge of modern transport - though he didn't have a clue what he was talking about.

"There's nae train ahead and nae points." Paul Jessop shook his grey head. "I've travelled back and forward on this line for nigh on 50 years. It's a single track. Only three trains a day, and this is the last. There must be an obstacle blocking the way."

Uallabh was on his feet and standing on the seat in an instant. He opened the little sliding aperture on top of the main window and pushed his head out.

"Careful noo mannie. This train starts up again, and you'll look like Headless Horace o' the Highlands. He was a famous bogle, you know."

The warrior's head shot in again, a tense look on his face.

"Lilly," he said quietly. "You better take a look."

The girl bounced onto her seat and stuck her head out of the aperture on the other side. The woman in the tweed coat lowered her magazine and tutted loudly.

"What do you see?" Charlie asked, sliding into the aisle. By now, the rest of the clan were on their feet, looking nervously at each other. Peazle climbed onto the rim of the lower window so he could get his head out of the narrow gap above.

"It's just fog."

"Nonsense." It was Paul Jessop again. "This is one of the windiest moors in the highlands. There's not been a fog here the whole time I've travelled this route. And that's nigh on 50 years," he reminded them.

"It's windy, right enough." The pickpocket was holding the bowler hat on with one hand. "But that fog isn't moving an inch. And it's a funny colour. Almost yellow."

Lilly withdrew her head and pulled Peazle roughly back in.

"Stoorhaar!" she gasped.

"Stoor what?"

"A Stoorhaar." The girl slammed the aperture shut and sank into her seat. "It's a mist that dark forces use to travel undetected."

Uallabh looked over at Duncan, anger spreading across his face.

"Why didn't I think of this?" He thumped the back of his seat, releasing a cloud of dust. "Morgana's not waiting for us to arrive anywhere! She's sent some of her forces to attack the train!"

"She wouldn't dare." Lilly shook her head in disbelief. "There are humans on board!"

"What do you think we are? Easter Bunnies?" Charlie was jumping up and down, trying to reach the luggage rack. His fingers scrabbled at the fishing holder containing Excalibur until he managed to dislodge it. Duncan caught the weapon before it hit the ground. He reached up, pulled his own holder from the rack and unsheathed his blade.

There was a strangled sob from further up the train. The woman in the tweed coat was clutching her two frightened children.

"What do you mean, attack the train?" she squeaked. "And why do you have *swords*?"

"How many carriages are behind the engine?" Uallabh was addressing Paul Jessop. The warrior already had a pistol in each hand. The woman gasped and hugged her children tighter.

"Three."

"Put the damned guns away!" Charlie snapped, looking across at the terrified family. The boy was staring at Uallabh, wide-eyed. He didn't seem all that much younger than Charlie.

"Please don't kill us," the woman whispered.

"We're not going to kill you. We're not going to harm you at all." Charlie moved towards her and the woman and children shrank into their seats. "We're on your side, madam. But there's something outside the train that means us all harm."

The woman tried to hide the whimpering kids in the folds of her voluminous coat. Duncan now held his sword in one hand and Excalibur in the other.

"Mrs McCusker." Paul Jessop obviously knew the petrified family. He got up shakily and pointed to the window behind her. "Out there."

Yellow-green banks of fog were drifting past the train, so thick they seemed to be scraping along the glass.

"These queer-looking folk are telling the truth." the old man said with utter conviction. He turned to Lilly.

"The Stoorhaar is an old legend in these parts, spun to scare wee bairns, but I know it is real. I came across one - a long time ago - and barely escaped with my life."

"You're all insane." Mrs McCusker's eyes were as wide as saucers, and she looked like she was on the verge of a mental breakdown herself.

The sliding door at the front of the carriage opened suddenly. Uallabh and Duncan whirled, weapons pointing. Mrs McCusker squealed.

The train driver stumbled into the carriage and sank to his knees.

"Monster," he croaked. "There's a monster in the fog."

The Stoorhaar

"Shadowjack, get the rest of the train's passengers into this carriage," Uallabh barked. "Do it now."

"Try not to panic them," Charlie added.

Shadowjack snatched the driver's hat from the man's bowed head and stuck it on his own curly thatch. He raced through the sliding doors at the other end of the carriage and vanished into the compartment beyond.

"Fire! Fire at the back of the train!" They heard him bellowing. "Everybody forward before you're burned to a crisp! Prawn Cocktail flavour, most likely!"

Charlie winced.

"You saw a Stoorhaar before?" Lilly turned to Paul Jessop.

"What's a stoohaa mummy?" the little girl asked pleadingly.

"It's just an old highland story, sweetie. Told by superstitious crofters and the like." The woman patted her daughter's head protectively and shot the old man a filthy look. "It's not real."

The girl looked across at Paul Jessop for confirmation, but he could give her none.

"I ran into one on Ben Armine in 1969." Jessop bit his lip at the memory. "Something in the fog took a sheep right in front of my eyes."

"You're lucky to be alive," Lilly said.

"If I didn't take my shotgun everywhere, I wouldn't be. Took both barrels to scare whatever it was away."

Mrs McCusker gave a groan of dismay at everyone's behaviour.

"You carry a shotgun all the time?" Uallabh asked.

"Of course. I'm a gamekeeper."

"Then get it!"

The sliding doors opened and a stream of people poured into the carriage, though they stopped in alarm when they saw the occupants. Uallabh and Duncan were standing in the middle of the corridor, bristling with weapons. Paul Jessop was perched precariously on the back of a seat, pulling a huge shotgun down from the luggage rack.

"What the hell is going on?" A large, heavy-set man with a bushy beard, fisherman's cap and weatherproof jacket threw his arms wide, stopping the rest of the bewildered passengers from coming any further into the compartment.

"Come on in, Ben Harper," Paul Jessop said, lowering his gun. He seemed to know everyone on the train. "The engine appears to be under attack."

"Attack ye say. By these jokers?" The big man glared suspiciously at the clan.

"No, no. These folks are eh.... circus performers," the old man replied quickly, showing his mind was agile, even if his body wasn't. "The tall one's Honest John Plain the Wild West Sharpshooter. And that one with the long hair throws swords."

The clan looked at him with astonishment. Uallabh recovered first, whirling both guns expertly around his fingers.

"Howdy," he said laconically. Charlie did a perfect back flip in his seat.

"I'm an acrobat." He gave a low bow. Five or six juggling balls suddenly appeared in Lilly's hand, spinning through her blurred fingers before disappearing again. Mrs McCusker's daughter giggled.

"And the big eejit who's running around shouting fire?"

"Circus strongman," Charlie said without hesitation.

"We asked him to get everyone in here." Paul Jessop was unable to keep a roguish smile off his face. "We appear to be in a wee bit of trouble."

Ben Harper motioned and the rest of the passengers began to edge into the carriage. There were another two men, a youth and a woman with a young boy.

"Aye. So you say." Harper stood with his hands on his hips. "What's aw this nonsense about an attack on the train?"

"There's a Stoorhaar outside." Paul Jessop looked unperturbed.

"Och, come on now, Mr Jessop." Ben Harper gave the man an incredulous look. "That's an old wife's tale. I'm surprised at…"

Mrs McCusker let loose a piercing scream, cutting the fisherman off. She was backing away from the window, shaking her head in disbelief.

The yellow mist had obscured the scenery outside, and total silence enveloped the train. They could hear no birds, no wind; even the noise of the idling train engine was gone.

"I saw something in the fog!" Mrs McCusker was pointing in horror. Her children had disappeared under the nearest seats.

A head appeared at the window.

It was a glistening grey, with dead fish eyes and pouting, tooth-ridged lips. But its sheer size was what horrified the occupants – the scaly cranium must have been four feet across. The head flicked quickly to the side, slick, papery skin squealing across the glass like a wet finger. A long body, resembling that of a giant eel, flashed past the windows, travelling the length of the carriage in seconds. Then the creature was gone into the pea-souper.

"Ye Gods. It's a sea serpent," Ben Harper hissed.

"On top of a mountain?" the smaller man behind him spluttered. He was wearing identical gear to Harper. In fact, all the men behind were dressed like him - Charlie guessed he was the captain of a fishing boat and the others were members of his crew. Either that, or everyone in the highlands shared the bigger man's fashion sense.

"It's a Stoorworm." Lilly was bouncing from seat to seat, slamming the upper windows shut. "They swim through the fog. Usually in pairs. And the mist itself is poisonous."

Shadowjack Henry appeared at the back of the little group.

"Shut every window and door on the train," Uallabh shouted to him. "Block up any vents. Do it now!"

The blacksmith nodded and vanished again.

Ben Harper turned to his crew.

"Karston, Davie, Sean. Go with the strongman. Give him a hand, then get right back here."

The two men and the youth turned and hurried back the way they had come.

"You, missus. Take your wee kiddie and put him under a seat." Ben Harper was obviously used to giving orders, and the second woman complied immediately. The captain strode over to Paul Jessop.

"I mind you telling me about thon Stoorworm in a pub in Thurso. I thought you were having me on."

"1969. I'll never forget it. I was on a hill in…"

"I apologise for no believing you, but mebbie now isnae the time for a wee story." Harper rounded on Lilly instead. "And how does a lassie like you know so much about yon beastie?"

"I'm a Gypsy," the old lie rolled easily off Lilly's tongue. "We have legends about the Stoorworm just as you do in the highlands."

There was a crash against the side of the train and the worm's head squashed disgustingly against the glass. Its skin flattened out on the window like a lump of ancient dough, then it was gone again, leaving a wide, sweaty smear.

"That's no legend!"

"Can it tip the train?" Mrs McCusker whimpered.

"It's a big creature, right enough, but this train weighs about forty tons," the driver piped up between coughs. His face was grey and his breathing laboured. "The lassie's right about the poison, though."

He hauled himself unsteadily to his feet.

"I stopped the train when I saw the fog and tried to close the cab window as it started seeping in, but I caught one mouthful and was almost out cold. The cab's full of the stuff. I can't get back in to move the engine again."

The head crashed into the window. This time, there was a chorus of screams and shouts. The children under the seats began to cry.

The fishermen and Shadowjack piled back into the front carriage.

"We've sealed up every crack, boss," one crew member barked, wiping perspiration from his brow. It was cold in the carriage and Charlie guessed the sweat was made more by fear than exertion.

Mrs McCusker was huddled between seats, holding a mobile phone to her ear.

"You have to help us, officer," she sobbed. "We're on the Wick train, being attacked by giant worms in a poisonous fog. No, it's not a practical joke!"

"Don't be daft, woman!" Ben Harper snapped. "The Lairg Police aren't going to believe that. Tell them it's a chemical gas leak or something."

It was too late. The head smashed against the train again and the window exploded.

Inspector Archer sat in the canteen at St Leonard's police station in Edinburgh, watching his plate of greasy egg and chips go cold. Occasionally, the uniforms in the room gave him a curious glance, but he didn't seem particularly friendly, so they left him alone. Most of them didn't even know Archer was a fellow officer. At the table next to him, a group of young recruits were talking about their strangest cases to date.

"So, I got to the graveyard and half the headstones had been pushed over," one constable was saying.

"Ach, that's just vandals."

"No. It was worse than that. The whole graveyard was… dug up. I mean every inch. There were bones and everything on the surface. A tree had been completely uprooted. And there were worms everywhere. Millions of them. It was totally raj."

"All right. It was… a lot of vandals."

"Aye. Well, a woman in one of the tenements did give a statement. Said she saw a bunch of kids and a couple of adults running away from the scene. Said one of the kids was wearing a bowler hat, of all things."

Inspector Archer's head shot up.

"Talking of worms…" a policewoman spooned a forkful of watery pasta into her mouth. "We just got the strangest report over the radio. Some hysterical woman called the police at Lairg a few minutes ago."

"Where's Lairg?"

"It's away up north, but the police there radioed us to ask if we had any reports of a chemical spill in the highlands." The policewoman waved her fork at the other officers. "She claimed the Wick train was being attacked by a poisonous fog filled with flying worms or something. Said a bunch of circus performers were defending it."

"Where's Wick?"

"Jeez? Did you not study geography at school?"

Inspector Archer pushed away his plate and stood.

"Excuse me," he said as politely as he could manage, though excitement coursed through every inch of his lanky frame. "Could you tell me where I can find your commanding officer? I need to ask him a big favour."

Fifteen minutes later, he was speeding north in an unmarked police car.

The Baggage Car

The Stoorworm forced its bloated, shimmering body through the shattered train window, blank grey eyes searching calmly for its nearest victim. Uallabh and Duncan threw themselves sideways, an instant before razor-sharp teeth snapped shut in the place they had been standing. Paul Jessop and Peazle sank silently onto the floor and Charlie and Lilly flipped over their seat backs, as the monster swerved, buried its jaws in the musty upholstery and ripped out a torso-sized chunk.

Shadowjack and the passengers from the other compartment were at the far end of the carriage, beckoning frantically to the kids under the seats. The Stoorworm veered back towards Duncan, but the highlander grasped the luggage rail and swung himself adroitly into the netting, as the gaping mouth sailed past. Mrs McCusker was screaming at the top of her lungs, trapped in her seat by the creature's slimy body, just behind what appeared to be gills. The Stoorworm tried to twist back round to get at her, but its bulk made it impossible to manoeuvre between the train seats, and the petrified woman's very proximity kept her just out of reach of its slashing teeth. Her children were sheltering in the iron framework under the seats, wailing hysterically.

The creature gave an ear-piercing shriek and began to inch its body out of the window to free itself for another attack. Great wads of flesh rolled into ridges behind the head as it fought to pull itself back from the confines of the broken aperture.

"Don't let the beast out!" Lilly shouted, flat on her back between two seats. "Its body is all that's stopping the fog getting in."

Duncan rolled out of the luggage rack and landed on the upholstery below. Using it as a trampoline, he bent his knees and flew into the air, sword held in front of him. He collided with the creature and his blade buried itself in the translucent flesh right behind the bony ridged head. The monster gave another screech and wrenched itself backwards, but the sword caught on the window fame, temporarily stopping its exit. Uallabh stepped forward and emptied both guns into the straining Goliath's flank. The creature hardly seemed to feel it. Charlie sprang up from where he had been hiding.

"Duncan. Excalibur! To me."

Duncan leapt nimbly back from the grinding jaws and tossed the second sword sideways. The boy caught it and launched himself over the top of the Stoorworm's body. Sliding headfirst down the other side, he plunged the sword into the monster and let go, landing upside down on Mrs McCusker's lap. She grabbed him

in a maniacal bear hug and held on, howling uncontrollably.

The Stoorworm bucked in agony. Excalibur was no
ordinary weapon and, though the monster was too big
to kill with one thrust, the Great Sword was causing it
extreme distress. It tried to reverse again, but both pro-
truding blades caught against the buckled window
frame and stopped the creature getting out. It gave up
trying to free itself and fixed its saucer-shaped eyes on
Uallabh, who was backing quietly away. The warrior
turned to run and tripped over one of Mrs McCusker's
children, crawling silently to safety along the aisle
floor.

The creature reared up over the prone humans, its
mouth widening to an impossible size. Uallabh's
mouth opened in a doomed plea. The child below him
covered its eyes.

There was a deafening roar, then another, and the
Stoorworm's head exploded. Gouts of green blood and
lumps of grey flesh fountained across the carriage,
showering the passengers.

Paul Jessop lowered his shotgun, acrid smoke floating from both barrels.

"It worked in 1969, too." He gave a wry smile.

Peazle rose up from between two gore-splattered
seats. A shard of window glass jutted from the side of
his temple and blood was running down his nose and
congealing under one eye. His face and clothes were

covered in green goo, and a large lump of oily flesh protruded from the top of his waistcoat.

"That was truly unpleasant," he said weakly.

"Fetch your swords and get ready to run." Lilly was down on her knees, peering under the seat. "Come, children," she said. "The Stoorworm is dead."

"I'm scared," a little voice came from the darkness.

"But we have to move," the girl gently urged. "When we pull the swords out of the Stoorworm, it'll will fall back through the window, and poison gas will flood in."

She hesitated, then decided that the truth was the best option.

"Plus, there's another one out there, and it's not going to take kindly to us killing its kin."

There was silence under the seats. Charlie prised himself loose from Mrs McCusker's vice-like grip and slid onto the floor, squeezing under the flaccid, bloody chin of the dead Stoorworm.

"My name is Charlie Wilson," he said to the wide eyes under the seat. "I'm hardly any older than you, and I'm really scared too. But the only way to get out of this is to be brave and pull together. Remember, you have your mothers to protect, don't you?"

After a long pause, the children emerged cautiously from the darkness, tracks of their tears streaking dirty cheeks. Mrs McCusker gave her offspring a timid smile and a little wave to indicate she was OK. She eased out of her seat and skirted the dead leviathan, never taking her eyes off it, as if she expected the creature to spring to life at any moment. Once she was clear, the children grasped her hands and led her towards the safety of the next compartment. The rest of the passengers followed.

Duncan grasped his sword hilt and put one foot against the slippery side of the worm.

"Ready, Charlie?"

The boy grasped Excalibur and signalled to the highlander that he was. He and Duncan pulled the swords out simultaneously. The creature's own dead weight pulled it back through the window, and a yellow torrent of fog cascaded into the empty gap, like water flooding a breached ship. Charlie and Duncan retreated, holding their breath, sprinting into the second carriage and shutting the door.

"What do we do now?" asked one of the crewmen.

"Same again, I suppose," Ben Harper said. "If we're lucky, these circus folk can kill the second one the same way they did the first. Then we shut ourselves in the baggage compartment and wait for help to arrive."

"I don't think..." the driver began, but Mrs McCusker was thumping him on the shoulder, fist crammed against her mouth. She pointed behind the uniformed man with a fluttering hand.

A second eel-like head, as big as the first, was watching them from the murk outside the window. Paul Jessop swung his gun again.

"No, wait!" Uallabh held up a hand. "Fire through the glass and the fog will get in."

"Dinnae worry, son. All my ammunition is in the carriage we just left."

"Damn. Mine too," the warrior admitted shamefacedly.

"This one's doing something different," Duncan said, cautiously lowering his sword.

The worm floated in the mist, regarding them with what seemed like cold indifference. Every few seconds, it inched forward, so it almost touched the window, then jerked back with a rippling motion. The children disappeared under a new set of chairs.

"It wants us to fire. Pretending to attack but ready to dodge away."

The passengers moved back and forth, mirroring the monster's subtle motions, ready to flee at any second.

"It's smart! It's trying to figure out a better way to get at us."

The Stoorworm slid slowly to the side and drifted off into the fog. Mrs McCusker heaved a sigh of relief.

"I don't like this one wee bit." Uallabh was twisting and turning, trying to look through every window at once.

"Maybe it's seen a nice juicy bus."

There was a quiet whoosh and the Stoorworm's tail slammed against the window nearest Mrs McCusker. The poor woman almost fainted on her feet. A thick blue crack appeared the length of the window, splitting the vanishing tail into a deadly double prism.

"Everybody into the last carriage!" roared Shadowjack, pulling squealing children from under seats and dragging them with him. "That window won't stand another blow!"

The passengers made a mad dash for the connecting door, pushing and shoving each other into the baggage compartment. As they ran, the Stoorworm's tail crashed into the damaged window again, breaking it into a thousand pieces. Uallabh, still in the doomed carriage, threw himself to the floor as shards of flying glass filled the top half of the car and embedded themselves in the opposite wall. He rolled over and emptied the last few rounds from his pistols at the ruined window. But the tail was gone, and yellow-green mist was already pouring through the hole. The warrior staggered to his feet and flung himself into the baggage compartment. Shadowjack slammed the door behind him.

"We're being outsmarted by a flying fog fish," the blacksmith said grumpily.

The baggage compartment was full of crates and boxes, lit only by overhead lights. To everyone's relief, there were no big windows in this carriage - only small, elongated portals of thick smoked glass near the top. Because it carried goods rather than people, the baggage car was designed with security in mind rather than giving a good view. The passengers sank gratefully to the floor, breathing heavily.

"Try the mobile phones again. See if we can get help," Ben Harper ordered.

"We've been trying, captain. The signal can't penetrate this fog."

"I got through once, but I don't think they believed me." Mrs McCusker gave a sorrowful sniff.

"When the train doesn't turn up at Lairg, they'll send someone. Eventually."

"I think we have to make a move before that," Lilly was looking around. "There's a definite greenish tinge to the air in here."

"The baggage car is built differently from the rest of the train." The driver still looked sick and pale, but he was finally able to talk normally. "Hasnae got any real windows, but it's not airtight like a normal carriage." He gave a racking cough. "No passengers, see, so it doesnae matter if it's draughty. Lots of little holes everywhere."

"Let's start finding those and plugging them up."

"That's impossible," the driver began to object. "There's no way…"

He caught sight of the cowering children and quickly shut up.

"C'mon now, kids," Shadowjack tore the lid off the nearest crate without the slightest effort. "You look for any wee gaps in the walls. Then we'll see if there's something in these boxes we can use to cover them - blankets and the like. Up and at em."

Terrified though the children were, they sprang to attention - Shadowjack Henry was almost as frightening as the Stoorworm. Charlie helped them rummage through the numerous boxes, while Mrs McCusker, Peazle, Duncan and the crewmen felt around the walls for cracks. Paul Jessop sat on the largest crate and directed operations. Eventually, the other woman joined in.

"I'm Mrs Mcnab." She offered her hand to Mrs McCusker. "Met you a couple of times in the Co-op in Thurso."

The driver crawled over to Uallabh and Ben Harper.

"This isnae going to work," he whispered. "The baggage compartment's got more holes than a sieve. Our only chance is to try and drive the train out of the fog. I left the engine running. All we have to do is release the brake and push the throttle."

"Only we can't get to the cab without suffocating or getting eaten," Uallabh pointed out listlessly. Since his double brush with death, the fight seemed to have been knocked out of him.

"I can run through the carriages holding my breath." Ben Harper got to his feet. "What do the brake and throttle look like?"

"Two levers on the control panel. Green and red. Push them both forward."

"Don't be daft," Duncan had overheard the conversation. "You'd never make it that far."

"I'm a captain." Ben Harper gave a nervous smile. "I'm supposed tae go down with my ship. Well... train."

"No." Charlie joined in. "These things are after us, not you. It's all our fault. One of us will have to go."

"Oh, thanks, boy," Uallabh said caustically. By now, the rest of the passengers were listening intently.

"Why is it your fault? What do you mean?" Mrs McCusker was still desperately seeking an explanation of the surrounding madness.

"Now's not really the time to go into it." Charlie indicated the faint layer of yellow slowly spreading across the floor. "But our... eh... circus is fighting some very dark forces. We didn't mean you to get caught in the middle."

"What in the name of Harry's knitting are these?" Shadowjack was still foraging in the crates. He hauled a double tank, topped with a gauge, out of the straw packing. A mask on the end of a short tube dangled from the cylinders.

One of the crewmen came over and inspected the equipment.

"Scuba gear," he said. "Must be on route tae Wick. Divers use them for minor repairs on oil rigs."

Shadowjack just stared.

"I didn't understand any of that."

"You use them to breathe underwater, big man." Ben Harper gave a broad smile. "Or, if you're desperate enough, in a poisonous fog."

The Fight at the Pass of Shin

While Ben Harper checked the diving equipment for faults, an unspoken question hung in the air, as unpalatable as the fog outside.

"Who's going to go?" Peazle said finally.

"I will." Duncan, as usual, showed no hesitation.

"No. I'll go," Shadowjack butted in. "These tanks are heavy. I can carry them faster than the rest of you."

"Neither of you know anything about modern technology." Charlie looked up from the crate he was rummaging in.

"I can push a couple of levers well enough. And I certainly know how to breathe."

"It's not as easy as that," Ben Harper broke in. "I should do it. I've had experience with scuba gear."

"So has Uallabh, I'll bet," Peazle said, but the warrior simply scowled and shook his head.

"It has to be someone small." Lilly's voice cut through the argument. Charlie and Peazle looked at her in alarm and the other children scampered behind one of the crates.

"The carriages are full of thick fog," the girl continued. "Try to go fast, and you'll be crashing into seats and debris that you can't see until the Stoorworm cuts you down. But someone small can crawl along the aisle, between the seats, even with the tanks strapped on. It's the only way anyone will reach the cab."

She looked around at the others.

"I'm the smallest," she added unnecessarily. "It has to be me."

"Naw. That's suicide, lassie," Ben Harper objected.

"Eh. I can… actually… ehm… make myself invisible." Lilly said tentatively. "Only for a little while, but I have that much power, at least."

Her voice petered out as she realised that the whole box car was staring at her.

"Invisible, is it?" Paul Jessop raised a white flecked eyebrow. Ben Harper took off his hat and scratched his head.

"You're a wee bit more than a circus performer, aren't you?"

"A wee bit."

"That's why you can't go." Peazle put an end to the awkward discussion. "What happens if you do come across the Stoorworm? Magical creatures can't fight each other, remember?" He tapped his thin chest. "I'm as small as you. Can you make *me* invisible?"

Lilly nodded.

"Then it's settled." The boy pulled his bowler hat tightly onto his head. "As a pickpocket, I'm already an expert at not drawing attention to myself."

"Nice try." As Charlie spoke, a fresh rivulet of blood escaped from under the rim of Peazle's hat and trickled down his forehead. "But you can't see properly, even without any fog."

The boy was still pulling items from crates and studying them, stuffing some into pockets and discarding others. He straightened up, compared a fish knife he held in one hand to a grappling hook in the other, then gave both a tentative swing.

"I'm small. I've done scuba diving on holiday with my parents. Strap the tanks on me." The boy turned and spread his arms wide, weapon in each hand. "Go on, before I change my mind."

"The mist in here is getting thicker," Mrs McCusker said, furiously stuffing paper towels into a drill hole in the floor. "Whoever is going, better do it fast."

"I don't like this." Ben Harper picked up the tanks with a grunt and began to fasten them to Charlie's back. "Sending a wee boy."

"Really? I'm just loving it," Charlie replied acidly, his knees almost buckling under the weight of the tanks. He stood erect, not without some difficulty, and took a deep breath.

"Take Excalibur."

"He can't. The stupid thing is made of faerie silver and isn't affected by my weak magic." Lilly said irreverently. "I can't make it invisible."

"Hell. I've got half a dozen weapons." Charlie was wedging the fish knife in his belt and looking for somewhere to fasten the grappling hook. "I could start a war with what's in those crates."

"A wee blade's not going to make much of an impression on that big beast," Peazle said doubtfully.

"What do you want him to do? Charm his way past it?"

"Stop it, all of you." Lilly raised her arms, took a deep breath, and then thrust both hands forwards, fingers spread.

"Get ready, Charlie," she said. "Take care."

The boy vanished. There was a gasp from the crewmen and the children. The mothers stopped blocking up holes and stared in amazement.

"I'd be the world's best gamekeeper if I could do that," Paul Jessop whistled. "Aye, an poach on the side."

"Am I invisible?" The boy's trembling voice came from nowhere.

"Either that, or we've all gone blind," Duncan replied in an awed tone. "Shadowjack, hammer on the back of the carriage, distract that big worm thingie. Give Charlie a chance tae get oot the other way."

Shadowjack motioned the children and together, they began to yell and bang on the back of the baggage car.

There was a clank, a grunt and the sound of hollow breathing, like someone sucking noisily through a tube. The carriage door suddenly slid open and shut again. Then the sound was gone and so was Charlie.

As soon as he was through the sliding doors, the boy dropped to his knees and began to crawl. The fog in the carriage was so thick and murky it was like moving along the bottom of some polluted sea - Charlie couldn't even see his hands in front of him. Then he realised he couldn't see his hands anyway and chuckled, despite himself.

Inch by inch, he felt his way, the scuba tanks already causing his arm muscles to ache and his lungs to strain. Shards of glass littered the carriage floor and stuck in his palms until the boy bit his lip in pain. By the time he was halfway down the carriage, he was leaving little smears of blood on the dirty floor and his breath was coming in ragged gasps. Every few feet, the air tanks caught on the seats flanking him and he had to reverse and free them before carrying on. The silence was as thick as the fog, making his laboured breathing thunder in his ears.

There was no sign of the Stoorworm.

A shin-high yellow film now covered the floor of the baggage car, forcing the occupants to stand. The children were huddled together on top of one of the crates. Mrs McCusker and Mrs Mcnab had wrapped scarves around their mouths but were still bravely stopping up holes in the carriage wall with rags and paper.

"I shouldn't have let that wee laddie go." Ben Harper had his ear to the carriage door, listening for any sound of Charlie. "He's helluva brave, though."

"He most certainly is." Peazle sat miserably on a box, rag pressed against his bloody forehead. "Used scuba gear on holiday? His parents haven't two pennies to rub together. I bet he's never even been in a boat."

Charlie's head bumped into something solid. He reached out on either side, as far as he could, but there was no way past the barrier. For a second, he felt a rising panic, thinking he had taken some kind of wrong turn. Then he realised he had crawled the length of the second carriage and reached the door on the opposite side. He gave a silent prayer, for his back was aching, and his arms felt as if they might not support him much longer. With his body flat against the wood panel, he felt around above him until one lacerated hand grasped the handle. He cautiously slid the door open, scuttled through and began crawling again.

The fog had now reached the thighs of those in the baggage compartment. Duncan paced back and forth, scowling, still holding a sword in each hand. He hated being powerless to act, especially while Charlie was out there, risking his life.

"Best stay still, lad," said Sean, one of Harper's crewmen. "You're using up mair oxygen, doin that."

With a muttered curse, Duncan went and sat on a crate, where he had to make do with tapping his foot impatiently.

"I don't understand," Shadowjack said suddenly. "That fog outside is so thick you can't see an inch."

"I know. But all Charlie has to do is follow the aisle and he'll get there."

"I'm not talking about Charlie." The big man got off his crate and looked up at the little misted windows above. "How do Stoorworms see in it?"

Lilly clasped a hand to her mouth.

Realisation slowly spread over Ben Harper's face.

"They must be like sharks - hunting using smell as well as vision." He tapped his thick, bulbous nose.

"They don't have to see prey. They *smell* them."

Charlie was halfway through the front carriage, wheezing like a pair of bellows, when the Stoorworm struck. The boy felt a blast of hot air across his neck and the fog around him darkened under a huge shadow. Something slammed into his back with a force that crushed him to the ground, almost knocking the scuba mask from his face. His chest whacked against the carriage floor and his lungs emptied of air. The round back of the grappling hook bounced off a rib with so much force it almost broke. Fighting to suck oxygen into his empty lungs, Charlie could hear the creature's teeth grinding across the surface of the scuba tanks, as it tried to gain purchase on his exposed flesh. Snapping jaws slipped off the metal cylinder, and the worm pulled back with an enraged shriek.

Charlie scuttled forward but only gained a few feet before the creature attacked again. The boy twisted his head in time to see the Stoorworm filling the broken window and lunging toward him. Its slavering maw clamped onto the scuba tanks again. This time, the monster held on.

The Stoorworm reared up, pulling Charlie off his hands and knees and into the air like some fish caught on a hook. With its prey firmly locked in its jaws, the monster reversed out of the window, dragging the boy with it. Charlie clawed at his invisible waistband, trying to reach the fish knife. But the straps of the scuba gear had been pulled so tightly against his chest he couldn't get it free.

There was a deafening bang and Charlie shuddered violently in the air. The Stoorworm's teeth had ruptured one of the tanks! A jet of compressed oxygen shot into the creature's mouth, and it swung sideways with a choked cry. Charlie spun into the air, hit the opposite wall and landed on his back in one of the seats. The tanks smashed into his spine for a second time, sending a searing jolt of agony through his body. A surge of nausea rose in his throat and the boy's head swam. Oxygen hissed from the tank and enveloped him in a pure cloud, clearing the fog away and giving him a proper view of his attacker for the first time.

The Stoorworm was thrashing its head from side to side near the roof of the carriage, exhaling the poisonous oxygen from its gaping jaws in mighty puffs. It dipped its slobbering head towards the helpless boy and prepared for a final assault.

Charlie put his hand inside his jacket and pulled out another object he had found in the baggage car crate. When it was visible, it was a small red cylinder with a warning label on the side - a ship's emergency flare.

"I'd say this was an emergency," the boy growled through gritted teeth.

He pulled the trigger.

A plume of red poured from the barrel and shot into the Stoorworm's snarling mouth. The creature reared upwards in anguish, its head almost demolishing the roof. Billowing crimson smoke and flames erupted from the mighty jaws as the flare ignited the oxygen and exploded inside its throat.

For a moment, Charlie knew exactly what a dragon looked like.

Then the pale malevolent eyes glazed over, and the Stoorworm slid lifelessly out of the window.

The boy rolled off the seat and stumbled along the aisle, a jet of oxygen forcing enough of the fog aside to let him see the carriage door ahead. But the tank itself was almost empty and the boy's head was aching. He burst into the locomotive cab, felt for the levers on the control panel and pushed them. There was a throaty roar from the engine and the train lurched forward. Charlie lost his balance, stumbled and fell. Then blackness closed over him.

He awoke, lying stretched out on one of the seats. Outside, he could see the tops of trees floating past and a welcome wind blew in through the shattered window. Around him, a ring of concerned faces peered down.

"We owe you our lives, laddie," Ben Harper said, ruffling the boy's hair. His crewmen nodded in agreement. Paul Jessop winked at him. Mrs McCusker and Mrs Mcnab looked like they were ready to swoon with gratefulness and their children regarded him with something akin to hero-worship. Behind them, he could see the clan waving.

Only Uallabh held back, an odd expression of distaste on his face. Lilly pushed her way through to Charlie's side, leaned over and gave him a kiss on the lips.

"You are a real hero," she whispered.

The cab door slid open and the train driver's beaming face appeared round the frame.

"We've left all trace of thon fog behind," he announced happily. "The train will be arriving at Lairg station in a few minutes. Late as usual."

"You have our deepest gratitude, son." Ben Harper fingered the cap in his hand. "There are things going on with this strange band of yours that we cannae pretend tae understand. But, if we can do anything to help, we surely will."

He looked around.

"That means all of us."

The crewmen, women and kids nodded in agreement.

Charlie studied the ring of faces and a wild idea began to form in his mind. Ben Harper was big and had a beard. Sean was tall with a moustache. Mrs McCusker and Mrs McNab had three children between them. And now that the youngest of Harper's crew had removed his cap, Charlie saw that he had long black hair, like Duncan.

The boy sat up, wincing at the pain in his back.

"You want to help?" he said brightly. "As a matter of fact, I know exactly how you can."

Lairg

Inspector Archer was parked by the side of the road, mobile phone pressed to his ear, in a vain attempt to combat the devastating effect the surrounding mountains were having on reception.

"Is this Lairg station?" he yelled. "I'm trying to get some information about the Wick train… Wick! No. I'm with Birmingham CID… Yes, that's in England, I know. But I'm not there, I'm…"

Inspector Archer squinted through his windshield. Rich pastureland swept upward, fading into jagged peaks on either side of the single track road, as far as he could see. The tops of the mountains were drifting in and out of a rainy mist.

"I'm in the highlands somewhere… Look, I need to know if the Wick train has arrived in Lairg yet… Ah… right. Two hours late."

The Inspector held the phone away from his head as the station master launched into a shouted tirade about the disruption to the schedule making him miss his tea.

"Was there anything odd about the train?" Archer interrupted. "Broken windows, you say? Dents in the roof."

He grabbed his notebook and flipped it open. The station master had begun another heated monologue about how he had to clean up broken glass, that the carriages had been covered in muck that smelled of fish and how the train wasn't fit to continue its journey, so the passengers were going to have to wait till morning for the next one.

Inspector Archer took a deep breath.

"I'm looking for… certain individuals that might be among the passengers." He looked at the description of the graveyard party scribbled down by the Edinburgh police.

"I haven't got many details, but there are a couple of men. One is big with a beard. There's a girl, two boys and a youth with long hair." He hesitated, then plunged on. "Eh…. one of the children might be wearing a bowler hat. They're there? You're sure?"

The Inspector beeped his horn in triumph and a few startled sheep popped their dirty heads out of the gorse.

"Listen very carefully. I want you to call the local police. Give them my name and ID number and tell them to hold on to these people till I get to Lairg… No, I don't know where I am, but I'm on my way."

Inspector Archer gunned his car to life and spun back onto the road.

Darkness was finally falling. A narrow road skirted the edge of Gruid's wood. Beyond that, the River Shin was turning into a strip of ink. Duncan could no longer see the tree-lined embankment across the water where the clan had left the train. The engine driver had stopped briefly, a mile before Lairg, to let them off in the most thickly forested area he knew. They had waded across the river and hidden among the trees until dusk - the driver assured them this area was rarely visited. Then they had tried to snatch some sleep while they waited for night.

Half a dozen yellow streetlights sputtered to life in the distance, marking out Lairg's solitary main road. Duncan slipped back into the trees and began shaking each slumbering member of the clan.

"It's time tae leave," he informed the others, as they crawled reluctantly from the warmth of their sleeping bags. "It's dark enough, so nae birds will be flying, or unable to see us if they do."

He offered around a flask of ice-cold water from the river.

"I hope you got some sleep, for we'll have tae travel all night and quickly too. Leave everything that's not essential."

"Like our sanity," Charlie grunted. But Duncan was already heading out of the forest to keep look out on the narrow road that led in the direction of Lairg. The rest of the clan emerged warily from the trees.

"Wait a minute. Peazle's not here," Shadowjack glanced around. "His sleeping bag's empty."

"Och, that's all we need." Duncan snarled. "Does he no realise we have tae make thirty miles on foot this night and get through Lairg without being spotted besides? His wee legs winnae appreciate that, *withoot* any delays."

"Hush. Something's coming." Lilly held up a hand. They heard the sound of an engine, faint but steadily growing louder. The clan scattered, flattening themselves into the long grass on either side of the tarmac, watching a pair of headlights appeared over the brow of the hill. Monochrome fence posts, trees and scraggly grass bobbed in the double beams, as a tractor and trailer zigzagged erratically down the lane, drew alongside their hiding place and sputtered to a halt.

"I have to say, this is one of the biggest things I've ever stolen." A little light went on in the cab and Peazle's beaming face winked into existence. "Uallabh. Would you consent to take over? I've never really driven before and I can only work the pedals by standing. I can't see properly out the window either."

He hopped down from the cab and the warrior silently took his place. The rest of the clan climbed into the long, flatbed trailer, filled with bales of straw and covered in tarpaulin. Once they wriggled underneath the plastic covering, they were invisible from the air. If Morgana's spies were on the wing, they would see nothing more suspicious than a man driving through the night to make a dawn delivery.

Uallabh floored the accelerator and the tractor trundled off at a sedate but respectable speed. It rolled down Lairg's silent main street, encountering only one car on the way, then headed into the darkness again. The narrow road kept close to the shore of Loch Shin, though they could no longer see the water. The mountains on the other side of the highway had solidified into a black mass, craggy outlines only visible because they blocked out the stars.

On the tractor rattled, through Dalchork Wood and over Fiag Bridge, past the solitary Overscaig Hotel, its lights blazing at the rim of the dark forest. Fifteen miles further on, near the tip of Loch Shin, a tiny dirt track broke off from the road and headed west. Duncan sat up, tapped on the back of the cab and motioned in that direction. A few minutes later, they reached a scattering of lonely windows, curtains drawn, that marked the hamlet of Corrykinloch. Here, the track petered out, so Uallabh parked the tractor in a nearby field and the clan crept away from the last habitation that marked their journey. The highlander signalled ahead to where two solid chunks of blackness rose on either side of a near-invisible pass.

"Up there? In the dark?" Peazle's jaw dropped in disbelief.

"It's blacker than the Earl of Hell's waistcoat," Shadowjack chimed in.

"You'd rather wait till daylight? Get caught out crossing bare mountains withoot any cover?" Duncan shouldered his pack and fastened his sword to his side.

"Walk steadily and cautiously, and dinnae stray from my footsteps. If I can remember the way, we will reach the Falls by sunrise."

"And if you can't?"

"Then we'll end up dead at the bottom of a cliff." The highlander gave an uncharacteristic bark of laughter and set off into the night, eager to roam once more on the hills he dearly loved.

Inspector Archer pulled to a halt outside Lairg police station, a boxy two-story house with a single police sign on a pole in the garden. The door of the building opened as he walked up the path. A wedge of yellow light spilled over two begonias in plastic pots and a battered welcome mat.

"You made it safely then?" Lairg's only policeman, Constable MacDonald, shook the Inspector's hand and ushered him inside.

"Apart from almost getting run off the road by a tractor and trailer, I'm fine." The Inspector showed the constable his ID and badge, then removed his raincoat.

They were in a study that obviously doubled as the policeman's office. A child's push-along car lay, abandoned, in the middle of the floor and half a dozen wanted posters were tacked next to a picture of the Tweenies. With a jolt, Inspector Archer realised that the Tweenies actually looked more sinister.

"What's the story on the train passengers?" he said, quickly turning away.

"Not much." Constable MacDonald opened his notebook and scanned it. "Bunch of fishermen fae Wick. A Mrs McCusker, also from Wick, with her two children. Mrs McNab and her son are from just outside Tain. They all appear to be genuine."

The policeman shut his notebook and tossed it to the Inspector.

"And there's an old gamekeeper who wouldn't let go of his shotgun until I threatened to throw him in jail. But I wouldn't say he was the criminal type."

"Nobody called Charlie Wilson?" Archer frowned.

"Not as far as I know."

"Then I need to talk to whichever boy was wearing a bowler hat."

"There's not a lot of space - the holding area is full with that lot - but you can take him upstairs to my living room for some privacy. Tea?"

The constable plugged in an old electric kettle and got some chipped cups emblazoned with *Lairg Folk Festival 1987* from the cupboard.

"Mrs McCusker will have to be present too, seeing how it's her wee boy wi the hat and him being a minor."

The Inspector was standing in the living room, studying a dresser covered in family photographs and darts trophies, when Constable MacDonald ushered Mrs McCusker and her son in. He looked quizzically at Archer.

"I'm inspecting," the Inspector said. Constable MacDonald sighed and closed the door. Archer motioned for the mother and son to sit, and both sank nervously into an old floral sofa, which emitted a flurry of loud boings and almost swallowed them. The pair sat, pale and uncertain, hands trembling on knees which were now higher than their heads. There were a matching set of floral armchairs opposite that looked equally deadly, so the Inspector chose to stand and give himself a height advantage.

Archer had interviewed hundreds of witnesses before, but never with so little material to work on. He didn't even know what he was looking for - except Charlie Wilson, of course. Beside the dresser, a blue budgerigar in a cage puffed up its feathers and chirruped loudly. The boy was still wearing the bowler hat, as well as a bright yellow waistcoat.

"First, just let me just say that you're not in any trouble," the Inspector lied, leaning casually on the mantelpiece, his elbow lost among engraved China bells and miniature Wally Dugs. "I just need the answer to a couple of questions."

The boy nodded, wiping a tired, tear-streaked cheek.

"I need to know what you were doing in Birmingham a couple of days ago, that's all. With a lad called Charlie Wilson."

Mrs McCusker's lips tightened and the boy shook his head vehemently.

"I've never been south of Dundee, mister," he replied unhappily. "I live in Wick with my ma."

He looked at his mother for reassurance.

"Shouldn't we have a lawyer? I don't think we should say anything." The woman was sitting so rigidly she looked like her spine would fracture if anyone coughed.

"You have the right to remain silent..." the budgie whooped. Mrs McCusker glared at it.

"You don't need a lawyer. You're not under arrest." The Inspector addressed the boy again, ignoring Mrs McCusker, skilfully keeping the excitement out of his voice. He knew instinctively that the child was telling the truth - but both mother and son had given a small start at the mention of Charlie Wilson.

"Tell you what, I'll come clean with you if you do the same for me," he continued pleasantly. "What's your name?"

"Cormack."

"Mine is Walter."

The boy smiled.

"Yes. I don't tell many people that. Most call me Inspector." Archer smiled back. Then his mannerisms switched the way only an effective police officer's can.

"Charlie Wilson is in danger, isn't he? And he's only a kid, just like you."

He hammered home the point, even though he hated doing it.

"If something happens to Charlie because I can't find him in time, that *will* be your fault." He looked evenly at the boy, all trace of friendliness gone.

"Then you *are* in trouble."

Cormack's eyes opened wide and he gave a whimper. He looked at his mother again pleadingly.

"You say nothing, child." The woman fixed the Inspector with a steely glare. "But the policeman and I want to have a wee talk."

Cormack looked suddenly alarmed.

"Trust me, son," Mrs McCusker said gently. "C'mere."

She removed the bowler hat and kissed his head.

"Away to the loo and wash your face." She looked defiantly at the Inspector, daring him to detain her son further. When Archer gave no response, she gave the child a pat on the behind with the hat and shooed him out of the room.

"Nice young lad," said the Inspector once Cormack had gone. "You must be proud of him."

Mrs McCusker stayed silent.

"Strange that his clothes don't fit properly," the policeman added.

Mrs McCusker bristled but still said nothing. The Inspector sat on the coffee table across from her so that their heads were nearer the same height.

"I had a peep at the other passengers downstairs," he continued. "Some of their clothes don't fit either. Like they swapped outfits with someone else. As if they were decoys for a group that looked a bit like them."

The woman pointedly avoided his stare.

"I think Charlie Wilson and his... eh... friends were on your train. I think they got off somewhere before Lairg. I think you and the other passengers are covering for them. I just don't know why."

The Inspector leaned farther forwards, forcing himself into Mrs McCusker's line of sight.

"I think you called and reported a monster attacking the train."

Mrs McCusker looked down and the budgie blew a raspberry.

Archer moved closer to the unresponsive woman and whispered in her ear.

"And I think I'm the only policeman in the world who'd believe that phone call wasn't a hoax."

The Inspector picked up the bowler hat from the couch and removed a shard of glittering glass.

"I investigate cases of missing children, Mrs McCusker," he said softly, still inches from her ear. "I *believe* in monsters. For once, I'd like to save a child from once, before it's too late."

Tears glistened in Mrs McCusker's eyes.

"Everything *I* believe in has been sorely tested, Inspector," she said finally. "If Charlie Wilson and his friends are being chased by something evil, and I know they are, I've no proof it's not you."

She struggled to get out of the low-slung couch and the Inspector stood and offered his hand.

"As a matter of fact, I think you are genuine," the woman said breathlessly as Archer pulled her to her feet. "But I promised my son I wouldn't talk and I don't think any of the rest of the passengers will either. So, if we're not under arrest, my kids and I will be finding a hotel room for the night."

Mrs McCusker turned to see her son smiling at her from the doorway, his face washed and hair combed.

"Keep the hat." She took Cormack's hand and swept out of the room.

"Fair cop guv," the budgie squeaked.

Archer collapsed wearily into the patterned armchair, bowler on his knees, passing the rim idly through his fingers. He tried it on his head but it was too small. On impulse, he turned it over and looked inside. A tiny bit of paper was sticking out of the crepe lining. With trembling fingers, the Inspector unfolded it.

It was a small section of a touring map showing the area around Lairg. One name had been circled in black pen.

Eas a Chual Aluinn Falls.

He got out his mobile and dialled. It was answered at the first ring.

"Mrs Wilson?" he said. "I think I know where your son is going."

Heading for the Falls

Charlie had almost come to terms with leading a dangerous life. You tried not to think about it until something bad actually happened - then you simply responded. If you responded by not running away, you were considered brave. Charlie didn't think he was particularly brave and his courage was now being sorely tested. Climbing these highland hills, with nothing but cloud riddled moonlight to light the way, brought on a slow creeping dread. The clan were moving across steep, uneven terrain pocked with hidden holes and warrens that would have been perilous in broad daylight. After a couple of hours, everyone's legs, lungs and hearts were aching, but that was not the worst part. Hostile inclines with summits that vanished into the blackness loomed on every side, creating a world of sinister shadows - and every crack of a twig had Charlie's heart in his mouth. Twice, they found themselves feet away from the edge of a near-invisible cliff and retreated in panic.

As he walked, the boy kept repeating one of the last things his father had told him.

There are two great virtues that a man can have. One is knowing what is right. The other is doing what is right.

The words comforted and kept him going, even when he longed to give up and lie down, exhausted, in the heather.

He had obviously paid more attention to his father than he realised. The boy missed his dad all the more for that.

Duncan walked at the head of the clan throughout the night, worried in a different way. He had only been in this area twice before, both times in daylight - and that was almost two centuries ago. But he had taken time to memorise the lay of the land on Peazle's map - which was a good job, since the pickpocket had left it in Lairg by mistake. And he had a highlander's natural sense of direction and feeling for how the mountains lay.

Unerringly, he led them along the side of Creag Riabhach and up and around Loch Nan Sgaraig. They slid on their backsides into the black unknown that finally levelled out at the waters of Gorm Loch Mor, then followed its tributary along the floor of a steep valley that Duncan hoped would come out near the Falls.

He was right. After hours of stumbling through the midnight ravines, they heard a low hiss, rising to a rumble that eventually turned into a roar. Duncan signalled a halt.

"Well. We cannae see the Falls, but there is nae doubt we are close."

Charlie looked at the luminous dial of his watch.

"There's still a couple of hours till dawn," he said. "Maybe we should try and catch a little kip."

"Excellent suggestion." Shadowjack and Peazle already had their sleeping bags out of their rucksacks and were climbing in. Charlie opened his own pack, his frozen fingers fumbling at the strings. With an exhausted groan, he unrolled his sleeping bag, climbed in, and immediately fell asleep.

The boy woke to see a narrow grey light outlining the horizon. He forced his gummy eyes open and looked around. The clan were strewn around him in an array of red and blue bags, only the tops of their heads visible. The boy propped himself up on one elbow. In front of him, the valley opened out into a flat glen ringed by mountains, though it was still too dark to make out more details of the landscape. Still, there was no mistaking the area. This was once the home of Gorrodin - the same place he had seen after drinking Jack Thane's potion.

Uallabh was sitting on a rock, with his back to the rest of the group, staring at the cold glow of dawn spreading across the east. Charlie wriggled out of the bag and crawled over to him.

The warrior was wearing the long oilskin coat that used to belong to one of the fishermen. Wrapped around him like a cloak, it didn't look much different from his normal attire. Charlie sat on the wide rock next to him.

"You are a brave fighter indeed, lad," Uallabh said without looking at him.

"So are you."

The warrior remained motionless.

"I have fought to keep alive, that's all."

"No. You could have handed over the cup to us and gone safely on your way. You didn't."

Uallabh began to protest, but Charlie held up his hand.

"You are a truly noble warrior." The boy hesitated. "You've just lost your nerve."

Startled, Uallabh glanced sideways at him.

"What gave me away?"

"Yesterday on the train. You jumped when a branch hit the window. It was more than just a reflex. You were scared."

"I was." The warrior turned and fixed cold grey eyes on Charlie. "Over the centuries, I have seen all the horrific things people can do to each other. I don't like humanity, and I long ago grew tired of this world. Yet, I have also travelled the globe and seen its natural beauty. I have fought so many times to stay breathing that maybe living is just a habit."

He unfastened the buttons on the weatherproof jacket.

"Whatever the reason, I'm afraid to die, son."

Uallabh brought out a gun from inside the coat and began to check the mechanism with the practised motions of an expert in firearms.

"I was once a fearless fighter. Now I'm just a killer, scared of where his next enemy will strike."

His voice held no trace of pity, either for his victims or for himself.

"Wait here." Charlie got up and ran back to his sleeping bag. He pulled Excalibur from its holder and returned.

The rising sun was beating back shadows across a beautiful heather covered valley. Beyond that Eas a Chual Aluinn Falls cascaded down the mountainside - half in darkness, half in light - its upper waters sparkling like molten silver.

"You can't be tired of all the people in this world." He indicated behind him where the clan were beginning to stir. "Not all of us are bad, are we?"

Once more, an image of Charlie's father sprang into the boy's mind. His dad, who had offered to give up the life he had chosen, to waste away in some bank for the love of his son. The boy had never thought of it that way before.

"If there comes a time when nobody is willing to sacrifice themselves for those they care about," he said. "Then you can truly give up on humanity."

The warrior looked morbidly across the lightening landscape.

"You know as well as I that Morgana won't have left this place completely undefended," he said.

The boy reached out his hand for the gun.

"Why don't I take that?" he asked. "And you take the sword. Like you used to when you were with King Arthur. We'll go and fight together."

Uallabh picked up Excalibur and held it in front of him, watching its blade glint in the crisp radiance of dawn. The warrior slid the gun back into his coat and stepped down off the rock.

"No. If this sword ever belonged to someone other than Arthur, it surely belongs to you." He knelt before Charlie, holding out the weapon, hilt first.

"My Lord," he said, bowing his head.

Surprised, Charlie took the handle. On impulse, he laid the blade gently on Uallabh's shoulder. The warrior clasped both hands together in acknowledgement, then stood and looked out across the valley.

"Let us go to battle."

And he turned and walked into the rising sun.

Gorrodin

The clan stared up at the sheer face of the mountain called Leiter Dhuibh. Light inched across the valley floor, pushing the last shadows into mossy corners as the sun gained height. Half a mile to the left, Eas a Chual Aluinn Falls arced over the top of a sheer incline, then dropped in drifting plumes of white, five hundred feet into a churning river. The air was damp with spray, even at this distance, and the clan shivered in the shady strip at the base of the cliff. Lilly stood in front of the group, Gorrodin's talisman held tightly against her body.

"Where's the cave?" Shadowjack Henry scrutinised the craggy precipice but could see no sign of an entrance.

"Hidden." Lilly's voice was tense, her face a mixture of anxiety and anticipation. "One simple word will open and close it, but not without the key."

She held up the glowing wooden cup.

"This is the key."

"What's the password?" Peazle asked. "It's not Open Sesame, is it?"

"That's two words."

"It is my real name," Lilly said simply. "Nimve."

"Heather. Lilly. Nimve." Peazle smirked. "How many handles do you *have*?"

But the others were staring past him. The pickpocket turned and his eyes widened.

The bottom of the cliff was slowly peeling open, bending back on itself like burning paper. The ground began to shake and, with a tooth jarring reverberation, rock parted from solid rock, until a crack the height of a two-story house snaked up the stone face.

A few loose boulders fell and rolled onto the grass, then there was silence. The clan shuffled around uneasily while Lilly stood immobile, staring intently into the dark fissure.

Gorrodin emerged.

He was tall and thin and wore a dark green cloak over a silver tunic. A battered leather bag hung by his side. His face was pale and drawn, but his eyes were as bright and green as the most precious emeralds.

He saw his daughter. And, for the first time in nearly a thousand years, Gorrodin smiled.

Lilly dropped the Grail and ran to him, launching herself into her father's arms, laughing uncontrollably. Gorrodin swept her round, holding her tight, his grateful face pressed against the girl's cheek. Eventually, he put her down and knelt, both hands resting on her shoulders.

"You have remained a child, Nimve," he said softly, stroking her hair.

"I did not want to grow up without you," she replied. Gorrodin clutched her to him again, as if he would never let the girl go.

Charlie felt his own tears welling and Peazle wiped at his eyes with a grubby sleeve. Uallabh and Duncan looked at the ground and Shadowjack coughed and patted his chest, trying to stop emotions getting away with him.

"I'd say our quest was worth this moment alone," he croaked.

Gorrodin finally released his child.

"I feel I have slept for an age," he said to her. He had not even looked at the rest of the clan. "You must show me all, Nimve."

"It's Lilly now, Father."

"Very well, Lilly. Let me see." He placed willowy fingers on either side of the girl's head and stared into her eyes for a long time.

"He's doing his magic thingie," Peazle explained.

At last Gorrodin relaxed, letting both arms fall to his sides.

"Ah," he said sorrowfully. "I see."

He stood up, placing a protective hand on Lilly's arm, and faced the others.

"I can never thank you enough for what you have done. What powers I possess will always work in your favour. You have my word."

He spotted the Grail lying in the grass. Taking his daughter's hand, he walked over and picked it up. But he did not look pleased to see his talisman.

"Morgana will not have left my place of imprisonment unguarded." The wizard looked quickly around. "There was a Thin Place on yonder hill. I sense it is still open, so we must make haste towards it. I have a lifetime of love to shower on my daughter and more thanks to give you, which will all be for nought if we do not flee."

"But you hae your Grail," Duncan broke in. "I'm sorry, wizard, but I dinnae understand. Surely you can use it tae defeat Morgana?"

The wizard looked unhappily at the cup in his hand.

"No, highlander," he said. "I allowed her to control it, too. She had my blessing." The wizard clenched his teeth, remembering his own gullibility. "It belongs to her as much as me and I cannot turn it against her."

He took a deep breath.

"My friends… the situation is far worse than that."

"It can get worse?" Peazle asked incredulously.

"The Grail is glowing." Gorrodin held out the cup, which pulsed with unnatural light. "The Dolorous Stroke has been struck."

The wizard stuffed the cup roughly into his bag, as if he could no longer bear to look at it.

"Come with me to the Thin Place," he said. "I will tell the story as we walk, for it is one you must know.

But gather round close and keep constant watch for danger."

The clan bunched around the wizard. Gorrodin set off across the valley at a brisk pace, talking as he went.

"Long ago in Galhadria," he said. "There was a terrible civil war. When it was finally over, the greatest sorcerers of the land plotted to make sure it would never happen again…"

"Master Gorrodin, I've… eh… already told them the story of the Dolorous Stroke," Peazle interrupted. "That it means one magical creature has killed another."

"Have you, child?" Gorrodin's bright green eyes darted from place to place, scanning every rock and hollow. "Did you know I added my own small enchantment to the Great Spell?"

The pickpocket shook his head.

"My talisman would begin to glow if ever the Dolorous Stroke took place. A warning of impending doom, you might say."

He stopped. The others were still looking expectantly at him.

"Ah. You do not understand," he said. "It will shine only if the fatal blow was struck by one of my own kind."

"You mean…" Lilly began.

"I mean, a Galhadrian has slain one of the Gorrodin Rath." Gorrodin placed a hand gently on his daughter's head. "Though we may escape through a Thin Place, it will only delay the inevitable." He quickened his stride. "Galhadria is doomed."

"The cup began to glow eight months ago," Uallabh said. Lilly shot a startled look at Charlie.

"Wasn't that... around the time you killed Mordred?" she muttered.

"It could not be the boy," Gorrodin cut in. "Excalibur is magical, and they obviously have a bond - but he is only a human."

He squinted at Charlie.

"Unless you have used the Grail to change yourself."

"Not a chance." The boy shook his head.

"He has not, father. I can vouch for that."

Gorrodin allowed himself a resentful sneer.

"Then I suspect Jack Thane's hand in this. He was always too rash, and I imagine he dealt the Stroke himself. He may think otherwise, but his arrogance will lead to a war that, ultimately, he cannot win."

"What should we do?"

"What Thane wanted from you in the first place," the wizard said. "We must escape to Galhadria and keep the Grail out of Morgana's hands. Even if we cannot defeat her, it will slow her down and give us some respite. "

"Gorrodin." Peazle pulled at the wizard's bag. "There are children in the valley."

The Changelings

They looked in the direction the pickpocket was pointing. A crowd of little figures were pouring into the valley, jabbering and singing, heading towards the clan. All looked thin and malnourished, their hair wild and matted, bodies wrapped in rags. But they scampered across the heather with a skipping run, yelling to each other like normal youngsters at play.

"Get ready to fight," Gorrodin whispered. "I am weak from my captivity and it will take time to replenish my strength. Yet I may be able to hold them at bay until you reach the safety of the Thin Place."

"No, father!" Lilly whispered, clutching his hand.

"They're just children," Shadowjack grunted. "Not much of an adversary, I'd say."

"They are not children," Gorrodin snapped. "They are Changelings."

Beside the wizard, Duncan bristled.

"What are we dealing with here?" Charlie gripped Excalibur tighter, his palms sweating.

"Galhadrians can be... thoughtless." Gorrodin's face was stony as he searched for the right words. "It was worse in days gone by, though I have no time for explanations." He looked towards the laughing crowd.

"Occasionally, Galhadrians would bear children in which magic had gone wrong." His expression was still blank, but he could not keep the shame from his voice. "When this happened, the parents might... steal a human baby and leave their own in its place."

He was barely whispering now.

"The humans named these impostors Changelings."

"I'd say that was a devil's sight more than thoughtless," Duncan growled, and Gorrodin hung his head.

The children had begun to spread out in a line, still chattering and waving to each other. The clan kept a wary eye on them.

"Most Changelings were killed by the humans as soon as they realised what had befallen their real offspring," the wizard continued in a contrite tone. "But some escaped to the desolate parts of the highlands, and there they banded together in packs - cursed with a ravenous, never-ending hunger."

"How could they have survived here undetected?"

"Morgana must have locked them away too, to be set upon me if I was ever released."

"I don't understand." Peazle looked at the mangy children, now standing in a line between the clan and the Thin Place. "They don't look like much."

"Not until you see their teeth."

Then the row of children opened their mouths, the jaws stretching wider and wider until they seemed to come unhinged. The movement wrinkled up their noses and narrowed their eyes into slits. From each innocent face, two rows of drooling fangs thrust forwards. They roared in unison, a desolate, terrifying ululation that echoed through the valley. It sounded like the end of the world.

Uallabh dropped his pistols and ran.

"Uallabh, no!" Charlie shouted, but the warrior was already sprinting across the heather. The Changelings, seeing the clan weakened, moved forwards with grotesque prances, surrounding them in a snarling ring.

"Forget him," Duncan snapped, clutching his sword in both hands. "Form a circle facing out, all of you."

Peazle snatched up Uallabh's guns, cocked them and handed one to Lilly. The ring of Changelings began to slowly tighten, as the creatures moved towards them, baring naked fangs.

"Your weapons will do little good against these creatures," Gorrodin said grimly. "Nor a sword made of steel, highlander."

He glanced at Excalibur.

"That will cause some damage, but not enough to save us, I fear."

"I will fight with what I have," Duncan replied and Shadowjack flexed his huge muscles, preparing to defend his friends with bare hands.

"As will I," Gorrodin agreed. But defeat hung heavy in his tone. The wizard ran his fingers tenderly through Lilly's curly hair.

"I am sorry for this, my daughter. All the oceans of this world cannot match the depths of my regret."

Lilly kissed her father's hand and held it against her cheek.

"I will work what defensive magic I can." Gorrodin reached into the bag hanging by his side for his talisman. A look of panic spread across his face.

"The cup is not here!" He rummaged inside the empty satchel. "What treachery is this?"

The clan looked at each other, equally mystified.

"I took it." Peazle stepped forward. "Not difficult for a pickpocket." He indicated the advancing Changelings, creeping ever closer. "You were all rather... distracted."

"Where is it, boy!?"

"I gave it to Uallabh." Peazle looked at the angry faces all around him. "It was his idea! He said he had a plan!"

The clan spun around. The warrior was still running, his long red hair streaming behind, growing smaller with every yard he covered. With a start, they realised he was heading for Gorrodin's cave.

The Changelings were looking in the same direction.

Uallabh reached inside his coat and pulled out the Grail. Without breaking stride, he hoisted it above his head. A furious howl rose from the circle of sinister children. As one, they streamed after the fleeing figure.

"No!" Charlie raised his sword and ran after them. With a flying tackle, Duncan brought him crashing to the ground.

"Let him go, Charlie," the highlander urged, lying on top of the struggling boy. "Uallabh is carrying out the oath he swore to Arthur. He is protecting the Grail."

The Changelings caught the fleeing warrior as he reached the mouth of the cave. Charlie's last sight of his friend was a tiny figure covered in clawing, biting creatures, disappearing into the crevasse. His final roar drifted out of the darkness, as the last of the Changelings poured into the mountain after him.

"Nimve!" he cried with his dying breath. The cup came flying out of the closing gap and landed on the grass.

There was a shuddering sigh, and the two sides of the cliff face swung shut. Charlie clapped both hands over his eyes to blot out the sight. The rest looked on, stunned.

"We are safe." Gorrodin's voice was a hoarse whisper. "But the cost was high, indeed."

"We made him leave his coffin behind," Shadowjack said to no one in particular.

Peazle stood apart from the rest, shaking uncontrollably.

"I didn't know," he whispered. "I didn't know he was going to do *that*."

Shadowjack put his arm around the trembling boy while Lilly fetched the Grail. Duncan stood and pulled Charlie roughly to his feet.

"I was wrong to doubt him," the highlander said quietly. "He was a fine warrior and a good man."

He tried to sound tough but his voice was uneven and his hands shook.

"Look!" Lilly indicated a nearby hillock.

A tall figure was striding towards them, a bowler hat under one arm. The stranger was covered in mud and tufts of heather - but under the grime, he appeared to be wearing a suit and raincoat. Duncan's sword was raised in a flash and the rest of the clan tensed to attack, their desperation replaced by anger.

"Hey, I'm one of the good guys." The man held up a hand in surrender. "My name is Inspector Archer of Birmingham CID."

"Nice to meet you," Peazle said. "I see you have my hat."

The clan sat on a grassy hill beside the Thin Place. They had told Inspector Archer their story and the policeman looked suitably stunned.

"What will you do now?" he asked the seated figures.

"With the Grail in my possession, Morgana no longer has any reason to pursue Charlie," the wizard replied. "You may take him home, Archer. I gather that is why you are here."

"What *will* Morgana do?"

"She will rally her army in Toth and prepare for war. Even without the cup, they are a mighty force, and the Dolorous Stroke means they will surely win."

Gorrodin smiled wanly at the others.

"The rest of you are free as well. You may return to Galhadria or stay on earth. You choose."

"I'll stay," Duncan said fiercely. "The devil himself couldnae find me in these hills, and I am done with Jack Thane."

"What about you, wizard?" Peazle asked.

"I shall go to Galhadria. The Lords will not welcome me, but they shall need my help in the battle that will soon come." Gorrodin looked fondly at Lilly. "First, I would have a little time to know my child again."

The rest nodded, understanding. Charlie looked at Gorrodin, arm still round his daughter, then at the Inspector. Archer caught his glance.

"God knows how we're going to explain this to your parents," he said. Charlie's hair was matted with blood and dirt and his clothes were in shreds. "Better start thinking up a good excuse."

He reached out his hand to the boy.

Charlie blinked hard. The rest of the group got up and gathered awkwardly around him, not knowing what to say. The boy choked back a sob and straightened his shoulders.

"Where are *you* going, Peazle?"

"To Galhadria," Peazle said. "I shall help Gorrodin prepare for war against Morgana. For all the Lord's faults, their home is my home now."

"Then take this." Charlie handed over Excalibur. "I won't be needing it anymore."

"I will go with you, Peazle," Shadowjack said. "I understand there's not much work here for blacksmiths these days.

They both looked round at Duncan.

"Ach, so will I," the highlander sighed. "You'd be lost without me and fighting is what I know best."

"Naturally, I will accompany my father," Lilly said.

"I hae a brother," Duncan turned to the Inspector. "He went missing when he was just a baby. I've not found him so far."

Inspector Archer looked at the spot where the Changelings had been trapped. He reached out and shook the highlander's hand.

"I'll keep my eyes open."

"Then let us depart.

"Wait." Peazle looked ashamed. "Before we leave, there is something I must tell you."

His face had gone bright red.

"I have kept it to myself and had no intention of carrying it out. But I fear it may be important."

The rest of the group looked at him quizzically.

"I was given a secret mission by Jack Thane." Peazle sat down on a rock. "And I have the horrible feeling it was the real reason he sent a former pick-pocket to find Charlie."

"Out with it, young man," Gorrodin commanded.

"I was told to steal a silver bear on a chain around his neck and give it to Thane."

Gorrodin went white.

"A silver bear?" he repeated quietly. "That cannot be."

"I'm afraid it can."

The voice came from behind them. Charlie whirled, recognising it immediately.

"*Mum*?"

"Hello, my boy. I cannot tell you how delighted I am to see you."

Charlie's mother and father stood a few feet away, as if they had appeared from nowhere.

The Reunion

"Mum!" Charlie ran over and squeezed the woman. "I'm sorry! You must have been so worried."

He turned awkwardly to his dad.

"I have a good excuse, I promise."

"I don't doubt it." His father hugged him. "And it's us who should apologise."

"What? *Why*?"

"We have been in hiding for a long, long time." His mother said sadly. "And you have become the victim of our deception."

"I don't understand." Charlie looked at his parents, but they were staring at Gorrodin.

"I never thought to set eyes on you both again," the Wizard smiled.

"Wait." Charlie felt like his head might explode. "You *know* each other?"

"Very well." Gorrodin strode forwards and threw his arms around Charlie's mum. "This is my sister Ganieda, one of the Lords of the Western Wilderness."

He released the woman and clasped Charlie's father by the hand.

"Words cannot express how glad I am to set eyes on you again, my liege."

"My *liege*." Charlie almost fell over. "That's my father."

"Is it, now?" Gorrodin regarded the boy with something approaching awe. "I know him by another name."

He gave a small smile.

"This is the great warrior king, Arthur."

"Just hold on a minute!" the boy stammered. "I saw Arthur when I drank the potion Peazle gave me. He didn't look anything like dad!"

"A potion Peazle got from Jack Thane," his mother replied grimly. "I'm sure he added his own little enchantment to make sure you did not recognise your father and discover your true lineage."

"Why would he do that?"

"Using people is Jack's speciality," Charlie's mum said. "Which is always easier if he keeps vital information from them."

There was a stunned silence from the rest of the group. Finally, Peazle knelt, taking off his bowler.

"I am at your service, my liege."

The rest followed suit.

"My dad is King Arthur, and my mum is one of the Little People," Charlie muttered. "I'm finding this a bit difficult to take in."

"Sit, all of you." Charlie's mum plonked herself on a flat stone. "My boy deserves to hear the truth about us, and the rest of you must know it too."

They dutifully sat.

"I have hidden my powers for longer than I can remember," she said sadly. "Concealed my talisman so none could ever find me. Never thought I would need it again, but that time of innocence is obviously over."

She held out her hand to Charlie.

"May I have it back for a while?"

"Here." The boy pulled the chain over his head and handed the silver bear to her.

"I will return it in due course for, as my heir, I bestowed it upon you." She cupped the talisman in her hand.

"You sound different, mum," Charlie said anxiously.

"I love you with all my soul," the woman replied. "But please refer to me as Ganieda, or my Lady, from now on."

"*Seriously?*"

"Where we're going, mum doesn't sound powerful enough." She winked at him. "And I must assert myself with the other wizards of Galhadria. So, I better get used to their stuffy way of talking again."

"You are coming with us?" Gorrodin asked.

"We are. For the fate of both worlds hangs in the balance."

She waved a hand in the air.

"But first, you must know our story."

"Go on then," Charlie said. "It might help me get my head around the fact that my mother is a sorceress and my father is king bloody Arthur."

Sparks flew from Ganieda's fingertips and the clan watched as a picture formed in the air.

Arthur lay dying on the battlefield. Clustered around him were his few surviving knights: Lucan, Bedivere, Griflet, and Blioberis. Morgana and the remaining Gorrodin Rath had fled, and the battlefield was awash with blood and bodies.

"My king's wounds are too severe for him to live much longer." Lucan shook his head miserably. "The Round Table is no more."

"This need not be so." A woman appeared beside them, dressed in an emerald dress. "My name is Ganieda and I shall tend to his injuries."

She placed slim hands on the gaping wound splitting Arthur's chest and a strange glow emanated from her fingers. Slowly, the gash began to heal.

"You are Galhadrian," Griflet gasped. "Like Gorrodin, Arthur's old adviser."

"Why did your people not aid us when we needed you most?" Lucan spat. "We thought ourselves your allies."

"I stood by and watched when they banished my brother, Gorrodin," Ganieda replied bitterly. "Now he is imprisoned and I do not know where."

She bowed her head.

"And yes, we did nothing when you were slaughtered fighting a race that will become our enemies."

She stood and waved her arm. A glowing blue circle appeared a few yards away.

"And so, I am done with my people," she said defiantly. "Belvedere, gather all the silver and use it to block up the tunnels where the remaining Gorrodin Rath hide. I shall take Arthur to a place of safety and give him time to heal properly."

"Thank you, my Lady."

"It is I who should thank you. I shall shield my talisman, remain in the world of men and the Lords of the Western Wilderness will never find me."

She picked up Arthur as if he were feather light, stepped through the portal and vanished.

"I tended to Arthur until he was fit and well. In the process, we fell in love." Ganieda glanced at her husband, who blew her a kiss.

"Oh, please don't do that," Charlie blushed.

"Had I any thoughts of returning to Galhadria, they were gone."

"Ganiedia's magic kept me young," Arthur said. "We changed our names and travelled the world for centuries, with no plans other than to live our lives in peace."

His wife's face clouded.

"The Lords of the Western Wilderness *did* have plans, however." She waved her hand again. "They always do."

Now, the clan were transported to Galhadria, where Jack Thane was addressing the other wizards.

"We made a grievous error in allowing Arthur's knights to be destroyed," he said. *"It prompted Ganieda to leave us and we cannot locate her."*

"Then we will do without," Tom Lincoln shrugged. *"We are weakened but no one dare challenge us."*

"There will always be potential enemies on our borders," Thane countered. *"Yet we cannot subdue them without risking the Dolorous Stroke."*

"Do you have a solution?"

"Yes. We will resurrect the Round Table."

"That will be a feat, indeed," Mabon scoffed. *"There are only a handful left."*

"Arthur was sometimes called The Knight With 1,000 Eyes," Thane countered. *"Do you know why?"*

"We have no interest in human gossip."

"Because he sent 500 of his most upright warriors far and wide. They were dispatched to do good deeds and fight oppression wherever they went."

"That is noble, if rather pointless," Math said. *"What of it?"*

"It was brilliant," Thane sighed. *"On one hand, it ensured that Arthur was known and revered in the most far-flung lands. It also showed his strength. If he could afford to send his finest men so far from home, how mighty must his kingdom be?"*

"So, he was a fairly able tactician." Prestor John was unimpressed. "What use is that to us?"

"When the Round Table was destroyed, the 1,000 Eyes saw no point in returning. Instead, they settled where they were and raised families of their own."

"I begin to see what you are getting at," Math said.

"Suppose we were to... take descendants of these knights to Galhadria? Raise them to be mighty warriors from birth?" Thane paused to let the idea sink in. "We can send them to Alabarra, The Wooded Kingdom and Monshorn. Anywhere that potential enemies might lurk. There, they can perform the same function for Galhadria as they did on earth."

"That is very clever."

"They will roam the wilderness, dispatching our foes and earning the gratitude of the inhabitants. And, because they are not magical, there will be no Dolorous Stroke."

He tapped his chin slyly.

"If one knight should be killed, we will simply replace him with another."

"That is a shrewd idea indeed," Tom Lincoln chuckled. "Let us put it to the vote."

Every one of the Lords raised their hands.

"The wizards *did* take my brother," Duncan cried. "And then lied tae me about it!"

He looked angrily at Charlie's mum.

"Could ye no have done something?"

"I have been in hiding for centuries," Ganieda shook her head. "Even if I had not left, I would have been outvoted and powerless to stop it."

Her eyes glinted with steely resolve.

"But things have changed. My own brother is free again and the Lords are in dire straits. They need us. That gives us leverage."

She laid a hand on Duncan's arm.

"I will unite you with your brother. You have my word."

"I will hold ye to that."

"What about Charlie?" Peazle asked. "Where did he come into your plans?"

"My wife and I have always been happy with each other," Arthur said. "But, eventually, our lives felt incomplete."

"So, we had a child," Ganieda finished his sentence. "Who we love dearly."

"And who is half Galhadrian." Gorrodin paled. "A magical creature."

"Why, thanks," Charlie blushed. "But I don't have any spell casting abilities. I must take after my dad."

"It doesn't matter." Lilly put a hand to her mouth. "You killed Mordred."

"Who was also a magical creature." Gorrodin clasped his hands together.

"Charlie. It was *you* who delivered the Dolorous Stroke and doomed Galhadria."

Castle Alclud

"How was I to know?" the boy objected. "Honestly, I get the blame for everything."

"Nobody is blaming you, son," Arthur assured him. "The fault is ours for hiding your lineage."

"We just wanted you to have a normal life," Ganieda said. "It did not work out quite the way we'd hoped."

"You *think*?"

"Galhadria may be condemned but I'm going to fight for it, anyway." Duncan stuck out his chest. "It's the only way to find my brother."

"Speak for yourself," Peazle frowned. "I'm certainly having second thoughts now."

"The Lords are a rum bunch, I'll agree," Shadowjack rumbled. "But the common folk of Galhadria always treated me well. I cannot stand by and let them die."

"You don't understand," Ganieda snapped. "Jack Thane has no honour or scruples. I am sure he has thought of a plan to achieve victory."

"That's good, isn't it?" Charlie asked. "What do you suppose he intends to do?"

"All I know is that he was desperate to get his hands on your cup, brother." His mother held up the silver bear. "And my talisman."

She turned to Peazle.

"He asked you to steal it for him, did he not?"

"He did." The boy went red again.

"Either would greatly increase the Lords' power." The wizard tapped his long nose. "But nothing can break the Great Spell. The Dolorous Stroke means the Gorrodin Rath cannot lose."

"Then, why did Thane want our talismans so badly, if they would do him no good in battle?"

"I have no idea."

"Nor I. And the only way I can find out his scheme is to go to Galhadria with you."

Inspector Archer coughed loudly and they all stared at him.

"Can I come too?" he asked. "This seems like a once-in-a-lifetime experience, plus I've still got a few days of paid vacation left."

"Ye certainly may." Duncan clapped him on the back. "Do you have a sword?"

"Sorry, no."

"Nae matter. We'll pick something up when we get there. Are ye right or left-handed?"

"Does it matter?"

"I dinnae suppose so."

"When we arrive, follow my lead," Gorrodin commanded. "No matter what may transpire."

He clapped thin hands and a misty blue glow spread across the top of the hillock.

Jack Thane faced the rest of the Lords in the Whale Room. Each one regarded him stonily.

"The Gorrodin Rath will attack any day now," Baubi Ross said. "You have run out of time to deliver on your grand promises."

Thane shuffled from foot to foot.

"There has been a delay…" he began.

"You have nothing!" Tom Lincoln snapped. "If we did not need you to help us fight, you would be in chains right now."

"I have recalled the Round Table from the far-flung corners of our lands. They are formidable fighters."

"That will do no good!"

"I… Eh…" For once, Thane was lost for words.

A shimmering glow appeared in the corner of the room. As the Lords gaped, Gorrodin and Ganieda stepped through, followed by Arthur, Peazle, Duncan, Shadowjack, Charlie, Lilly and Inspector Archer.

Jack Thane recovered quickly.

"I believe reinforcements have arrived."

Jenny Haa and Will Thorn were on their feet in an instant.

"You dare invade our hall, Gorrodin. You have been banished."

"Nor are *you* welcome, Ganieda," Prestor John spat. "You deserted us long ago for some human."

"You will address my wife as *Mistress* Ganieda or my Lady." Charlie's dad stepped forwards, calm and collected. "And refer to me as King Arthur of Tane-borc."

"Arthur. The Knight With 1,000 Eyes." Jack Thane bowed to him. "Welcome, Sire."

"We are here to help in any way we can," Gorrodin said. "We would not desert Galhadria in its hour of need and I imagine you could do with our assistance."

"I strongly suggest we let bygones be bygones." Jack Thane smiled disarmingly. "I require either Gor-rodin's cup or Mistress Ganieda's talisman to ensure victory. Having both is even better."

He bowed to them as well.

"I presume you have brought the bear and the cup?"

"We didn't get here on a flying carpet."

"Then I welcome you," Lincoln said brusquely. "For beggars cannot be choosers."

He pointed at Jack Thane.

"I will know your strategy, right now. And brook no more secrecy or delay."

"Of course, Master Lincoln." The wizard beckoned to Charlie and the boy trotted forwards.

"This is Charlie Wilson, son of Mistress Ganieda and King Arthur. As such, he is half Galhadrian."

"Pleased to meet you, I think."

The Lords looked far from pleased.

"It was this boy who killed Mordred, son of Morgana and so delivered the Dolorous Stroke."

The Lord's demeanour passed from outrage to outright hostility.

"You have given us the cause but not the solution," Will Thorn shouted. "This changes nothing."

"Charlie Wilson is also half-human." Thane smiled slyly. "Which means there are *two* races the Gorrodin Rath are certain to defeat in any war."

"I begin to understand." As always, Math was quickest to catch on. "With Gorrodin's cup and Ganiedia's bear, we are back to our former strength."

"So, it will take the Gorrodin Rath a little longer to defeat us," Prestor John fumed.

"We would have enough power to open up all the Thin Places to earth again." Thane countered. "Combine them in front of the Great Wall, just as the enemy reaches it."

"Of course!" Mabon breathed. "The Gorrodin Rath would never reach Galhadria. They'd be transported all over earth instead!"

"Then we shut the Thin Places again, forever this time." Mabon clasped her hands. "Morgana and her race will conquer humanity instead, and we will be saved."

The clan stared at the Lords in horror. Yet, before they could voice their opposition, Ganieda spoke.

"That is an excellent plan," she said. "I commend you, Master Thane."

"You're welcome." But the wizard looked suspicious. "I thought you might object, having lived there so long."

"I only care that my family is safe." The woman did not bat an eyelid. "In return for our help, Gorrodin and I wish to be returned to our rightful places with the Lords and would ask that our children be welcomed as well."

There were mutterings from the gathered sorcerers.

"I shall reluctantly grant that," Lincoln replied. "And who is this?"

He scowled at Inspector Archer.

"My son's protector. He also stays."

"Agreed."

"I have a request as well." Arthur stepped forwards. "I wish to be put in charge of your army."

"That is a step too far," Lincoln growled. "We do not know you."

"You know my reputation," the man said coolly. "I have fought in countless wars throughout human history. When was the last time you engaged in battle?"

Charlie goggled his father. He no longer bore any resemblance to the man he had known all his life.

"If Thane's plan works, you will have no need of me," Arthur continued. "If something goes wrong, however, you will wish you had granted my boon."

"I see sense in that." Math nodded. "And this is no time for misplaced vanity."

"I shall let it be known that you will command our forces," Lincoln sighed. "Is that it?"

"Let us not call our foe the Gorrodin Rath anymore," Gorrodin spoke up. "For they have long abandoned my guidance. The Rath will do."

"I have no problem granting that wish."

"Then, I would like to retire with my party." Ganieda yawned. "The last few days have been quite an ordeal for us all."

"And I would spend some time with my daughter," Gorrodin added. "We have many lost years to catch up on."

"Very well." Lincoln held out his hand. "Give me your talismans. We will place them in the spell chamber with our own."

Ganieda slipped the chain over her head and surrendered the silver bear. Gorrodin hesitated, then passed over his cup.

"It is done." Tom Lincoln signalled the meeting was adjourned. "When the Rath attack, we will open up the Thin Places together and link them in front of the Great Wall."

"I fear it is our kingdom Morgana wants most," Prester John warned. "She will try to prevent them going through."

"When their bloodlust is up, even Morgana will not be able to stop the Rath." For the first time in weeks, Tom Lincoln smiled.

"We are saved."

The Decision

The clan were escorted to their rooms by a blue-coated attendant. As soon as he was gone, Duncan rounded on his companions.

"I cannae believe that…" he began angrily.

Lilly put a finger to her lips until he calmed down.

They waited while Gorrodin weaved a spell of silence to ward off prying ears.

"We cannot let this happen," Lilly said finally. "The human race has many flaws but they do not deserve such a fate."

"Neither do the Galhadrians," Gorrodin replied. "I fear we are stuck between a rock and a hard place."

"The Lord's plan is truly abominable," Shadowjack grumbled. "Though I have to say, it's pretty ingenious too."

"We have been outmanoeuvred." Ganieda slumped in a chair. "Unsealing a Thin Place takes great power. With our talismans, my brother and I might have managed to open one right here and let us escape back to earth. Now, we no longer possess them."

She looked lost.

"We have no choice. We must save Galhadria."

There was a chorus of objections from the rest of the clan.

"Mum?" Charlie pleaded. "You don't have to help Thane. You could sabotage his plan by not taking part."

"Do you not understand?" his mother sighed. "We are stuck here. If we do not aid the Lords, the Rath will destroy us all."

She laid a tired hand on his shoulder.

"I will not let you die, no matter what the cost."

"That's no your decision tae make," Duncan shot back.

"I'm truly sorry, but nothing can change my mind."

"Remember what you told me?" Charlie looked at his father. "Sometimes virtue is its own reward."

"I also told you that wearing glasses would make your eyes recede into your head."

"Don't be flippant, dad. You must recall what else you said."

"There are two great virtues a person can have." Arthur straightened his shoulders. "Knowing what is right and doing what is right."

He kissed his wife on the top of her head.

"The Lords cast the Great Spell and Galhadria is prepared for war. Humanity is not. Though they will lose, it is *this* land where the battle should be fought."

"I agree with Lord Arthur," Gorrodin nodded. "I usually do."

"Arthur, no!" his wife cried. "Our son!"

"I will have two of my new knights escort him to the farthest corner of the realm."

He indicated the rest of the clan.

"You can go with him, if that is your desire."

"I dinnae run from danger," Duncan said angrily. "I will fight."

"I'll stick around too," Shadowjack raised his hand.

"And me," Peazle sighed.

"I may as well stay," Inspector Archer said. "I don't really know my way around."

"Lilly will accompany you, Charlie." Gorrodin sounded relieved.

"Lilly shall do no such thing." The girl stamped her foot. "I will not abandon my friends."

"Or me." Charlie hugged his mother. "I appreciate what you're doing, but I am the son of King Arthur. He was willing to give his life fighting the Rath once before. I can do no less."

"He's picking up Galhadrian speak quite well," Arthur remarked.

"You joke at a time like this?" Ganieda shot him a filthy look.

"I agree that humanity has many flaws." Arthur held her stare. "Sacrificing themselves to do what is right is not one of them."

His eyes took on a hard spark.

"This is something your Lords have obviously forgotten."

"Surely humanity cannot lose," Peazle piped up. "The Rath army is great but humans number in their millions. They have weapons the enemy cannot conceive of."

"The Rath also have a secret weapon," Arthur replied. "It was part of the enchantment they wove for themselves long ago. Why do you imagine there are so many of them? Why are the Galhadrian forces still heavily armoured with fairy silver, as my knights once were?"

"I think I can guess," Peazle gulped. "The Rath do not breed, do they? They have another way of reproducing."

"Yes. The creatures' bites are infectious and will turn anyone on the receiving end into one of them. Let a few of them loose in a human city and Morgana will have another army within hours. A scenario that will be duplicated all over earth."

Peazle caught on first.

"The Rath did not wipe out the inhabitants of Toth. They *turned* them."

"You're kidding," Charlie stammered. "Like in a zombie film?"

"Exactly."

"If we allow Jack Thane's plan to go ahead," Gorrodin said. "He will be seen as Galhadria's saviour and, most likely, its ruler. Is that something you could accept, Ganieda? He is as bad as Morgana."

"If the Rath took Galhadria, how long would it be before they moved on Alabarra, The Wooded Kingdom, Monshorn and then lands beyond?" Ganieda looked pleadingly at her brother. "Turned the inhabitants into monsters? Even if they fled, our children would never be safe."

Gorrodin was silent for a long time.

"You are right," he said finally. "We have no choice but to go along with Thane's plan."

There was a chorus of objections from the clan.

"Enough!" Gorrodin raised a fist, crackling with light. "It is decided. Return to your rooms."

Arthur said nothing, but his lips tightened.

The clan were awakened at dawn by bells ringing.

"The Gorrodin Rath are massing to attack." The blue-coated attendant ran from door to door. "Morgana herself has been sighted."

The occupants stumbled into the corridor.

"I thought they would come at night." Shadowjack rubbed sleep from his eyes. "I was dreaming about being on a pirate ship and only having one leg."

"It is a fear tactic," Arthur replied. "They are no longer repelled by the sun and wish the Galhadrians to fully understand their increased power."

He grabbed the attendant.

"Bring silver armour for my companions and me, then lead us to my knights."

500 mounted men were stretched out on the plain behind the Great Wall, sunlight glinting off their breastplates and helmets. Behind them were massed ranks of armed Galhadrians. Charlie estimated there were upwards of 5,000 fighters.

On the hill above, Castle Alclud towered above the army.

"Quite a formidable array." Duncan looked impressed. "I doubted there would be so many."

"I'll wager they were never told the Dolorous Stroke had been struck," Gorrodin said. "They think they have a chance at winning. Even if they were aware of the true situation, however, I dare say they would fight to the last man to defend their land."

"Yet not one of them are trained for battle," Arthur grunted. "They have not fought a war in centuries."

"They won't have to, will they?" Charlie remarked sourly. "The Rath will never reach the wall."

"Gorrodin and I must go to the spell chamber and prepare." Ganieda kissed her son's head and glanced at her husband. "I hope, someday, you will both forgive me."

"I would ask a small spell from each of you before you go," Arthur asked. "Gorrodin, can you amplify my voice so the troops can all hear me?"

The wizard snapped his fingers.

"It is done."

"And I want to know which of these knights is Duncan's brother."

Ganieda pressed a palm to her forehead, scanning the ranks in an instant.

"Front row, second from the left," she said. "There is a man who looks just like him."

"They're all wearing helmets."

"I'm a sorceress, aren't I?" She beckoned to Gorrodin. "Let us not put off this sorry spectacle any further, brother."

She clapped her hands, and the pair vanished.

"Off you go, lad," Arthur said. "We will wait for our steeds."

"Steeds?" Charlie looked horrified. "I've never sat on a horse in my life. The closest I ever got was a donkey on Brighton beach."

"Can't say I've been on one either," Inspector Archer added. "Never fancied being in the mounted police. Those buggers have teeth like paving stones, and that's just the riders."

"I can provide better transportation." Peazle pointed to a small copse of trees at the edge of the valley. "It's stashed over there."

He bowed to Arthur.

"With your permission, my king."

"Every little helps, as they say at Tesco's."

"I've no idea what that meant, but I'll go get it."

He took off at a run.

Duncan reached the ranks of knights and stopped in front of the one Ganieda had picked out. Now that the moment he had waited for so long had arrived, he had no idea how to proceed.

"Hello, Caleb," he said, finally. "You've grown up a wee bit."

The knight removed his helmet, revealing a shock of ginger hair.

"Oh." Duncan was taken aback. "You definitely take after oor father's line. He had a head like a thistle."

"My name is Sir Galahad, not Caleb." The man looked puzzled. "Sorry, but do I know you?"

"You do not," Duncan sat. "It is a long story, and this is not the time tea tell it." He paused.

"You are my brother."

"Of course. We are all brothers here."

"No. Though, I cannae prove it, I am your flesh and blood. Your real brother."

"You look just like me, apart from that dark hair." The man hesitated. "I don't understand."

"Explanations will have tae wait." Duncan stepped forward and laid a hand on Galahad's leg. "Just know that I have searched for you for centuries and prayed for this moment."

The man looked into Duncan's eyes.

"Then I believe you. Brother."

"Those are words I have ached tae hear for longer than I can remember."

"Your timing could be better, however."

"Dinnae get me started on that."

"Stay close and I will defend you." The man leant down and clasped Duncan's hand. "When this is over, I will seek you out. We have much to talk about."

"That we do." Duncan let go and marched back to his companions, wiping tears from his eyes.

The attendant had arrived with a group of white horses. Shadowjack heaved himself onto a charger.

"Sorry, beastie," he apologised. "I must be quite a weight to carry. I've not bothered with a helmet, or else your legs might collapse."

Duncan arrived.

"I am ready." He leapt onto his steed in a single bound.

There was a throbbing hum and Peazle appeared over a rise.

"Is that an... armoured car?" Charlie gasped.

The boy drew up alongside them and switched off the engine.

"This is a Patria AMV XP personnel carrier," he said proudly. "Armour plated with a 12.7 mm machine gun, 30 mm cannon, 7.62 mm coaxial machine gun and two guided anti-tank heat-seeking missile launchers. Plus, it's filled with automatic weapons."

He jumped out and patted the sides.

"Jack Thane turned the whole thing silver to pack an added punch against the Rath." He shrugged. "He does like his modern toys, though the other Lords frown upon his collection and made him stop."

He shrugged.

"I hid this wee beauty from them."

"Where the hell did you get it?"

"Stole it from an army base in Finland. There's still a Thin Place open there, so I drove it through."

"I'll be getting in that for sure," Lilly clambered up the side, Inspector Archer right behind.

"What's the point?" Charlie protested. "We're not actually going to fight."

"Your father is King Arthur." Lilly peered down at him. "You honestly think he's not going to do what he believes is right?"

"Dad?" Charlie looked up at the mounted man.

"I intend leading my forces to war." Arthur nodded sadly. "You must take the carrier in the opposite direction, for we are sure to be defeated."

"But I can't lose you!"

"Fate has played its hand, boy. I will meet my end happily if you stay alive."

"I love you, Dad." Charlie climbed into the armoured vehicle. "Please don't die."

"I shall do my best."

Arthur took a deep breath, then addressed his troops.

"I am your commander, Arthur of Taneborc." His voice rang loudly and clearly through the valley. "The Rath are about to attack so, normally, I would line the Great Wall with archers - for it *seems* an impenetrable barrier. But Morgana is leading them and she is no fool.

Therefore, I must assume she has a way to bring the barrier down."

There was a collective gasp from the assembled army.

"If she does, we will be at a grave disadvantage. The Rath will scramble over the rubble in their thousands and our cavalry will be useless, with no room to manoeuvre. They will be forced to dismount and fight on foot."

A few of the knights nodded, understanding their limitations in such a situation.

"Therefore, we will do the last thing Morgana expects. We shall attack first." He raised his hand. "Open the gates and reform on the other side of the wall."

The attendants stared at him. But he was the leader of their forces. Reluctantly, they unbarred and swung open the huge gates.

Arthur's army marched through and began to take up their places.

Inside the armoured carrier, Peazle turned to his companions.

"What is it to be, folks?" he asked. "Fight or flee?"

"I'm not leaving mum and dad." Charlie folded his arms. "I just can't do it."

"I'm a policeman," Inspector Archer rubbed his bald head. "My job is to take on bad guys. And I know how to drive."

"Looks like we're staying," Lilly said. "I'll man the cannon."

"I shall take the machine gun," Peazle grinned wryly. "Wish I'd stolen a helmet too. This bowler hat isn't going to be much protection."

The armoured carrier roared to life and rumbled after the Galhadrians. Arthur swung round on his mount when he heard the commotion.

"Aw, no, you little fool," he groaned. "You could have gotten away."

But it was too late. The gates swung shut behind them and were barred.

Betrayal

Gorrodin and Ganieda wound down stone steps to the spell room, where the Lord's talismans were kept. As the most precious artefacts in Galhadria, they were locked away in the deepest dungeons of Castle Alclud and closely guarded. An attendant unlocked a heavy wooden door, protected by magic, no doubt. The spell room was small, with ancient stone walls devoid of windows. The other sorcerers were gathered around plinths, each holding their most precious objects.

"Are you both ready?" Math urged.

"We are."

The pair took their places and placed their hands on the silver bear and the Grail cup.

"The Rath have gathered," Tom Lincoln said. "They have no patience and, therefore, an attack is imminent."

"When they charge, we will cast our spell on my signal," Jack Thane said. "I have calculated the exact location to open the giant portal in front of the wall."

"It must be timed to perfection," Prestor John added. "They will cross the valley floor at a run, and they are fast."

"Then let us prepare." Lincoln bent over his talisman, a long clay pipe. "This will take our utmost concentration and skill."

The pipe began to softly vibrate.

"How will we know when the Rath move?" Ganieda interrupted. "When we are concentrating all our powers down here."

"There is a watcher on the wall." Jack Thane held up a walkie talkie. "An acquisition from your young friend, Peazle, on one of his forays."

Tom Lincoln tutted his displeasure, but the rest held their tongues.

"So, you found humans are good for something, eh, Master Thane?" Gorrodin grunted.

"I have no desire to destroy the kingdom of men and I grieve for what will happen," Thane replied defiantly. "But it is them or us. Now focus."

The Lords bent over their talismans and, one by one, each began to radiate with soft light. As if on cue, the radio crackled to life.

An attack has begun, Master Thane.

"We are ready. Let us know when the Rath are moments from the wall."

I do not understand, the voice fizzed back. *It is our side who are advancing. Was it not at your instruction?*

Tom Lincoln's eyes widened. He swept his arm in an arc and the pipe before him faded.

A vision appeared in the air. They could see the Galhadrian army spreading out slowly across the plane of Toth, Arthur and his knights in front.

"What is this treachery?" Thane gasped. "They are in the way! There is nowhere for us to open the portal."

The Lords broke into a panicked babble, and Thane rounded on Ganieda and Gorrodin.

"You have betrayed us," he spat. "I will have you thrown into our deepest pit for eternity."

"We knew nothing of this." Gorrodin put a hand on his chest. "Use enchantment to look into our hearts if you doubt it."

"This was not my doing." Ganieda had turned pale. "I swear."

"Our forces are under the command of your husband!"

"My husband, not me!" the woman retorted. "Do you think I would knowingly put my own son in the firing line?"

"I say we lock them up," Prestor John grunted. "Who knows what other mischief they will cause?"

"Do not let your anger overcome common sense," Ganieda retorted. "You are going to need us for the coming fight."

"A fight we cannot win!"

"You'll lose a damned sight faster if Gorrodin and I are locked up," Ganieda retorted. "Arthur has taken command of the army and gone against my wishes. I see no course of action but to support him."

"This is a coup," Thane roared. "Do not listen to them."

"It's no coup. It's the opportunity to regain the honour you obviously lost long ago." Ganieda's voice was laden with sorrow. "My husband has determined this war will be waged honestly and he and my son shall lose their lives because of it."

"Well spoken, sister," Gorrodin said. "Arthur has forged his own path. Like it or not, we must follow where he leads."

The Lords looked at Tom Lincoln. The wizard's mouth worked silently as he struggled to contain his rage.

"You cannot allow…" Thane began.

"Enough!" Lincoln shouted. "There is no more time for debate. Let us make haste to the Great Wall."

He picked up his talisman.

"We will show these traitors we know how to die with dignity."

Toth-Haden

Tom Lincoln and the other wizards materialised on top of the Great Wall. Below them, the two armies faced each other.

"Where are our archers?" Mabon demanded. "This is the perfect vantage point to fire down on the enemy."

"Grouped at the back of the troops below." Mabon pointed down. "This Arthur is an incompetent fool!"

"He is a brilliant general," Gorrodin countered. "If there are no defenders up here, it is for a reason."

"What possible reason could he have?"

"Think!" Ganieda urged. "Morgana did not know about your plan to open a portal. Why would she send her minions against a barrier they cannot breach?"

"She would not," Gorrodin concluded. "Therefore, she must have a way to bring down the wall."

"Impossible!" Tom Lincoln laughed. "It is reinforced with our magic. Even if she had the Grail, Morgana's powers would never be strong enough to raze this mighty structure."

He slammed his hand against a stone nacelle.

"Because of Arthur, the Rath will wipe out our forces without having to even tackle it."

"He has a point." Gorrodin glanced at Ganieda.

"Arthur knows he must lose," she replied. "But he would never throw away the lives of those he commands to make a point. He's far too clever for that."

"I agree." Gorrodin turned to the other Lords. "I trust my king. My sister and I will fight below. You are fools if you stay here."

The siblings stepped off the parapet and floated down, cloaks flapping in the wind. They soared across the Galhadrians and landed beside Arthur.

"Hello, dear. Sorry about this."

"Hi, mum." Charlie waved from the top of the armoured carrier. Ganieda gave an agonised groan.

"Stay out of the fighting," she commanded. "Or else."

"Bit late now."

"If we survive, you and I shall be having serious words," she rasped at her husband. "You allowed our son to come with you!"

"It seems I'm not the only one who won't do as he's told," the king faltered. "I did not think…"

"You never do." Ganieda turned on her heel and walked towards her son, casting a hate-filled look at Arthur. "I'll never forgive you."

Arthur blinked back tears. Charlie was about to climb down in a vain attempt to smooth things over when a shadow fell across the valley.

"Oh, my stars." Gorrodin looked up. "It *can't* be."

A gigantic shape rose over the mountains, filling the sky. It was twice the size of a jumbo jet, kept in the air by wings that stretched the width of the valley.

"What the hell is that beastie?" Duncan whispered.

"Toth-Haden." Gorrodin's voice shook. "The greatest of the Black Dragons – a race that was supposed to have died out millennia ago."

"I presume he's bad news," Arthur shielded his eyes with one hand.

"It's a female. And she could annihilate half your army with one blast of her fiery breath."

"I'll take that as a yes." The king raised one arm and motioned for his men to move slowly forward.

"You're going to attack now?" Shadowjack's eyes were on stalks. "After what the wizard just told you."

"I'm moving my forces away from the wall," Arthur replied. "For that will surely be her first target. Thank God the Lords are up there to defend it."

"Dragon magic is the most powerful kind ever discovered." Gorrodin shook his head. "They cannot hope to match it, though I fear they will try."

Toth-Haden flapped her wings and moved swiftly towards the Great Wall. Tom Lincoln and his fellow wizards launched a dozen bolts of lightning at her, but they simply bounced off the scaly black hide.

The dragon opened her mouth.

An avalanche of molten fire roared towards the Lords. They crouched, clenching their fists and a protective bubble appeared around them. The flames slid

off and poured down the wall. Toth-Haden took another huge gulp and breathed again. This time, the
conflagration hit the structure full on.

"Oh my God," Charlie croaked from the carrier.
"It's melting."

Slowly, the Great Wall caught fire and began to dis-
solve, collapsing in on itself. The wizards vanished,
screaming, into a molten crevasse. Toth-Haden rose in
a leisurely arc, one rolling eye turning to the Galhadrian troops. The Rath leapt up and down, gurgling and
spitting with glee.

"I fear it is our turn," Ganieda balled her fists and
raised both arms, determined to go down fighting.

Two white plumes shot into the air, twisting and
turning, hitting Toth-Haden in her underbelly. There
was a huge explosion and the dragon roared in agony,
sending a spout of fire into the air. Before she could
recover, another pair of vapour trails raced into the sky.
They arched at the last moment and vanished into the
beast's maw.

There was a muffled rumble, and the creature's
throat exploded, bone and guts raining over the landscape. Toth-Haden plunged down, crashing into the
remains of the Great Wall and demolishing the structure completely.

''Heat-seeking missiles.'' A cover slid open on the
front of the armoured carrier and Peazle's eyes appeared in the slit. "Like I kept telling Jack Thane,
humans have a completely different kind of magic."

The jeers and laughter of the Rath had turned to horrified silence.

"The enemy are confused and demoralised." Arthur raised his arm again. "This is the moment to strike."

He spurred his mount into a gallop.

"Chaaaaaarge!"

500 horses thundered across the plain towards the Rath, Galhadrian forces running behind, screaming defiance. The front ranks of the enemy tried to retreat but had nowhere to go. Then Morgana was among them, cursing and spitting, urging her followers forward. The Rath broke into a shambling lope.

The gap between the forces narrowed. 1,000 yards. Then 500. Then 200.

Arthur's knights suddenly halted. The centre section moved aside and, into the gap, rumbled the armoured car driven by Inspector Archer.

Two more missiles sped into the Rath's massed ranks, blowing them apart. The 30 mm cannon and co-axial machine gun opened fire. On top of the turret, Charlie let loose with the second machine gun, sweeping it in wide arcs. Spent casings bounced and pinged around him.

"Say hello to my leetle friend!" he crowed. "Saw that in a movie once."

The first 20 or 30 lines of the Rath were annihilated. The rest tried to surge forward, using sheer weight of numbers to reach their foe. It did no good.

Rank after rank went down as they floundered against a wall of bullets and artillery shells. Morgana let out a cry of rage, pushed her way back into the throng and disappeared. She knew, only too well, that she was not impervious to silver bullets.

With a wail, the Rath turned and ran, leaving thousands of bodies behind.

"That went well." Peazle jumped down from the vehicle and saluted Arthur. "We've got them on the run."

"We've simply made them more cautious," his king replied. "I imagine the next attack will come after dark."

"That is perfectly fine by me," the boy smiled. "This thing has night scopes and headlights."

Night Falls

"Morgana has great influence over dark creatures," Gorrodin said. "But she must have truly formidable powers to be able to wake and command a dragon."

"Got any good news?" Charlie asked.

"Toth-Haden must have been the last of her race. If not, another would be among us by now."

"Thank heavens for small mercies."

The clan were gathered in a hastily erected tent. The rest of the army had built small fires and were resting. Some were roasting dragon meat, renowned for giving strength and vitality to those who ate it.

Duncan sorely wanted to go and see his brother but this was a war council and he felt he should be part of it.

"How are you for ammunition?" he asked Peazle.

"Four missiles left. Enough shells and bullets to pull off the same trick one more time. Then we will be out."

He pulled a silver handgun from his pocket.

"The small arms haven't been touched yet. We'll use them once the armoured car's weapons are spent."

"The Rath favour the dark and Morgana won't be fooled twice," Gorrodin said. "If we can hold off a night attack, we will stand a better chance the following day."

"That's a big if." Duncan looked up to where the sun had almost sunk below the hills. "If we're gonnae come up wi a plan, we'd better do it fast."

''What about launching a sneaky attack ourselves?" Shadowjack asked. "Morgana won't expect that."

"With good reason," the wizard snorted. "Further back, where the plain narrows, the mountains are riddled with caves. And no doubt, they are filled with Rath. If we ventured too far, they would pour down and surround us. We have no choice but to wait for them to come at us once night falls."

"You and I can light up the sky," Ganieda said. "Make them a better target."

"That would help," her brother conceded. "But use up most of our strength. We'd be useless in battle."

"It is far from ideal." Arthur was hunched over a table, looking at a map of the area. "But we have little choice. Archer?"

"Yes, sir?"

"When they charge, use up the rest of your ammunition, then retreat immediately."

"Understood."

"Galhadrians have sharper eyes than humans. I will station them along the foot of the mountains, for the Rath will try to sneak along that way, sticking to the shadows. My knights will stay behind the armoured carrier, ready to take over once it departs."

He turned to Archer.

"You *will* leave on my order. You have my son and Gorrodin's daughter with you."

"Not going to attempt any heroics, don't worry."

"Then let's get a couple of hours rest."

"May I go see my brother, Sire?" Duncan leapt to his feet.

"Of course." Arthur went back to his map. Charlie tapped him on the shoulder and the man looked around.

"Sorry, boy. I've been a bit preoccupied." He embraced his son. "I want to say how proud I am of the way you've acted."

"Thanks, dad. Now, how about making *me* proud?"

"What do you mean?"

"I mean, you saunter into battle without flinching, but you're scared of talking to your own wife."

"Too right, I am."

"Do it for me." Charlie took his dad's hand and led him over to his mum. Ganieda was seated in a corner of the tent, a picture of misery.

"We have been together forever, it seems." Arthur knelt beside her. "And never disagreed before."

"This is more than a disagreement." The woman's face was pinched with fury. "I tried to protect my boy. You put him in the middle of a battlefield."

"Right," Charlie snapped. "Stop using me as an excuse, you two."

His parents' eyes widened.

"You are each other's worlds," the boy continued. "Sure, you love me, but not as much as each other, and I have no problem with that. In fact, I think it's rather wonderful."

His parents began to object, but Charlie cut them off.

"Mother? You did what you thought was right, despite the cost. Father? You did what *you* thought was right. Your aims were at odds but neither of you were wrong. So, let's cut to the chase."

A frown clouded his brow.

"How dare you both deny me the opportunity to do the same? I am the son of a Lord of the Western Wilderness and the fabled King Arthur. I have fought the Rath and won. I hold the Great Sword. Quite frankly, I expect to be treated as an equal and it disappoints me greatly that you do not."

"Told you he was picking up our way of talking," Arthur winced.

"Move on and stop acting like teenagers in a playground spat." Charlie wagged a finger at them. "Bloody well kiss and make up."

Arthur and Ganieda looked into each other's eyes. Finally, they both smiled. Charlie was right. They had been in love for centuries, and nothing could change that.

"My king." Ganieda stood and opened her arms. Arthur sank gratefully into them. He motioned for Charlie and the boy joined their embrace.

Gorrodin looked around. Lilly was standing a few feet away.

"Come, daughter." He held out his hand. "Let us walk and talk, as we used to, long ago. I would hear of your adventures."

"You read my mind back at the falls," Lilly said shyly.

"A poor substitute for hearing them from your own lips. My heart is sore at the years I have missed and how little time we have to be together."

Lilly took his arm and they strolled across the darkening plain.

Duncan found his brother seated beside a campfire with his mount.

"So, what dae I call you?" he asked. "Caleb or Galahad?"

"I am Galahad to everyone here," the man replied. "But I know it is a name borrowed from another, long dead warrior. To you, I am Caleb, and that is good enough for me."

Beside them, his horse nibbled at the grass.

Now that Duncan's great quest was at an end, he wasn't sure how to proceed.

"I'm not much of a talker," he admitted. "I dinnae rightly ken what tae say."

"I do not see that we stand much chance in the coming fight." Caleb patted his steed's nose. "Therefore, I am grateful for your company, even if you stay silent."

"No. You are my only kin and I cannae hold my tongue, even if you may not want tae hear what I have to say."

And he told Caleb everything, including what he knew of the Dolorous Stroke.

When he was finished, the man sat quietly for a long time.

"If you were tae ride away now, I would understand," Duncan said.

"I will not desert my comrades nor abandon my brother," Caleb replied. "But there is one more story I would like to hear."

"Anything."

The knight moved closer until his shoulder was touching Duncan's.

"Tell me about our father and mother."

The Sky Aflame

There was a commotion outside the tent and Peazle burst in.

"Two people seek an audience, my lady," he said. "Demand it, in fact."

Ganieda let go of her family.

"Who is it," she asked. "I am rather preoccupied."

"Oh, I think you'll recognise them."

The tent flap opened and a pair of figures pushed their way through. Ganieda exhaled loudly and Arthur's hand went to his sword hilt.

"Yes. It takes more than a damned dragon to kill us."

Jack Thane and Math stood before them, clothes tattered and torn. Their gashed faces were caked with blood, and Thane leaned heavily on an ash staff. One of Math's arms hung limply by her side.

"Where are the other Lords?" Arthur rose to his feet.

"Dead." There was no emotion in the wizard's voice. "And we are grievously hurt, as you can see."

"I will heal your wounds as best I can." Gorrodin and Lilly entered behind them. "Stay still."

"Do not waste your magic, old man." Math waved him away. "The Rath are massing as we speak."

"I will muster the men." Arthur got to his feet. "My love? You and Gorrodin must light up the sky, as we discussed. Lady Math and Lord Thane? I beg you to assist them."

"That is a poor plan," Thane sniffed. "We cannot match the sun and, despite our best efforts, many deep shadows will remain for those creatures to hide in."

"It's the only move open to us," Artur retorted. "Unless you have a better idea."

"I always do." Thane cast a glance at Math and she nodded.

"I know you think me a monster," he continued. "But I swore an oath to do my utmost for Galhadria and my resolution has always been firm. I would have ruled in the same way."

He stood as erect as he could manage.

"You may have despised my methods but times change. I merely reflected that." He turned to Ganieda. "I wished to kill two birds with one stone, as humans say."

Charlie's mother could not meet his gaze.

"Humanity is as great a threat to us as the Rath and I feel you know that in your heart. One day, I will be proved right."

"You were talking about a plan?" Arthur was unmoved.

"Save your troops until morning, when they stand a chance, no matter how slim. Math and I shall hold Morgana at bay until daylight."

"That is suicide." Gorrodin shook his head. "I will not hear of it."

"With Tom Lincoln gone," Thane snapped. "I lead the Lords, or what is left of them. I am not asking for permission."

He gave a thin smile.

"I used to love travelling this land, singing ballads," he said. "It would have been nice to hear one was written about how I met my fate. Just a shame there will be nobody left to recount it."

"And you, Math?"

"I cannot sing a note." The woman kept her face straight. "I will go with Master Thane. He would have made a great leader, you know. Though, it seemed only I could see it."

"I'm beginning to get an inking." Gorrodin stared at Thane. "You still could be, for we are not dead yet. You could both transport yourself somewhere else."

"As could you."

"My place is here, I am afraid."

"Mine too. A ruler with no kingdom will never recover from the pain of its loss." Thane winked at Arthur. "Isn't that right, my Lord?"

It was Arthur's turn to look away.

Charlie watched his dad's reaction. Here was a man who had gone from being the saviour of a nation to a circus acrobat, entertaining small crowds. That must have hurt deep inside.

"Once, we were good friends." Gorrodin shook Thane's hand. "I consider us to be so again."

"I suppose. Pity you're rotten at playing the lute."

Thane and Math put up their hoods and left without a backward glance. The clan trooped out and watched the pair limp across the plain, until darkness swallowed them.

Duncan and Caleb piled more hastily gathered wood on the fire. In the distance, they could hear the growls and grunts as the Rath gathered.

"Why have no orders come from our king?" Caleb looked pensive. "We should be on our horses and ready to repel the enemy."

"I dinnae ken." Duncan was equally puzzled. "But I swear I saw two figures heading towards them."

"It cannot be an attempt to parlay." Caleb stroked his nervous steed. "After what you told me, we know Morgana will settle for nothing but total victory."

A flash lit the night and the brothers jumped. The nearest horses backed away, snorting in panic. The other knights clasped their muzzles, calming them.

A sea of flame leapt up in the distance and they could suddenly see ranks of creatures writhing and burning. In the centre of the conflagration were Jack Thane and Math, laying waste to the foe. Bolts of lightning shot from their fingers, lancing through the enemy.

As the beasts shrank back, Thane and Math staggered forward, pushing into the screaming mass. Soon they were encircled and hidden from sight, still emanating death and destruction.

"I have seen many acts of bravery in my time," Caleb lamented. "But none like this."

"Whoever they are, they met their death tae give us a chance,"

Duncan unsheathed his sword and held it up. One by one, the 500 knights did the same, the reflections of firelight mingling with the far off inferno, flickering along the blades.

Jack Thane and Math were almost spent. The Rath were warily closing in around them.

"It is time." Thane pulled his talisman from inside the folds of his cloak. His companion did the same.

"Mistress Math? It has been one of the great privileges of..."

"Oh, shut up." The woman grabbed Thane's head and kissed him on the lips. "You and I need no words."

She stepped back and smiled.

"Been wanting to do that for a century or more."

Seeing their chance, the Rath charged. As claws ripped into them, Jack Thane and Math smashed the talismans together.

The explosion lit up the plain with the force of a dozen suns, a dazzling lethal luminescence that spread for half a mile. It annihilated thousands of Morgana's forces, scorching grass and sending rocks tumbling down the mountain screes, burying hundreds more creatures inside their caves.

As the darkness descended again, the Rath retreated once more - until the valley was silent - save for the cheering of Arthur's men.

The clan watched the deaths of Jack Thane and Math with open mouths.

"Surely they'll give up," Inspector Archer ventured. "Morgana must have lost more than half her force by now."

"She cares not for casualties," Arthur corrected. "Not when she is guaranteed victory."

He motioned for the rest of them to follow.

"Into the tent," he commanded. "Peazle? Fetch Duncan and his brother. I have a story to tell you."

Daybreak

The clan waited until Duncan and Caleb joined them. They sat down, all except Arthur.

"When I was king," he began. "The Round Table and I fought the Rath, as most of you know. They lost and we won but it was a pyrrhic victory."

"What's that then?" Shadowjack asked. "I get enough big words thrown at me from Peazle."

"It's a victory that inflicts such a devastating toll on the winner, it negates any true sense of achievement." Peazle was always quick to show off his knowledge.

"Aye. That doesn't help. I don't know what negate means either."

"It means the king won, but his men were almost wiped out in the process."

"Indeed." Arthur nodded. "The Rath's reign of terror was ended, yet the toll on us was immense. Only four of my knights were left alive. I was mortally wounded and the Round Table destroyed. Without us, the country slipped back into lawlessness."

"I see what you are getting at," Gorrodin nodded. "We must do to the Rath what they once did to us."

"They are destined to win," Arthur agreed. "But what if we take almost all of them with us? Say we managed to kill all but a handful?"

"They would be still the victors," Duncan said. "But without the numbers tae do any further damage."

"They will simply breed again," Ganieda pointed out. "Or infect others left in Galhadria."

"Then we must act quickly." Arthur motioned for Duncan's brother to rise.

"You will ride back across the land. Tell the remaining inhabitants to seek refuge in Alabarra, The Wooded Kingdom and Monshorn."

"They aren't exactly friends of ours," Peazle reminded him. "They consider the Little People to be arrogant and insular."

"They are not exactly enemies either," Caleb argued. "For I have travelled their lands and rid them of many a monster."

"They are not warlike and have sat on the fence so far," Duncan added. "But news travels fast, and they will soon ken what the Rath are capable of, if they dinnae already."

"Then urge them to raise a force quickly and ride into Galhadria," Arthur said. "Wipe out the few creatures we could not defeat before the Rath gain a foothold and come for *them*."

"Tell them they *can* secure victory." Charlie snapped his fingers. "For none of those kingdoms were involved in the Dolorous Stroke."

"Precisely," Arthur smiled solemnly. "This army will not live to see it, but Galhadria will be saved."

"I should have trusted you." Ganieda beamed. "Charlie and Lilly can accompany him. All the kids can."

"I do not wish to seem ungrateful, My Lord," Caleb said. "But my place is by my brother's side."

"Of course it is. So, the rest of the clan will go with you. I trust only the best."

A silence descended as each member considered this. One last chance to avoid certain death.

"I can't." Charlie was the first to speak. "I am the guardian of Excalibur."

"The Great Sword is rightfully mine, boy."

"Not anymore. It has chosen me." Charlie refused to back down. "Besides, how would it look if the king's own son fled and left his forces to their fate."

"Oh, please, no." Ganieda pleaded.

"Those Luddites you command don't have a clue how to operate an armoured car or work a machine gun." Peazle fastened his waistcoat. "I'm staying."

"I'm the designated driver," Inspector Archer rubbed his bald head. "Been in many a high-speed chase, too."

"I man the cannons," Lilly cracked her knuckles.

"We're not leaving our pals," Shadowjack and Duncan shook their heads.

"This is the wish of your commander!" Arthur pulled himself up to his full height. "You will do as I say!"

"You're my father, not my commander," Charlie retorted. "In fact, none of the clan are actually in your army."

Arthur's shoulders slumped.

"What if I said please?"

"Sorry, dad. My mind is made up. I'm not deserting you and mum."

"I *am* bound by your orders, Sire." Caleb got to his feet. "Though I beg you to reconsider."

"As you said, you have travelled the lands of Alabarra, The Wooded Kingdom and Monshorn. If the clan will not go, take the three Galhadrians with the fastest steeds instead."

"As you wish." Caleb cast a lost look at Duncan. "I am truly sorry, brother."

"I'm not, for at least you will be safe."

Caleb saluted Arthur, lips tight, and pushed his way out of the tent.

"I don't suppose you and Gorrodin would consider accompanying him?" Arthur knelt down by Ganieda. "Galhadria will need new Lords to rule in the coming unstable times."

"And leave you and Charlie. Not a chance."

"We can wreak more havoc on the Rath than all your knights combined." Gorrodin put his arm around Lilly. "So, no."

"Not much bloody use being king if nobody does what I say," Arthur grumped, sounding remarkably like his old self.

"Pull yourself together, dad." Charlie pinched his father's cheek with false bravado. "You have a pyrrhic defeat to engineer. Get thinking. It's almost daybreak."

The clan trooped out of the tent, leaving Arthur and Ganieda alone.

"I tried, dear." The man sank to the ground beside his wife. "I really did."

"I know." Ganieda kissed his weary forehead. "Our son is as stubborn as us, and I love him all the more for it."

"I must lead from the front, as I always have." Arthur spread out a map of the valley on the ground. "You stay by Charlie as much as you are able. Protect him to the end."

"Of course." His wife shook her head miserably. "We've been terrible parents, haven't we?"

"Absolutely." But Arthur couldn't keep the pride from his voice. "Yet what an incredible son we managed to raise."

The king rode to the front of his army. He was resplendent in silver armour, a plume of red spouting from his helmet. On the other side of the plain, the Rath were gathering once more.

There was no sign of Morgana. He assumed she was wisely staying at the back. She was powerful but not indestructible.

"We are still vastly outnumbered, as you can plainly see." Arthur began. "But why would we want more soldiers?"

Sitting on top of the armoured carrier, Charlie frowned. This seemed an odd way for the king to raise his troop's spirits.

"If we are going to die, the less of us the better, is that not so? But the fewer the men, the greater share of honour."

Arthur lowered his voice, though the troops could still hear him perfectly.

"Still, if any of you want to leave, you are free to do so."

This time, Charlie groaned out loud. What was his dad up to? Many of his troops certainly looked tempted by the offer. But Arthur wasn't finished.

"Think about this, though," he yelled. "Our battle shall go down in history. It will be remembered forever in legend, and so will you, just for being here."

He stood up in the saddle.

"Your descendants will sing songs and tell stories of how we few, we happy few, became a band of brothers. For anyone who fights with me today *is* my brother!"

A whoop rose from the ranks.

"When other Galhadrians try to boast of the great things they have achieved," Arthur continued at the top of his lungs. "Your children can make them fall silent and bow their heads by simply saying these words."

He raised a gleaming sword in the air.

"I fought alongside my king against the Rath!"

The army roared and stamped their feet. Charlie gave his father a thumbs up.

Standing next to him, Ganieda raised a shapely eyebrow.

"Yes, yes." Arthur winked at her. "I knicked most of that speech from William Shakespeare."

He slammed down his visor.

"Let us commence battle."

Lancelot Du Lac

The Galhadrian army took the same formation as they had the day before.

In the vanguard were the 500 knights, with the armoured carrier at its centre. Behind that were Ganieda and Gorrodin, flanked by Duncan and Shadowjack, who had abandoned their unfamiliar mounts and were now on foot. To the rear were the Galhadrian troops.

Arthur sat astride his steed, a few yards in front of his army, horribly exposed. Yet, he seemed to show no fear. Once again, Charlie marvelled at the change in his meek and mild father. He was beginning to see that a true leader could wear many faces.

Opposite them, the Rath sensed triumph and Morgana was encouraging them from the safety of the back. This time, the creatures were determined not to run, no matter how high the casualties.

Which was exactly what Arthur hoped and feared in equal measure.

His men knew what to do. Gorrodin had spirited the plan into their minds, using magic, in case Morgana had spies watching. It had used up precious power, but it meant she had no inkling of their strategy.

In essence, however, the idea was simplicity itself. Kill as many of the enemy as possible before they were overwhelmed.

The Rath whooped and screeched, making little runs and then retreating, trying to unnerve their foe. Arthur knew any delay would only weaken the morale of his troops.

"I am the Knight with 1,000 eyes," he shouted across the valley. "And I see your doom!"

He charged towards the enemy and the 500 galloped after him. Archer revved the armoured car into life and the Galhadrians followed, roaring a battle cry.

With blood-curdling screeches, the Rath scampered out to meet them, bristling with claws and teeth.

Arthur veered left and, once again, the knights split in two, heading for the enemy flanks, as close to the steeply rising cliffs as they could manage, leaving the armoured vehicle in the centre.

Morgana's forces were not going to be fooled twice. They parted and surged towards the mountains to meet the knights, leaving as few in the middle as they could, waiting to be annihilated by machine gun fire.

The last two rockets streamed from the armoured car. But they were not aimed at the Rath.

The creatures looked up, astonished, as the white plumes soared high over their heads and kept going. Near the end of the valley, the missiles crashed into the sheer cliff faces and exploded three-quarters of the way up.

As the sonic boom faded, it was replaced by a sound like nails being dragged across a blackboard - and rocks cascaded down onto the Rath. Both cliff faces sagged and collapsed, burying hundreds of the streaming creatures under tons of falling rubble. Huge boulders filled the valley floor, effectively cutting Morgana's forces in half.

The armoured car shot forward through the gap in the middle of the Rath, spitting lead in all directions. Its cannons roared, and more of the cliff face peeled off and fell. The knights wheeled around and headed back the way they had come, while Galhadrian footsoldiers crashed into the Rath, sweeping them away.

As the enemy centre collapsed, the flanks tried to circle the gap and trap the Galhadrians. Instead, they ran into a hail of machine gun fire. The knights wheeled again and joined the fray, slamming into the creatures from either side.

The rear half of Morgana's army began scrabbling over the barrier of rubble, but the guns switched and raked the top. The front half of the Rath tried to retreat but found themselves trapped between Arthur's troops and the wall of boulders. By the time the guns ran out of ammo, it was too late.

Within ten minutes, it was over. Not a monster was left alive.

Arthur spun his hand. His army turned and headed back to the remains of the Great Wall.

There, they regrouped and waited.

The clan whispered to each other, casting glances at Arthur, who sat calmly on his charger. Finally, Duncan strode over, the rest bunched behind him.

"Your plan worked perfectly, my Lord." He bowed. "But we dinnae understand why ye retreated."

He indicated the barrier of slabs and boulders between them and the rest of Morgana's forces.

"Thon beasties will have to climb up that and doon the other side tae engage us. We could easily pick them off as they do so."

"True," Arthur said. "And Morgana knows that, as well. There is no rule to say she has to win this battle today. If we stayed, she would wait for nightfall again, then begin removing the rocks under cover of darkness."

"So, we're just going tae let her entire army climb over and get intae formation, withoot doing anything?"

"Correct." Arthur smiled. "I used the same trick when I first encountered the Rath. They will only attack if they are confident of success. If we are lucky, they will think we retreated because the armoured car ran out of bullets."

"Well... it has."

"So, they will commit everything to one last foray. They do not know Ganieda and Gorrodin are with us. And, this time, they will have a wall of rocks at their backs."

"Meaning they cannae retreat."

"Nor can we." Arthur dismounted. "This is the end game, my young friend. Take the opportunity to rest. The enemy does not have that luxury."

"I will not have another chance tae say it." Duncan saluted. "But thank you for saving my brother."

"You are most welcome."

Arthur's army sat and talked nervously, watching the Rath climb over the rubble and slowly gather on the plain.

"There's a lot less of them than before," Shadow-jack Henry peered over his shoulder every few minutes. "But they still outnumber us five to one."

"All the more tae kill," Duncan grunted.

"You're a bloodthirsty wee devil, aren't you?"

Arthur was moving through his army, praising and thanking them. Charlie sidled up to his mother.

"Still mad at me, my Lady?"

"Oh, God. Just call me mum." The woman embraced him. "I am still mad at you but also incredibly honoured that you are mine."

She pointed to Peazle, Duncan and Lilly.

"They look like youths but have lived a long, long time. What would make a boy like you sacrifice himself when you have your whole life ahead?"

"Galhadria is full of children with their whole lives ahead. I'm just one person, and this is where I am needed."

He rested his head on his mother's shoulder.

"I don't mind admitting I'm terrified, though."

"It's not too late for…"

"I told you," Charlie interrupted. "I'm staying."

He paused.

"And maybe I'm hoping for a miracle. How come I don't have any magical powers? I'm half Galhadrian, after all."

"I'm afraid you take after your father. Human. A dreamer. Someone who cannot bear to see wrongs without trying to right them."

She pulled him tighter.

"And the noblest man who ever lived."

"I guess that will have to do."

The Rath were almost ready, a few final stragglers lurching over the wall. In the far distance, they could see Morgana, a tiny figure hurrying them along.

The clan gathered for a final farewell. They shook hands and hugged but were mostly silent. Then they sat in a ring, lost in their own thoughts.

"If you don't mind, I'd like to say a few words." Inspector Archer got to his feet. The rest stared at him in surprise. He was normally so quiet it was easy to forget he was there.

"Go ahead, my friend." Arthur motioned for him to continue.

"I'm a true outsider here," he said. "None of you even know my first name. And so, I look at you all from that perspective. Earlier, I watched you debate who to save, Galhadria or humanity."

"It was no easy decision…" Gorrodin began.

"No," Arthur commanded. "Let him say his piece."

Archer cleared his throat.

"I'm a policeman," he said. "That in itself means nothing. There are good and bad cops. But it doesn't alter what we're supposed to do. Protect innocents from those who'd prey on them."

He brought out his badge.

"Right and wrong are complex concepts and painful to uphold - yet underneath is something very simple. Help others. Don't put yourself and your desires first."

He glanced around.

"Here I see humans, Galhadrians and those in between, held by a bond. Friendship. You talk of losing, but that's also a concept. We'll be wiped out, yes. But we won't have lost. Our names may vanish. But what we did will live on."

He dropped the badge into the mud and sat down.

"I don't need a symbol to remind me of what I do. I fight monsters."

There was a stunned silence.

"What *is* your first name?" Peazle asked quietly.

"Walter."

"Not anymore." Arthur stood and drew his sword. "If you would do me the honour?"

He placed the blade on Inspector Archer's shoulder.

"Of all my lost knights, there was one I favoured above all others. He was humble, brave and principled beyond all calling. You remind me of him."

He raised the weapon and placed it on the other shoulder.

"From now on, you will be known as Sir Lancelot Du Lac, Knight of Joyous Gard."

The Final Battle

The opposing forces faced each other for the last time. Once more, Gorrodin sent out a subliminal message to Arthur's force, conveying his new strategy. Again, there was a simple underlying message. Fight to the last man.

The king rode to the front of his army.

"I have no great speech to give this time," he cried. "We have reduced the Rath from one hundred thousand to ten thousand. Now, all we can do is buy time for our families."

He lifted his sword.

"Are you ready?"

The din of blades rattling on shields was deafening.

"Bowmen, let loose!"

All Galhadrians knew archery. But Gorrodin had used magic to transform their simple hunting weapons into longbows. Arthur knew how powerful a firearm they could be. He had fought at the Battle of Agincourt.

The sky turned dark with arrows. They fell among the Rath like black rain, decimating them. Before the monsters could recover another deadly hail sailed into the air and landed among them.

The beasts charged.

Arthur's archers had time for one more volley. They dropped the bows and picked up their swords and shields.

This time, the knights stayed where they were and half the Galhadrian force charged instead, two tightly packed ranks stretching across the valley floor. The enemies raced towards each other, screaming war cries.

Twenty yards from their foe, the Galhadrians skidded to a halt. Each man locked eyes with the creature heading toward him, as if daring it to come on. The mass of Rath showed no hesitation, eager to break this thin line of resistance. They were so focused they did not notice the 500 knights gathering in a V formation, like the point of a spear, with Arthur at the front. Did not see them break into a gallop.

As they reached their prey, each Galhadrian thrust his sword forwards. But not at the creature they had been watching so carefully. Instead, every thrust was aimed at the monster to the right of them. It was a blind blow but could not fail to connect with such a tightly packed group.

The entire front line of the Rath fell.

The Galhadrian vanguard turned and fled, leaving the next line exposed. But they did not attempt to fight, for their swords were still sheathed. Each man threw a spear at the second rank of the enemy. Another swathe of the creatures collapsed, clutching impaled throats and chests.

The second row of Galhadrians spun and retreated as quickly as they could run.

The creatures attempted to catch them but had to scramble over the bodies of their fallen comrades, stumbling and sliding in pools of blood. By the time they had done so, The Galhadrians were twenty yards ahead.

The Rath gibbered and jeered. The enemy was fast but they knew they could outpace them. Besides, the Galhadrians were heading right for the hurtling knights, and the two groups would surely collide in a tangled mess of armour and bodies. Victory was theirs at last!

The Galhadrians suddenly dropped to the ground and rolled onto their backs, shields braced across their torsos. The 500 hundred knights dug in their spurs, and the horses leapt over the prone bodies of their comrades.

In a flash, the Galhadrians were on their feet once more, joining the rest of their force sprinting behind the 500.

A forest of lances impaled the Rath and were quickly released as armoured warhorses slammed into the enemy. The knights drew their swords and began to hack and slash. The V widened, forcing the creatures apart and the armoured car surged into the gap, crushing beasts under its tracks. It was followed by the entire Galhadrian army.

It was every man for themselves.

Arthur was an unstoppable force, slicing and cutting in all directions. The Galhadrians fought with the fury that only those defending their homeland could muster. Gorrodin and Ganieda leapt down from the rear of the armoured vehicle, bolts of lightning shooting from their fingers, burning smouldering paths through the shrieking monsters.

But the numbers they were facing were insurmountable. Rath surrounded the armoured car and swarmed over the top, trying to prise open the hatches. Others began to rock the vehicle from side to side. Ganieda and Gorrodin did their best to destroy them but were pushed further and further away, forced to defend themselves, rather than protecting their children.

With a screech of tortured metal, the armoured car toppled over. The turret hatch opened and the Rath whooped in triumph, ready to worm their way inside.

They were met with a hail of silver bullets. Charlie and Peazle crawled out, firing as they went, followed by Lilly and Inspector Archer. Charlie and Archer held Thompson M192 Machine Guns, while Peazle had an Uzi in each hand. They got to their feet and advanced, spraying death in all directions.

Lilly didn't need a weapon. Though her powers could not match that of Gorrodin or Ganieda, she was perfectly capable of defending herself. She thrust out both hands and a dozen snarling creatures dissolved in front of her.

Flashes of light showed where Ganieda and her brother were holding back the foe. Arthur was nowhere in sight. Charlie spotted Shadowjack and Duncan to their right. Duncan was whirling like a dervish, his sword a blur, while Shadowjack swung his blacksmith's hammer, breaking heads as if they were eggs.

Incredible as it seemed, Arthur's army was holding its own.

Morgana finally appeared.

She headed for Gorrodin first, sweeping men and horses from her path. The wizard understood her intentions immediately. She was coming after his talisman.

"Hold her back," he hissed to Ganieda, for he knew his powers were useless against his former wife. Once again, he cursed himself for sharing the Grail with her.

Ganieda rubbed her hands together and sent a blast of light pulsing towards Morgana. It lifted her into the air and sent the creature flying back several yards.

But Morgana had grown too strong. Within seconds, she was on her feet and lurching forwards.

Gorrodin threw the cup in the air and batted it, as if he were playing tennis. It sailed over the heads of the battling throng and found its way to Lilly. She plucked it from the sky and hid it in the folds of her cloak.

With a scream of fury, Morgana changed direction and headed for her daughter.

The clan had formed a tight circle, back-to-back, with Lilly in the centre. They struck, parried and fired, enveloped in a haze of oily smoke and spattering blood.

Morgana was cutting her way through Arthur's forces as if they were flies to be swatted. At the sight of her, the Rath were invigorated, doubling their efforts.

"Concentrate your fire on Morgana," Charlie shouted. "Cut her down!"

Her minions leapt in the way, hiding their leader as she dodged and weaved, using her forces as inhuman shields. This gruesome game of hide and seek continued until Charlie, Archer and Peazle finally ran out of bullets.

Morgana rushed forwards and batted Archer's gun from his hands, raking savage claws across his chest. The man groaned and sank to his knees in the mud. Morgana leapt away from the swords, grinning maniacally.

"Save yourselves," Duncan commanded. "We'll deal wi this horror."

He and Shadowjack advanced.

From the corner of his eye, Charlie saw Peazle dart back to the armoured car, worm his way inside and shut the hatch. Charlie couldn't blame him. The boy wasn't a fighter and no longer had a weapon.

Shadowjack swung his hammer but Morgana ducked, sank her talons into his side and flung the giant away, knocking over assailants as if they were ninepins. Duncan advanced, trying to reach her, but this determination was his undoing. He went down, four of the Rath clinging to him like leeches.

"Run, Lilly," Charlie hissed. "You can't let Morgana get hold of the Grail, or we'll be finished in minutes."

"Don't you dare die," Lilly blasted open a path and fled through the hole she had made in the enemy ranks. Charlie dropped his empty gun and pulled out Excalibur. At the sight of the Great Sword, the Rath shrank back, snarling and making tentative lunges at the boy. A few lopped-off arms had them retreating again.

Their leader showed no such hesitation, taking off after Lilly. Her soldiers parted to allow faster passage.

"Hey, ugly!" Charlie yelled. "I'm the one who killed your son! You going to let that go unavenged?"

Morgana stopped in her tracks. Tiny malevolent eyes fastened on the boy and a chill ran up his spine. But he had to give Lilly a chance.

"That's right!" he shouted. "The big bully cried for his mum as he died."

Morgana started towards him, claws twitching. Then, for the first time, she spoke.

"When I am finished, I ssswear I will make you do the ssssame."

"Got an identical stupid lisp as Mordred, eh?" Charlie grinned. "Must run in the family."

Morgana drew in a deep breath and ground two rows of vicious teeth, trying to control her anger.

"He isssss not to be harmed," she rasped to her underlings. "I will return and make him beg for death myssself."

Then she chased after Lilly.

"Damn!" Charlie raced to cut her off. To his astonishment, the Rath refused to touch him.

"At least being on Morgana's bad side makes it easier to get around."

He found Lilly, trapped in a ring of snarling creatures. Her magic was at an end, weak sparks emanating from her fingers. The Rath parted to let Morgana through and she advanced on the girl.

"The cup isssss mine," she gurgled. "Give it to me."

Lilly pulled the Grail from inside her cloak. For a second, she considered handing it over. Yet, she knew Morgana would not spare her. In desperation, she looked for someone to throw it to.

"Not yet, Toothy Mctoothface." Charlie appeared between Morgana and her daughter. "In a long line of mistakes, you just made another."

He held Excalibur out.

"Want to try your luck against the Great Sword?"

"You are indeed a worthy adverssssary." Morgana sounded surprised. "I have underessstimated you, as my sssson did."

"It's no use, Charlie," Lilly sobbed. "I have no talisman of my own. And you have no magic."

Then it struck the boy. A simple, obvious fact. He recalled Jack Thane's words from long ago.

You have formed a bond with the weapon for reasons I do not comprehend. It has chosen you.

"I may not have magic, but I *do* have a talisman," he cried. "And I share it with you."

He handed the Great Sword to Lilly.

"Now, get us the hell out of here."

The girl tapped Excalibur against the cup and muttered an incantation. A blue, glowing portal opened behind her and Morgana gaped.

"Kill them both!" she screamed.

Lilly and Charlie leapt into the light. Morgana scooped up an axe and threw it after them. Then she dived through the closing aperture.

The light faded and the creatures milled around in confusion.

Charlie, Lilly and Morgana were gone.

The Whistle

Charlie sprawled, headfirst, in long, lush grass, then jumped to his feet. Excalibur was sticking out of the damp soil. He grabbed the hilt in time to see Morgana emerge from the closing portal. There was no sign of Lilly or the Grail.

"Looks like it's you and me again," He pointed the sword at her. "Another stalemate, eh?"

"Sssso it would sssseem." To his astonishment, Morgana smiled, revealing two rows of jagged teeth. "I fear the Great Sword but I do not tire, like you. I will wait for night to fall and then you will be mine."

"I seem to remember Mordred saying much the same thing. But I'm still here."

"Taunting me will make revenge all the sssweeter. In the meantime, I ssshall hunt for the cup."

Her grin faded as she looked past the boy.

"Where are we?"

Charlie risked a glance over his shoulder. The mountain of Leiter Dhuibh soared upwards and Eas a Chual Aluinn Falls sparkled as it cascaded down one side.

"You don't recognise it?" He masked his own astonishment. "The talisman has taken Lilly to the last place and time she was truly happy."

"It cannot be." Morgana's tiny eyes registered shock. On the other side of a wide swathe of pastureland dotted with wildflowers was a stone cottage. Smoke rose from the chimney, and a few chickens pecked and scuffed around the front door.

It was her daughter's home. *Her* home. Confusion flickered over the creature's face.

"I do not wisssh to be here."

"Neither do I," Charlie admitted. "I think I know what happens next and it's not something I ever wanted to experience again."

"What do you mean?" Morgana tapped her head with a yellow claw. "It is ssso long ago that I cannot remember."

"In that case, you're in for a hell of a shock."

Lilly appeared in the meadow, playing with a dog. She did not resemble the tired and bloodstained girl Morgana had chased through the portal. This was a younger version, happy and carefree, singing a song and picking daisies.

They heard a rumble in the distance that transformed quickly into the thunder of horses' hooves.

Morgana emerged from the house, into the sunlight. Not the abomination she would become but a beautiful woman in a velvet dress. Her hands shot to her mouth as she spotted whooping horsemen galloping across the moor towards her daughter. Their faces were daubed with blue and all were heavily armed. Their savage cries sounded remarkably like those of the Rath.

"Picts!" she breathed. "A war party!"

Lilly had spotted the horsemen and was sprinting back towards the safety of the house - but it was obvious the Picts would catch her before she reached shelter. Morgana was about to head for her daughter then, realising the same thing, turned and darted back indoors.

Lilly was still racing for safety. Her dog turned and bounded towards the attackers in a desperate attempt to save his mistress.

The hound didn't stand a chance. After a few desperate lunges, it vanished under the oncoming hooves.

Lilly skidded to a halt, rage written across her childish face. She stretched out her hands and the leading Pict was catapulted backwards off his steed. She thrust her arms forward again and another rider went down. The remaining warriors yelled louder and spurred their horses on - there were far too many in the raiding party for the girl's fledgling magical powers to stop.

Lilly turned to run again, but a wooden axe came hurtling through the air and embedded itself in her back. She fell forward onto a patch of gorse, a gout of blood erupting in the air.

With a triumphant whoop, the leading Pict dismounted his horse and advanced towards the dying girl.

He never reached her.

There was a rippling in the air. Ferns and heather curled in on themselves, as if subjected to immense heat. The shimmering path reached the Picts, turning them instantly to black outlines that broke and drifted into the sky.

Morgana stood in the doorway, holding Gorrodin's Grail. She ran to her daughter, still clutching the cup, and knelt beside her. With a shudder, the woman pulled the axe from Lilly's back and placed her hand over the spurting wound. She drank from the cup again, whispering hysterically to herself. The blood pouring between her fingers instantly stopped and, when she removed her hand, her daughter's wound was gone. Lilly's shallow laboured breathing evened out until it became deep and regular.

"Sleep, child," Morgana whispered. "When you awake, you will forget this dreadful thing." She hesitated. "Nor will you remember that I broke my sacred promise to your father and used his Grail."

She clasped, then unclasped, her fingers and a small, glinting object appeared in her hand. She fastened it around her sleeping daughter's neck.

It was a tiny silver whistle on a chain.

"If you are ever in trouble again, my child, blow the whistle and I will come to save you."

She carried her child into the house and closed the door.

Charlie and the monster that was once a woman stood a few feet apart. But Morgana no longer seemed interested in him.

She padded over to the house and peered into the window. Her human self was pressing a cloth to Lilly's head, tears streaming down her cheeks.

Charlie walked up behind her.

"Your son is gone," he said. "And you should be ashamed of what you turned him into."

Morgana stayed silent,

"But you still have a daughter. You made a vow to protect her. Remember now?"

The creature whirled around.

"Do not try to trick me, boy."

"Where's the trick?" Charlie kept a respectful distance. "A thousand years without a mother or father, can you imagine that? You were both her world."

He leaned heavily on his sword.

"Go and find your cup, then. Let the Rath destroy Galhadria. But answer me one question first. *Why*?"

The boy sounded defeated.

"To rule? Over what? For revenge? Against who?"

Morgana stared at him.

"That girl is your heir. You should be fighting *for* her, not trying to kill her."

"Where *isssss* my daughter?" Morgana began to search and Charlie joined her, making sure to stay several feet away. But there was no sign of the girl.

Then they heard the sound of a whistle, so faint Charlie wasn't sure if he imagined it. But Morgana's bat-like ears pricked up and she padded into a thicket of long grass.

Lilly lay on her side, curled into a ball, motionless in a pool of blood. The whistle had dropped from her lifeless hand, for the axe Morgana had thrown through the portal was buried in her back.

"Oh, no. no." Charlie knelt beside his friend, cradling her head in his arms. "Not again."

Morgana shuffled on the spot behind him, looking uncertain. She dropped to all fours and began hunting through the greenery.

When she finally stood, she was holding the Grail.

"I have it," she hissed triumphantly.

"Keep the damned thing." Charlie rocked back and forwards, stroking Lilly's matted hair. "You have all the power you could wish for now. Open a portal and go back to your conquest. Wipe out your foes."

Morgana clutched the cup to her chest like a scolded child.

"Now you can spend eternity reigning over your precious Rath, who know nothing but carnage and primal urges. How much satisfaction will you feel with nobody left to love or to love you?"

"The cup is not ssssomething humans can resissst," Morgana protested.

"Aw, stop pretending you're a victim. You haven't been human for a long time. The cup is yours to command, not the other way round. It's just a bloody object that has brought nothing but misery to everyone who possessed it. Including you."

He picked up the whistle and flung it at her.

"Here's another object. Keep it as a reminder of the monster you've become. Not because of how you look or what you did to the man who adored you. Not because you fell under the spell of the Grail."

He laid Lilly gently down.

"Because your only daughter wasted her last breath blowing it."

"That was a very eloquent ssssssspeech," Morgana muttered.

"Eloquence is for liars," Charlie shot back. "You know when someone is telling the truth because it always hurts."

Morgana picked up the silver whistle and stared at it. Then she slid the chain over her misshapen head.

"Move." She hunkered down and pushed the boy out of the way. She held the cup to Lilly's lips and poured some of the liquid into her mouth.

"She's gone, Morgana."

"Lilly is a magical creature, like me. We do not die so easssily."

She rolled the girl over, placed taloned hands on her back and began to mutter incantations. An orange lambency spread between her claws and the wound began to close.

"It isssss done," she said, exhausted.

Lilly drew a sharp breath and began coughing.

"My God." Charlie stammered. "You did it."

He couldn't be sure, but the creature's fanged lips seemed to turn up at the corners.

Lilly sat up and spotted Morgana. She gave a cry of terror and raised her hands to ward off the creature. The expression vanished from Morgana's face.

"It's all right!" Charlie grabbed the girl's shoulder. "Your mum saved you."

"Mother?" Lilly asked hopefully. "Is that true?"

"Ssstay here and remain hidden, for you are too weak to move." Morgana reached out for the girl, then quickly withdrew her malformed hand. "We must leave, but Charlie will return for you."

"*What?* You two are mortal enemies!"

"I believe we have come to an… undersssstanding."

She spoke a few words and a portal opened behind them. Morgana nodded at the boy.

"Come with me, child, before my will fails."

"That's it?" Charlie sheathed Excalibur. "Aren't you going to tell Lilly you love her?"

"Sometimes wordssss are not enough."

Morgana locked eyes with her daughter. The girl started as if she had been slapped. Then she smiled.

"I love you too," she said weakly. "I always did."

Morgana leaned over and whispered in Charlie's ear.

"Before we go, you must know sssomething. My daughter did not blow the whisstle to ssssummon *me.*"

She stood and pulled the boy towards the portal.

"She wanted you."

Morgana

They arrived back on the battlefield to a scene of utter carnage. Exhausted Galhadrians, men and monsters were trading blows in a sea of mud, neither side willing to give an inch. The air was filled with the screams of wounded and dying.

At the sight of their leader, the Rath let out a triumphant roar, quickly changing to confusion when Charlie emerged from the blue light behind her.

"Where isssss Gorrodin?" Morgana demanded.

One of her minions pointed to a far off knot of battling figures.

"Thank you." She sliced him open with one swipe.

"Oooh, that's harsh." Charlie winced.

Morgana took off, barrelling through her own ranks, cutting and tearing their flesh as she went. Charlie ran alongside.

"Don't harm her," he shouted over and over to his side. "She's with me!"

Within minutes, Morgana had reached the clan, or what was left of them. Arthur and Ganieda were badly hurt, leaning feebly against each other. Shadowjack and Gorrodin had fared no better, blood pouring from multiple wounds. The wizard's head was bowed in pain and the blacksmith was holding him up. A handful of knights had formed a defensive ring around them, but their circle was growing ever smaller.

Charlie sprinted past Morgana, holding up the Great Sword.

"Let her through!" he shrieked. "I command it!"

The knights hesitated, then reluctantly parted, allowing Arthur's son and their worst nightmare passage to their leader.

"Charlie!" Ganieda cried. "You're alive!"

"And I brought reinforcements."

Gorrodin raised his head and his eyes widened.

"I return your talisssman." Morgana held out the cup to him. "And relinquissssh all claim to it."

The wizard reached out and touched her scaly cheek.

"My darling," he said softly. "This moment is worth all the tortures I have endured."

He took the Grail and drank.

The change was instant. He straightened his back and his eyes blazed with renewed energy.

"Goodbye, husband," Morgana said. "Try to forgive me."

She turned and charged into the Rath, arms whirling, flinging them asunder, jaws fastening on one body after another. As the stunned creatures threw themselves upon her, she vanished into the melee.

"Morgana has changed sides!" Gorrodin's voice carried across the battlefield, loud and clear as a bell.

"Since the Dolorous Stroke was struck against her, the Great Spell is now working for us!"

A wail went up from the Rath.

"One more push and the day is ours," the wizard continued. "Victory is assured."

Arthur's men moved forward with renewed vigour. Broken and disheartened, the Rath turned and fled.

They reached the wall of rubble with the enemy on their heels and attempted to climb it. But they were too late. The Galhadrian army swarmed over them.

Fifteen minutes later, the greatest threat Galhadria had ever known had been annihilated.

Ganieda pulled Charlie into her arms.

"I thought I had lost my son," she whispered. "And my heart was torn asunder. I did not realise just how much I loved you."

"I am ashamed to say I was the same." Arthur kissed the boy's head. "My joy at finding you knows no bounds."

"Then, may I ask a boon?" Charlie wriggled out from their embrace.

"Anything."

"Please, let's go back to talking normally. It's driving me crazy."

"You got it, kid. Call us mum and dad."

Shadowjack and Arthur were allowed small sips of the Grail to speed their recovery. As a Galhadrian, Ganieda healed quickly. She gave her son another kiss then left, to use what magic she had remaining to aid the injured. Arthur went with her.

Gorrodin approached the boy warily, a sorrowful look on his face.

"Where is my daughter?" he asked. "Is she…?"

"She's alive," Charlie said. "Back at her old home. And when I say back, I mean a thousand years or so. I imagine the Grail knows exactly when."

"How did…"

"Maybe later, eh?"

"I shall use my cup to fetch her immediately." The wizard beamed. "A thousand thanks to you."

He opened a portal and vanished.

Charlie looked around. Bodies were strewn in every direction and the ground was a red pool of gore. Moans and cries drifted through the air. Now and then, a hand was raised pleadingly.

"So, this is war." The boy sighed. "What a bloody waste."

He stepped gingerly over corpses until he reached the armoured car.

"You can come out now, Peazle," he shouted, clattering the handle of Excalibur against the metal side. "It's all over."

The hatch opened and Peazle crawled out.

"Did we win?"

"As a matter of fact, we did." Charlie helped him to his feet. "I'll explain later."

"Excellent!" the boy straightened his bowler and took in the scene at a glance.

"By my oath." His face fell. "Is this all that is left of our army?"

"Could have been worse."

"Where is Duncan?"

"I don't know. You should go look for him."

"I'm on my way." Peazle gave a half-hearted grin. "He will be fine, I'm sure."

Charlie avoided his hopeful stare.

"That fellow is imperishable, eh?" Peazle's voice cracked. "Isn't that right?"

"I have to go."

Charlie made his way back to the portal just as Gorrodin emerged, Lilly leaning on his arm. She hugged Charlie and kissed his cheek.

"Where is my mother?"

"She went this way." Charlie led them across the battlefield towards the wall of rubble. The Rath were so thick on the ground it was impossible to proceed without stepping on them.

They found Morgana leaning against a rock, half-buried under the creatures she had once commanded. She was covered in lacerations and bite marks, her breathing coming in ragged bursts.

Charlie helped them pull the bodies off, then Gorrodin and Lilly knelt beside the creature.

"You saved us, my darling." Gorrodin cried freely while Lilly squeezed what was left of her mother's mangled hand. Morgana's eyes fluttered open.

"Daughter," she groaned. "I am ssssorry."

"Please don't die," Lilly wept. "We can be together at last."

"I shall use the Grail." Gorrodin yanked the cup from his cloak. "All is not lost."

"Do not usssse that thing on me!" Morgana pushed him away. "You were always too hopeful, husband. Do you never learn from your misssstakes?"

"Of course." Gorrodin nodded.

"Use my fate as a lesson, I beg you." Morgana's eyelids closed. "And please do not think too harshly of me. I tried."

She let out a long breath and passed away.

Charlie left Lilly and Gorrodin grieving and went to help his mother tend to the injured.

Caleb finally arrived with a ragtag army made up of men and women from the lands surrounding Galhadria. But the battle was long over. Instead, Arthur requested they help bury the bodies.

They toiled for days, side by side. Gorrodin and Ganieda, restored to full strength, used magic to pile rocks over the remains of the enemy. Then they fashioned the remains of the Great Wall into a giant monument. It was a simple design, tall and unadorned. Written at the bottom was an equally plain inscription.

Here Lie Those Who Fell Defending Their Homes and Families Against the Rath.

Beyond that was a sea of white crosses, each with a name carved on it. The Galhadrians were still making their way back and would mourn fathers, mothers, uncles, aunts, sisters and brothers when they arrived.

But, before that, the clan held a private ceremony.

Arthur, Ganieda, Gorrodin, Lilly, Caleb, Shadowjack, Peazle and Charlie stood over a row of graves.

Ganieda stepped forwards.

"You had no stake in this battle, Walter Archer," she said. "Yet you gave your life. On earth, nobody will know what you have done. But, from this day forward, the plain will be known as Archer's Rest. Proof, if it were needed, that some humans are decent to their very core."

"Farewell, sweetheart." Gorrodin placed a wreath on the second mound. "I will never know what torment you suffered. But you overcame it. I loved you and always will."

"Goodbye, mother." Lilly pushed her silver whistle into the earth. "I called and you came."

She began to cry and Gorrodin wrapped her in the folds of his cloak.

Arthur motioned Caleb forward but the man shook his head.

"I would give worlds to have more time with my brother but, truth be told, I barely knew him."

He glanced at Peazle.

"His best friend should speak."

"Really?"

"I think it fitting."

Peazle took a huge breath.

"I have always wanted to be a man of learning," he said. "Spent decades acquiring knowledge."

He plunged Duncan's sword into the grave.

"You taught me more than any book could, Duncan MacPhail. How to be a good person."

His voice broke.

"I would trade everything I know if I could have you back."

His legs gave way and he sank to his knees, sobbing.

Arthur laid a hand on his shoulder.

"It's Sir Duncan," he said. "King's Champion and Knight of the Round Table."

Camelot

Arthur's official coronation was a subdued affair, for Galhadria was still lamenting its losses. Even so, the main hall was packed with grateful subjects lining the walls. The human who had suddenly appeared to snatch victory from the jaws of defeat was fast becoming a legend once more.

At Arthur's side sat Queen Ganieda, radiant in white and gold, while Gorrodin stood behind the throne. Once again, he had used sorcery to send his king's message to the crowds thronging outside.

"Castle Alclud is no more," Arthur stood. "From now on, it will be called Camelot. Gorrodin will be my trusted adviser, as he was in happier times."

The wizard nodded solemnly.

He clenched his fist, and an enormous object began to solidify in the centre of the room. Everyone moved back, talking in hushed whispers.

It was a round table encircled by high-backed wooden seats.

"Will my knights take their places?" Arthur asked.

Thirty men stepped forward, all that was left of the 500 who had gone into battle. Caleb went to join them, but Ganieda waved him back.

Not yet, she whispered.

Her husband addressed his subjects.

"I understand that many of you who fought with me have families to return to. Those who do not, however, are welcome to join."

Fifty or so Galhadrians took seats, smiling broadly.

"There are still many empty places," Arthur said. "They will eventually be filled by those who have proved brave and true. Not just humans and Galhadrians but those of Alabarra, Monshorn and the Wooded Lands - or anywhere else, for that matter."

There was a shocked silence from those in attendance. Then a cheer went up.

"Arthur! Arthur!"

The king waved for them to be silent.

"I have thought long on this and decided I cannot lead them. My job is to stay here and ensure peace and prosperity in Galhadria."

He beckoned to Charlie.

The boy walked over, casting a surprised glance at his companions. He knelt in front of his king, holding up Excalibur.

Arthur took it and placed the blade gently on the boy's shoulders.

"Arise, Sir Charlie. Commander of my forces and Guardian of the Great Sword."

The cheering grew louder as the boy stood and took back the weapon.

"I will need a second in command," he said in a loud, clear voice. "Therefore, I choose Sir Galahad. Or Caleb, as he prefers to be called."

Caleb looked stunned. Then he took his seat at the Round Table.

"Now it is time to celebrate," Arthur said. "We have all lost people we loved and will grieve for them tomorrow. Tonight, we honour them with music and dance, as is our way. For we are all Galhadrians now."

The wooden doors burst open and men entered, bringing food and wine.

"Do we have bards here to sing us songs?"

A dozen hands went up.

"Come forwards and play," Arthur said. "However, tomorrow, I have a task for you."

"What do you wish, my liege?" one asked.

"Together, you will write a ballad about Math and Jack Thane. How they sacrificed themselves that we might live."

"We will pen the most beautiful tune this land has ever heard, with words to match."

"Please do." Arthur smiled sadly. "Jack Thane would have liked that."

The dancing and merriment went on long into the night. Halfway through, Arthur and Ganieda retired to their chambers, motioning for what was left of the clan to follow.

The king and queen sat on their four-poster bed while the others lounged on huge, embroidered cushions.

Now that they were alone, Arthur and Ganieda lapsed back into the way they had talked on earth.

"God, I'm pooped," Arthur said. "I never got this tired jumping around in spangly tights."

"I knew you missed it," Ganieda grinned. "You could always introduce sequins as a fashion statement. You're all the rage right now."

"I'll pass." Arthur lay back on the bed and rolled over. "You can take over while I have a snooze."

"Get up off your lazy butt." Ganieda gave it a slap. "This is important."

"Suppose." Arthur sat up again. "We have a few urgent matters to discuss."

"You have a choice, Lord Peazle," Ganieda pointed at him.

"Did you say, *Lord* Peazle?"

"Don't get all flustered. You deserve it."

"I locked myself in an armoured car while everyone else was fighting. I'll never forgive myself for that."

"It just proves how smart you are." Ganieda shrugged. "You are welcome to become our chief adviser, along with Gorrodin."

"Free library pass forever." Charlie nudged him.

"You said I have a choice."

"Or you can return to the world of men and keep an eye on them." Ganieda grew serious. "You were right, as usual. They have a different kind of magic and, someday, they *will* be Galhadria's greatest threat."

"I presume that's what you really want me to do."

"You'll be able to drink as much Coke and coffee as you like," Arthur cajoled. "Ever have a deep-fried Mars Bar?"

"You had me at Coke." Peazle saluted. "I accept."

"May I go with him?" Shadowjack asked. "I've become very partial to prawn cocktail crisps and skinny boy here will probably need some protecting."

"Of course."

"I shall spend some time with my father," Lilly said. "Then I will go too."

"Are you sure, daughter?" Gorrodin's face fell.

"The truth is, I miss the place. I belong to two worlds and, finally, I am contented with that." She gave her father a hug. "We will return often and tell you of our adventures."

"At great length," Peazle added.

"I shall look forward to each reunion." The wizard kissed Lilly's curls.

"Will you come, Charlie?" the girl asked hesitantly.

"I'm the king's Commander," Charlie shook his head. "I suppose I have commanding to do."

"And your mum has pointed out that mankind is our greatest threat," Lilly persisted. "You might want to help us watch their movements. I'm sure Caleb can manage to keep a few rogue trolls, dwarves and giants in line."

She lowered her eyes.

"I miss Duncan terribly but he was a friend. To be honest, I have grown to love you."

"Holy smoke." Charlie blushed from head to foot. "You probably guessed I feel the same way."

"Wouldn't have asked otherwise." Lilly winked at him. "I've got my pride, you know."

"Do what your heart dictates, son." Arthur glanced at his wife. "Love is the engine that drives us all."

"My heart soars to hear you say that," Charlie took Lilly's hands. "But my father is wrong. Doing the right thing is what always drove him and I can ask no less of myself."

"Now, I love you even more. But please stop talking like someone's granddad. It's freaking me out."

Charlie chuckled.

"OK. I got a task to complete. Then wild horses couldn't keep us apart."

"And what is that?"

"I'll take my men to scour every kingdom we know, offering the hand of friendship. Then beyond, to places we have never been. Galhadria's time of isolation is over."

"He is wiser than his years, my liege." Gorrodin smiled approvingly. "And courageous with it."

"Courage is a choice," Charlie said. "It's time to explore. Embrace other cultures and forge alliances. It's time to belong."

He kissed Lilly on the lips.

"I'll be with you someday soon. For now, I've got to take on the task my dad started."

He raised Excalibur and saluted his king.

"I am the knight with 1,000 eyes."

END

ABOUT THE AUTHOR

Jan-Andrew Henderson (J.A. Henderson) is the author of 40 childrens', teen, YA, adult and non-fiction books. Published in the UK, USA, Australia, Canada, and Europe, he has been shortlisted for fifteen literary awards and is the winner of the Doncaster Book Prize, the Aurealis Award and the Royal Mail Award.

www.janandrewhenderson.com